SKi / B...

1 hr North Vegas

> 9,000

sunny
snowy
outside

HAWaii Flys Las vegas

NiKON class

Dance class

Ski MondAys +

3pt Harmony ♩♪ Honolulu

3 bros.

life at these speeds

Makaha
Sans

Aloha

jeremy jackson

picador
new york

life at these speeds

www.picadorusa.com

Picador® is a U.S. registered trademark and is used by St. Martin's Press under license from Pan Books Limited.

For information on Picador Reading Group Guides, as well as ordering, please contact the Trade Marketing department at St. Martin's Press.
Phone: 1-800-221-7945 extension 763
Fax: 212-677-7456
E-mail: trademarketing@stmartins.com

ISBN 0-312-28808-5 (hc)
ISBN 0-312-31366-7 (pbk)

Designed by Lorelle Graffeo

Chapter 1 appeared in The Greensboro Review in slightly different form as "It Didn't Bother Me" in 1996.

First Picador Edition: July 2003

10 9 8 7 6 5 4 3 2 1

for my parents

life at these speeds

part one

one

"*Hold,*" said Jarhead. He reached back from the driver's seat
as Bobby came near. Bobby was exiting the van. Jarhead grabbed
Bobby's shoulder and said, "You're doing high jump."

Bobby hated high jump.

"Okay," said Bobby.

Jarhead was coach. We called him Jarhead because his head with
its crew cut mimicked a mayonnaise jar's shape. We didn't know "jarhead" was a nickname for soldiers. We were thirteen or fourteen years
old, at an eighth-grade track meet in Bryceville. Tonight was the night
I was going to win the 800-meter run. I was going to win because
Jamie Torffelson wasn't there. Jamie Torffelson was a redshirt from
Portertown who had run a 2:04—two seconds off the Missouri junior-
high record.

I was the real high jumper, better than Bobby Sickle. But I also ran
fast, and tonight Jarhead needed me in the 1600-meter relay, the
3200-meter relay, and, of course, the open 800. I could only enter
three events, so I couldn't do high jump.

That was fine. I hated high jump. But then, I hated the 1600-
meter relay, the 3200-meter relay, and the open 800, too. Basically, I
hated running and jumping. But I ran fast and jumped high.

"You're headed to state finals next year," Jarhead had told me.

Next year I would be a freshman.

"That doesn't bother me," I said.

Jarhead was a big fucker. Something like six feet eight. He was blond haired, but his eyebrows were brown. Those were scary, his eyebrows. When he told Bobby Sickle that he was doing high jump, Jarhead nudged his brown eyebrows together in a way that said, "You're going to do high jump." It was intimidating, and I felt for Bobby. I was sitting near the back of the van with Ellie Butterbit and Ellie Butterbit's boobs. Trolley Catchell was back there, too, sitting in the very last seat sleeping or jacking off. He was fat. He threw shot put.

Jarhead told Bobby he was doing high jump. Bobby tromped off the van and walked past my window, cussing. I admired his vocabulary. He and I were mild rivals only because we were too much alike to be friends anymore. But I had always known that somewhere, somehow, Bobby Sickle was just *wrong*, just a notch or three below me. This year I had evidence: I was faster, jumped higher, and had Ellie Butterbit.

"Would you suck Bobby's dick?" I asked Ellie.

She threw her sweatshirt at me. I picked it up and smelled it. She laughed. Jarhead stepped out of the van and the van rocked. Ellie was still laughing at me.

"He's one big guy," Trolley said from his seat. He was lying down, so we couldn't see his face.

"That's darn tootin', Trolley," I replied.

It's amazing that Trolley Catchell never kicked my ass. I made fun of him every day. But then, I was popular, funny, and friendly when appropriate. I was an egomaniac, but I didn't know it.

Being an egomaniac didn't bother me. After all, who else had fooled around with Ellie Butterbit?

* * *

We were lying on blankets on the slope above the track, talking about how cold it was, saying things like, "It's really cold," and "Shit, I'm going to freeze." It was me and Ellie and Greg French and Heather Garnet and Will Wynsom and Gina Daley and Hoover Garfield.

Me and Ellie were keeping warm enough under a blanket, but I went along with the conversation.

"Frickin'-ass cold," I said.

Ellie thought that was funny.

Jarhead walked up like a blond-and-blue totem pole. He held clipboards.

"Jamie Torffelson *is* here," he said. "In the 800 with you."

My best time in the 800 was 2:10, but I had beaten Jamie last week at Helias with a 2:13. That was the only time I'd beaten him. Jarhead wanted me to win tonight. He wanted me to smash Jamie Torffelson into the cinders. Jarhead hated Portertown.

Jarhead said, "I want you to win tonight. I want you to smash Jamie Torffelson into the cinders. I hate Portertown."

"I'll win," I said. "I'll break 2:10."

"What size spikes you got?" asked Jarhead. He crouched down next to me. I had to reach an arm out from under the blanket to check my shoes.

"Quarter-inch."

"Well," said Jarhead, "you'll do what you do."

"It will be done did."

Our uniforms were blue. We yawned. Daylight saving time had not yet arrived this year, so the sun had set as our team van pulled into Bryceville, and our meet was held beneath the darkness. High schoolers' cars wheeled through the white-gravel lot beside the track. And why was there a muddy smell, hanging in the chill?

I ran the 3200-meter relay as a warm-up, testing my tendons. We placed third after Porterville and Bryceville. I was the anchor, the fastest, and Bobby Sickle ran well, too, but Greg French and Jason

Blick were slow, so our relay rarely won. Other than the 1600-meter relay, this was the only relay race our team entered. After the race, I walked through the finish area. Georgia Teeter sneered at me. I blew her a kiss. I walked into the infield, where Jarhead stood alone like an abandoned chess piece. Jarhead had kept our splits in the relay. They were: Jason Blick, 2:32; Greg French, 2:31; Bobby Sickle, 2:19; and me, 2:17. I hadn't been pushing.

Jamie Torffelson ran third-leg with a 2:07.

"He'll wear himself out," said Jarhead.

Then Jarhead told me he was pulling me out of the 1600-meter relay. He put Bobby Sickle in. "We're keeping you fresh," Coach told me. He and I were still standing far from anyone, in the middle of the infield. The field lights shone from the dents in his forehead.

"How's the track?" he asked.

"Loose. Dry."

"Oh *yeah*," he said, as if loose, dry tracks were the plague of his years.

Bryceville had the standard shit-school cinder track. They let us wear quarter-inch spikes. Bryceville was bigger than our school, Carton. My entire class contained sixteen kids. Fourteen of us had joined the track team.

Jarhead pulled a white bag from his jacket. "Here," he said. "Half-inch. No one will notice."

So I sat in the infield and screwed the half-inch spikes into my Nikes while Jarhead stood above me. Then he sent me to the high jump pit to tell Bobby he was running the 1600 relay so I could rest up.

"I hate that relay," said Bobby. He was being real royal about getting all the shit that Jarhead didn't want to put me in. Bobby was jumping well. I watched him clear 5'4".

"Good jump. Nice approach," I told him, knowing nothing is worse than middling compliments from someone who is better than you.

Jason Blick came up. "Hey," he said to me, "your parents are here."

They were. In the top corner of the bleachers, sitting on their little butt-saver cushions.

I went to my parents.

"Hey," I said.

"Well, how's it going?" asked Mom. She pulled open a cooler.

"Okay," I said.

"You already run the 1600 relay?" asked Dad. He was looking portly.

"No. Coach took me out of it to rest up for the 800."

"Ah. Good," said Dad.

"We're keeping me fresh," I explained.

Mom handed Dad a braunschweiger-and-cheddar sandwich. She poured him coffee from a thermos and offered me some.

"No," I said. "Chemicals, you know. Not for an athlete."

Lying on the blankets again.

"Ellie," I said, "go talk to my parents."

They thought Ellie was so nice and pleasant. Ellie was good with adults. She was smart.

"Fine," she said, and stood up. I heard runners crashing through hurdles. Behind Ellie's blue sweatpants the track's rust swath circled the pool-table infield. Beyond that was night, come comfortably up to the chain-link fence.

I looked at Ellie's face. She was smiling at me. One time we had met in the woods between our houses, and she had taken me to the cliffs above the floodplain and shown me how the view encompassed the hills of three counties. Often I had daydreamed of following her on more treks through the woods. We could pack snacks to eat. By road, our houses were four miles apart; but through the woods only one mile separated us.

"When I come back," she said, "you will have decided between Boston and Montana."

See, we were planning where to live. We were planning our adult persons.

"Okay," I said and clicked my teeth. I watched Ellie's smile turn and watched her walk with her hands swinging selflessly. Steadily she moved, crossing the track, the infield, and the track again. She rose into the bleachers. I pictured her walking right off the back of the bleachers, but she didn't. As she approached my parents, she opened her arms wide, like Jesus might have done at the end of his "Don't worry" parables. What was she saying to them?

I wanted her to come walking back.

As far as Boston and Montana were concerned, I liked Boston, but knew Ellie wanted Montana. My answer was both.

While Ellie visited the bleachers, me and Will Wynsom went behind the restrooms and smoked. Jamie Torffelson walked by with two buddies. I don't know what they were doing just walking behind the restrooms.

"How does it feel to be a loser?" asked Jamie.

I thought he was talking to Will, who was a genuine loser. But then he stopped in front of me.

"It doesn't bother me," I said, exhaling. I should have said, "How does it feel to have a woman's name?" but I didn't particularly want to be beaten into pulp.

The two things the backs of restrooms were made for: smoking and beating people into pulp.

Ellie came back as Will and me walked from behind the restrooms. "You were smoking," she said. "Mm, let me kiss you!"

I pushed her off. "Kiss Will," I said.

Will smiled.

Ellie screamed and slapped my shoulder. I grabbed her ass. It was a lovely thing to do.

"How are my fossils?" I asked.

"Your parents are *nice*," she said. "You should be *nice* to your parents."

Since my parents were there, that meant no van ride home. That meant no neck sucking with Ellie.

Ellie pulled her sweatshirt hood up. She began reading a book by someone dead.

Trolley Catchell loped up to our blanket camp and sat on the grass. "How'd the throwing go, Trolley?" I said.

"Third," said Trolley.

Bobby Sickle approached and sat with Gina Daley.

I was the official spokesman.

"How'd the jumping go?"

"Third," said Bobby. He picked dirt from his spikes and started unscrewing them. He was done for the night. He'd run a 1:15 in the 1600-meter relay—a poor time by any measure. Hell, Ellie could run a 1:06. I could do 59.

"My parents here?" Bobby asked, looking to the bleachers. We all looked. We were trained to spot parents. At any public event, it gave us great glee to tell another kid that his parents were present. Such news was a subtle slap, and we loved violence.

Greg French said, "They look like war ships."

I wondered whose parents he was insulting. I thought it was the kind of insult I should have gotten to first, but then I realized he was simply offering us a painfully uncreative description of the bleachers.

I saw my parents blobbed together in their parkas. They waved. I saluted them.

"Hippy, dippy, do," someone said.

"My parents were supposed to be here," said Bobby. He actually liked his parents to come to the meets. He actually liked his parents. Publicly. "I have to ride the fucking van," he said.

"Fuckity fuck fuck," I said. I was getting tired of waiting to win the 800. "Fellows, all this third-place taking has earned us a smoke." I looked around at Ellie and Bobby and Trolley and Jason and Greg and Heather and Will and Hoover. They were gazing at their laps.

I jumped up. I snapped at Will. He was the one with the cigarettes. He rose.

"Trolley," I said, "you deserve a break. Come on."

"No," he mumbled.

Bobby stood.

"Coming?" I asked.

"No doubt. I got something."

Behind the restrooms we lit and dragged.

"Fricking-ass cold," said Will, but no one laughed.

"Guys," said Bobby. "Look at this." He dug into his jacket, then froze.

Jamie Torffelson and two guys had come around the corner. One of the guys had a mustache. We didn't say anything, and they didn't say anything, but they came right up to us where we stood against the white cinder-block wall.

A toilet flushed inside. It made me bold.

I said, "I'm going to break 2:10. That would leave you in second, I guess. Or third."

Jamie's face fluttered. At my side, I felt Will cringe—he hated a fight.

Jamie shuffled a bit and looked over his shoulder. Then he pointed to Bobby. "You hold your cigarette like a fag," he said.

This was true, I admit. It was true.

"What?" said Bobby, and he dropped his cigarette. "You want to say that again?"

I kept smoking, slowly. Tact, I felt, was the key. "Come on guys," I said. "I have a race to win." I snuffed my cigarette with my heel.

"No way," said Bobby. "I want this *prick* to repeat what he just said so I can smash his face in."

"I'd love to, buttfucker."

I put my forearm across Bobby's stomach. "Come on," I said.

"No *fucking* way."

"Give me a cigarette, boys," said someone. I looked. It was Trolley Catchell, walking like a barrel, looking like a fortress, coming around the corner. "Give me a cigarette."

Will gave him a cigarette. Will was smiling.

"You all want a smoke?" Trolley asked Jamie's crew.

"No," said Jamie, and he left with his friends.

I scratched my eyebrow, put one foot up on the wall behind me.

"I saw them come back here," said Trolley, pill-rolling his Camel. He dropped it without even lighting it. He stepped on it. "Come on, they did first call for the 800."

I waited for Bobby to thank me. When he didn't, I followed Trolley.

The hair on my legs rose. The night was fifty degrees. I rubbed my calf muscles.

"Let me do that," said Ellie. "For good luck."

I let her do it.

Jarhead came up and smiled and said, "This is going to be good. This is going to be just fine."

"Good," I said. "Fine."

"Keep moving before the start," he said. "Keep jogging in place. This cold will lock your muscles if you don't."

"It's under control, Mister Coach Master, sir."

"Good," he said.

"Fine," said I.

Then I had to piss. I ran into the restroom. I ran out, jiggling my arms to loosen them, and Bobby came up. We jogged toward the starting line along the back part of the track. It was silent but for our footfalls.

"Let me run it," said Bobby.

"No way. I'm going to break 2:10."

"Shit," he said. He held something out to me. It was two joints. We had smoked pot a couple times, but didn't know who to get it from regularly.

"Where the hell . . . ?" I asked.

"Some kid over by concessions."

I smelled the joints. They were real.

"You can have them," said Bobby, "if you let me run this race. I want to blow Jamie Torffelson's ass away. I can do it."

"Bobby . . ." I said, but then I thought about next week's dance, and how it would be great to smoke with Ellie, and so on. I didn't care what Jarhead thought. I would quit the team if he wanted. I hated running and jumping anyway.

"Okay," I said.

"Give me your spikes," he said. "I already took mine out."

We sat on the track, traded shoes, then continued toward the starting line, wordless.

"Carton, Kevin Schuler," said the starter, "lane six."

Bobby stood in lane six. I looked around for Jarhead. He was on the far side near the finish line. The track wasn't standard size, so 800 meters wasn't two laps, but one and two-thirds.

"Hold your dicks, boys," said the starter. "I need caps."

A bouncing girl ran across the infield for more starter caps. Bobby motioned to me. I looked across the infield. Jarhead was striding right at us pointing at Bobby. Jarhead yelled. The bouncing girl ran past Jarhead and handed the caps to the starter; he threw one in, stood back, signaled the timers, said "Mark! Set!" and shot.

Then a wild thing happened: Bobby pulled out front, and when the lanes fell in he was in second, just off Jamie Torffelson's shoulder.

Jarhead stopped beside me, his head panning like a naval cannon, his lips loose and open just wide enough to hold a budding rose. As it quickly became apparent that Bobby was going to do fine, he said, "That's you out there."

"That's me," I agreed.

"You're doing good," he said.

"I'm doing *well*," I corrected.

Bobby stayed with Jamie around the first lap. He passed me and Jarhead. I checked the split on Jarhead's stopwatch. It was too fast for Bobby to hold. Jarhead didn't even check the split. "Kick it in!" he screamed. I followed Jarhead across the infield toward the finish line. I watched Bobby and Jamie. Bobby hugged Jamie's shoulder, moving up. I was almost impressed. But Jamie held him out on the curve. Then, as they hit the stretch, they were both tripping, windmilling, kicking up arcs of cinders. Jamie crashed. Bobby went on. He looked behind him as he sprinted in at 2:01.

Jarhead threw his clipboards into the bleachers and shook Bobby. "God damn yes!" he screamed. "God damn yes!"

When Jarhead released Bobby I expected him to crumple like canvas to the track, but he stood straight. He put his hands on his head, laced his fingers together. I cut toward him through the pack of coaches and timers. He was breathing through his nose. I saw he had more underarm hair than I did.

"Nice scuffle," I said.

Someone called for the official finish time. A timer referred to the starting roster: "Carton's runner . . . Kevin Schuler." It was then I realized that I, Kevin Schuler, now held the state record for the 800-meter run. It was my first record, and my easiest.

An official pulled Jarhead away. "Bring the runner," said the official, pointing to Bobby. I followed. Suddenly, Ellie had her arm around me. I didn't care about anything right then except her. I wanted to tell her about the joints in my pocket.

"Your runner spiked Jamie," said Porterville's wiry coach.

Jarhead shook his head. He said, "Your boy tripped him as he tried to pass."

The starter and three officials and several coaches and runners huddled around. Sitting on the ground, thirty meters up the track, Jamie Torffelson had wide gashes above his right ankle. Cinders and blood colored his knees and palms. As we watched, two EMTs wearing latex gloves lifted him and led him away. "Don't let them trick you!" he called.

"I saw it," said Jarhead. "Your runner tripped my runner. It was clear if you were watching."

"It's true," said someone. All heads turned. It was my father, hands resting on his yellow binoculars. "I saw the Porterville runner trip Carton's boy," he said.

There was silence.

"Now wait," said the starter. He was the starter at all the local meets. "Isn't this kid"—he pointed to me—"Kevin Schuler?"

"Uh, no," said Jarhead. He put his hand on Bobby's shoulder. "This is."

No heads moved. The starter crossed his arms. Bobby bent over.

I stepped out, pulling Ellie with me. She was smiling at my side. "Look," I said, "his shoes."

We all looked. Even Bobby looked. His shoes, indeed. There were stripes of blood on the left toe. And below, an inch from the view of the world, were the illegal, half-inch spikes that had cut Jamie Torffelson. I knew they would not be seen, but I knew they were there. I knew a thing the world didn't.

But what the world saw was notable: Across the heel of the spikes, written in my mother's round script, was *K. Schuler*.

Ellie squeezed my side.

The starter nodded. "Okay," he said, "all right. The record stands and we can go home. No need to dawdle in this flipping cold if we don't have to."

"Frickin'-ass cold," I said, and a few people laughed. Everyone turned and left. Ellie rubbed her head against my neck.

I rode with my parents in the beige sedan. We followed the van to McDonald's, and then passed by. I understood: The Porterville bus was already there. We headed to Hardee's.

"Best eatin' in town," said my dad.

Mom laughed.

I told them that I'd cramped up at the last moment and Jarhead had substituted Bobby. "Cramps, you know. Crazy."

"You can win next week," said Mom.

Dad nodded as we pulled into Hardee's behind the van. I kept worrying that someone would moon us if we followed the van too much.

Dad said, "I know what a raw deal it must feel like to get pulled at the last moment from the race you were going to win. I know that's no fun."

"It didn't bother me," I said.

My parents respectfully made themselves scarce in Hardee's. I showed Ellie the joints and she kissed me. "I'm kissing you," she said, "not the joints."

Our team had placed last in the meet, but all we cared about now was food and warmth and each other. "We're not much as a team," I admitted to Ellie.

"Come on," screamed Jarhead, "we have to get home before midnight. On board!"

In the dark behind the van Ellie kissed me and I sucked on her neck and she pushed me off and looked at my face intently. We stood so close together that to focus on my face she had to cross her eyes.

I said, "I remember when you brought that hen to the egg drop contest. Fourth grade."

"I did," she said, and bit her bottom lip. "Back in those days when I was shy."

"You're still shy," I said. I poked her navel. "We were up on the bleachers," I whispered, "and Miss Palmer was about to throw the hen and I had this sudden anxiety. I worried that the hen might not fly. Might get hurt. And I looked over at you, and I knew you were having the same last-minute worries."

"I thought I was a monster," Ellie said. "I took this hen from her quiet life and was about to throw her off the bleachers . . ."

"But the hen did fine."

Ellie said: "Floated down."

"I'll tell," I said, "what I saw: not that the hen fell, but that the earth rose to hold her."

Jarhead leaned from the van door. "In the van!" he yelled.

Ellie kissed me and turned away. "Call me," she said. It was a thing we did: call each other at two or three in the morning.

I pulled her back.

I said: "Montana."

I sat in the back of the sedan and Dad drove behind the van. "Coach Reese is speeding," he said, chuckling.

"Pass 'em," I said.

Mom slept.

I was still worried about someone mooning us.

"Pass 'em before the bridge," I said.

Dad passed them on a straight stretch, immediately before the bridge. Mom woke up.

"Slow down for the bridge tonight," she said. The bridge was damp. I could hear road-spray in the wheel wells. I looked up the moonlit Osage. It was a wide river. The bridge was high. I wondered if this was the bridge from which you could see all the way up to Bagnel Dam. I lay down, not worrying about mooning anymore, and dozed.

I called Ellie's house that night at two. Her dad answered. "Officer?" he asked.

"There, you see," I whispered to Trolley Catchell as he lay wrapped in gauze and dry sheets a week after the meet, "we're it now. We're the ones. We're the products. We'll go on to show the world."

But despite his cushiony mass—the weight that buffered him from the bent van seats and the bones of his teammates—he died too. In the sleepless nights of April and May I sat and counted the things I had lost: my spikes, my team, my girlfriend, my coach. I imagined the thrashing and bubbling of my teammates at the bottom of the Osage

River, and the wobble of Trolley Catchell floating to the surface. Soon enough, midsummer, I counted the things I'd gained: two joints, one state record, and Bobby Sickle's training shoes.

What bothered me: When you're at the top, there is nothing above.

"Don't look down," they say to people who fear heights.

Went my new motto: "Don't look up."

I feared depths.

B u t   m o s t   o f   t h e   time, no one was thinking.

In August even, no one was thinking. I walked right into Carton's school the day classes began.

As I tried to enter the gymnasium, Principal Brill manhandled me as if I were a wayward calf. "Now hold it there, son. Just what do you pretend to be doing here?" he asked.

"Learning," I said.

"Not here, you're not."

As he led me to his office, he reminded me there were only three people in my class—only three people who hadn't been in the track van in March. These three were Pim Blotto, Tom Poolcall, and myself. All our wonderful girls had been in the van.

I suggested that with such a small class we'd learn in an intimate environment.

"Intimacy has no place in this school," Brill replied. We entered his office. He stood in front of the air-conditioning unit in the window and dried his palms on the cool breeze. He eyed me, said, "I've seen kids sprout up over a summer, but . . ." Then he walked to his desk and sat. He picked up the phone, looked to me.

"Three two one oh," I said.

He dialed. I heard Mom answer like a door hinge.

Brill explained the situation to her: "Either he transfers to Bryceville, Sieland, Bend City, Loke, or he can join the class in front of him."

"Well, he's never been too smart," I heard Mother say. Mr. Brill cleaned beneath his fingernails with a bent paper clip. His mustache was narrower than his nose.

"I venture," Brill said, "our Kevin would be more comfortable elsewhere. That would be more comfortable for everyone. So talk to the other schools. They know the situation. They'll waive out-of-district tuition. I'm sure they'd be proud to have him."

"What was Plato's last name?" I asked after he hung up. If I raised my intelligence on the spot I wouldn't have to transfer. "And what was Marx's *raison d'être* for suggesting religion was outmoded by industrialism?"

"Do I look like I do comedy?" said Brill.

He flushed me into the outer office. I sank into a vinyl seat, enjoying the air conditioning. He shook his head. "No, no, no. Wait for your mother out front."

Carton did not wait until Labor Day to begin classes. Bryceville did, but because of their twelve snow days last year they had waived that requirement and started two weeks early. Sieland, loathing to be outdone by their flatland neighbor, did the same. Loke began the same day as Carton but evacuated the school after twenty minutes because of hornets in the cafeteria. Bend City High School, the biggest school in the state, began classes the day after Carton. So it was there I found myself, a thirty-minute drive from home, inside the secretary pool, at 7:30 A.M. Principal Brill had arranged for the superintendent to handle my transfer personally.

"Visitors for Superintendent Porphorhessohln wait in puce chairs," said a small male secretary.

I found a puce chair.

Three seats away, in another puce chair, sat a man made of four parts: beautifully long legs, a concave chest, a Mediterranean visage, and smoldering eyes.

He leaned away from me and flashed his eyebrows. "Yes so you wait for the Mister Porphorhessohln too?" he said. He enjoyed his own accent. I guessed he was either Spanish, Moroccan, Italian, or Libyan.

Perhaps he was a terrorist.

He stirred, unfolded his long body and moved a limp hand toward mine. "I am Gregory Altrabashar."

"Great," I said. He was too old to be a student. He was mustached, pock-faced, handsome, calm, and exuded a languidness I imagined arose from sexual experience. He reclined in his chair as if he were a light windbreaker that had been flung there.

"I'm Kevin Schuler."

"That is so," he said. He turned away and nodded at the array of vice-principal doors. He wore running shoes and tight black jeans. I checked his shoes. His lacing style and tread-wear indicated he had negligible pronation and probably ran exclusively on pavement. I judged from his wormy calf muscles that perhaps he had run marathons.

I was wearing brand new boots.

"You run," I said.

He smiled and let his eyes twinkle. He smiled on. "Yes, yes. I run."

"I ran," I said.

"That is a shame then. Past tense."

"I hated it," I said.

"Ah," he said, "then you were good?"

"Oh yes."

"Double good?"

"Yes," I said.

"Yes, yes," he replied.

"Good, good."

"Yes," he said. He nodded at an approaching secretary who motioned to me. "Good luck, then."

* * *

"Dear prospective student!" announced Superintendent Porphorhes-sohln, a man crowned by a great racket of white, brackenish hair—like a Hereford cow might grow if given her druthers. And his forehead was red and vertical—a brick wall.

I sat before his huge metal desk. I deemed it bulletproof. There was a peaceful cluster of seconds while the superintendent shuffled through my file from Carton. Then he said, "Call me Umber."

"Yes, sir, Mr. Porphorhessohln. Thank you. Call me Mr. Schuler."

"Okey dokers, Kevin."

He closed my file and placed a paperweight of clear Lucite upon it. In the paperweight was suspended a yellow scorpion and many wee bubbles. I pointed to the scorpion.

"Yow," I said.

"You know it!" he replied. Then his bookshelf eyebrows dropped and he slid forward in his leather chair and lowered his voice. "I like you. You remind me of my grandson, Will."

"Well, thank you, your honor."

He looked at the ceiling fan. I looked at the ceiling fan.

He looked back at me. I looked back at him.

He said: "You can't come here. You're too smart."

"You should talk to my mother."

"No, really, I see your file. You're too smart for our school."

"Honestly, Mr. Porphorhessohln, I'm quite average. Second rate. Bland."

"Well, I . . . The problem is, Kevin, that here at Bend City High we have two brackets: extremely talented and intelligent students and drastically poor, hopeless students."

"That's me. The latter. Hopeless. I hate hope."

"No, no. Your scores and reports put you just below the talented and intelligent students, but far, far above the hopeless bracket."

"I can become more hopeless. There's room to expand, to broaden myself."

"No. You see, the state grants us extra resources for each extremely intelligent student—to fund gifted programming—and they give us extra resources for each hopeless student—to fund vocational training, LD classes, handicap facilities, speech pathologists, blah, blah, blah. It's all very lucrative. We're a magnet school for the brightest and the dullest. We get no money for poor, average, or good students. Good students like yourself. I suggest you enroll across town at Lower Bend."

"Uh . . ." I said, trying to sound stupid. But I was led to the door. Mr. Porphorhessohln opened the door airily to reveal the lanky, gorgeous Gregory Altrabashar standing in an easy contrapposto pose and pointing at me with two fingers.

"Hold a bit," he said. Then, softly: "Are you coming here to this school, my Kevin Schuler?"

"No," said the superintendent. "He's unfortunately too smart."

Gregory addressed Mr. Porphorhessohln: "Do you know I much think that this is the same and very Kevin Schuler who in his eighth-grade season at Croop County R-5 Public School Southeast Central Western Division, Carton, Missouri, broke the state 1A record for the eighth-grade 800-meter run? A record, Mister Sir, that is less than four seconds off the current 4A 800-meter record for *high school*, set by Lower Bend's Deek Hazystrump in 1985."

"This true, Kevin?"

My record, I dimly recalled, stood far more than four seconds off the high school record. I couldn't see Gregory's motivation for lying.

"Actually," I said, "Deek Hazystrump set the 4A 800-meter record in 1984."

"Oh, I am a mistake," said Gregory.

But the superintendent would not stand for my evasion of the question and I did finally admit that indeed my name was in the record books. Within five minutes after that admission I was enrolled in the ninth grade at Bend City High School. Umber Porphorhessohln and Gregory Altrabashar stood on either side of me as I completed the paperwork.

"Tuition is waived, of course," the superintendent assured me when I reached the section of the form for out-of-district students. Mr. Porphorhessohln himself stamped and licked and signed and copied and sealed my papers. He gave me a small yellow card on which were written directions to my counselor's office.

"Proceed there, Mr. Schuler," he ordered me.

"And Godspeed," said Gregory, smiling to reveal attractive, unstraightened teeth.

The superintendent blurted, "Godspeed to us all!" and laughed heartily. But his eyes then became fixed on Gregory and his laugh faded. His lips cinched as he looked Gregory over rather slowly. "Who the . . ." he said. He gave a snort through his nose. "Just who the . . ." he said softly. He glanced at me as if for assistance, then looked back to Gregory. "Who the ding dong are you, anyways?"

Gregory blinked, pointed to himself.

"He's Gregory," I said.

"Gregory Altrabashar," Gregory stated. "Your new coach of track and cross-country."

Porphorhessohln's eyebrows jumped. "Oh! Oh! Yes! Error for the superintendent! Alteredbasher! But rein in your get-go: You're not hired yet. You're just here for the interview."

Gregory beamed and gestured toward me as if I were a washing machine the superintendent had won. "I have recruited, here," he said, "the next 800-meter record-setter for Bend City High School. This is a boy who set the 800-meter record six times in his eighth grade season."

I smiled on cue.

Mr. Porphorhessohln tottered slightly.

"I think it was just one record . . ." I said softly.

"How many years has the Bend City High School lost each and every track meeting with the Lower Bend High School?" Gregory asked.

Mr. Porphorhessohln's eyes went dim. He seemed to be far away. "Come—sign—the—contract," he said.

"I will see you March first," Gregory whispered as he pushed me toward the door of the secretary pool.

In Missouri, March first is the opening day of legal, coach-led training for the track season.

I should explain what Gregory Altrabashar and Umber Porphorhessohln saw when they looked at me. They did not see a scrawny eighth grader with soft patches of hair just beginning to creep up his ankles. They saw a fully developed young man who could have been mistaken for a college senior. Since March, my body had fulfilled a prophecy of perfection.

Consider: In March I stood five feet nine inches and weighed, in light clothes, one hundred and twenty-six pounds. The diameter of my biceps was ten inches; thighs, seventeen inches; calves, thirteen inches; neck, thirteen inches; chest, thirty-four inches; arm span, sixty-nine inches; waist, twenty-nine inches; penis (erect), five and one-eighth inches. My vision was 20/25. There was little hair on my body. I ate approximately 2,400 calories a day and slept at least nine hours a night, ten on weekends. I shaved with my father's Norelco once a week. To summarize, I resembled a row-end stalk of July sweet corn that has gone two weeks waterless and consequently achieved good height but no girth and stands slightly bowed under the weight of its own stunted, rust-silk ears.

I was scrappy-cute.

I recorded my physical dimensions regularly, charted the numbers on gridded paper and eagerly awaited each measuring in anticipation of growth. Some key data, such as weight, I tracked with line graphs. I am not the only boy to have kept such a record. These numbers are the diary of the teenage male—he eager to quantify the ascension into the trap of manhood.

I was following the only course that was allowed. There is one lane in that race.

And observe: By August I stood six feet tall and weighed one hundred and sixty-two pounds. The diameter of my biceps was fourteen inches; thighs, twenty-one inches; calves, fifteen inches; neck, sixteen inches; chest, thirty-nine inches; arm span, seventy-three inches; waist, thirty-two inches; penis (erect) six and one-half inches. My vision had reverted to 20/20. My honey-toned body hair was fully grown, but not overgrown (I had none upon my back). I ate 2,900 calories per day, slept under eight hours each night, and shaved with foam and safety razor each morning. My voice had dropped three whole steps. Perhaps the only thing that hadn't changed was my shoe size, but as a perfect ten it had no room for improvement.

My body had become an attractive paradigm of the well-toned ectomorph. I had dusty blond hair, left a little tousled and shaggy, and deep-set blue eyes that sometimes appeared gray. My teeth were straight and white, my nose cutely, slightly pug, my chin and smile strong, my manners typically modest, my posture good, my voice mellow, and my laugh quiet. True, I laughed and smiled rarely in those days, but when I did there appeared one dimple on my right cheek. Mother applied the nickname "Oak" to me and often stood before me and clapped my shoulders and said, "Your father never had such shoulders! Your father never had such a chin! Your father never had such eyes!"

Which left me wondering, what had my father had?

My school counselor happily relegated me into quiet classes: Drafting, English, Physical Science, Nations of Our World, Health, Practical Math, and Basic Structure (a construction-related class). I attended the Sundry Seeley half of the high school—the vocational half of the school. You could not walk far in the building without hearing the clacking of typewriters, the whine of a table saw, or seeing a splash of sparks from an arc welder. There was a wing of the school devoted to agriculture classes. There were indoor mechanic bays to allow twenty-four cars to be worked upon simultaneously. There was a fully stocked lumberyard. One section of the school held learning disability classes. For my part, I did my homework, kept my head down, and avoided involvement with any of the brute politics and iron-fisted cliques that ruled Sundry Seeley Vo-Tech-Ag-Special Ed.

From our small, triple-paned windows we could look out across the street toward the other half of the school, Zame Smith Woolstonecrapt, where future doctors and professors and marketing professionals studied Latin, fuzzy logic, macroeconomics, writing, philosophy, organic chemistry. During my fourth-hour science class some Zame Smith students ate lunch, and on nice days a group of them ate outside, within my view, beneath the wide umbrella of a grand elm tree, and as they ate they talked. They *conversed*, and I envied that.

But Sundry Seeley was glorious—the teachers expected nothing of my classmates and me. Without the pressures of steady achievement, I flourished and made excellent grades. The teachers enjoyed me because I was calm and didn't break things on purpose.

"Are you a chili fan or a pork-fritter-on-bun fan?" asked the boy behind me in the lunch line. It was late November and we were waiting for chili, carrot sticks, canned peach halves, a peanut butter sandwich, a sugar cookie, chocolate milk, and saltines.

"I suppose," I answered hesitantly, "that I am a fan of both." I knew that this guy's name was Jol Brule, and that he was one of the welding guys who spent half his days in the welding pits. He was very good from what I heard—could hold a torch in each hand—and he was also a starting receiver on the football team, even though he was a freshman like myself.

"That's very interesting," Jol Brule said. "Because I have found that in general a person is either a fan of our school lunch chili or our school lunch pork-fritter-on-bun, but not both."

I was nervous. It was remarkably unusual to have a somewhat normal conversation anywhere within Sundry Seeley, much less in the lunch line. Moreover, behind Jol stood the quartet of bullies known locally as Eeny, Meeny, Miney, and Mo, and they were monitoring our conversation with what appeared to be dissatisfaction.

"I must be an anomaly, then," I told Jol.

Jol shook his head. "Well, I'm a fan of both, too. But what about dessert? Let me ask you this. Are you a cream puff man or a honey bun man?"

We were all shuffling along in line, trays ready but empty. Jol looked me up and down as if he were trying to guess my answer from how I dressed. His skin was the richest coffee-brown you could find, and made my skin look like skim milk. But the bullies were waiting for my answer, and I was trying to decide which response would offend them least.

"Honey bun?" I said.

Miney laughed. I wondered if I was in for a relocation of my temporomandibular joint.

Jol turned to Miney. "What?" he asked. "What's your deal?"

"I just can't see," said Miney, who had a good fifty pounds on me, "how anyone could say honey bun over cream puff."

"Then you're a cream puff man?" Jol said.

"Absolutely," Miney said.

"Me too," said Eeny. And Meeny was nodding along.

"What about you, Mo?" Jol asked.

"Peach cobbler," Mo professed.

"Ah!" Jol and Meeny said together.

"Peach cobbler is great," Eeny said.

"I love peach cobbler," said Jol.

All of us were nodding now, happy in the way that only teenage boys can be when they are about to be served a hearty lunch.

"But you know what?" I said to them. "I like all desserts. Desserts are good."

"Kevin's right," Jol said. And I don't know how he knew my name, but he did. "Desserts *are* good."

"I," Mo remarked, "basically like eating in general."

We all voiced our agreement with Mo, then, and presently we came to the head of the lunch line. Our trays were loaded with food while we watched silently, the steam rolled off the bowls of chili, and the hour seemed splendidly adequate.

My dad was home the next weekend. The dispatcher had canceled his run to Spokane.

I suggested we go to the football game. Bend City was playing Lower Bend—that other school in Bend City, that school for poor, average, and good students that typically beat Bend High at every sport. But this year Bend City's football team had been doing well and was widely favored to give Lower Bend a good match. Our Zame Smith quarterback senior was a second-generation Chinese-American National Merit Scholar named Jonny Twe who always managed during interviews to discuss football in purely Aristotelian terms.

Dad agreed to go to the game. He winked at me. "I'll disappear when your girlfriends come 'round."

"Much appreciated," I said.

After dinner he stood up from the table and flipped on his green AC Delco hat. He nodded to Mother and said, "Off to the game."

Usually, mornings Father left for the road, he'd say this: "Off to the war."

In the dusk, Dad's maroon big rig occupied the driveway. The truck was taller than our house. And it sparkled even in the twilight, even for the lack of sun. Our pale sedan cowered before the truck.

Dad tossed the Buick's keys to me.

"You drive," he said. "I don't like to be so low to the road."

"I'm fourteen. Not legal." I tossed the keys back and he came to the driver's door.

"Oh, yeah," he said. "Which son are you? Jimmy, Rufus, Paul?"

No, there were no girls I wanted to see at the football game. It was Jol "Lojo" Brule I watched, number sixty-six. He was nearly the shortest man on the field, but what he lacked in height he made up for in speed and agility.

Dad and I spoke little during the game, and I knew Dad was watching Jol, too. The field lights always seemed to shine brighter on Jol's sticky hands than on anything else—though the features of his brown face, shaded beneath his helmet, were all but indiscernible. It wasn't that we were all so awed by his performance that we couldn't watch the whole game objectively; it was just that Jol always appeared wherever the game was. He had instinct, luck, intuition—call it what you may. He would pluck long, wobbly passes from the air as easily as if they were shirts hanging on a line. Then he'd outrun the pursuers. Or he would carry Jonny Twe's perfectly timed lateral passes or hand-offs through a thicket of defenders, ducking low sometimes to avoid a tackle (a signature move that explained his nickname). He was classified as a receiver, yes, but he sometimes played the role of tight end, and sometimes even running back. And we could all see Jol's father hanging over the handrail down at the front of the bleachers, cackling and hooting throughout the game, but not from joy. He derided his son after every play.

"What! Hey hey! Whoa! That's done lost the down, you fool! You shoulda tucked in by the thirty! Fool of fools!"

Though Jol stood only five and a half feet tall, his father was a full foot taller. Perhaps that is why no one told him to shut up.

Bend City won handily—the first victory over Lower Bend in twelve years, the announcer said. And I swear there was only one person in the stands who doubted that Jol Brule was the sole reason Bend City won.

Even after the final horn Jol's father could be heard over all the noise: "Coulda won with double those points if'n it weren't for such dumb rock-head playin' by number SIXTY-SIX!"

"Amen!" hollered someone sarcastically, some father wearing a Lower Bend sweatshirt.

I figured I couldn't blame Jol's father for being assholish, couldn't fault him, just as I couldn't blame my father for being his usual quiet self at the game and in the car on the half-hour drive out of Bend City and back into the country. And I was my usual quiet self, too. The engine knocked. Our bald tires whined. The heater fan warbled. We were silent, but the car conversed with itself.

At home, Mother came to my room where I sat reading and told me Mrs. Butterbit had left a letter for me from her daughter. "Who to who?" I asked. "From who?"

Mother smiled, then nodded, then stopped smiling as she stood in my doorway. Her hair was in rollers. "Ellie Butterbit," she said.

I recognized the name of one of my teammates. "I didn't know her much," I said.

Mother blinked at me, then began speaking quickly. "Now, I'll keep the letter. You just let me know. You're fine, Kevvy. Are you going to be up late? I've locked the front door. Your father is asleep. Do you need another blanket tonight? Tomorrow I'm going to the outlet mall. We could see if they have those shirts you like. I hate to drive the car when it rains. So I hear it might rain. Could you vacuum your room tomorrow? Of course you will. You keep it so tidy now. I'll leave you. You're fine, Kevvy. Door open, door closed? Door closed?"

She had said as much to me in thirty seconds as she often did in an entire day. And her eyes roamed the floor through the whole speech and her hand flapped like a starling at her shirt collar.

"Closed," I said, and she shut the door.

three

Only on paper is February the shortest month. Something in the cruel precision of a month with exactly four weeks lends to the trickery and grind of its wintry sinkhole. In central Missouri, spring typically arrives in March; but in the midst of February, during the clash and glare of purchased sentiment on Valentine's Day, March and its green announcement seem farther away than next Christmas, than next February even.

It was on Valentine's Day that Gregory Altrabashar appeared in the doorway of my drafting class. He looked like an ill Russian in his fur-trimmed parka. I wondered if indeed maybe he was a Soviet, from the south, the Muslim kind of Soviet. Georgian? Azerbaijani? He handed me a small foil-wrapped chocolate heart, then said, "If you will please, then, you must get your person examined physically by a doctor of medicine in front of beginning track practice in March." He gave me the physical exam form.

"Thanks for reminding me," I said, "but I won't be running track."

Then, there, Gregory's mustache drooped below his lips.

* * *

"Heya, hey! Hold it!" someone belted as I walked out of Sundry Seeley after the final bell. It was Superintendent Porphorhessohln, wearing nothing but a brown suit in the February wind. On his lapel, a Valentine pin proclaimed HUGS FOR ALL!

"I do believe you'll be running track this spring," he told me.

"An interesting enough proposition," I said, "but no."

"Yes."

"Uh," I said. I spotted Mother waiting for me in the Buick.

"Yes," he repeated.

"I can't."

"You will and you can."

I stood captive.

"Don't assume I don't know about the accident last spring," the superintendent said. "Do you think you're the only one that's had a scrape with suffering? Do you?"

I was not set to answer.

"Come by my office sometime and I'll tell you about my friend who died five feet in front of me in Inchon in 1950. Then I'll elucidate some of the finer points of my teenage days and nights in the coal mines in West Virginia. I'll show you a picture of my cousin Rex who didn't see fit to continue his life—and just after his third son was born. I've got a pocketful of little pities and dreggy guilt I could pour on you, son. And none of it false and none of it fit for the glory of movies or TV or rock music. How 'bout let's face ourselves and learn a little?

"You weren't even on the bus," he said.

"Van," I said.

Now his hand was on my shoulder. Now his other hand pointed at me—all four fingers and the thumb, jabbing my chest.

"I will see you *on* the track *on* the first day of March with your completed physical form in hand. And if you are not there—and I don't care if you have to miss your momma's funeral!—you will receive, on the second of March, a bill for the entire year's out-of-district tuition."

* * *

But things are not simple.

"I'm here wonderin'," said Dr. Rory Spittle, who yearned to be a farmer and not a doctor, "if I can let you run track when your heart rate is forty. I'm wonderin' how your brain's gettin' the air it needs. Do you feel dizzy or lightheaded sometimes, like you're gonna' slip off?"

"No," I said. "I guess I'll skip track this spring."

"Hot hell—skip walkin'! Take up bowling, golf, darts, or skeet shooting—some sport that doesn't flex your heart muscle over-much. Don't be limiting yourself at such a green age to just one sport. Don't box yourself in like that. Look at me, in here doctorin' and talkin' in the same little three-room office four days a week and two in the hospital, plus call hours and emergencies and whatbeezulbeedoo, when I could be out seven days a week tractorin' and plantin' and sprayin' and feedin' and truckin' and diggin' and spittin' Skoal at the bluegrass. Damn. That's what I *want* to do. But I'm done trapped. Think about that and tell me it doesn't make your noodle wiggle. Do you know what kind of stale air my lungs breathe fifty hours a week? Do you feel how soft my hands are, how pale my skin?"

And so I *was* on the track March first and *did* have my physical in hand, but it was not a passing physical. Gregory took the paper greedily, said, "Speed up and change," and turned away.

"Read it," I said.

He faced me. "Bean dip?" he said.

"No—read the physical."

He looked at the half-sheet for the longest time as if trying to remember English. Then he looked up into the grandstand. At the top stood Superintendent Porphorhessohln, silhouetted against the overcast sky. Gregory shook his head ever so slightly, and on that signal the superintendent came slowly down the steps, watching his toes all the way. Behind me I could hear the Volvos and Civics leave the students' lot at Zame Smith Woolstonecrapt. Further up the hill, at Sundry Seeley, the rasp of glass-packed mufflers rode the breeze as Camaros and

Silverados and Chevelles and all manner of knightly V-8s ignited and fled the school.

Porphorhessohln read the physical and looked at me flatly. His suit jacket was unbuttoned and he wore no belt.

"This doctor may be a fool," said Gregory. "Athletic prodigies sometimes have a tiny heart rate. Their heart is that much efficient. What variety of doctor is this"—he read the signature—"Dr. Glissat?"

"Spittle."

"Skittle?" asked Gregory.

"Dr. Spittle is a GP," I said.

"Where?" said Porphorhessohln.

"Carton."

"No, no, no," Porphorhessohln said.

He and Gregory stepped away and conversed beyond my hearing. They came back after less than a minute.

"You'll run this week," Porphorhessohln said, "since physicals aren't officially required until the first competition, and before then we'll find you a doctor who knows athletes."

"I know people," said Gregory.

"And I know people," said Porphorhessohln.

"We know double people," said Gregory.

I did not know people, but I knew how much I hated running. I spoke up: "Listen, my physician and I have decided it would be in my health's interest to forgo running in exchange for nonstrenuous sports, such as darts or pool or pinball."

"Oh!" said Gregory. "I play the pool! The billiards!"

It flashed in my mind that he might have been Indian or Pakistani.

I asked the superintendent a question then. "Have you checked for my *six* records in the official register?"

"I did that back in August, the day we signed you up."

It saddened me to see him lying. For if he had indeed checked the record books, of course, he would have seen I held only one record.

"Schuler," said Porphorhessohln, "you're running this year. Unless there's a damn hole in your heart!"

"There are four."

The superintendent wore a stone face. I noticed a scar on his chin-line. He said, "I have no qualms about hand-delivering a five-thousand-dollar tuition bill to your parents tomorrow morning. And I certainly have no qualms about making your passage through Sundry Seeley a smothering hell unless you are on the track in ten minutes busting your ass for Coach Altrabarass."

"Altrabashar, sir," corrected Gregory.

"Altrabasher."

"*Shar—*"

I headed to the locker room.

A week later, I was on the track after school, training with the eleven other mid-distance runners. We were running what we incorrectly called a chain fartlek—a drill where everyone runs in a single-file line at a moderate pace and then the person at the back of the line sprints to the front and takes the lead and then the new person at the end of the line sprints to the front and takes the lead, and so on. The drill reminded me of a book from my childhood in which hundreds of dogs are racing toward a canine festival in hundreds of tiny cars. They, in their general clownishness, probably executed maneuvers very similar to chain fartleks. But they were going to a canine festival and therefore their antics were quite excusable. We, though, were running in circles. Or ovals.

Above us, around us, it was one of those March days in Missouri that aspires to be a June afternoon. It was warm, and the sky was rudely blue and packed full of infant cumulous clouds. A man had pulled his white Cadillac up on the grass at the end of the track and was watching us closer than Gregory was. Gregory's black hair was being blown about today, and he seemed to be sapped of focus. As we passed Gregory on the straight stretch, Todd Halverstadt asked him what our split was—we were supposed to keep on a 1:45 quarter mile. Todd repeated his query.

Gregory looked up. "Oh," he said, and we passed him, and he called out no split.

Billy Sommers, a senior, said, "He's wandering today."

"Back in Iran maybe," Todd said.

"I heard he had a wife and daughter there," Ezekiel Bly said as he sprinted up the line to take the lead position.

All the distance runners but myself were students in Zame Smith Woolstonecrapt.

"I heard he had two wives and ten daughters, but in Turkey," Orson Vik said.

After we'd completed three miles of fartlek, Gregory sent us to the weight room. "But you," he said to me, "have an appointment with the man who stands beside that car." He pointed down toward the man by the Cadillac.

"Who is that?"

"He is a sports doctor from the state university and has agreed to see you free of charge. He is very busy and you are honored he will take his time for you."

"I am honored he will take his time for me," I said.

I approached the man. The door of his Cadillac was open and I could see a cellular phone resting on the tan leather seat. He wore khaki pants, a purple oxford shirt, penny loafers, and two beepers on his belt. He held out his hand while I was still ten feet away.

I shook the hand—it was as broad as a skillet.

"Kevin, I'm Dr. Brake."

"Fine to meet you."

"Do you mind if I feel your pulse right now—you only finished the run a minute ago."

He felt my pulse in my wrist. He then took my blood pressure, listened to my heart and my lungs, and felt my glands. He took my temperature, looked into my ears, eyes, nose, and throat, tested my reflexes, felt many of my tendons, and asked questions about my sundry body fluids. His queries continued.

"Do you ever feel your heart skip or hesitate or beat one huge beat?"

"No."

"Do you ever feel that your breathing is raspy after running, especially after running in cool air?"

"No."

"Do you cough after running?"

"No."

"Have you suffered from shinsplints?"

"No."

He asked me if I'd ever had pain in my feet.

"Nope."

"Those shoes of yours look to be way past retirement," he said.

I looked at my dingy training flats. It suddenly struck me they weren't really my shoes at all. They had belonged to a kid named Bobby, I recalled, and Dr. Brake was right that they appeared to have about two or three seasons of use on them. I did not clearly recall how I had come to wear the shoes of another boy, but I did know that when I had first acquired the shoes I walked a bit stiffly because the shoes were rigid, almost new. I couldn't figure how the shoes had become so worn.

"You've only been training one week this season, right?"

"Yes."

"Then are some of your muscles still sore from starting training?"

"No."

"Up here?" he asked, pointing to his thigh.

"Nope."

He asked me more questions before finally putting his equipment into his trunk, filling out a new physical form for me, and then getting into his car and rolling down the tinted window.

"You leaving?" I asked.

"No. I like talking from the seat of my car."

He lit a cigarette then, this doctor, and I noted how when he was seated his gut hung well over his belt. He told me to step away from the car so I wouldn't inhale his smoke, and then he talked.

"I observe from your running that you are an exemplar of biomechanical efficiency. You do not pronate or supinate. Your stride is well-matched to your height and your knee-lift is picture perfect. Your heart rate reveals your tremendous cardiovascular capacity, and your testimony that you have felt no soreness during this first week of training suggests remarkable things."

He dragged on his cigarette twice.

"And yet, you appear to be a mediocre runner. I saw you run the four quarter miles before the chain drills, and you consistently came in eighth or ninth—your times hovered above 1:15. Can you explain that? Were you holding back?"

"Holding back?" I asked. "I was just running—I wasn't thinking about speed, really. I hate running, you know."

"Some of the best athletes contain great pools of hatred within themselves. And when they channel that hatred into the sport—well, they do well."

"You mean to suggest that I use my hatred of the sport to excel at the sport that created the hate?"

"Sure."

"I don't know what I think of that. I might think that's poppycock. Running pulls me down."

"Makes you depressed?"

"It pulls me into low regions."

"Low regions," the doctor mouthed.

"Yes."

"I'm not a sports psychologist, Kevin, but when I saw you run last year, I saw energies flowing through you that made you excel. You were running faster as a scrawny eighth grader than you are now. Tell me: Is there a silent space within you when you run? A quiet place from which your discipline flows?"

"I don't have discipline."

"No?"

"And no quiet place. There's never quiet."

"Then what's inside you?"

"Commotion."

The doctor said nothing.

I explained: "Like kids babbling or whispering and giggling when they're supposed to be quiet."

"Kids?"

"I am mediocre," I insisted.

Dr. Brake blinked dully at me. His cigarette ash had grown half an inch long. After many seconds, he said, "You have to face your aptitude." He dropped his cigarette into the car's ashtray. "Maybe you have to face the forces behind your aptitude."

"When did you see me run last year?"

"I don't recall exactly, but sometimes I check up on athletes I hear about. I had heard of your sudden accomplishments, heard of you tearing the cinders off those 1A tracks, setting records. I came to see you. April or May."

"I didn't compete after March of last year."

Brake shook his head. "What do you mean? I saw you. You were in the papers."

Dr. Brake told me he would come back to check on me and drove away over the grass, up the straight stretch of the track, past Gregory—who waved timidly and dropped his whistle—out the field's gate, and down the street.

Perhaps I cannot describe my native land objectively. The trees are smaller than those on the coasts, I think. Our only common evergreens are cedars, really, and they turn drab in the winter. From November through March, the grass is tan—when not covered by snow—except for the tufts of orange broom sage that announce the tired soil of our region.

Carton lies twenty miles west of Bend City, in the Ozark borderlands. My parents' gray ranch house is five miles northeast of Carton. It is a two-bedroom house with electric strip heating and no garage. Half an hour to our south, the hills are huge and wooded and the soil unfit for crops except in creekbottoms. A few minutes to our north the

land is flat and open, with old hedgerows of Osage orange—good soy-
bean country, good pasture. So we live between the plains and the
Ozarks, caught between the flatlands and the knobs. The hills around
our house are relatively large—some are wooded, some cleared. Within
a mile of us are cornfields, bean fields, wheat fields, hog lots, cattle pasture, hay fields, and virgin woods. One of our neighbors grows pump-
kins in a low field beside Keen Creek. Another neighbor has
strawberries that draw pickers out from Bend City each June. Around
our house grow silver maples that rustle through the summers and
drop branches when a wind storm comes through.

Mid-March, a Saturday morning, Father drove me into Carton. We
went to the garage to buy a used tire for his semi, then we drove to the
hardware store. I looked at the revolving display of pocketknives. A
short man wearing an apron stopped beside me.

"Hiya, old Kevin," he said.

I recognized him and his sag-lid eyes, but didn't know who he was.

Father stepped around the corner of the aisle. "You remember Fitz
Sickle, Kevin," he said.

I shook this Mr. Sickle's dry hand, and when he asked how the city
folk were treating me, I told him they were doing fine by me.

"I've been just a bit afflicted for a while now, you know," Mr.
Sickle told me, then he leaned hard on his broomstick, dropped his
voice down into his chest so far I almost lost it, and spoke these next
words real slow, "for almost a year now, you know," then he pushed his
shoulders back and reclaimed his voice, "and I wondered if you might
be interested in doing some little farmwork and yardwork up at our
place. Some chorework, you know. I'd pay you fine. I'd like to see you
around, and Mrs. Sickle, too. No one's been fishing the ponds there for
a long time, and you're free to come do that anytime you want, and
your dad too, you know. We'd pay real good for any work. We still like
you, Kevin. We do."

* * *

After I left the strange Mr. Sickle in the hardware store, I walked down the hill through Carton in the mist. The houses around me were the older part of town and they were all white and squat. A pair of blue sweatpants lay in the ditch. The sidewalk was cracked all along the way. No birds called here.

I came before the Carton schoolhouse.

Outside the front doors of the school stood a pillar of red bricks upon which was fastened a plaque cast with the names of those who had died in the accident one year ago:

JASON BLICK
ELLEN BUTTERBIT
TROLLEY CATCHELL
GINA DALEY
YOLANDA EISEN
GREGORY FRENCH
HOOVER GARFIELD
HEATHER GARNET
ELISA PAULSON
ROBERT REESE, COACH
ROBERT SICKLE
GEORGIA TEETER
JENNIFER TEETER
WILLIAM WYNSOM

I touched the metal plaque as if it carried some tactile code, but the only message I received was that the metal was cold. On top of the monument sat a pair of bronze shoes. I watched Mr. Arkass screw the shoes into the brick. He was the oldest, wisest janitor in the world. He smiled broadly at me when I met his eyes, the kind of smile you give someone you know so well you don't have to speak a greeting.

The bronze shoes looked familiar.

They were Nikes. They were spikes.

I rubbed their heel—no *K. Schuler* written there.

Then I peeked beneath. Illegally long spikes.

"My shoes are golden," I said.

"Who?" asked Mr. Arkass. Tyler, we kids called him.

"Those are my shoes. In there." I knocked on the bronze with my knuckle.

"There's nothing in there—it's just a cast of the shoes."

I tried to enclose the shoes in my hands.

Tyler pulled the bill of his engineer cap up and then snapped it back down. He was head bus driver, head mechanic, head janitor.

"Lead me," I said, and he dropped his screwdriver and masonry screws and took me into the empty school, through the dark gymnasium where our footsteps echoed, down the tiled hallways with no windows. Behind the classroom doors, radiators clicked. Tyler guided me up and out and back and then up again, to the highest, darkest room in the school, an attic lined with boxes and piles of old trophies. Insulation hung in loose strips from the ceiling. Old flagpoles huddled in the corner. In this room, beneath the light of one bare bulb, Tyler Arkass pulled my Nikes from a box and restored them to my hands. They looked as if they'd been soaked in dishwater and then caked with toothpaste. I scraped the residue away from one shoe with my fingernail and showed Tyler my name written across the heel. I scraped again to reveal the clean, ice-blue racing stripe.

"This is just fine," I said. The shoes made my hands tingle and my head light.

"Why were your shoes in the van?" Tyler asked.

I smelled the shoes, wondering if I could scent the river.

"I don't know why they were in the van," I said. "Why, why, why?"

Tyler was still looking inquisitively at me.

"I loaned them to some kid for a race," I said. "I think."

"What's that?" Tyler asked. He pointed to the toe of one shoe, where the residue had fallen away to show a brown stripe, a stain of some sort.

"I don't know that either," I answered. "There's not much I know."

"You ran barefoot that spring," Tyler said.

"What?" I asked.

"In the races, I mean. Not in training."

"Is that some kind of metaphor?" I asked.

"It's no kind of metaphor."

"You're talking strange talk," I said. "Maybe you know more about me than I know about myself."

"Now, I'm not so grand."

"But no. You know the lives of this school. You have insight."

"I'm a janitor. And a mechanic."

"And you drive buses. For what, for twenty years?"

"For twenty-six years. But I'm not much of a coach, right?"

"Don't limit yourself."

"Don't limit yourself," he echoed.

I ran home from Carton, as planned—six miles from the school to my house—holding one of my spikes in each hand. As I ran I watched the hills in the mist and sometimes they seemed to be rolling toward me and sometimes they seemed to be retreating. Dad passed me in the sedan, honking, weaving down the center of the blacktop, spraying water on me. His weaving made me think of the Missouri River, which rolled along about ten miles north of our house, which rolled through Bend City, but which I never gave much thought. But rivers sometimes made their own way into my thoughts, flowed right into me, right over me.

four

My mother.

My mother is the kind of mother who buys five gallons of black-berry jam from the wholesale club on the access road beside the inter-state in the university town of Hibernia, forty miles to our north, and then spoons the jam into Mason half-pints, seals each jar with a flat canning lid and band—beneath which she places a foam-backed, lace-edged circle of flower-print material purchased pre-assembled at the craft store in the mall in Bend City—and then slaps onto each jar a computer-printed, self-adhesive label she ordered from the back pages of a women's magazine that reads, in what I suppose is an imitation of Victorian-era handwriting, FROM THE KITCHEN OF EMELDA-LAYNE SCHULER.

She was busy at this project on the evening of that Saturday I recovered my spikes. I approached her and asked her what I had done all the spring and summer following the accident.

"Besides making lists each day of the things you'd lost and gained and posting them above your bed?"

"Besides that."

"You didn't do much," she said.

"What little did I do?"

"I think it's healthy you're not dwelling on it."

"I've always been a healthy boy."

"You became an early riser."

"How's that?" I asked.

She stopped her busywork then and looked at me.

"You ran," she said. "You ran a lot."

She told me that beginning only a few days after the accident, I arose each morning at dawn and ran, a different route each day: I ran down our gravel road, or down to the creek, or across the long pastures and over the ford, along the narrow, hilly lane that ran through Bert Kahl's farm, out onto the county blacktop that traced the ridgeline. Some mornings, I ran to school. I ran on roads and cross-country. I hurdled barbed-wire fences. Even in rain I ran, and on wet mornings Mother drove behind me in the sedan, making sure a storm didn't knock me over or strike me dead with lightning.

"In one storm you turned onto Vance Ridge Road—like you were looking for lightning. So I pulled in front of you and you ran into the ditch to avoid the car and kept on running and so I pulled up in front of you again and opened the back door and pushed you right in there. You didn't struggle, but lay there across the backseat. I asked you why you wanted to run in such weather, why you kept running so much. But you didn't answer—you didn't answer much in those days. On nights after you got home from track meets I'd feed you some soup and ask you how you'd done, but you would just answer, 'Fine,' or 'Good.' I'd have to call Tyler the next day to find out how well you really did."

"Tyler Arkass?"

"He drove you to all the track meets for the rest of the season. He took you in the big bus."

"I don't remember any of that, Mom."

"Well, Kevvy, you won every race you entered!" she said. "I can't see why you wouldn't remember—you were so good! Your father took his vacation in May just to see you run. You were good and you *should* remember it!"

Mother left the kitchen then and came back with a shoe box. She set the box on the table and opened it and inside were blue ribbons, gold medals, and six certificates stating I had set new state 1A records in the eighth-grade 800-meter run. The certificates were dated from late March to mid-May.

"We found these all in the trash, in June," Mother said.

"I guess I didn't want them," I said.

"Why did you run, Kevvy?"

I stood blankly.

"Why did you run, Kevvy?"

"What was I supposed to do?" I asked. "What can a boy do? Look how good I was."

I searched my room that night and found, far within my closet, a folder full of loose-leaf notebook paper on which I had listed, over and over again, the names of the people who had died in the accident. There were twenty-nine pages that each listed all the victims. And further back in the folder were many pages that listed only some of the victims. And further back still there were pages that listed only a few people. Interspersed with these lists—all written in ballpoint in my tight script—were pages that at first seemed to be nonsense, but eventually worked themselves straight.

Like this:

W-
W-
E-
WE-
WEE-
WE-
-
VI-
WI-
WHEE-
WHEAL-
WHEEL-
WEUL-

WAEUL-
WIL-
WI-
WILL
WILLEE
WILLIUM
WILLEEUM
WILLYUM
WILLYIM
WILLIAM.

William.

A-
AE-
AIN-
RAIN-
RAINEY-
RANA-
RANAIL-
RAYNI-
RAYNOD-
RA-
R-
 -
R
 -
REYNODSL-
REYNOLDS.

Reynolds.

SOL-
SOLI-
SOWL-
ISOWL-
INSO-
INSA-
 -
IN-
INT-
WINTSOL-
 -
WINS-
WINSUL-

WINSOM-
WYNSOM.

Wynsom.

William Reynolds Wynsom—my teammate.

Now I remembered that this is how the names came to me throughout the spring and summer: in a quiet spelling that made me sweat. The names came in no particular order, and once they came, they stayed.

But though I had recovered the names, I had no images, no faces, no persons. These were just names to me. They meant nothing to me. In that respect they weren't really even names, but just words, just letters strung together with nothing standing behind them. So I could look at these pages, juxtapose different names next to each other, pick names at random from the list, even speak names out loud at random, and I felt no attachment to any of them. The names were all equal.

One odd thing: Mixed in with these pages and pages naming my dead teammates was a page on which I had reconstructed my own name.

I walked, that weekend, into the hills to our south. I walked out across Jim Toto's pasture, then across the creek, and into the woods. Crows were about in pairs. The trees carried gauzy yellow and red banners—thousands of buds coming forth.

I walked along the lip of the cliff that stood above the floodplain. From there I could see the hills across Keen Creek—the hills bobbing and bumping as if they were afloat on some river of their own. The fields below me lay stretched out and barren. They had not been tilled or plowed or planted yet, and last year's corn stalks covered some of them like the rubble of a forest after a fire.

I recalled that from this point, locally called Cissy Point, the view encompassed three counties, but today I could only count two counties before me. I counted again and again. Two counties. Just two.

* * *

Several nights later, on March twentieth—the first track meet of the year—I stood at the starting line of the 800-meter run, wearing my old spikes—now cleaned and bright once again—wondering why Gregory had even put me in the race when there were ten runners on our team who were faster than me at that distance. My best training time that spring for the 800-meter had been 2:26—downright paltry.

I stood on the far outside of the track on the stagger-start line. The starter mouthed instructions to us, but I ignored him. And when the gun went off I tripped a little because the shot surprised me, seemed to come right inside me and knock on some door I'd forgotten. Then, in the wake of the gunshot came silence—I didn't even hear the shot echoing back from the grandstand. I didn't hear the home crowd cheering, though I saw mouths gaping and hands clapping.

I was inside myself. I barely recognized the territory, but it was myself and it felt good to meet that person again.

Because of my poor start, I ran in last place as we entered the first corner. One of my teammates, a sophomore girl who did long jump, cheered me on from the infield—she was bent at her waist, arms straight at her sides, hands made into fists, face crimson, mouth open and black—but I heard nothing.

I held on to the silence. Or maybe it held on to me. It was solid. It was bedrock. I found a pace, and my body let me know that I could win this race. So I moved up in the outside lanes, careful to avoid being boxed in, not even hearing my own footfalls or my own breaths. My feet felt hot and light, and the breeze that played across my face and arms and legs was a breeze of my own making, the breeze of my speed.

I passed my teammate Brad Himmelstur, a senior whose personal record in the 800 was 1:56. He uttered one word as I overtook him, but I didn't hear it. Perhaps it was "Go!" or "Nice!" or "Fuck!"

As I passed the two Lower Bend runners on the back stretch of the final lap and thus secured the lead, I thought to myself, *This is me out here.* I thought, *I'm doing well.*

Now there were no runners before me, just bare track, white lines leading me, the lines so easy to follow. And likewise my stride felt easy to me, even though it had put me into the lead. I didn't even need to kick in the last forty meters. I cruised in. I breezed in. I blew through.

And crossed the line with a time of 1:55.11—a school record. Gregory shook my hand limply in the infield. I could hear again. I could hear the crowd. I could hear the traffic on the street beyond the track. I could hear my smooth breathing.

"Some fine, grand running," Gregory said. "You did this for yourself, Kevin? Did you do it for you?"

I did not answer Gregory because I suddenly found myself in Carton schoolhouse, in the boys' bathroom the night of my sixth-grade Christmas concert, watching Bobby Sickle pace before the sinks. We were due onstage immediately. Bobby's face was flushed, but his ears were red as radishes and he kept pressing his palms onto them.

"I'm all right," he said.

"I know."

"I mean it," he said.

He entered a stall and vomited.

Seconds later I stood onstage amidst my classmates, I the only one who knew Bobby was missing. I could see our bald director's head bobbing before the stage. Beyond him, the gymnasium yawned in darkness. Out there, on the basketball court, were ranks on ranks of folding chairs holding parents, grandparents, siblings, uncles, aunts. We sang "Deck the Halls." Lovely. Our second song was a contemporary novelty piece that described the tribulations Santa Claus faced in entering modern houses—the lack of chimneys and all—and detailed one incident in which Mr. Claus had nearly been arrested for breaking and entering and another occasion when a farmer shot at the reindeer:

> *The sleigh stuck thusly in the rut, the buckshot bit into Blitzen's . . .*
> *But Santa didn't let this onslaught bar him from his saintly duty . . .*

In the middle of the song came a place where the piano accompaniment stopped and one of the girls spoke loudly, "Why don't we just leave him a key?" This was the point where Bobby Sickle was supposed to speak, the setup for his punch line. This was the moment Bobby Sickle had trained for in music class since October. This was the task that had made Bobby ill through anticipation.

I delivered the line in his stead: "I gave him three, but I still got coal!"

All the heads of my classmates swung toward me in surprise, but presently the piano re-announced itself and the singing went on.

When I saw Bobby after the concert he appeared healthy. He did not thank me.

Thus I remembered the boy whose shoes I trained in.

five

Eight nights later, our Bend City team took four buses to the first big invitational meet of the season: two girls' buses and two boys' buses. The chaperones and assistant coaches arranged us in our buses according to class year and which half of the school we attended. So I rode on the Sundry Seeley bus, very near the front of the vehicle, surrounded by other freshmen boys. I sat, in fact, with Jol Brule, the infamous football star, who ran sprints on our team. Though we had smiled at each other in greeting, Jol and I said nothing until our bus—a lumbering diesel—rolled up alongside the track where we were to compete. We were a long way from home, in the suburbs of Kansas City, and the sun had not yet set. Jol said, "I'll win my race tonight," and I said, "Me too." Most of the boys on the bus had listened to music on their headphones during the drive. Jol had stared straight ahead for the entire ride, almost meditatively. I stared out the window at the characterless interstate landscape. I had been thinking of my father, who spent his days and nights on the interstates. I wondered if he felt free out there. The interstate did not speak of freedom to me.

Jol and I were correct in our predictions. Jol won his race, and I won mine. I ran the 800-meter again that night. Again silence followed the gunshot; again I set a winning pace; and again I crossed the finish line with a school record: 1:54.78. In the crush of bodies behind the finish line, I remembered an odd thing: another track meet, from another time.

When I was a seventh grader—and an only slightly better than average runner—our seventh and eighth grade track teams competed together at a school far to the south. This school was relatively wealthy because it sat in the middle of a district made rich by tourism—it sat near one of those huge man-made lakes that are common in the Ozarks. This school's track had an expensive, spongy black surface. Their track team wore shiny, body-hugging singlets, like a Scandinavian team might wear. Their public announcement system was loud and easily understandable from all parts of the field and stadium—not the tinny portable system that most teams we competed against owned.

It was a warm May afternoon. The wind spun through the tree-tops of the dense woods below the track. Flags flanked the football scoreboard and snapped in the breeze like banners on an oceanliner. Our team fared poorly. I myself botched a baton pass in the 800-meter relay, causing Jason Blick to stray out of our lane and disqualify us. Our stellar eighth-grade sprinter, Johnny Jakobi, pulled his hamstring. Hannah Halsey, the sure-thing eighth-grade high jumper, balked twice at the qualifying height of four feet and then twisted her ankle on her third attempt.

What an evening. I found a nickel tails-up beneath a urinal—I left it there. Vance Laloosi was disqualified for false-starting in both the 800 and 1600. Perry O'Hara's left shoe flew off his foot in the middle of the 200-meter dash and landed on his head. Sonny Smith's pole—the school's only pole—cracked in the pole vault. Ellie Butterbit tripped on the approach to the long jump and was spitting sand for the next hour.

Then, from the clear sky, a wall cloud approached—black and yellow like a bad banana. Wind came. Rain interrupted the 3200-meter run—officials couldn't even see across the infield. Instinctively, our team flocked to the bus. Many of us hadn't changed out of our spikes and so our shoes clicked and clattered as we crossed the asphalt lot toward the bus. There sat Herschel Nubbit, our squat driver, greeting us as we dashed in from the rain. He opened and closed the bus door for each of us. Almost the entire team was assembled there when Brandt Paul, our 3200 runner, dashed onto the bus. The humidity inside the bus was remarkable and the smell—wet shoes, wet hair, wet bodies—was simply tropical. Brandt stood at the front of the aisle and we all quieted down and Brandt said, "Well, I was on the fifth lap, on the second curve, and I just left the track and ran up the bleachers toward all of you."

Jarhead stepped onto the bus then. We knew Jarhead was a man with scant supplies of sympathy and fear.

Rain pummeled our bus top like pennies. The world was very dark now, and wind began pushing the rain.

We waited for Jarhead to chastise Brandt for leaving the race, but he didn't. Jarhead just looked at us. Water dripped from his jowl. He laid his hand on Brandt's shoulder, then removed his hand and stepped back into the rain.

All the buses were parked alongside each other, like sardines, and on one side of us was a bus from Essyville with no one on it, and on the other side of us was a bus from the state school for deaf children. Some of the kids on that bus were watching us. And soon some of the deaf girls wrote messages on their fogged-over windows.

HELLO

WE ARE TIRED

HOW YA DOIN?

Some of our girls wrote back. Heather Garnet wrote, WE WANT TO GO HOME. Ellie Butterbit, one seat in front of me, wrote, YOUR TEAM IS VERY GOOD! Then Hannah Halsey, so gorgeous, so kind—the eighth grade girl I adored most—used sign language to spell out her name: I AM HANNAH. I was surprised I remembered the sign language alphabet from grade school.

The girls on the other bus grew excited, signed frantically to each other, smiled broadly. They had good toothy smiles. They waved at us, and many of us waved back.

I AM PATTY, signed one girl.

I AM FREDONIA, signed another.

A VERY PRETTY NAME, Hannah slowly spelled.

THANK YOU.

The girls on both buses sat still for a bit. The deaf girls signed a little to each other. Hannah and Heather and Ellie talked softly. Then one of the deaf girls waved to catch our attention and wrote RAIN on her window, pointed to the sky, then sign-spelled RAIN, then made what must have been the sign language gesture for rain, a gesture not dissimilar to the one made to symbolize rain when singing "The Itsy Bitsy Spider." Heather and Hannah repeated the sign back to the deaf girl, saying "rain" aloud as they did so. The deaf girls nodded. Their ponytails bounced.

By this time, more of the students on the deaf bus were watching us, waving. One deaf boy was moving from window to window, drawing clouds on any windowpane that remained covered by fog. Another boy held up different CDs of popular music toward us and some people on our bus indicated which ones they liked by giving thumbs-ups and nods.

"I know sign language," Bobby Sickle said.

All those kids in the other bus were watching us now, all of them smiling.

"I know sign language," I heard Bobby repeat.

I waved toward the other bus, finally. But as I waved, the faces in the bus windows just six feet away from our own windows stopped smiling and a few of the girls were suddenly shouting and apparently angry—the girls who had originally been communicating with Hannah and Heather and Ellie.

I looked up the row to see Bobby Sickle and Johnny Jakobi flipping off the deaf bus.

"*That's* sign language," Bobby said, laughing, still sporting the bird.

Then, God bless her, Hannah Halsey rose and smacked Bobby so hard on the back of his head that Herschel Nubbit, a man quite deaf himself, turned around in the driver's seat to survey us for a moment.

The rain increased in intensity. We could see that the kids on the deaf bus were ignoring us now, facing away. We could also see that a couple of the girls were sobbing.

Ellie Butterbit wrote a note in her notebook, ripped it out, walked to the front of the bus and asked Herschel to let her off. He looked at her for a long time but finally did open the door and Ellie dashed out of sight, into the rain.

Almost immediately after Ellie left, Jarhead stepped onto the bus.

"They're waiting for it to blow over, and then we'll continue," Jarhead said.

We sat quietly, every one of us. We knew our team was in last place. The only event left was the 1600-meter relay—one of our weakest races. It was a Friday, and some of us had sleep-overs planned. And some of us had partaken of great quantities of spicy french fries at the concession stand and found ourselves now suffering silently through a balky brand of intestinal distress that was not made easier to bear by the storm rocking the bus.

Then Jarhead said a thing: "Do you want to go home now?"

In that moment, our team was unified. Yes, we answered.

We waited for Ellie—she returned quickly, note still in hand. She sat down with Hannah—right in front of me. She told Hannah that the deaf kids wouldn't open their bus door for her. She had tried to stuff her note under the door, but the paper was wet and wouldn't slip through the crack.

Our seats suddenly shuddered as Herschel Nubbit started the bus's engine. Ellie rose and walked to the back of the bus and began to write SORRY on each fog-covered window facing the deaf bus. As she bent over me to write on my window, rain water dripped from her dark hair and onto my bare knees. Hannah helped write on the windows, and by the time our diesel had warmed up and we pulled away, they had filled every window on one side of the bus. But it didn't seem that the deaf kids saw the apology—they were all still facing away from us.

The bus was our nation, and we fled in it.

six

When it rained—and rain it did that April of my freshman year—I ran alone, splashing along the streets of Bend City. The smell of my wet self, the smell of automobile exhaust in the humid air, the road spray thrown by passing cars—these locked me into an endorphinergic fugue, a blissful groove I left unquestioned.

I didn't mind wet feet. Rather, the water enlivened my pace. I didn't mind water in my eyes. Rather, the water cleared my vision, made the infant leaves in the trees appear to me with crystalline detail, like sculptures made of sugar, like green lace. I didn't mind cold ears, cold shins, cold hands, blue fingernails. Rather, my blood became refreshed by the coolness. I loved the sensation of splashing through puddles—I never avoided one.

I would run out, up to the top of the school's hill, around the ivied walls of the oldest section of Zame Smith, across the road toward Midstate State College, then over the highway and out along the streets of three-storied Victorian houses that surrounded the prison. Or I'd run the opposite direction, cut through downtown, past brokerage offices and restaurants, past city hall and the library, then follow High Street, parallel to the Missouri River. Sometimes I would make it all the way out to the newer subdivisions by the mall; I would run their districts of curving streets, their landscaped hillocks, their cul-de-sacs and willow tree corners. On dry days, when the whole long distance team would go for street runs, we kept close to the school, on prearranged routes, while Gregory lurked behind us in his blue hatchback with a hole in its muffler. So those wet days, those days I could choose my own route, no matter how dangerous or long, were treats.

One drizzly day in the middle of the month, I was only a mile away from school when a girl ran up beside me.

"Hi," she said, breathing too heavily for the pace, "I'm Henny Bulfinch."

"Right," I said, "you run the 800 too."

"Yeah." She smiled.

We ran on for a bit. She avoided a puddle. Her breathing grew raspy.

"I'm Kevin Schuler," I said.

"I know."

The rain had made her blond hair nearly black, and above her ears delicate tuft-wings of hair had escaped her tight braid and held upon themselves many tiny droplets of water. Her high-lidded eyes beamed, even on such a gray afternoon. I had once seen her run second-leg on the freshman junior-varsity 3200-meter relay, and her plodding heel strikes made me cringe. She was a delightful small person, a birdlike beauty, an Alpine maiden, a nymph, but not a runner.

"I just think you're an excellent runner," she said.

"Thanks."

"You blow them away." She took several labored breaths. "It's good."

"Thank you. It's just running."

"Can I run with you now? Do you mind? Because—" *breath, breath, breath,* "—I could really fix myself up if I train with you," *breath, breath,* "you know." *Breath, breath, breath, breath, breath.* "I don't mean fix myself up—" *breath, breath,* "—I don't know why I said that. I don't know . . ." *Breath, breath.* "I meant," *breath, breath,* "I could really," *breath, breath,* "get much better."

"It would be lovely if you could run with me," I said.

She stayed with me, running off my shoulder. I swapped places with her so that I would be running close to the traffic and she could have the curb. We came into a neighborhood of white and yellow bungalows, a flat post-war neighborhood on a sycamore-lined street. The sycamores leaned eastward, and in that neighborhood peonies had begun to bloom early, and their pink-syrup odor hung across the street. For a while there a young, collarless golden retriever ran with us, tongue to the breeze, toenails tapping the pavement, but soon dropped away. Not long after the dog left, Henny lagged several paces behind me, and before I'd completed the next half-mile, she was out of sight.

On those wet days, the rest of the track team ran inside Sundry Seeley—its halls were wide and abandoned after final bell. One particular loop route through the school measured a half-mile, and was favored by my long-distance teammates. Gregory sat by the glass doors in one of the lobbies and kept tabs on the team. But on these rainy days he seemed farther away than usual and we were essentially on our own to construct a good workout.

Perhaps because of Gregory's fluctuating effectiveness, Orson Vik approached me one rainy day and asked if I would run with him inside Sundry Seeley. I was laced up and had already decided on a nine-mile course across Bend City, a course that passed through six of the city's parks, strung them together like a string of pearls.

"You're a good pacesetter for us," Orson told me.

Orson was a sophomore from Zame Smith, shorter than me, scrawny. His long hair was nearly white. He had a tic in his left eye. Today his tic was spastic.

I agreed to run with Orson; six of the other long-distance runners came with us. I set a light pace through the dim halls. We passed the welding pits, the garage, descended to the cafeteria, cut through the underground hallway that led to the enclave of special ed classrooms, passed computer classrooms, passed air-conditioning repair classrooms,

classrooms filled with drafting desks, classrooms filled with typewriters and Dictaphones, then ascended to the short hallway of academic class-rooms, passed the south lobby—where Gregory waved and said, as we passed around the corner, "Mr. Duck Man Water Runner has come inside to help us out. . . ." But after three easy laps of the course, I had left my teammates far behind. The halls were crowded with runners from the entire track team: sprinters, field athletes, mid-distancers. Many of them greeted me as I passed. "Kevin!" they'd say. Or they'd stress the second syllable: "Ke-*vin!*" "Go go Ke-*vin!*"

It was on my fifth mile, after many runners had quit, that I entered the cafeteria-cum-basketball court and found Orson Vik being held up against the wall, his feet not touching the ground, by a group of three Sundry Seeley students.

"Whoa!" I shouted across the court.

All turned toward me. I wasn't sure how I had fallen into the hero role all of a sudden, and I realized it might quickly become the smashed-head role.

I stopped running and walked up to the students. The thugs were in street clothes, and they were of considerable size. They were, in fact, Eeny, Meeny, and Mo. Miney was not present. And it was Mo who held Orson aloft.

"Mo," I said, "let him down. There's no reason to bother him."

"What's the secret password?" Mo asked me.

I pondered this. "Peach cobbler," I answered.

"What he said!" barked someone behind us. It was Jol Brule, jog-ging up to us. He had been running the circuit, too.

Mo released Orson. Orson fell to the floor.

"Come on, come on," I said to Orson, and pulled him to his feet.

Orson sprinted across the cafeteria—glancing once back toward us—and disappeared down the hallway.

"Rainy day distraction," Eeny said by way of explanation, shrug-ging.

"All right," Jol said, "let's move along and be nice."

*   *   *

I found, that night, a handwritten note in the back of my desk drawer at home:

> Kev,
>   *I wrote your name on a piece of paper last night and put it under my pillow and I dreamed of you! Did you dream of me? Maybe we can both do this and dream together.*
>
>   *Lovey,*
>   *El*

seven

May first, as I exited the locker room at five o'clock, a white Cadillac sat idling on the street between Sundry Seeley and Zame Smith, where Mother's Buick usually waited. The Cadillac's tinted passenger window slid down and I saw Dr. Brake inside.

"Good afternoon, Mr. Kevin."

"Seen my mother?"

"I sent her home. Told her I'd drive you."

"All right."

"She said she was going to do some shopping," Brake reported.

"That's what she does all day. She drives me to school, shops until four-thirty, then picks me up."

"Very nice."

I got in the car. The leather seats squeaked against my jeans.

On the highway, headed west past the mall, Dr. Brake told me I would win the 800 at state this year.

I nodded.

"You'll be the first freshman to take a state 800. You're a hot topic in certain circles. Many of my colleagues want to meet you."

"Doctors?"

"Some. Others are coaches, others researchers. Do you know how far your 800 times are off the state and national high school records?"

"No."

"Do you know how far you're off the men's *world* record?"

"Sebastian Coe, 1:41.72," I said.

"Don't you care about breaking records?"

"I suppose I'm interested in breaking records. I suppose I'm supposed to be interested."

"You're very good at pretending to be aloof," Brake said.

The highway narrowed to two lanes. We crossed Lippenswitch Creek, which was in flood, lapping its banks. A sheet of high clouds blocked the sun. We turned onto a county blacktop. We drove at ridiculous speeds and suddenly came up behind a lopsided green pickup traveling at forty miles an hour. The wizened driver, like his vehicle, was off-kilter—one shoulder sagging, head cocked rightwise—but the road was too curvy for Brake to pass. It was the kind of narrow asphalt road with no lines down the middle and no shoulder. After a few minutes, we came into Carton and the truck pulled off at the filling station and Brake accelerated on down the road. When we turned onto my gravel road, though, the doctor slowed to a ridiculous crawl. Gravel pinged in the wheel wells and the doctor cringed. "Pretty far out here, isn't it?" he said. "I guess these pebbles won't chip my paint."

"Oh," I said, "they might."

The doctor slowed further, to what could aptly be called a walking pace.

We came into the short driveway of my home and Brake idled and stared at our house for longer than was polite and then asked if I had any health complaints after eight weeks of track season. None worth mentioning, I said. He named several ailments common to high-mileage runners: shinsplints, runner's knee, plantar fasciitis, cramps, et cetera. I admitted I did have some blisters. At his insistence, I removed my shoes and socks and showed him the sores.

"Those are in rough shape," he said. "Those are awful. You've been running with these for a while."

Indeed, there was blood on my socks today, even some blood on the inside of my shoes. But I told Brake the blisters didn't trouble me. Regardless, he demanded that I let him clean and dress the sores. As Brake knelt in the white gravel of the driveway and swabbed my feet, my lopsided neighbor, Carl Otto, drove by in his green lopsided pickup. I waved, but Carl didn't seem to see me, gawking as he was at the Cadillac and the man in the tailored suit kneeling before me, holding my feet.

"Those training shoes don't fit you perfectly," Brake told me after he was done.

"I like them," I said.

"They're played out. Too old. Can I measure your feet?"

I assented and he pulled a tailor's measuring tape from his bag.

"Your feet are identical," Brake said. "Usually, there's a size difference between feet."

"You're telling me I have special feet?"

"A statistical oddity, that's all. The thing is, even if you're as biomechanically efficient as you appear to be, you're headed toward injury if you keep these old shoes. Feel that. That midsole's compacted in the forefoot. And here, under the heel counter, the midsole's beginning to collapse."

"Not to mention how dingy they look," I said.

Brake looked at me, wasn't sure whether I was joking. "At the very least, you'll keep getting these blisters."

Brake put his supplies away, got in his car, and closed the door. I stood barefoot outside his window, bandages on my heels. Brake lit a cigarette.

"The scab on your knee looks good. Did they reprimand the guy who did it?"

"I don't think so," I said. "Some official came around to ask me about it, but I told him that it was my fault, that I should have been passing further out on the curve."

"Damn it, Kevin, you pass too far out in the lanes as it is," Brake declared. "Believe me, there'll be more roughhousing to come for you, especially if you let them get away with it, so you might as well get used to taking a stand, making sure the perps get knocked from the circuit. Any knucklehead could take the state title from you if they wanted— one guy is all it'd take."

"Perps?" I asked.

"What?"

"You said, 'making sure the perps get knocked from the circuit.' What are 'perps'?"

"Perpetrators."

"Did you make that up, that contraction?"

"I heard it on TV. You know, those cop shows."

"No, I don't know."

"Don't you get cable out here?"

"No."

"Satellite?"

"We're not flush with cash."

"But don't you get the networks over the air?"

"I think so. I guess I don't watch TV. It's a lot of babble."

Brake shrugged.

"I think I used to watch TV," I said. "If that makes you feel better."

"You think you used to? What kind of talk is that? It's just weird."

"Weird-talk Schuler," I said.

Brake lit another cigarette before the first was gone. He looked again at our house, our yard. Swallows had built a mud-nest below the gutter and crapped a white streak down the house's siding. Molehills ringed our yard like a chain of lilliputian mountains.

"Well, Kevin, how do you explain your performances this spring?"

"I wouldn't know how to do that."

"Why are you suddenly a track prodigy?"

"I don't know. I don't think I train very hard."

"I saw you in practice. Your times were average."

"Maybe I just wasn't really trying."

"Is that it? And now you're trying?"

"Perhaps there's nothing else to it."

"So simple," he said, and laughed a little. "Do you know, though," he said, "that if I hadn't talked to your coach, he wouldn't have put you in that first 800 race you won. I thought for a while that I would have to bribe him."

"Gregory," I said, and rolled my eyes.

"I guess it's like last year, right? I checked up on this. Your 800-meter and 400-meter times were okay for your first two meets, but at your third meet—in Bryceville, right?—you broke that record in the 800, and all your performances after that were spectacular. The competition engages you, draws out your talent."

"Lucky me," I said.

At meets I sat by myself, far from the various clots of my teammates, and read magazines beneath the field lights until it was time for me to perform. I never suffered from nervousness. I suffered from disgust. If I looked around the field, I grew nauseated. If I watched a race for too long, I would start to grind my teeth unconsciously. The clatter of a hurdle race evoked a great vertigo in me. I resented the narrowness of the events, the simplicity. I resented the lines. You must stay within the lines. You must stay within your lane.

I ran for silence. In all the races that spring, the silence followed the gunshot, and I won each and every race, even the 800-meter race in which a runner from Bloom City had tripped me, even the race where I had been boxed in. Even in the 3200-meter relay, where I ran the anchor leg, the silence followed the gun and I would wait trackside, ensconced in that unbreakable silence, until my leg of the race came and I took to the track and brought in the victory.

All along, during and after my victories, I did remember more of my old classmates. I recalled faces, antics, sleep-overs, games. Many of my memories were unremarkable. Snippets. Will Wynsom sitting on a pencil. My square-dance partner, Yolanda Eisen, wearing clip-on earrings. Gina Daley crying every morning of kindergarten. Jennifer

Teeter's extensive sticker collection. Trolley Catchell liberating the class gerbil into the cedars at the edge of the playground.

What thrilled me was that the silence had begun to appear in my training runs. Particularly on long runs on rainy days I noticed that the silence often welled up after a few miles, as if it were a force coming from within me, instead of something arising only from within the constraints of competition.

One afternoon Bend City lay under an impending thunderstorm but I ran into the rain anyway. Before I'd left campus, Henny Bulfinch had joined me.

"I love thunderstorms, really," she said. "I love that part in *King Lear* where he's wandering in the storm. What a strong metaphor."

"Yeah," I said.

We were headed down the hill past Midstate State College. Across the shallow valley, toward the north, I could see up into the older part of town, along High Street, perhaps a mile away. Henny and I were running in a light rain, but the sky was darker in the north, and I noticed, as I watched, that the trees there were suddenly swaying about vigorously. Then they were obscured in rain. Thunder rolled around us and Henny emitted a short hoot and then went silent.

I could see the sheet of rain approaching. Cars on the streets had their headlights on. The air was oddly warm, ridiculously humid. We ran past a parked car with its theft alarm wailing. Though the street was wide, I switched over to the sidewalk, worried that the visibility in the rain would be poor enough to make running on the street quite risky. Henny kept running in the street, and I dropped back beside her and took her by the arm and pulled her onto the sidewalk just before the wind hit us. Henny screamed in the wind, and our pace slowed remarkably as we ran into the gale. Henny was smiling and shouting.

"Go back to school!" I yelled. "Go back!" I waved her away with my hand. The rain hit us at an angle, drenched my front immediately, left my back dry. I looked at Henny. She ran just behind me, pushing her wet hair from her face. She gave me a thumbs-up and shouted something that was lost within a clap of thunder. She was grinning.

I ran on, head down, and soon recognized that I was running within the silence. I watched my feet splashing on the sidewalk at a fast pace. I ran my palm across my drenched head. I removed my T-shirt, heavy with rain. I concentrated on paying attention to street crossings, but realized that almost no cars were on the roads.

I recalled:

Standing in Carton's gymnasium during a downpour—rain roaring on the metal roof—I shook my head at Trolley Catchell.

"Ya bastard," I said. "Ya tub of butter."

Trolley wore a white shirt and red tie and black, beltless pants that hung dangerously low. He stood beside a pasteboard display explaining the details of his 4H project. On the display were many photographs of pigs. The display's title was PRODUCTION OF LEAN SHOATS ON WINTER CORN DIET.

Georgia Teeter stood near me, against me.

"Ya fat ass," I said to Trolley.

"Kevin . . ." Trolley said and sighed.

"Production of Fat Trolleys on Lard Diet," I said.

Georgia laughed.

"Boy Raises Porkers in His Likeness," I said.

Georgia guffawed and took my hand. The rain fell harder.

I looked over the display. Trolley's handwriting slanted drastically to the left. Most of his display I could not read. One picture showed Trolley standing inside a shit-floored pen of pigs and smiling without inhibition. I pointed to that picture and said, "Pig Boy Attracts Followers."

"Oh, Kevin," Georgia said, laughing. Her cheeks were red, her dainty elf cheeks. "Stop it," she said, out of breath from laughing.

"Yeah," I said. I pulled my hand from Georgia and slapped my own knuckles. "Stop it," I said to myself. "Meanie."

As we turned away from Trolley, the fluorescent lights that lit the gym blinked out. Immediately, in that darkness, came a tremendous peal of thunder. When the lights returned, seconds later, Georgia Teeter had her hand beneath my T-shirt, and Trolley Catchell was standing with his fists clenched, arms straight at his side. He bit his lip.

"Hey hey," I said gently. "Trolley . . ."

The roar of the rain became gaseous then, as if it inhabited the room and entered my lungs with each breath, filling me with dread.

As I watched, Trolley swung his right arm and stuck his pig project display board with such force that it became airborne—impressively so—and began dropping thumbtacks and photographs onto us. The posterboard crashed to the floor, the thumbtacks bounced on the wood court, the photographs rained down.

My feet splashed through ankle-high water. Then I crossed a section of drier sidewalk on which lay many maple buds and a few pale earthworms. I was running down Beal Street, east of downtown. It was still raining, but not as hard as before. I heard a splashing behind me. I turned and saw Henny Bulfinch there, running quietly, breathing hard. Her face was a washed-out salmon color. But she had kept up with me, even through the storm. I checked my watch, judged how far we had come, how fast.

I slowed, dropped back beside Henny.

"Come on," I said, "let's go back to school." Henny nodded. We headed south. The rain lifted.

"That was crazy," Henny said. "I didn't know what was going to happen. On that one corner the water must have been a foot deep, and it ran so fast. But we went through it. . . . Then when that branch fell I thought it was going to trip you but you jumped right over it. . . ."

"Henny," I said as we neared school, "I'm not in Zame Smith, I'm in Sundry Seeley."

"Oh, I know."

"You do?"

"Sure."

"I'm not smart like you," I said.

"I think you are."

We remained silent for several seconds. We were running up the hill toward the school.

"I *know* you're smart," she said. "I see the magazines you read. They're not kid stuff. They're not *BMX Weekly* or *Kung Fu Journal.*"

"*Kung Fu Journal,*" I said. "That sounds pretty good."

Henny laughed as we stopped before the doors of Zame Smith. I checked my watch again. We'd held a six-and-a-half-minute pace for about four miles. I couldn't believe Henny had kept up. Color was returning to Henny's face now and she looked at me with a certain kind of openness in her features that tripped a connection in my head: She was a member of that clutch of Zame Smith students who ate their lunches outside on fair days. I had noticed her before and longed to meet her.

"I have another circuit to run," I said, and reset my stopwatch. I crouched to tighten my shoelaces.

"Kevin, will you come with me to the May Ball?"

I stood back up.

"Oh, I can't," I said.

"Okay."

"I'm sorry," I said.

"No, no. It's okay."

"It's not me," I said.

Henny repeated, "It's okay."

"I mean it's not you," I said.

I ran away.

I inspected, after supper, this sheet of paper:

> C-
> CB-
> CEEB-
> KEE-
> KEAL-
> KEBE-
> KEBEAL-
> KE-

-
KEB-
KEBIL-
KEI-
-

KEBIN-
KEDIN-
-

KEDDEL-
KEDDIN-
KEBIN-
-

KEVIN.

Kevin.

KEVN-
KENN-
KIN-
KINT-
-

INTRICKED-
-

KINTRI-
KENDRICKED-
-

KENDRINY-
KENDRICKY-
KENDRICK.

Kendrick.

SPOON-
SPOONER-
SOONER-
SPOONY-
OONIE-
OONER-
OOLNER-
OOL-
OOLER-
-

SPOOL-
-
S-

-
SOK-
SKO-
-

SK-
SKOONER-
SKOOLER-
SHOO-
SKOOL-
SKOOLI-
-

SKSH-
SKO-
SKULER-
SCHULER.

Schuler.

Kevin Kendrick Schuler.

I took this page and placed it under my pillow.
    My sleep was dreamless.

eight

At the district track meet—the qualifying event for the state meet—I ran the 800 and 3200-meter relay, as usual, and the 1600-meter run—the metric mile. Gregory pulled Orson Vik from the 1600 and put me in. Though I had not run a 1600-meter in competition before, I placed first with a good time. I also won the 800-meter and our team won the relay. Thus I qualified for all three events at the state meet.

The 3A-4A state track meet fell on the last Friday and Saturday in May. Track teams from all over the state bused into Bend City on Thursday night and checked into the hotels. Because Bend City sat nicely in the center of Missouri, the state meet was always held there, in Midstate State College's stadium, right across the street from Bend City High School. Our team was lucky: We didn't have to ride the bus anywhere or sleep in hotel rooms or eat fast food. We just showed up. Historically, though, our hometown advantage had not boosted us enough to place us within the top five teams since the early 1960s. Lower Bend High School, on the other hand, had won back-to-back team championships only a few years ago and still remained one of the strongest teams in the state.

On Friday, the opening day of the meet, the temperature

reached ninety-five, but the grandstand was packed anyway. Many people held umbrellas to block the sun. Our team set up camp low in the bleachers—a prominent place—right next to Lower Bend's team. I sat on my blanket on the grass near the north end of the track, far from any bleachers. Superintendent Porphorhessohln, decked out in a Bend City Track T-shirt, black shorts, canvas deck shoes, and brown socks, reserved two seats in one of the VIP tents at the very bottom of the grandstand for my parents—neither of whom even owned a pair of shorts, thankfully. Occasionally, as I glanced toward the stands, my parents and Porphorhessohln would wave vigorously to me with their scorebooks and hats. I waved back with my magazine, gave a thumbs-up.

The first event of the meet was the 3200-meter relay, and we won it. When Brad Himmelstur handed the baton to me we were in third place, behind one of the old Kansas City schools and a private St. Louis school. But I brought in the win. Later in the afternoon, I won my heat in the 800-meter preliminaries, coming across the finish line with a state record. The crowd thundered at the sight of it—the first record of the meet.

Just past the finish line, young boys leaned toward me over the railing at the base of the bleachers.

"Hey! Hey! Guy! Sign my scorebook!"

"Hey! Sign for me, too!"

I walked over and scribbled my signature for the lot of them. A girl walked down the steps of the grandstand and stood behind the boys, quietly waiting. The boys, who had already received my autograph, blabbered on.

"How fast do you go? Do you go about sixty miles an hour?"

"Not quite that fast," I said.

"Those are fast shoes. Where did you get those shoes?"

"A river."

"You know, you know, I'm really fast too. I won my school's one-lap race."

"That's very good."

"Why do you have the short hair? Are you in the army?"

"No, I'm not in the army."

"Do you want to be in the army?"

"No."

"I do," the boy said.

The girl, slightly older than the boys, didn't have a scorebook for me to sign, just a scrap of a paper sack.

"Here," I said, and I removed the large registration number pinned to the front of my shirt, signed it, and gave it to the girl. She wore her brown hair tucked behind her ears. About her neck hung a thin gold chain. When she smiled there appeared two dimples on her cheeks and she avoided my eyes.

"Thank you, Kevin," the girl said, and turned to walk back into the stands.

"Aw, man!" the boys clamored. "Why'd you give her that?"

"Give me the number off your back!"

"Give me your watch, man!"

I couldn't account for how the girl knew my name—the program only listed my last name. But as I stood watching her ascend into the grandstand the announcer's voice broke over the PA, and I realized that perhaps my full name had been announced earlier, too.

"Now we call it official, folks. With a time of 1:51.38, Bend City freshman Kevin Schuler has set a new 4A and overall state record in the 800-meter run—one of our oldest records. Of course, Mr. Schuler's time also represents a new state meet record, surpassing Jimmy Windey's 1986 performance of 1:51.92. Everyone put your hands together for Ke-vinnn Shooo-ler!"

The crowd responded then. I finally lost sight of the girl I had signed my race number for. She had faded into the crowd in the nether sections of the stands—the very highest rows. I now turned away and walked north toward my blanket, but before I'd walked ten paces Gregory tackled me from behind, held me momentarily in some kind of half-nelson, then took my hand and thrust it above my head—a championship gesture. The crowd's clamoring reached a crescendo, and Gregory spoke softly into my ear:

"Hear them calling for you!"

When I made it back to my blanket to wait out the afternoon, Henny Bulfinch, who had not qualified to compete at the meet but served as a field volunteer, approached me and congratulated me on my relay gold medal and the 800 state record, and sat with me for her fifteen minute break from the long jump pit. We sat in silence. She watched the runners. I watched the traffic beyond the chain-link fence. And out of the corner of my vision, I watched Henny. After we'd been sitting together for ten minutes, a camera-laden reporter approached us and asked if I was Kevin Schuler.

"I think he's up by the courtesy tent," I said, and the young man thanked me and left.

Henny looked at me quizzically.

"What the hell kind of interesting article could anyone write about running?" I asked.

"Maybe he's a good writer."

A heat of the 1600-meter relay reeled past on the curve. The hollow relay batons held by the runners hummed the same way a soda bottle hums when you blow across its top.

"And what the hell is a courtesy tent?" Henny asked.

"I have no idea. I just invented it. But it sounds like a good idea."

Henny sighed. "I'm just glad I've decided not to run track next year," she said.

As we drove home after eating at Golden Corral—Father's favorite restaurant—Mother, at the wheel, said, "I saw you talking to Tam Butterbit after your 800."

"Who?" I said from the passenger's seat. Father lay across the backseat, snoring softly, his stomach churning audibly.

"Tam Butterbit," Mother repeated.

"Butterbit," I said.

"Ellie's little sister."

"Right, right," I said. "I signed my race number for her."

"That's nice."

"It is," I said. "Yeah."

"You know, I still have a letter that Mrs. Butterbit left for you. I nearly forgot about it. Do you want it now?"

S a t u r d a y   d a w n e d   d i m l y   as a line of thunderstorms passed through mid-Missouri. They rumbled tirelessly and tossed the tree limbs about, but did not loose a drop of rain until almost nine-thirty, by which point I sat alone on the track below Sundry Seeley, stretching my muscles. Against the advice of Gregory, I wanted to run a little bit before my noon 1600 final and two o'clock 800 final. Though there was little thunder and no wind now, the rain came heavily, vertically, as if it were a tropical rain, and set a full inch of water upon the track. I removed my training flats and socks and jogged the circuit barefoot. The track was soft beneath my feet.

I had not yet run a mile when I looked into the bleachers and saw Jol Brule coming down wearing his running gear—shorts, shoes, but no shirt. On his brown chest I could see, even from this distance, even through the rain, two short scars that I assumed were related to the broken ribs he had suffered in the last month of the football season. I remembered his injury had attracted front-page coverage from the school newspaper and the *Bend City Gazette* and that local doctors had treated him free of charge.

"I don't know if this is a bright suggestion, to run in the water like this," Jol said as I passed. I stopped and Jol came down onto the track, stepping reluctantly into the water.

"I saw your heats yesterday," I said. "I think you've got it wrapped up."

He said, "You're the one with it wrapped up, with your records and all."

"Oh yeah. I'm godlike."

He smirked.

"Do you want the outside sprint lanes?" I asked.

"No, I'm just out for a slow run."

"Good idea." I took off and Jol began stretching. Two laps later, Jol started running behind me and we stayed rather evenly distanced, keeping a similar pace. The rain had not ceased nor lightened but in fact increased its intensity. As we passed the concrete grandstand, sheets of water poured off its bottom lip. I cut across the lanes and ran through that wide waterfall. I looked back at Jol.

He smiled and shook his head.

The track was now covered by more than two inches of rain and in order to run on it we had to lift our knees high and drop our feet more vertically than usual. I could hear no distinct sounds over the roaring of the rain. I removed my sodden T-shirt and threw it onto the bleachers.

Jol shouted something unintelligible.

I dropped back and ran beside him.

"What?" I screamed.

"Why're we still running?"

"It's filling us with speed!" I said. "The rain! Soak it up!"

Jol shook his head again.

"Last lap," I yelled. "Just one more. Kick it in!"

"Okay," he said.

I looked around. There was no one in sight. The street that passed near the back side of the track was vacant of traffic. Even if a car had passed they couldn't have seen far through the downpour.

"Watch!" I screamed and I stopped and pulled my shorts off, tossed them toward my T-shirt, then ran, bare as the day of my birth, taking the lap at a good pace, feeling the raindrops tap madly against my skin. I completed the circuit and put my shorts back on. Jol came in twenty seconds behind me.

"Motherfucker," he said, laughing.

"Now I can't lose my races," I told him.

"Motherfucker," he repeated.

"I'm fortified by the waters of the sky," I said.

"Motherfucker," he said.

At ten-thirty, I walked through the rain from the high school's track to the Midstate State College grandstand—little more than a half-mile walk. Father was on the road today, so I made sure Mother was situated with Porphorhessohln in the VIP tent then went out onto the wet red track and loosened up by running four laps—1600 meters. Midstate's synthetic track was much better drained and graded than our school's and so the water did not stand upon it. Most of our team had already arrived and resigned themselves to getting wet by sitting out in the open of the grandstand. As I passed the team Jol yelled from beneath the hood of his wet sweatsuit, "Take it off, baby!" A few kids hooted.

"Go Ke-*vin!*" someone shouted, and immediately many others echoed this call and whistled.

At eleven o'clock precisely, as the first race took to the starting blocks, the rain halted. Within ten minutes, the sun was out. I waited on the wet grass north of the track, as I had yesterday. The grandstand, hulking like a military bunker, sat on the east side of the track. Beside it was the parking lot, wrapping around the far curve of the track—windshields reflecting the sun toward us—and the rest of the track was ringed by wide lawns. Behind me, further away from the track, dark woods climbed a hill—the undeveloped fringe of a city park. Those woods still dripped water, but by noon, when the first call for the boys' 4A 1600-meter run came across the speakers, everything else was nearly dry—the sun had evaporated the water off the grass and track as the temperature broke ninety.

I won the 1600. I set a state record. I gave many autographs to kids, then went into the grandstand.

"Hey, big champion!" Mother barked when I approached her tent.

"That's solid work, boy," Porphorhessohln said.

"Oak!" Mother said.

I suggested that the nickname "Oak" did not particularly befit a runner.

Mother gave me money for lunch and let me borrow the binoculars. I ate in the cool bowels of the grandstand, leaning against a huge concrete pillar far from the flow of traffic. Pigeons roosted in the dark heights inside the grandstand and I could hear their beating wings but not see them. Sprinters practiced their starts in the shadow of the grandstand. As I made my way back down through the stadium, many people recognized me and I signed a few copies of the day's *Bend City Gazette*—which bore a front-page photograph of my record-setting run from yesterday. I wasn't inundated by fans or anything. They didn't try to rip my shirt off or tear out a piece of my hair or drape brassieres around my neck, but for some reason my presence made some fathers feel as if they had good reason to tell me how fortunate I was to display such talent as a freshman, and how they had once learned so much about life by running track or playing another sport in high school—and they hadn't been half-bad, actually; actually pretty good—and how Junior was just a sour little delinquent who had no work ethic or sense of discipline because he wouldn't take on any sport. It took me thirty minutes to get back to my blanket, by which point I only had twenty minutes until the 800.

There I sat, then, stretching, when a pack of six Lower Bend runners approached me across the wide lawn. Their yellow shorts fluttered as they walked, and I could see that they were the distance runners of their team. Among them walked Rye Bledsloe, a senior who was their best runner and the second-place finisher behind me in the 1600.

The boys came up to me, gathered around my blanket. Rye reached down. "Can I see?" he asked, and I handed my magazine to him.

He flipped through it slowly, nodding here and there, then commenced tearing single pages out. "This is crap," he said, and ripped a page. "No, no, no," he said as he ripped another. Many pages he ripped in silence and when he handed the magazine back to me I saw that he had ripped out everything but the advertisements. The other pages of the magazine lay on the lawn, some swelling and flapping in the breeze at Rye's feet, others already blown far away. Rye's red hair caught the sunlight and shone like copper, but there was not one single hair upon his legs. Not one hair.

The boys were sweating and I was grateful to be reclining within their shadows.

"See," Rye said, "we didn't quite expect you to be in the 1600. I mean, because of the split district system, we didn't run against you at the district meet. Some of us had designs on the 1600, and we're not particularly pleased to find you impeding our plans. Oh, of course it's not personal. We don't know you so how can we really judge you? You're probably a great guy. We're all Bend Citians, right? We're all young white men. We're all talented and can compete at the college level if we wish. But some of us are idealists. And some of us are dreamers. It's difficult for us to compete in one of the least glamorized, least appreciated, least popular sports, knowing full well that this sport indeed is the most primal, the most symbolic, perhaps the most meaningful of all sports. We don't receive the recognition we deserve—and you know this as well as we do. Yes, we all like a good show, we all like a good struggle, we want to be pushed, to be challenged from unexpected quarters. We want a certain quantity of the unknown to rear before us periodically so that we might wrestle it down or, more likely, be knocked flat by it and stand up and train harder in order to finally conquer that which had defeated us. That random element is part of the mythic essence of track and field; it evokes a tang of recognition from within the dim tones of our feelings; it strikes great resonant chords upon the strings of our hearts. Nonetheless we dislike to see our designs foiled by a freshman who had hitherto limited himself to the 800. Do you comprehend?

"Oh, I hate to sound harsh—hate, *hate* it—and I don't intend to imply that we wish to limit any person's liberty or shackle an element of the very energy that drives the excitement and pure scheme of our gorgeous sport; but I'm standing here, having whittled my times down through six years of year-round training to the point, finally, where I am ranked first in the state in the 1600—twenty-second in the nation, mind you—and have come here hoping to crack my PR and the state record in the final 1600 race of my high school career. And I *did* set a personal record and that PR *would* have broken a state record if you, Friend Schuler, had not won the 1600 and set your own record."

Rye threw up his hands. "What is second place? I mean, what is it? What? It is defeat. It is shame. It is embarrassment. At best it can amount to nothing more than a motive to train harder, reach deeper. Track is a sport of losers—only a very few are consistent winners. But my, what those winners symbolize!"

Rye looked at his watch.

"It's frankly disheartening," he said. "I'm screwing two girls on my track team and one on yours and they're all sitting over there watching me lose to a freshman who had not even entered a 1600 time until districts. I hope you know that I do have it within my power to have you tested for drug use and I do have it within my power to take your 800-meter final away from you—and I admit that the 800 is *your* race, you've proven that, just as the 1600 was my race. No, don't worry about me making any rash moves in the race: I won't do anything myself because though the 800 is not my signature event I am favored to place in the top three and don't need to jeopardize my chances. I do hope you see that I'm not a person of low values but much the opposite and therefore unwilling to tolerate unreasonable gains by people who don't work for or deserve such success. Maybe I'm asking for a kind of justice that doesn't exist anymore. Maybe my idealism will undermine anything I attempt in this jaded world. Maybe I've always been on the wrong path. That's possible. Sure, it's possible."

Rye looked up into the sky, as if trying to remember what else he had to say. Finally, he nodded and said, "But I thank you for listening. Thank you very much for letting me communicate my thoughts to you. I didn't want to leave you uninformed, no. That would be callous. Do you have any questions?"

"Not at this time," I said.

"All right, then, we'll see you on the track."

"Good-bye," I said. "Good luck."

"Bye-bye."

The boys retreated. I watched an orange ladybug climbing my shin, having a rough go of it, shouldering through my leg hair. The bug eventually reached the summit of my knee, and before I could bid her hello she spread her wings dramatically and flew in a rising arc toward the woods.

I smelled popcorn on the breeze. And chalk dust.

I laced up my spikes.

The 800 was an eight-man final, with a one-turn box alley start. We started cleanly, came off the curve, fell in toward lane one and found ourselves bunched tightly together. The pack was so thick I could not take the pace I wanted. Rye ran directly before me—his red hair bobbing madly—and his teammate ran on my shoulder, pushing me hard against the inside. I treaded the line carefully; one misstep into the infield would disqualify me. And there were runners directly behind me. In other words, I was boxed in, completely at the mercy of the pack. Before we'd even completed the first two hundred meters, it was obvious that this would be a tactical race, that our pace was slow, and the pack unpredictable.

Then, at four hundred meters, in front of the grandstand, Rye's teammate began dropping off my shoulder. At five hundred meters, I saw the opening and surged forward. But as I made my move, Rye's teammate clipped my right ankle and my shoe popped off my heel. My balance broken, I sank down, placing my left hand on the track to brace myself against a full fall. The jumble of feet and falling torsos then was too much to follow, and too fast. I was trod upon; runners tripped over me, some tumbling into the infield; but I succeeded in keeping my fall from bringing me to a full halt. In fact, I rather miraculously and accidentally executed a move quite like a somersault and regained my feet.

The tumble cost me precious seconds, though, put me at the end of the pack with little more than a half lap to go. As I sped up, I felt myself become bolted down onto the foundation that was my silence, and from such a position I set a remarkable pace and soon joined the pack on the final curve. I moved to the third lane to pass the pack. I had no sensation in my body, no awareness of my footfalls or breathing or sweat. I was stable and saturated with energy. I felt that I had an excess of energy. I watched myself move into second place, then come up onto Rye Bledsloe's shoulder as we entered the head of the home stretch. My passage down that final sixty meters frightened me because it appeared that my pace was still increasing—not decreasing—even past a point where I hardly recognized the speed as mine, as something coming from within myself. But where does it come from, then? I asked myself. I left Rye behind. I broke the tape at the finish line and with that action the silence collapsed and the screams of the crowd entered me with a force that unhinged me. Those screams seemed to be the noise and commotion of my nightmares—an excruciating amplification of noises familiar to me. I put my hand upon my face. I brought my legs to a halt. And when I finally reached a standstill I did not feel stillness but only a sense of turbulence that toppled me onto the track.

Footsteps approached. A timer screamed out my time to me. It was no record. Many hands suddenly touched me and I opened my eyes. Two medics knelt beside me, unwrapping large packs of gauze.

"This is ridiculous," I said, "why am I lying here?"

Gregory appeared and sat beside me. He said, "He has his own doctor."

I smelled rubbing alcohol and felt cool swabs on my legs, arm, hand.

"Get this shirt," someone said, and I heard the snip of scissors and suddenly I was shirtless. They rolled me up onto my side and swabbed my back. They pulled my shoes and socks off.

"Maybe you push yourself too hard, Kevin," Gregory said.

"I didn't push anything," I said.

I sat up, per their instructions.

Dr. Brake jogged up the track to where I lay. I realized that I was some thirty meters beyond the finish line, near the end of the sprint lanes.

"I got spiked," I said to Brake.

"Yes," he said.

"He's fine," one medic told Brake. That medic pointed out the wounds, all of which had been cleaned already: the heel of my right foot, my right ankle, my right knee, my left hand, left shoulder, upper back.

Brake wiped my face with a wet swab.

The crowd was hushed, and many of them watched me, but most people stood looking south. On that end of the track sat an ambulance and I watched the EMTs there attend to a runner on the ground. I looked back into the crowd and my eyes became unfocused on the multitude and my vision darkened and I could see my pulse strobing in the periphery of my vision. I blinked and my vision cleared and I immediately noticed a face, far up in the stands, that reminded me of my Carton days. The face evoked a sensation of well-being in me, a desire to act kindly toward others. I surprised myself by putting a name with the face: Hannah Halsey. She had been a year ahead of me at Carton. She had been an angel in my eyes.

My glimpse of Hannah was blocked as a tan, short-haired woman of about fifty crouched by me and handed me one of my shoes. "You left this behind," she said.

"Behind?"

"It came off when you got clipped," Brake said.

"I ran with one shoe?"

"That is yes," Gregory told me. "You ran like a demon."

"A demon?" I said. "Is that good?"

"I don't know," Gregory said.

"Are you suggesting that my speed has unholy sources?"

"You ran fast, Kevin," Gregory said, "that is everything I meant."

"You're lucky this track has such a short spike limit," Brake told me.

"What we need to know," the woman who had handed me my shoe asked, "is do you suspect there was foul play involved in this incident?"

"No."

"There will be a full investigation, of course, but we needed a preliminary statement from you."

"I got clipped. The pack was tight. That's it."

"Thank you," the woman said, and she stood.

"Wait," I said. I waved my shoe toward the far end of the track, toward the ambulance. "Who went down?"

"Named Dennis Poultry, Kansas City Southeast."

"He was behind me?"

"He tripped over you, then was hit by another runner. Looks to have broken his ankle."

The ambulance cruised around the track and out a side gate. The announcer reported the runner's condition. "We're still waiting for word on Kevin Schuler's injuries," the announcer said. Soon after, with the help of Gregory and Brake, I stood up. The crowd applauded through the entire two minutes it took me to walk into the stands, where I reassured Mother and Porphorhessohln that I was fine, even as some of my bandages became saturated with blood and were dressed again, on the spot, by Brake. "I wonder if this one shouldn't get a stitch or two," Brake said, wiping the puckered gash on my shoulder. "They were stepping on you like a doormat," Porphorhessohln proclaimed. Moments later, Gregory pulled me back down onto the field. Trackside, two girls from our team met us and took over Gregory's job of supporting me. The girls were both high jumpers from Zame Smith and I walked with my arms slung around both of them and hobbled across the track toward the winner's stand.

"We're going to name our children after you," one of the girls said.

"We're going to have our children by you," the other said.

"We're going to cut ourselves so our wounds match your wounds."

"We're going to buzz our hair in emulation."

The last suggestion, I objected to.

The girls led me across the grass and up onto the medal stand. There I stood with the girls, at the top of the stand, surrounded by the scent of their clean hair. The gold medal was placed around my neck and the official photographer walked out in front of us. I still didn't have a shirt on, and bulky white bandages covered my wounds. Rye Bledsloe stood on the step below me. He wouldn't make eye contact with anyone and the photographer had to ask him to look toward the camera.

After the picture, the girls led me down from the stand, waited for the 200-meter dash to pass—Jol Brule zoomed by—then took me back across the track. "Actually, I'm sitting out there," I said, and I pointed away toward my blanket.

"Take us where you will," one girl said.

They walked me to my blanket and offered to stay but I suggested that I needed to rest. They wanted to bring me a drink or food. I asked instead if they'd pick up the scattered pages from my magazine. They did so and then said good-bye.

"She's Beth," one said in parting.

"And she's Finn," said the other.

After I dispatched the girls, I saw the reporters approaching. Cornered, lame, unable to deny my identity, I answered their questions.

When finally the reporters left, the 1600-meter relay was on the track—the last event of the meet. I scanned the grandstand with Dad's binoculars. I sought one particular face.

There was Mother, lips compressed in excitement as she watched the relay.

There was Porphorhessohln, toting his own binoculars.

There was Jol Brule, cheering the relay.

There was Henny, leaning against the railing, glancing back and forth between the race and me.

And there, up, up in seats—inhabiting the upper strata of the grandstand—stood Hannah Halsey, that angel of Carton, packing her backpack. I had watched Hannah for only a few moments when a blur obstructed my view. I lowered the binoculars and saw Dr. Brake and a short, block-jawed man standing before me.

"Kevin," Brake said, "how are your cuts?"

"Not so bad."

The shoulder cut—the one that had bled most—was now closed up and dry. Brake complimented my blood's clotting abilities. He advised me how to clean the cuts each morning and night, to watch them for signs of infection or slow healing.

"This is my colleague Dr. E," Brake said, and the short man reached down to shake my hand. "He is a colleague of mine at the university, a sports researcher."

"How do you spell your name?" I asked.

"E," the man answered.

"Oh," I said.

"No," he said, "Just E."

"Your name is a vowel."

Dr. E said, "Kevin, I am most impressed by your accomplishments, and most interested in the efficiency of your body."

"Thank you." I crouched and began pulling my blanket into my duffel bag.

Brake spoke. "Dr. E would like to study you, Kevin."

"What do you mean?"

"Study your body, your athletic capacities, your biomechanics, et cetera. Your body."

"This thing?" I asked and slapped my chest.

"We get few opportunities to study athletic prodigies, if you don't mind my using such a term," Dr. E said.

I laced on my training flats, despite the wounds on my right foot. I stood.

"I need to go," I said.

Brake put a hand on my shoulder. "We can compensate you, Kevin."

"Compensate? For what?"

"For letting us study your body as you exercise," E said, "about an hour a week, we can pay you many thousand dollars a year."

"I can't do that, can I? Accept money for athletics?"

"We're not paying you to compete for us or promote our product or anything like that," E said. "We're paying to study your body, that's all, much as other doctors pay subjects to test new treatments for asthma or depression or what have you. Your amateur status as a runner would not be compromised."

The grandstand was emptying.

"I can talk later," I said.

Brake said, "If we had an answer now, we could get you a check within a week."

"Fine," I said. "Fine. Go ahead." I pushed between the two men.

"I'll call you," Brake said to my back.

I looked into the grandstand as I approached. I could see Hannah standing, peering out at the infield. Just as I climbed the first steps into the grandstand, though, Porphorhessohln blocked me.

"We need your picture, too, trooper," he said.

"What?"

"For the team trophy picture. We won second place, thanks to you and Brule."

Finn and Beth appeared and wrapped themselves against me.

"I don't need crutches, actually," I said as they turned me toward the infield where most of the boys' team already stood rank and file.

"Don't think of us as crutches," Finn said.

"Think of us as nude," Beth said.

"Look, you scared him," Finn told Beth.

We neared the team.

"We're just lonely seniors," Beth explained. "We won't be around to see you grow up. We would love to see you grow up."

"He is needing a shirt," Gregory said.

Beth removed her team jersey, revealing her shapely torso and bosom clad only in a black athletic bra.

"Wear me," Beth said and she pushed her balled shirt into my gut and then leaned hard into me and kissed me below my ear so that I lost my balance just enough that I had to wrap my free arm around her.

My palm held her hip. That soft, unmistakable feel of woman-flesh.

When Beth drew back, Finn said, "Schemer."

"Poor envious dear," Beth countered.

Finn then yanked my head down and kissed me full on the lips.

"We are not attending a kissing derby!" Gregory said.

I disentangled myself from the two of them, pulled Beth's shirt over my head, and took my place in the middle of the back row of the team.

"And this is yours to hold," Gregory said, and handed me the team trophy.

"Can't I share it with someone?" I asked.

"No," said Porphorhessohln.

"You earned the thing, man," one of my teammates said.

"Who won the most points for the team?" I asked.

"You, Mr. Winner," Gregory said.

"Oh."

"Jesus, son!" Porphorhessohln yelped. "Don't you know you deserve it?"

"Who won the second most points for the team?" I asked.

"Jol," Gregory said.

"Then get him up here—we'll both hold it."

"No," Porphorhessohln said. "Don't wave that trophy around! Someone will lose an eye on one of those points!"

"We aren't needing blind runners here," Gregory said.

"Sorry," I said.

"There will be no rearranging of the group," Porphorhessohln said. "We've got everything here nicely arranged based on height."

"Based on height?"

"The rows are arranged aesthetically," Porphorhessohln said.

"It is very pretty and that is the truth of it!" Gregory proclaimed, becoming more aggravated.

"Wait," I said. "I don't even want to co-hold the trophy. I don't want to hold it at all. It's a team trophy. Gregory should hold it. Or Superintendent Porphorhessohln should hold it—it's his school."

Porphorhessohln cussed mildly for several seconds, ordered me to wear my three medals, planted the trophy in my hand, and signaled the photographer. Beyond the camera, I saw Hannah Halsey standing at the bottom of the grandstand, watching the picture. Just a few feet from Hannah stood Henny.

After the fifth photograph, Hannah began walking up the stairs.

After the ninth photograph, Hannah had exited the stands.

After the twelfth photograph, the team was released and I tossed the trophy to Gregory, removed my shirt, passed it to Beth—who immediately smelled it—and ran into the grandstand, taking three steps at a time. I passed Henny, I passed Mother, gave her my duffel bag. I ran into the dark underside of the grandstand, my footfalls echoed in the cavernous, cool air. I ran out the back of the grandstand, ran down the road toward the main parking lot. My medals clapped against my chest. Cars filled the road, locked in a standstill as everyone tried to leave the stadium simultaneously. I ran past dozens of brake lights, I ran through the thick car exhaust. I ran past rows of idling school buses, those yellow vessels of youth.

"Hannah," I called, but she kept walking.

"Hannah," I called as I neared her. She unlocked her car.

"Hey, Hannah," I called, but she closed the car door.

I tapped on the window. She looked at me briefly, then started the car. The hatchback purred.

"Hannah," I said, "it's me, Kevin Schuler."

She sorted through some cassette tapes on the seat beside her, put on sunglasses, shifted the stick into reverse.

I stepped away from the car.

I stood there for perhaps a minute. Hannah stared straight ahead but made no move to leave. Eventually, she rolled down her window.

"I know who you are," she said sternly.

"Go Ke-*vin!*" someone yelled at me from afar. *"Go go!"*

I smiled, sensing Hannah's jesting mood, but when she removed her sunglasses, I saw there was no joking within her eyes.

"And I'm not particularly interested in knowing you anymore," she said.

"What do you mean?" I said.

She sat with her fingers tight upon the wheel and didn't look at me for several seconds. When she turned to me, I backed up involuntarily and bumped the car behind me.

"I'm a rational person," she said. "I'm a sensible person. I'm not quick to condemn. I'm not judgmental. Yet I found it difficult to imagine a rational explanation for why you didn't attend a single funeral or vigil. I find it difficult to imagine why you did not come to the dedication of the memorial. And I never heard any explanation for why you kept running track that spring except for what you told me after I saw you win a race and set a record at Loke. Do you know what you said? Do you know? You said, 'The median performance of our team has improved.' That's all you said! I asked you questions but you wouldn't answer. I thought you were joking! But a joke in such poor taste! And you weren't joking. Then I heard such weird things about your visits to Trolley Catchell in the hospital. People told me that you just said bizarre things to Trolley, as if you didn't care about any of it. And that's not the Kevin Schuler I thought I knew. That's not the Kevin Schuler I had fixed in my mind when Ellie Butterbit came to me right before Christmas that year and asked my advice and I told her what I thought was true: that beneath the tacked-on attitude and fading immaturity you were the most genuine and smartest guy in your class and would be an excellent boyfriend who would only get better with time, become more willing to show your sensitivity and more accepting and less smartass."

"I am less smartass," I murmured.

"When I saw you tumble in that race today, I thought, Good, he needs to take a fall. But you got right back up and ran like a machine and won and that made me sick to the stomach, I admit, to see you win that way despite you bleeding everywhere. Most people feel pain, Kevin. Most people *feel*."

"I am falling, Hannah," I said softly. "I have been."

"Good-bye, Kevin Schuler, you son of a bitch." She rolled up her window.

"Go Ke-*vin!*" a teammate screamed at me across the parking lot.

"I'm running home," I told Mother.

"You don't like Shanghai Pagoda?" she asked. "Do you want to go somewhere else?"

Mother and Gregory and Porphorhessohln and I stood at the foot of the grandstand. Porphorhessohln had offered to take us all to dinner.

"I want to run home."

Porphorhessohln laughed. "A nice long cool-down, eh?" He laughed more.

"Let's get you a shirt," Mother said, and she opened my duffel bag.

Gregory said, "I think he means it."

"I am running home," I said.

I started walking up the stairs.

"Is this a joke?" I heard Mother say. "Kevvy?"

I ran again through the parking lot. The sun warmed my bare chest. There were no clouds in sight. I ran up Donnestal Road, then turned onto Bob White Avenue. A car pulled in front of me. A figure left the car and walked toward me and pushed me over. I skidded into the gravel on the shoulder of the road. I looked up at the man who had knocked me down. It was Rye Bledsloe. As I lay on my side, he kicked me twice on my back. Then he left—I heard the car accelerate away. I regained my feet, commenced running.

By the time I turned onto the highway that led west toward Carton, I was wrapped in silence. I watched jet contrails fade and drift above me. I watched my feet. Gregory now followed me in his blue hatchback, hazard lights flashing. My pace was steady. The sun mired above the horizon. The sun became lodged in the limbs of an elm. I saw a beautiful plastic soda bottle on the roadside. I saw two beetles waiting to cross the road. Here was a snapped fan belt; there a lost shoe. Broken glass glittered. Leaves sighed. The humidity of the evening curled the hair on my legs. Hay fields stood roadside. The rains earlier in the day had knocked down thick patches of fescue grass. From those fields, fireflies rose.

And images rose from within me:

We were now locked in the Lutheran social hall. Twenty-nine kids. My host, Will Wynsom, followed me like a puppy.

"Go ask when they'll start the movie," I told Will, and he left me.

Georgia Teeter and Gina Daley sat on the concrete steps leading into the basement. I walked past the building's front doors and saw the orange sun impaled on a low elm branch. I descended the stairs and sat hip-to-hip with Georgia.

"Can you stay up all night?" Gina asked.

"I can if Georgia stays up with me," I answered.

"What's in the basement?" Georgia said and she stood and walked down the stairs, into the dark.

"We'd better find out," I said and followed Georgia.

Gina stood and looked after us.

Georgia and I walked into the dim light of the basement kitchen. Georgia leaned on a counter. I approached her.

"What's down there?" I heard Will Wynsom say, and I looked back toward the stairs and saw him pass Gina and come into the basement.

Later in the evening, Will asked me to come to his birthday party.

"I can't make it," I said. "My aunt and uncle are coming to visit."

"When?"

I didn't know when Will's birthday was. "Well," I said, "they're coming tomorrow and staying through July."

"Oh," he said. "Maybe you can come next year."

"I hope," I said. "Because I don't want to miss the festivity."

Will fell asleep promptly at ten o'clock. Now I had my run of the place. Reverend Peacelilly removed the movie *Romancing the Stone* from the VCR after it had played for an hour because it was too racy. He put in a movie called *Blade Runner* and removed it after twelve minutes. He put in a movie called *Time Bandits* and removed it after nineteen minutes. He put in a movie called *Pete's Dragon*. *Pete's Dragon* played all the way through, though I left in the middle of it and went into the basement. The basement was lit now and Johnny Jakobi had plugged in his boom box.

"I heard that you break dance," Johnny said to me.

"Yeah," I said.

"Well, go ahead."

I moonwalked. I did a few arm waves.

"I can't do any real moves on this concrete floor," I told him. "Concrete's no good for that stuff."

"Uh huh," Johnny said.

I looked in the basement storage rooms. I went back upstairs, looked in the room behind the community hall. The only person there was Ellie Butterbit, reading. I couldn't find Georgia. Then I went back down into the basement and there was almost everybody, including Georgia, gathered around watching Will Wynsom break dance. Apparently, Will had only been napping.

"He's really good," Johnny said to me. I watched Will's robotic gyrations for a moment. He didn't attempt any real moves. What stupid curly hair he had. I stealthily positioned myself behind Georgia and pinched her ass. She glanced at me and elbowed me in the gut.

I went back upstairs. No one was watching the movie. Reverend Peacelilly slept in a chair. I wondered what he thought the purpose of this lock-in was. I went into the room behind the hall. Ellie Butterbit looked up from her book as I stood in the doorway. Globe lights hung from the ceiling and lit the clean honey expanse of pinewood floor.

"Hey," I said.

"Hi, Kevin," Ellie said.

I felt the clarity of her gaze. I backed out of the room. Then I entered.

Late in the night, many hours after I had arrived home from my run—from Bend City—I opened the envelope Mrs. Butterbit had left with my mother months ago. Inside was a folded piece of notebook paper that was wavy as if it had been wet. I opened the paper. There was a hole through the paper, as if a pen had been pushed through it, and the handwriting was faded.

> Kevin,
>
> I just said good-bye to you outside the van and you told me Montana and now I am so happy I have to write you now and tell you what a good boyfriend you are and how I love you love you love you love you love you. The cabin it is! The cabin on a lake! The mountains! The lake! The baby grand piano! I'm writing in the complete dark of course and the van is bumping around all crazy-like so I doubt you can even read this but I'll tell you all this on the phone later tonight anyway. I do want to walk in the woods with you again, Kevin. That would be so nice. Kevin, I'm so glad you broke up with Georgia to go with me. I think you're glad too. Tam thinks you're really great—you're so sweet with her, and I appreciate that, you know. That was so wild what Bobby did in the race. But you're my

Just like that, the letter ended.

I turned off my lights and sat by my window. The moonlight came and lit the note I had spread on the floor.

I placed beside the note these three sheets of paper:

E-
E-
E-
E-
E-
-
ENDY-
GOGO-
TATA-
E-
-
-
ENDIBIE-
ELE-
-
E-
-E
E-E-E-E-
-
ELBOW-
EGLY-
ELASTIC-
ELECTROCORTICOGRAM-
ENGILD-
EXPRESS-
EEBEE EEBEE-
-
EEBEE SEESEE-
EEBEECEEBEELEENAH-
-
EBEE-
ELE-
EEELEE-
EE-
EELEE-
EELLEEN-
ELIEN-
ELENE-
-

ELLEN.

Ellen.

OKO-
OROYO-
ORO-
-
Y-
ONY-
YONY-
ONIE-
-
NY-
INY-
ANY-
INNY-
INNIE-
AETHINNIE-
ATHINY-
ETHANY-
ET-
-
BETHANY.

Bethany.

UMBI-
OMNI-
CAELI-
HIMMEL-
AMI-
AMIT-
UMBIT-
BIT-
BIT-
BIT-
BITBIT-
-
BITTBIT-
BITBITBIT-
BITBITBITBUT-
BITTERBIT-
BI-
-

BUTTERBIT.

Butterbit.

Ellen Bethany Butterbit.

Ellie.

ten

"Curious that you should visit me," Porphorhessohln said. "I was planning to call you in this afternoon."

I sat in the superintendent's office, before his gun-blue desk.

"I expressed my great admiration and gratitude toward you Saturday afternoon, did I not?" Porphorhessohln asked.

"I believe you did."

"Good. I don't want that to go unsaid. You secured our school's first state track trophy since 1949. Do you know how many phone calls we've received about you?"

"No."

"After your picture came out in the Sunday paper, we had about one hundred and fifty messages with our answering service this morning and already we've had two dozen more calls today."

Porphorhessohln was referring to a picture that had been taken of me as I lay on the track immediately after my 800-meter run Saturday. My right calf and foot were coated with blood. I had no shoe on that foot. Most remarkably, I stared at my bloody hand, and my face was marked with a bloody handprint.

"All these callers, checking on your well-being and congratulating you. Gregory talked to some reporters yesterday, so I expect today's papers will put to rest most of the rumors that you're in shock and nearing death. But hold on, I've got something for you."

Porphorhessohln ducked his head under his desk for a moment and then reappeared holding a new letter jacket.

"For you," he said. "My gift."

I took the jacket. It had a black wool body and white leather sleeves.

"You can put your medals and letters and all on there. You'll get patches soon for your wins at district and state. What am I saying? You know what a letter jacket is."

"Why is it black and white?"

"Our school colors."

"Our colors are red and white."

"Not anymore."

"Black and white aren't colors. They're tones."

Porphorhessohln laughed.

I thanked him for the jacket.

"My pleasure. You know, I was once a state champion runner, too."

"Is that so?"

"Yes. Umber Porphorhessohln, from Bend City High School. I won the standing broad jump and the 220- and 440-yard dashes as a senior. That was 1949."

"Ah," I said. "This school's last state trophy."

Porphorhessohln touched his index finger to his nose.

"But I thought you grew up in West Virginia."

"I moved here in '47 to live with my great aunt after my mother died. And a blessing it was—I would never have graduated from high school if I'd stayed in West Virginia."

"Life takes us where we need to go, leads us through our own blindness," I said.

"Now that's well said, Kevin. Well said."

"Oh, I heard it somewhere. Or read it. On a greeting card maybe."

"What's that on your hands?" Porphorhessohln asked.

"Bandages," I said.

"You hurt both hands? Your palms? I thought you got spiked on the back of your left hand."

"I tripped and skinned my palms on my run home Saturday."

Porphorhessohln tugged on his hair for a moment. He shook his head. "That was quite a run," he said. "Gregory told me it was quite a run."

"I was excited from the track meet," I said. "I needed the run to calm down."

"A twenty-mile calm-down—you are a zinger, Kevin."

"Eighteen miles."

Porphorhessohln shrugged.

"I have a question for you," I said.

"That's right—why did you come to see me on this fine spring morning?"

"I want to transfer to Zame Smith."

Porphorhessohln shook his head. "Can't do it."

"I'm smart enough."

"Probably," he said calmly. "But the workload at Zame Smith would pinch your training schedule. Just look at our track team. Most of the long-distance runners are from Zame Smith, right? And most of the sprinters from Sundry Seeley. And who wins more races? The sprinters. They have more time to train. It's a simple equation."

"I never thought of it in mathematical terms before," I said.

"Part of my job," Porphorhessohln said.

"Couldn't one make the argument, though, that students that succeed in Zame Smith are more likely to have developed a sense of discipline and self-control, skills which are directly related to athletic success?"

"One could make that argument," the superintendent replied, "but I wouldn't be swayed."

A week after school ended, I received in the mail a check for five thousand dollars written on Dr. Brake's personal account. Two days later, Brake drove me north to Hibernia, led me through a secured entrance at the rear of a concrete building connected to the state university's massive medical complex, and took me into Dr. E's laboratory. It was a low-ceilinged room lit by fluorescent lights and crammed full of filing cabinets and exercise equipment and boxy instruments with tubes hanging off of them.

Dr. E handed me four Twinkies. His face was as flat and triangular as the plate of a steam iron.

"Thank you," I said, "but Dr. Brake has already paid me."

"These are for today's experiment. We are seeing how you react to sugars and such."

"I like how you said that: 'sugars and such.'"

"Sugars and such," E repeated.

"Sugars and such," I said.

"Sugars and such," he said again.

"Sucrose," I said.

I ran on a treadmill while my heart rate and blood pressure were monitored. After twenty minutes at a seven-minute pace, Dr. E and his Japanese research assistant, Bob Popincock, scraped sweat from my legs and torso and stoppered it into a tiny vial. Then I ate the Twinkies and repeated the drill.

Dr. Brake waited for me through the experiment and then drove me home.

A week later, I returned to Dr. E and operated an exercise bike while slides of baby animals flashed on a screen before me. Electrodes glued to my head measured my brain waves. Also, my heart rate and blood pressure were monitored again, and my sweat was collected twice during the exercise and once immediately afterward.

"Which babies did you think were the most vulnerable?" Bob Popincock asked me after I had dismounted the bike.

"Well, I guess the little chicks were very vulnerable. Though I do admit that something about the baby elephant, despite its size, really touched me as fragile. Maybe something about those floppy ears."

"Okay, good," Bob said, and he wrote on his clipboard. "Which babies do you think were the most intelligent?" he asked.

"The baby Holstein and the box turtle twins struck me as particularly bright."

"Okay, good," Bob said. "Did your opinion of their intelligence fluctuate from the beginning of your ride to the end?"

"As a matter of fact, Bob, I did at first think that the turtle twins were obviously the smartest of the lot, but later realized the calf exuded a subtle air of sophistication—and not a pompous affectation, but the self-assured attitude of a being adept at employing complex critical thinking skills."

"Okay, good," Bob said. He bowed to me. "Thank you, Kevin Schuler."

"No," I said, "thank you, Bob Popincock."

That summer, I visited Dr. E nine times. One time he tested my reactions to running with one of my shoes untied. Another time he painted my hands blue and made me stare at them as I rode a stair-climbing machine. And yet another time he placed two treadmills face-to-face and had a lovely college female run on one treadmill as I ran on the other. The rules of that experiment were that I had to maintain eye contact with the female at least 90 percent of the time, and every two minutes, on Bob Popincock's cue, the female said, "I love you, Kevin Schuler," immediately after which I was supposed to pick a number between one and fifteen and tell Bob Popincock this number. As it turned out, I picked the numbers four and fourteen much of the time. One time, though, I picked the number fifty-two—far out of the test range—and heard Dr. E whisper "By God!" to Bob Popincock.

As the female ran, sweat gleamed like sugar glaze on her upper lip and a vein in her neck bulged healthily. She was gorgeous.

When I arrived home after that visit to Dr. E's, I found a small note in my duffel. It said, "I am the girl who ran opposite you. Call me. Janine 342-1019."

I asked Dr. E, later in the summer, "These experiments, they will help you tell me why I run so fast, they will tell you what's inside me?"

"These experiments . . ." E said. "We are seeking clues. It's like throwing rocks into a forest and hoping you hit one of the animals in there so that it will come running out and you can see it. You can't just walk into the forest and walk up to the animals and label them and prod them and ask them questions. That doesn't work. The animals will hide, run away, or even attack you. We're throwing rocks into a forest. The forest is you."

On one drive home from Hibernia, Dr. Brake stopped at a shoe store in Bend City, bought me a pair of expensive training shoes, and demanded, once we were back in his parked car, that I hand Bobby Sickle's training shoes to him. I declined.

"If I don't take those shoes, you'll just keep running in them till you've worn the soles clear away."

He threatened not to start his car until I handed the shoes to him.

"Well," I reasoned, "they're not really my shoes, so I don't have authority to give them away."

One of Brake's eyebrows rose momentarily, he touched his hairline, shook his head, then started the car.

Thus I retained the shoes of Bobby Sickle.

That summer, I ran each morning. I started before dawn and sometimes continued running until eight or nine or even ten.

Every morning, as I left the house, I said to my mother, who sat at the kitchen table drinking coffee from her green mug, "Going for my morning run."

That summer, the sun rose as I ran and often cast my shadow far ahead of me—maybe fifty paces, maybe a hundred, sometimes more. Sometimes I could wave a hand and the shadow of my hand would brush a hilltop. Or the shadow of my torso might occlude a herd of cattle. By late August, we had gone seven weeks without rain and the dust lay thick upon the roadside weeds. Dust rose at my every footfall and when a car or pickup passed—even if it was a neighbor who recognized me and slowed to pass—I ran then through a cloud of brown dust for many seconds. Sometimes I became so coated with dirt that the sweat that ran down my legs and arms made clean rivulets across my brown skin.

Perhaps it was the dust that made the August air seem yellow. No, the morning light was not the clean, white light one expects as one nears the cusp of the year—where the warm months end and the cold arises. The morning light was yellow, and seemed to me to carry some sense of warning.

On one particular run, as I passed through the yellow light, I remembered the stoplight my elementary principal, Mr. Peeve, had mounted in the corner of our lunchroom. At the start of the lunch hour, the light was green. But if we were unnecessarily rowdy or loud, or even if one kid pulled a stupid antic, Mr. Peeve switched the light to yellow—a warning. If conditions did not improve, the light went to red. When the light was red we were no longer allowed to talk or laugh or touch one another.

That dry summer, my shadow head sometimes wore the crowns of oaks and ash trees. My shadow fingers could touch the crows who sat hunched a quarter mile down the road. My shadow torso slid across pastures. But my shadow feet never went far from my real feet. My feet beat the dry roads and summoned dust from the brown gravel that had been dredged from creeks.

part two

eleven

The Saturday was foggy. Dew shone on the golf course's fairways. The putting greens held moisture like sponges. Yesterday, a cold front had knocked leaves to the ground, so that now the woods displayed much gray, and suddenly we could envision December, though it was only early October.

I ran out front in this race, as I did in all cross-country races. I ran in silence. To me, cross-country resembled a training run more than a race. There were no lanes to bind me. I rarely saw other runners after the first half mile. In track races, we ran in circles upon a synthetic surface; in cross-country, our course was determined by the landscape. This particular race ran the perimeter of Bogg Hills Golf Club in Springfield. I ran across a broad fairway, skirted a sand pit. The course then took me beneath the oaks that bordered a cemetery. Spectators leaned toward me as I passed. They clapped and chanted encouraging words in what appeared to be the same manner one would egg on a dim-witted hound—"Good boy! Good boy! Go on! Go boy! All right, boy! All right!"—though of course I didn't actually hear them.

I rounded a corner marked by a dead elm. A volunteer in a yellow slicker pointed the way for me, pointed toward a long, golf-cart-wide wooden bridge that crossed a muddy gulch. I passed over the bridge.

The wood vibrated under my feet. I wondered if the course supervisors realized how much damage a few hundred spike-footed runners could inflict upon such wood—the planks were already pocked from the varsity girls' race. Across the bridge, a heavy rain started. I ran along a thick row of bushes. A clutch of sparrows burst from cover. Then the course swung left and I saw before me the same gulch I had just crossed, but without a bridge. I did not hesitate. I followed the white line that had been painted on the ground. I took the incline. During warm-up, this ditch had presented no problem—just a bit soft at the bottom—but now, after a minute of torrential rain, the slope was muddy. I could not open my stride. I held back, my heels slipped, my momentum increased. I tumbled, skidded, slid on the spare grass. My stomach suddenly became clenched, as if in anticipation of vomiting. The mud was cold beneath me as I fell onward, downward.

At the bottom of the slope, where the mud lay deepest, I came to a halt on my back. The rain beat my chest. I could see spectators peering over the lip of the gulch's other side. The spectators held brightly colored umbrellas. In the ditch, the light was dim. Surrounding hickories had not yet relinquished their leaves. A sour rubber smell resided in the air. And presently, on the slope, appeared my nearest competitors—perhaps a dozen boys. They encountered the same problems I had. They slipped. They had no hope. They were running too close to each other and brought one another down like a set of bowling pins. They slid and tumbled toward me with a speed greater than what their running pace had been. I squirmed in the mire. The mud kept me down. My shin collided with someone's skull. A stranger's hands pushed against my back. My own hands encountered someone's hot, rain-slick shoulder. Mud was flung into my face. An elbow met my neck. A foot wriggled before me like a beached fish, clad in one of those nefarious neon orange and green Nike spikes from years ago. And now I saw more runners spilling into the gulch, tumbling toward us with toothy grimaces upon their faces. I observed at close range the freckles on another runner's biceps.

Briefly, then, I envisioned the scene as if I were suspended above it all; and from that vantage point I could not discern my own body among the jumble of torsos and twitching legs. This vision put terror in my bones. I scrambled like a cornered pig. I pushed down my fellow runners in my struggle to rise. Finally, I stood, stepped through the thicket of bodies. But someone grabbed my ankle and yanked, brought me chest-first into the mud again. I looked back into the melee and saw that the hand that had tripped me belonged to a runner in a yellow shirt—a Lower Bend runner. I twisted my leg around to loosen the runner's grip, I kicked, pulled free, and clambered up the slope using my hands as much as my feet. I did not look back into the gulch, and ran on through the increasing rain.

This was one of the few courses of the year that did not loop back on itself for a second or third circuit, so I did not have to cross the gulch again. If I ran faster this day than most others, perhaps it was because I was running away from the gulch. By the time I crossed the finish line in first place, the rain had washed me clean of mud. They handed me the square of paper with "1" written on it. Gregory emerged from the crowd and we walked away together and waited beneath the dripping trees for my teammates to finish. Gregory had grown a beard, a bulbous thing, and he commented that I appeared pale. Twenty minutes later, when we received word that the race results had been nullified on account of the problems in the mud pit, Gregory and I both shrugged. Henny approached me wearing gum boots much too large for her and silently handed me a note. Just behind Henny walked an official. He told me he had received reports that foul play had been directed toward me in the mud pit.

"Mud was directed toward me in the mud pit," I said, "nothing else."

Henny's note read, *There is more to Kevin than running.*

I was cold and sluggish enough that I did not evade the reporters.

"Are you disappointed that your victory has been voided? I heard that your finishing time was a course record."

I waved off the man.

"Any news on the twisted ankle you suffered in last week's race?" someone else asked.

As I stepped onto the team bus, another reporter shouted, "How do you think the impending shut-downs of Bend City's automotive plants will affect the city?"

I received, in the mail, a photocopied excerpt from the unabridged minutes of September's Carton school board meeting. There was no indication who had sent them to me. Handwritten arrows directed me to a particular section of the text:

> Board President Barry Griffon and Board Member Dena Perquizzit brought forth the issue of the dangerous length and sharpness of the spikes on the bronze cast of the running shoes that sits atop the Track Team Memorial in front of the school.
>
> District Resident Deedee Rausch testified that her son Thatch, a first grader, had received lacerations from the spikes while climbing on the memorial after school on 3 September.
>
> Second Grade Teacher Victoria Orr reported two similar accidents that had occurred while she and her class were waiting for a field trip bus in front of the school on 9 September. "Children desire to touch anything within reach," Ms. Orr testified. "The [Track Team] Monument poses a danger to all our younger students."
>
> Superintendent Robert Oligarchy related that his office had received "at least six but no more than eight" other complaints about the monument's sharp spikes and pointed out that the monument was placed in an area of the campus where young students often waited unattended after school. One course of action, Oligarchy said, would be to move the monument to a more secure place, or a place where younger students wouldn't be likely to encounter it.
>
> Ms. Orr suggested that an All School Memorandum could warn faculty and staff of the monument's threat.

Board Member Randall Tarkio proposed placing a decorative barrier or fence around the monument.

Superintendent Oligarchy asserted that a warning sign on or near the monument would also aid in averting future injuries.

At this time, Board President Barry Griffon reported that he had measured the spikes himself and consulted with Coach Teddy Freeday. The spikes, Griffon said, were a half-inch long, a length that Coach Freeday assured him was extremely rare, even on cinder tracks. Coach Freeday told Griffon that none of the tracks Carton competed on allowed spikes greater than three-eighths of an inch in length.

Superintendent Oligarchy asked Board President Griffon just what was the point of his point.

Board President Griffon replied that he hoped to show that the spikes were not a "realistic representation of the standard equipment of Carton's junior high or high school track teams" and therefore should, in fact, be removed entirely from the monument or filed down to a more reasonable length. Or, Griffon stated, the spikes could have their tips blunted.

Board Member Dena Perquizzit made a motion to assign a Special Ombudsperson to the issue at hand. No Member seconded the motion.

At this point, the Board and Advisors unanimously carried a motion to enact an immediate ten minute recess and dispatch Board Secretary and Stenographer Linda Parson to brew another carafe of dark-roast coffee.

Following recess, Superintendent Oligarchy asked if the identity of the owner of the illegally long spikes was known.

District Transportation and Maintenance Chief Tyler Arkass answered in the negative.

Board Member Dena Perquizzit asked Superintendent Oligarchy why he was particularly interested in punishing the students of a class that no longer existed.

Superintendent Oligarchy declined to answer.

Tyler Arkass then testified that Board President Griffon's proposal to shorten, blunt, or remove the monument's spikes could be easily realized, consuming between twenty and forty minutes total of preparation, work, and clean up—with no foreseeable Materials, Outside Contract, or Special Advisory Fees.

Board President Griffon put forth a motion to vote on the complete removal of the monument's spikes.

Board Member Alan Lore seconded the motion.

The vote passed five to one.

Board Member Thomas Merchant requested that he be recorded as the sole dissenter on the grounds that complete removal of the spikes would alter the monument's authenticity in representing the acts and details of the junior high track team. He explained that regardless of legal spike length limits, the shoes had been retrieved from the van after the accident and therefore offered a most authentic and appropriate representation of the track team.

The Board adjourned at 1:07 A.M.

The Saturday after the mud-pit race, I returned home from my morning run to find a red two-seat convertible in our driveway. As far as I could discern, the car had been generated on the spot—it showed no signs of wear. The clear-coat paint shone like fingernail polish; not a single particle of dust clung to the bumper or wheel wells; the carpeted floor mats exhibited no scuff marks or dirt; even the treads of the tires were black and unmarred, held no pebbles, and still bore fragile, hair-like nubbins of rubber left over from the casting process. The leather seats glowed as if they had been waxed.

Mother walked out of the house. It startled me to see her outside without her purse. Here she was, pale in the sunlight, wearing elastic-waist jeans.

"How'd this get here?" I asked.

"Brake sent it!" she said. "He just called."

I nodded. "But how'd it get here?"

"It's part of your payment for the university study! Brake thought you'd want a car now that you're almost sixteen."

"I'm not sixteen until May," I said.

"Look how new it is!" she said.

"May first, if you recall."

"You're going places!" she said.

"Half a year away," I said.

"Red was always your favorite color."

"But how'd the car get here? The odometer reads one mile."

"Get here?" Mother said. "They rolled it off a truck."

Inside the house, I dialed Brake's cellular phone number.

"Thank you so much, but I didn't ask for a car."

"Kevin, you're too modest to ask for the things you really want."

"I don't want a car. My mother thinks I'm some kind of celebrity now."

"Is she wrong?"

"Take the car back, find out when my birthday really is, send me a card."

"It's easier at the moment to pay you for the next six months by giving you this gift."

"What do you mean easier? It's easier to buy a car for me than write a check?"

"It's complicated—taxes, appropriation reports. You're dealing with a university here, not a business."

"This university is very good at handing me money, but their research of me seems to have nothing to report."

"Be patient."

"Take the car back or I will breach the contract."

"Okay, okay."

"Today."

In the afternoon, when the flatbed arrived to retrieve the car, Mother watched mournfully from the kitchen window.

"Your father won't believe this story," she said. "It will be like a fish story: 'A glittering fish as long as my leg jumped into my boat and I threw it back—splash!' We could have at least taken a picture of the car!"

"That fish story is a very beautiful fish story," I said. "Can't you hear the joy in the splash?"

twelve

A week later, another Saturday, I left the house at 6 A.M., ran
down the road, crossed Blank's Ford over Keen Creek, passed up the
long hill beside Quint's dairy farm, entered the cedar knobs, continued
down Bell Lane past the old settlers' cemetery, past the abandoned
farmstead where the half-dozen outbuildings leaned toward the still-
stout house like children reaching for a parent, came back into the
broad apron of flat cropland in the north creekbottom, then turned
onto the grassy access lanes that led through Carl Otto's cornfields, and
eventually made my way across the fields in a very indirect manner to
where I intersected Bell Lane again and turned toward home. This
route, in fact, had been the exact route I had followed last Saturday
morning, and the sky was the same steely overcast shade today as it had
been during that run, and my sweat was cold upon my brow, as it had
been last week, too. The similarities between last week's run and
today's run were sufficient to discombobulate me to the point where
my first thought on returning home and seeing a new silver coupe sitting in the driveway was that the car should be red and convertible and
Japanese. I regained my wits, though, and looked the machine over. It
was European. It at least had some wear on the tires, some dust on the
body, but it was still obviously the kind of car meant to impress

teenagers—sunroof, dual overhead camshaft, spoiler, tinted windows, custom sound system.

I walked into the house enraged, walked toward the phone in the kitchen.

"Kevin?" Mother called from within the house.

"What?"

She sang: "There's a young lady to see you."

Mother sat in the living room with a girl my age. They rose as I entered. It was chilly outside, so Mother had put the "Carefree Fireplace" tape into the VCR and as I stood there after entering the room, in that moment before any of us spoke, a knot on a log in the television fireplace popped and sprayed sparks.

"Kevin, this is Andanda Dane from your school newspaper. Andanda, this is my son."

I shook the girl's hand. She was dressed rather businesslike, in dark slacks and a silk blouse.

"Andanda has been telling me how interested her paper is in writing about you."

"That's very flattering."

"We're excited to tell our readers about you," Andanda said.

"I'm sure she'll write a lovely article—nothing tasteless like some reporters," Mother said.

"I'm sure she's an excellent writer," I said. "Are you from Zame Smith?"

"Yes."

"That would explain why I've not seen you before."

"I've seen you," she said. "But then, you're rather renowned around campus."

Mother slapped her hand to her chest. "Oh! *Renowned!* I— Don't let me intrude, I've got wash to sort in the basement."

"We don't have a basement, Mother."

"Yes, well, I just didn't want Andanda to feel uncomfortable knowing I was in the house listening to you two . . ."

"Perhaps she and I could talk outside," I said.

On the lawn, Andanda removed a cigarette from her corduroy jacket and lit it. She held the cigarette between the very tips of her fingers. "I'd offer you one," she said, "but I don't imagine an athlete like yourself smoking."

"A very smart assessment," I said. "You are correct. You can print that in your interview."

"Let me say, it's not so much that I want a single interview with you. Really, I have in mind following you around for some time and getting a broader picture. In light of the recent publicity you've received after being ranked the top cross-country runner in the state, my editor has been gracious enough to grant me a large word-count for the article. Plus room for pictures. I am a good photographer, too. Do you assent to the article?"

"Where would you get the idea that I wouldn't assent?"

"Perhaps from Jerry Pontif's attempts to interview you and our frequent written queries to you and various reports in the media about your avoidance of press."

"Ah, yes. So to ply the reluctant subject you get into his house and charm his mother."

"Not only that, but Superintendent Porphorhessohln yesterday pledged his full support of this article and does hope you can see the logic of following through with it."

"Very nice," I said. "Well played."

"Kevin, I am not a hack. I will do my job efficiently and produce an excellent article. Furthermore," she said, "I am not in the least impressed by athletics."

She flicked her cigarette ashes onto our brown lawn.

"I am not impressed by athletics," she repeated, "or athletes."

She had won me.

I leaned toward her. I said, "I hate athletics."

For a week, Andanda arrived at my house before dawn and followed me on my morning runs. "No questions this week," she promised me.

The first morning, she crept behind me in her silver coupe, sipping latté from a take-out cup. The next morning, a perfectly clear morning with a colorless sunrise, she showed up with her mountain bike on a rack atop her car and so followed me by bike. She stayed behind me on my runs and I admit that I usually forgot I was being trailed. One time, I happened to glance back to see her coasting along on her bike, cigarette planted firmly in her mouth at an angle that brought to mind a cigar.

On Thursday I arrived back at the house from my run and Andanda was nowhere in sight. She walked in the driveway with her bike ten minutes later.

"Why didn't you stop?" she asked.

"What?"

"I had a flat tire and asked you to stop. I *yelled*, for Christ's sake."

"I didn't hear."

I explained that sometimes when I ran I was enclosed in silence. I waited for her to ask me why, to ask me the nature of the silence, its source, its meaning. Instead, though, she nodded and said, "You focus so intently on your running that you cut off nonessential sensory input."

"Okay," I said.

After the morning runs, while I showered, Andanda left. I would eat and then Mother would take me in to school.

"What a beauty!" Mother told me late in the week as we drove along. "She's gorgeous, Kevin!"

"I have eyes."

"*She* has eyes! You don't see green eyes like that very often! Emeralds!"

"You haven't been talking to her while I shower, have you?"

"Oh, no. Not really. She asks small questions, nothing worthy of being in print. She's just being courteous. I think she's very interested in you. She's in your grade, you know."

"I know."

"She's Editor-At-Large for the newspaper—sounds very impressive."

"Sounds like a fugitive."

"And what hair! Those curls aren't fake. She's very pretty."

"Her eyebrows, though—plucked," I said.

"There aren't many women as tall as you, Kevin."

"I like short women," I said. "Short like my mother."

At a home football game, Jol Brule called me down onto the sideline. With Jol in top form and a strong core of experienced seniors, our football team sported an undefeated record for the year.

"I get sick of this game," Jol told me. "I don't know what the point is."

"I understand," I told him.

"I don't know anyone else who does."

We sat on the grass away from the team. For the rest of the game, Jol would take to the field with the offensive team, wow the crowd, come off the field, confer with the coach, then walk over to sit with me. Behind us, we could hear Jol's father cajoling him. "This is how *not* to play football!" I heard Mr. Brule yell after Jol caught a twenty-yard pass and then ran another sixteen yards before being forced out of bounds. "This is how not to play football!"

"Why doesn't your father come to track meets?" I asked Jol after he returned from the play. "He could add pizzazz to our cheering section."

Jol smiled, shook his head. "He doesn't think track's a real sport. You know, there's no contact in track."

"He hasn't seen my races," I said.

"That's true. I should describe to him that race where the guy in front of you stopped cold and you just plowed him over."

"I tried to dodge him."

"My football coach is hoping you'll try out for defense."

The field lights were reflected in the lenses of our eyes. The temperature settled toward fifty. A wind blew off the grandstand, down through the bundled crowd, and on that breeze I smelled whiskey.

"When I'm out there," Jol said, pointing to the field, "I kind of imagine that all of the opponents are my father."

"And then you dodge them," I said.

Jol nodded.

When the time came to deliver fabrications, I didn't hesitate.

Andanda and I sat in her car, parked in Breaklee Park, in clear view of the muddy Missouri River and the broad, brown October fields that covered the floodplain north of the river. She asked me if I thought often of my Carton teammates. This was the first time she had mentioned Carton.

"They won't leave me," I answered. "And I can't leave them."

"Do your memories comfort you? Are you stronger now than you were two years ago?"

"I've worked through it. Counselors declared me remarkably unscathed. I hope I have taken on some of the vitality and goodness that existed within my classmates."

Andanda waited many seconds before speaking again.

"The investigation of the accident is ongoing, correct?"

"I think," I answered.

"Are there any theories you hold?"

I didn't answer. I watched the river roil far below.

She said, "Investigators continue to focus on the bus's steering mechanisms. But that reporter from St. Louis—oh, I can't remember his name—"

"Clarence Phee."

"Right—how do you feel about his theory?"

"It's sensationalistic."

"It implicates you and your parents in the accident. Is that why you and your parents refuse to talk to Phee?"

"We don't speak with any reporters."

"Does that include me?"

"You're offering me editorial power over the article."

"Right."

"Then why are you pursuing this line of questions if you know I won't let you write anything about it?"

"I'm looking at you from as many angles as I can. You're not a translucent subject. Perhaps I can locate you by process of triangulation."

I looked at her face. Yes, she was beautiful. Mother was right.

"You've really done your research," I said. "Hardly anyone in Bend City seems to know about the accident. *Carton* knows. They know."

"What do you mean?" she asked.

"I'll tell you why I don't believe Phee's theory. I was in the car that night, and there was almost no water on the bridge. So the idea that our road spray hit the van's windshield is just wrong. Nothing against Phee—I applaud his calls for top-hatch emergency exits in Missouri school buses."

"But isn't the point of Phee's theory that when the driver tried to find the windshield wipers, his eyes strayed from the road just long enough that the bus nicked the right guardrail, which then caused the driver to make an exaggerated steering correction? That wouldn't require much road spray, right? Especially considering that the driver was your coach and not a very experienced bus driver. And he hadn't driven that particular bus before because it was almost brand new."

"Van," I said.

"What?"

"You keep saying 'bus.' It was a van. It wasn't even yellow. It was gray."

"But what about Phee's theory? What do you think?"

"There wasn't any road spray is what I'm saying."

"But a minute ago you said there was *almost* no water on the road."

"Is someone supposed to bear the whole weight of the thing?" I asked.

Andanda shook her head after a moment. "I don't mean to bring up bad memories," she said.

"No, no. It's no problem. It's not your problem. It's all fine. Smooth sailing. You're doing a perfect job."

I told Andanda to take me back to the school then, lied that my mother would be picking me up in five minutes when in fact it would be another half hour. At school, I wandered the halls of Sundry Seeley. I spotted Jol in the welding pits. I went in. The concrete floor was burnt in patches. An after-school supervisor sat inside the glass-enclosed office across the room.

"Hey K. V.," Jol barked as I approached. He sat on a metal foot locker. "Go Ke-*vin!*"

"Maybe I should change my name to Go Kevin Schuler," I said. I pointed to a small metal cage Jol held. "What's that?" I asked.

"A dodecahedron," Jol said.

"A twelve-planed object."

"That's it," Jol said.

"Fun with welding," I said.

"It was challenging to figure out all the angles."

"I've never seen you in here after school."

"No football practice today. Game tomorrow. And I'm in no scurry to get home 'cause my dad's out of work now."

"Sorry to hear that."

"Well, half the town's on the same downriver barge next month, right, with these plant closings? They just let my pop go early. So he sits at home being sour—a good reason to avoid the place."

"What did he do at the plant?"

Jol held up the dodecahedron.

"Welder?" I said.

"Yep."

"How's your toe?" I asked. He had fractured a toe in a game two weeks ago.

"It'll be fine as long as it doesn't get stepped on tomorrow."

"People thought it would slow you down."

"Nope. Hey, you don't drive, do you?"

"Not yet."

"Shoot. I need to go out to the store and buy more ankle wrap. That stuff just starts to reek after you wear it for a few weeks."

"Doesn't the football trainer wrap your ankle for you? I mean, don't they supply you with ankle wrap?"

"Yeah, but I'm trying to keep this injury secret—I haven't told the trainer."

"You want Valapraso's Athletics?"

"Yeah, that's where I like to go. Or a drugstore, I guess. Dad won't drive anywhere now. Saving gasoline."

"My mom will be here in a few minutes and we can take you out there."

Mother was flattered to meet the famous Lojo Brule. She drove us to the athletic store, then back in toward the center of town.

"This is fine, Mrs. Schuler," Jol said as we neared the school.

"Well, which house is it?" she asked.

"This corner's close enough."

"Whoop—let me get up closer to the curb."

Jol thanked Mother, left the car, walked up the street.

"Imagine," Mother said as we drove away, "you two being buddies. The two little star athletes."

thirteen

Since the end of freshman year, letters came weekly from Henny, and I answered every one. This letter came mid-October, written in fountain pen on her usual unlined stationery:

Kevin,

I'm glad you like for me to be at your cross-country races. I lurk around the race's course. I duck behind trees and cars and trash cans to play our hiding game (once I ducked behind that doctor of yours, Brake, and felt quite secure behind his ponderous girth) and after the race is done, after you run down that little roped-off funnel at the end of the course and they hand you the piece of paper on which is written "1," I lurk some more while you cool down, while you stretch, then I pop up, as if I had only just arrived. And you tell me in your last letter how it makes you happy to know that I am there but hidden.

I love this time of year. Everything is preparing to bend toward winter, everything shares the same state of mind. Frogs have burrowed into the mud. Walnuts litter the ground and their husks have gone brown and soft. I envy you and your country home where you can ramble in the hills. Here in town I must ramble up the slope of our backyard to where Mother has piled the pine cones against our back fence. Or I can go across the block to the cemetery, which exudes a lovely, autumn-type vibration.

I have chased just such a vibration on my clarinet and have not succeeded in cornering it. I can chase it uphill with arpeggios and sometimes I can even emulate its promise of warmth by twiddling around the low notes of my instrument. But I can't get it! Do you know the tone I mean? But you don't play an instrument, Kevin. You should play an instrument. My clarinet helps me communicate things I cannot or will not put into words.

At the moment, Father is boiling onions and so food is entering my mind. Out my window, I can see the orange sunset pulling itself over the city like a flannel sheet. I've got ninety pages of Hume to read tonight—and you know how I get the Sunday-night ache and can't concentrate on anything. I don't know what this ache's about. It's an ache that makes me look at maps and wonder and get caught up in visions of future landscapes of my life.

I'm sliding toward sentimentality so I'll cut the letter here. Weary in town I remain—

> *Faithfully yours,*
> *Henrietta*

Her letters made me fear my own youth, and they made me tremble sometimes as I read them. She communicated so freely on the page. She poured herself toward me in a selfless, honest way that made my return letters seem stiff, a tad formal. But she commended my letters, remarked on my pastoral vision and something she called my "detachable imagination"—by which term I think she referred to her perception that I could empathize with anyone. "This ability must frighten you sometimes, yes?" she wrote once. "Or does it let you draw the line between yourself and tragedy? Or does it occlude all lines? Does it let you cast yourself into disaster or pain? Does it let you forecast? Revise your life? Please tell me, I who have such a plodding imaginative life."

At school, Henny and I saw each other rarely—she spent her days in Zame Smith, I spent mine in Sundry Seeley. During second hour, though, as I sat in my mathematics class I could see across the street to the gothic windows where Henny's macroeconomics class met. On dark, rainy mornings, I could even see into her class's lighted room, and discern individual figures, but could not tell which one was Henny. Occasionally, when I was out on a run, I would see her walking home after school—she loved the half-hour walk as much as she had hated running and as much as she hated riding the bus—and I would run past her and we'd both say nothing. We enjoyed that sense of knowing we knew each other but hadn't spoken—a shared secret. Sometimes I looped around the block and passed her a second time— though on a second pass one or both of us could rarely resist laughing.

When Henny invited me to her birthday party, I explained my reluctance to meet strangers in groups. I explained that her party fell on the night of the cross-country state championship race and I'd be exhausted. "It will be a small party," she assured me in a letter, "and there will be no potato sack races or egg-in-spoon races or crab-walk races—there will be no races at all. And as for strangers, there will only be Tinka and Mark, who are as intimidating as cottage cheese." Still I declined, and she wrote back, "I only want you to treat yourself right, and so I am happy for you to not attend my party if that means you are listening to your instincts and telling me the truth."

Andanda had heard that I had become Jol's sideline companion, and asked me if I could get Jol to invite her down onto the sidelines, too. Come Friday night, Jol did let Andanda come down to sit with us.

Andanda sat in the wet grass right next to Jol, asked well-informed questions about the football team's prospects. Soon, the two were whispering to each other, laughing together.

"Am I that hilarious?" I finally asked, near halftime.

"If you'll excuse us," Andanda said, "I'd like to talk to Jol alone."

"So you've used me to get an interview with the football star and now you're ready to lose me?"

"I interviewed Jol back in September," she said. "You must not read our paper."

"She's here to interview me *about you*, Kevin."

"Oh," I said. I stood up. "Be warned that he lies," I said.

"Lies are good. I want lies," Andanda said.

I wandered around the track toward the end zone. A Styrofoam cup rolled before me in the wind. I followed it and finally it became trapped below a yew shrub on the outside of the track's corner. As I bent to pick up the cup I saw that the shrub held many pieces of trash—newspaper inserts, a streamer, a plastic shopping bag, even a greeting card. The greeting card depicted an artificially pink sunset over a shallow, rocky river in a mountain valley. The inside of the card said, "Congratulations!" I used the plastic bag to carry the trash to a garbage can, then walked to the far side of the track and watched the game from there until Andanda and Jol waved me back toward them.

fourteen

Andanda had arranged to spend the entire day of the state cross-country meet with me, so when I dressed and came down the hall at five-thirty on that first Saturday in November, there she sat at our yellow Formica kitchen table. She asked me about the breakfast I ate, about how I had slept, about my state of nervousness. Most of the time, she sat back and observed.

Mother bustled around the house humming Burl Ives tunes. The electric strip heaters clicked as they warmed. The sun rose and illuminated the faux stained-glass hummingbird suncatcher above the kitchen sink. The faucet, this morning, cooperated by not dripping, and Mother drank her coffee from a cup and saucer instead of her old green mug.

By and by, Mother brought out a large gift box, wrapped in white tissue paper.

"It's a race day present for my Kevvy," she said.

Inside the box was the black-and-white letter jacket Porphorhessohln had given me in May. I had hung the bare jacket in the hall closet and given it no further thought but Mother had found it and sewn onto it my name, my varsity letter and pin, my eight patches from the district and state track meets, and all my medals from seventh grade, eighth grade, freshman year, and my cross-country medals from this year.

"Your dear mother's little fingers put it together, piece by piece. It's a coat of armor for my son."

"The rows of medals," I said, "sewn in straight lines, at such a tasteful, thirty degree angle."

"Kevin just doesn't show respect for his medals," Mother told Andanda. "He used to try to throw them out. And when he ran home last year from the state meet he dropped all three of his medals into the ditch and Gregory had to stop and pick them up. A strange kind of modesty."

I shrugged.

"This jacket will tell the world who you are," Mother said.

I pulled it on.

"Oh, this will be warm—perfect for a day like today," I said.

"Yes!" Mother said. "And see it sparkle in the sunlight! I mean, that's bright! You'll wear it *everywhere!*"

Mother picked lint off the jacket's shoulder. "Wait," she said. "Wait a pop." She walked down the hall and into her bedroom.

"These are all yours?" Andanda asked.

"I did this," I said, and I spread my arms, modeling the jacket, letting the medals clink gently against each other as I turned on my heel. "Are you impressed?"

"What's the difference between the medals? Which ones are gold and which silver and which bronze?"

I looked down at the jacket.

"They're all gold," I said, "except these from my seventh grade year. Silver, silver, silver."

Mother came back into the room. "Your father left this for you," she said and handed me a key.

"A key to Bethany Anne," I said.

"You recognize it!" said Mother. "I told him you would."

The key was worn and tarnished.

"Your father has carried it with him since he sold Bethany Anne.

But now he says it's yours and it will keep you running on the right course."

"Bethany Anne?" Andanda asked.

"The first truck my father owned," I said. "It was a battered, secondhand thing, but ran for years, fed our family."

"It happens to be the truck Mr. Schuler proposed to me in," Mother said.

"Furthermore," I said, "rumors suggest I was conceived in the cab of that truck."

"Kevin! Dear! Let's not reveal all our secrets!" Mother said. She laughed.

I said, "I would carry the key with me when I run, but that's really not practical."

"Hm," Mother said.

I handed the key to Mother. "Sew it on the jacket," I said.

"Perfect! That's it!"

"Sew it right next to my name—sew it right now."

This she did.

In the race, I ran perfectly. My stride opened up easily, my feet felt as if they weren't even touching the earth. The day was clear and the sun shone down on the race at a low angle. We ran along the lakeshore of a county park just west of Bend City. Geese scattered before us. I followed the white line that had been painted onto the sparse grass to mark the course. I saw Gregory nodding in the crowd as I came up the slope from the lake and entered the woods. The woods trail was rough—roots and acorns and packed mats of fallen leaves. I trod carefully, left the other front-runners, and licked the sweat off my upper lip. The course came out of the woods and cut through a meadow dotted with squat cedar trees. Here many people stood. I saw Andanda and Porphorhessohln standing together. Cameras were aimed at me. I smelled woodsmoke. I saw Tyler Arkass's leather face beaming at me.

Back in the trees. Few spectators. Occasional course officials. I ran alongside a dry creek. I ran between a limestone bluff and the lakeshore. A squirrel panicked before me. I felt light, impervious to gravity. But as I entered a lonely stretch of tall woods, the muscles around my eyeballs tightened; a heaviness hit my brow and flowed into my torso and limbs. I felt myself sliding backward into a recollection of a night during the summer after my seventh grade year.

At Hoover Garfield's farm, cans of creme soda lay on ice in a galvanized metal tub. Two bowls of melon balls sat upon a picnic table, trays of crackers and summer sausage arranged alongside. It was Hoover's birthday party, and the entire class was invited. All came. The girls surprised the boys by wearing shorts. Extension cords provided power for music. We had bathed especially for the occasion, and the July dusk tickled our necks. As the baked air of the day lifted away, we could smell pollen on the wind.

I walked with Georgia Teeter to see the horses. Two young Arabian horses sniffed our hands.

"That's gross," Georgia said. "I don't want horse snot on me."

"There's no snot."

The mare's chin whiskers tickled my knuckles.

"I'm going back," Georgia said.

"Okay."

I stayed and patted the mare's shoulder. I moved over to the stallion and began to pull his mane onto his left side, but the mare nipped his haunch, and he moved away. The mare leaned her heavy neck against my shoulder. Barn swallows floated over the pasture.

Little Tam Butterbit walked up to my side. "Hi, Kevin," she said.

"Howdy, Tam. Ellie here?"

"Yep."

"You here for our party?"

"Our parents are going to Bend City for a play and so Ellie said I could come with her to the party instead of being babysat by Mrs. Blick."

"I'm glad you're here," I said.

"Give them some grass," Tam said, and she bent and pulled some grass and held it toward the mare. The mare's lips made plopping sounds as it took the grass.

"I got an idea," I said. I took Tam back toward the party and we filled our hands with melon balls and walked back to the horses and fed the balls one by one to the mare. I imitated the mare's lip-smacking and Tam laughed.

"Give the other horse some," Tam suggested.

"The mare won't let him," I said. "She'll bite him if we give him attention."

"Then you keep feeding the mare, and I'll sneak over and feed the other one."

This plan worked, and as we stood feeding the horses our last bits of melon, Ellie appeared, looking farmy in her ponytail and plaid shirt.

"You guys," she said, "feeding the horses sweet food. You're bad."

"They like it," Tam said.

Ellie looked to me.

"They like it," I said.

I had one melon ball left. I moved the melon slowly toward Ellie's mouth. I said, "Perhaps the rare and skittish Ellen Butterbit, seldom seen without a book behind which to hide, could in fact be won by so simple a treat as a single piece of melon."

Tam laughed.

"Researchers have long speculated just how this gorgeous creature maintains—"

Then I dropped the melon ball.

Later in the party, Georgia Teeter pulled me behind the grain silo.

"You want to jump my bones," she told me. She inhaled and held her breath.

"I left my hat on the picnic table," I said and walked back to the party.

In the center of the barnyard, bales of straw were arranged in a circle. Tam and I danced in that circle. I let her put her feet on top of my feet—as I had seen done in movies—and we waltzed to country music.

The sun was gone. A bat etched across the sunset. Two huge spruce trees rose toward the evening star, their boughs bent as if loaded with fruit. The Garfield farm was west of Carton, where the land lay flat. Cornfields bordered the yard and barnyard. A rusty swing set stood beside a hay wagon. An abandoned, three-story farmhouse sat near the gravel road, and a trailer home lay beside it. In the barnyard was a tremendous hole—a foundation hole dug for a new house during an optimistic season on the farm, but abandoned now for a few years. Into this hole Mr. Garfield had piled the remains of an old wooden chicken house and a spruce tree that had fallen after an ice storm.

Presently, as we chanted "Bonfire! Bonfire!," Mr. Garfield lit the remains of the chicken house and tree. When the fire took, it grew so quickly that we jogged away from the pit. We were driven past the refreshments, past the stereo and straw bales. We watched the fire sprout from the hole, and for a while we didn't talk but squinted into the flames. Behind us were cornfields illuminated for hundreds of feet.

The flames towered and leaned toward the two spruce trees that stood near the pit. Streams of sparks rolled through their boughs. Finally, a spark gained purchase and lit one tree. The spruce burned quickly, a nexus of many tiny flames growing into one. Hoover stood sullenly in his conical birthday hat, shielding his eyes as he looked at the burning tree: his huge birthday candle. He looked as if he were saluting the tree.

Tam and I went into the barn. We climbed into the quiet loft and scrambled over the hay bales to where a window looked out onto the scene of the bonfire and burning tree.

"I would like to see this fire from the sky," Tam said. "But I do not fancy the view from earth. No I don't."

I looked at Tam. I put on an English accent. "Where, dear, did you learn to speak so melodically?"

"In the hills and in the fields," Tam said dramatically, "with the bees, in the sunlight, in the sweet breeze."

"You're magic," I said. "Like your sister."

As soon as the tree had burned out, the party was over. Parents arrived. Tam and I came down from the hayloft and stood next to the driveway. "Let's go say bye to the horses," Tam said, and so we went into the dark pasture and found the horses and Tam patted them each upon their snout.

"We'll be missing you," I told the horses. I patted them both on their shoulders.

"I see why my sister likes you," Tam said.

Hoover engaged each arriving parent in conversation. Stay stay stay. Too much food left. Night so young. Stars so clear. Fire so charming. Bonus: smoldering tree! Our parents were polite, but wouldn't be persuaded. The sedans and pickups continued to arrive and pull my classmates down the road toward the county blacktop. Most of us would not see each other until late August, when school began.

We lived in the country, see, and distance separated us—air, fences, creeks, woods, light. Distance.

I came across the finish line in first place, with a course record. My feet retained a heavy feel. I talked briefly to the reporters. Andanda hovered nearby in her leather jacket. After all our runners had come in—most of them ran well—Gregory put a towel around me and walked me away from the crowd. We walked quickly to keep me from cramping up. "I can't make decisions for you," he told me, "but if you are hurting, you need to show me." I nodded and we kept walking. After the trophy presentation, my teammates lifted me up on their shoulders for some pictures taken by our yearbook photographer. Andanda took pictures for the newspaper. Other newspaper photographers, spectators with cameras, and television cameramen quickly became attracted to the photo-op. Mother asked Gregory to take a picture of her and me and the individual and team trophy. Many other photographers snapped this picture, too. "Up with Mother!" I screamed. "Up with Mother!" And my teammates vaulted her onto their shoulders while she squealed. "Down with Mother!" she yelped.

I went to Henny, who hung behind the crowds, behind the flash-bulbs. I handed her a small, folded piece of paper.

"Open it now," I said.

She unfolded it and read it silently.

It said this:

> You deserve your birthday wish, whatever it may be.
> Happy birthday.

"The paper's damp," she said.

"I carried it during the race," I said. "I was hoping I'd see you somewhere along the course where I could hand it to you."

Porphorhessohln called to me. I rolled my eyes. Porphorhessohln had pictures taken of him and me and the team trophy. He complimented the letter jacket, complimented my mother for assembling the letter jacket, complimented my victory.

After Porphorhessohln left, Jol wandered up, clapped me on the shoulder.

"Another win for the Go-Boy," he said.

"Oh boy," I said. "I didn't see you here," I told him.

"I drove out."

"Your dad let you take the truck?"

Jol shook his head. "I drove out without permission. Then Dad took a taxi out here and drove the truck back to town." Jol smiled, flapped his hands in the air, smiled with his lips closed.

"You need a ride home?"

"I don't really want to go home at the moment."

So Jol rode with Mother, myself, and Andanda back to our house. Mother kicked into hostess mode and brought out the Tupperware party tumblers and served soft drinks and sour cream chip dip. Then she announced a lunch of grilled cheese sandwiches. I showered. As I dressed I saw Jol and Andanda walking toward the house across the pasture. They looked odd there, the short black boy and the tall white girl, surrounded by tall grass.

"Just showed Jol part of one of your cross-country training routes," Andanda said when they came inside.

Jol nodded for many seconds, then said, "You have a beautiful training ground."

Andanda drove Jol and me into Bend City at six. We stopped beside Jol's house.

"Do you want me to come in with you?" I asked him. "Maybe your dad won't be mad at you if I'm there."

"He'll just wait till you leave."

Jol's house was square and brown. The porch sagged.

I opened the passenger door, got out, and pulled my seat forward. Jol climbed out from the backseat.

"Wait, Jol," Andanda said, and she handed him a slip of paper.

"What's this?" Jol asked.

"It's my cell phone number," Andanda said. "In case you ever need a ride."

Andanda and I drove down Jol's street. A garbage can lay toppled against the curb. Andanda turned and drove toward school. We came onto the stretch of road beside the track. Abruptly, Andanda turned into the parking lot that abutted the track.

"I don't know where I'm going," she said. "I was just driving."

Night was upon the city, but in the west I could discern the last shreds of sunset.

"Where do you want to go?" Andanda asked. "I'll treat you to anything you like, take you anywhere. Bowling? Movie? Coffee? Bookstore? What? Do you want to go home? This is your day. Your night."

"Can I see," I said after a silence, "your house?"

Therefore, we came onto the streets of Andanda's subdivision, streets wide enough for five cars to pass abreast. The houses hulked upon knolls, set far back from the curb, sheltered by broad pines and bare maples. Andanda swung into the driveway of a long, angular house. I saw broad planes of glass shining in the darkness. Andanda stopped the car in the circle drive. "No reason to park in the garage," she said.

Inside were foot-wide floorboards, ceilings vaulting into the darkness, exposed beams, a graceful, curving staircase. Andanda's room was scented. Her walls were covered by framed posters and photographs. Her overstuffed comforter slouched from her queen-sized platform bed onto the floor. Skylights peered down. The basement contained a pool table, another fireplace, a widescreen entertainment center—identical to the one upstairs in the den—an exercise room, a bathroom, two bare but finished rooms, and a stretch of French doors. We stood at the doors. Andanda flicked a switch and floodlights lit the flagstone patio, the pool, and sloping lawn. Birches rose in the lower yard.

"My brother's supposed to cover the pool up," Andanda said, "but of course he doesn't."

"Shouldn't it be drained this late in the year?"

"Oh, well, it's heated," she replied.

I admitted to Andanda that I often ran in this neighborhood and had noticed her house before.

"I've seen you run past," she said.

I had Andanda drive me to Henny's house. I did not tell her why I wanted to go there, or even who lived there. Andanda asked no questions. Henny's house, a single story Craftsman, sat up on a steep hillside, surrounded by low trees, and yellowish light glowed from the windows of the house. Quite soon after we stopped the car, Henny stepped out onto her stoop, peering down at us. Soon she came walking down the steps from her house and waved to me. I rolled down my window.

"I thought you might surprise me," she said. "Come in."

"Only for a while," I agreed. I had not intended to even see Henny, much less go in to her party. I had simply wanted to sit outside her house for a moment.

Henny bent down to see further into the dark cabin of the car.

"Who drove you?"

Henny insisted that Andanda come inside, too.

Inside, Henny's willowy friend Tinka greeted us, knife in hand as she bent over a birthday cake. The candles were still smoking. "Perhaps now we will have enough people to properly consume this cake altogether," Tinka said. The only other guest at the party was Mark Marchinson, the first-seat French horn player whose glasses were always reflecting light so that you could never quite see his eyes. I knew from Henny's letters that Tinka and Mark were a couple. Henny handed me a small newspaper clipping that she said her father had clipped from an East Coast newspaper. I admitted to her that I'd seen the piece—a newswire article about me.

Henny's parents had absconded for the evening, gone north to Hibernia for dinner and an opera, leaving the birthday soirée unencumbered by adult supervision. But rather than exploit the situation by acting like reckless teenagers, our group instead oscillated between modes of conduct that befit retirees and grade-schoolers: after cake and tea, after Play-Doh experiments, after many rounds of canasta, we found ourselves in the front room—a large room—playing a silent kind of hide-and-seek in the dark. There, as I crouched beneath the grand piano, listening to the floorboards creak as Mark crawled around the room trying to find one of us, I heard someone breathing quite near me, and presently a hand lay upon my back and then that hand ran onto my shoulder. Then this person gently kissed the back of my neck and moved away through the dark room. I smelled ginger. Very soon after this occurrence, I lost my balance as I squatted there and fell against a leg of the piano, which caused the piano to roll a bit on its casters—a sound sufficient to notify Mark of my position.

fifteen

On Monday, Andanda let me read the final draft of her article. I asked for no changes or deletions. Wednesday, the article appeared on page one of the school paper, *The River Messenger*.

LIFE AT THESE SPEEDS

By Andanda Dane, Editor-At-Large

As sophomore Kevin Schuler cruised down the final hundred-meter straightaway of Saturday's state cross-country championship meet at Jeffer Lake, not a single other runner was in sight, his victory was assured. To the last, Kevin's face remained relaxed and calm, his hands lightly clenched, his gait smooth and fast. He won the competition by fifty seconds, turning in a time—15:21—twenty-four seconds below the course record and bringing home Bend City High School's first-ever number one finish in the state championship race.

BC's cross-country coach, Gregory Altrabashar, clenched his jaw as he watched Kevin complete the 5-kilometer race. "His stride is simply a gorgeous thing," Altrabashar said. "I don't know where he found it—I worry where he might have found it—but . . . it is a gorgeous thing." In contrast, the other runners in Saturday's race, including high-placing Bend City runners Todd Halverstadt, 13th, Ezekiel Bly, 18th, and Bobolink Crustacean, 21st (see p. 6 for detailed results), exhibited extreme fatigue as they completed the race—grimacing, head bobbing, arm swinging, choppy strides—very much the usual result of this most grueling of high school footraces. Many runners collapsed after finishing the race. A few vomited.

Twenty miles west of Bend City, in rural Croop County, Kevin trains on the gravel lanes surrounding his home. Some of these roads are no wider than a pickup truck, and in a few remote stretches crabgrass grows down the middle of the road. In late September, waist-high goldenrod blooms in great patches along the fencerows and in the pastures. Crickets buzz in the ditches. Cattle ignore the blond-haired boy running past. In training for cross-country, Kevin runs long, slow distances in the morning before school, including an extended run of up to twenty miles on Saturdays. In the afternoons, he runs shorter, faster distances in Bend City or sessions of what he calls "speed play." On one afternoon he ran north across Bend City to the Old State Cemetery, sprinted up the cemetery's well-known Navy Slope, then walked back to the bottom of the hill and ran up it again. He ran the hill nine times.

Kevin also runs along trails that cross his neighbors' lands, passing along the edges of cornfields, mounting the knobby hills near Keen Creek, winding through deep hickory woods.

Kevin is quiet. He will not babble or banter. He will not brag. But he will answer questions. If you inquire about the dark scars on his knees and shin, he will tell you they are racing injuries. He will admit that his skin scars badly, forms keloid scars that will never fade. If you ask him if he has other scars he will say yes, but he will not reveal these scars unless you press him. There are scars on his ankles, the top of one foot, the sides of two toes. One of the biggest scars is high on his back, another on his arm. Three small dot-scars are on the back of his hand. All of these injuries came during races, the results of being spiked by other runners. Kevin's signature track event, the 800-meter run, is one of the most dangerous track events, he says, because the runners often run very close together. And the 800 is the fastest track event where the runners are not confined to their own lanes. Ask Kevin if he has any scars not caused by racing and he'll shake his head. Ask Kevin if he worries about being seriously injured—he is, after all, only a sopho-more, with many racing years ahead of him—and he'll say softly, "No."

But running is not usually a dangerous sport; it is not a contact sport. Most runners don't suffer so many injuries. Why is Kevin so battered? His reply: "Most runners don't win every race they enter."

Spike wounds are not the only running injuries Kevin carries. He admits to enduring, at one point or another, shinsplints, runner's knee, severe sunburn, respiratory infection, gastrointestinal disturbances, and Achilles tendonitis. These ailments are relatively minor—Kevin contends—common, treatable, and have not interfered with his training or racing.

"Kevin is a guiding spirit for the team," senior Todd Halverstadt, cross-country team captain, says. "True, he lives in his own world and does most of his training by himself, but his *presence*, his *aura*, his *example* strengthen the team. I can't duplicate the tremendous mental toughness that Kevin has, nor can I match his remarkable leg speed or inborn talent; but I can cultivate my own toughness, I can follow Kevin's speed training example, and I can make maxi-mum use of my own genetic abilities. Kevin's great-ness lies on a different plane than mine or my other teammates, but Kevin inspires us toward our *own* greatness. He inspires the team. He inspires our coach. We can't say we know Kevin very well. We can't say we're chums with him. We can't say we know where he's coming from. But we can jump in behind him, catch his draft, and follow him."

"Kevin's not a small bit aloof at all," coach Gregory Altrabashar states. "People would come to me last spring after Kevin's races and sometimes say, 'Why doesn't he smile when he wins? That boy, he is feeling no joy, we think.' Later in the season, people would

complain also that Kevin did not appear to be trying
so hard as he could—even though he was beating the
field by five seconds. They'd say, 'We see him slow
down and lean back before he gets to the finish tape.
Why doesn't he keep trying?' They'd say this even
when he broke state records! So I spoke to Kevin and
said, 'We're as afraid of your speed as you are, Kevin;
but you have to break through that fear and run the
race all the way through or you'll never know what
satisfaction is, what contentment is, what peace is.
You *own* these races, so accept that and treat the races
with respect.' I told him that, and now he no longer
reins in at the end of the race. He hasn't broken the
fear, but maybe he's finally *meeting* it." Asked about
the specific nature of Kevin's fear, Altrabashar shrugs.
"I can only speculate. Many outstanding athletes carry
a weight that pushes them to excel. With Kevin,
everything is internal, everything within himself. He
is a pressure cooker. He builds great pressure inside—
this propels him to win races. But such pressure can
cripple a person. Pressure can become uncontrollable.
Where is Kevin's pressure coming from? What is it? I
don't know, so I watch Kevin and wait."

In the hallway of Kevin's parents' house hangs a
picture of Kevin bundled in a snowsuit. He has con-
structed a fort in the snow and stands grinning beside
it. Kevin is thirteen in the photograph, an eighth
grader, and he is slightly gawky, quite skinny—not
the model of fitness and good looks that he is today.
Located at the end of the hallway, Kevin's room is
small, square. There is one window, facing north. The
white walls are bare. The closet holds unpretentious
button-up sport shirts, which Kevin wears tucked into
his store-brand jeans. Kevin's bed is neatly made. On
his desk are schoolbooks and a pile of recent magazines. Kevin subscribes to twelve magazines—an
eclectic mix of political monthlies, news weeklies,
high-brow general interest magazines, a conservation-
minded outdoor magazine, a literary journal, and a
well-respected environmental periodical. A glance at
this pile of magazines assures you of Kevin's left-of-
center politics. Against one wall of his room are stacks
of back issues of his magazines. Against another wall is

a bookshelf packed with over a hundred titles, from contemporary fiction and history to a few swords-and-sorcery titles and a small cache of running books. The only touch of decoration in the room sits atop Kevin's dresser: a collection of four scale-model tractor-trailers that Kevin built from kits as a child. Kevin's father is a cross-country truck driver.

When does Kevin read? After all, he trains over twenty hours per week, touts a perfect attendance record at school, and has made the Select Honor Roll in Sundry Seeley each semester. Where does he find the time?

Well, aside from watching no television and listening to no music (his room lacks the teenager's obligatory stereo), Kevin suggests he reads a great deal for three reasons: he is a fast reader; he sleeps little; he does not socialize. Indeed, his ideal Saturday night includes a session of hill running, a shower, dinner with his mother (and father, too, though Mr. Schuler is on the road well over two hundred days a year), a game of gin rummy with his mother, and then a long evening of reading in his room. Kevin hasn't had a girlfriend in well over a year, and anyone who has seen or met Kevin can assure you that his monastic lifestyle is one chosen of his own volition, not for a lack of attractiveness on his part.

Certainly not for a lack of attractiveness.

"Truth is," Jol Brule, infamous varsity football receiver and friend of Kevin, says, "Kevin won't admit he's a hot item. I've seen him throw away notes every day—girls slip notes into his locker. He gets asked out to every dance. In Sundry Seeley, everyone knows him. The girls salivate over him, and most of the boys wish they were him—that's the truth. Even though he's so withdrawn, he has somehow created a huge reputation as one of the nicest and smartest guys in the school. I can't think of anyone who dislikes him. Except the runners he competes against, perhaps, although a lot of them actually worship him." Jol tells of going into Valapraso's Athletics store with Kevin and watching all the clerks ask for Kevin's autograph. "Now you'd think," Jol says, "they'd go for the football star, right? They'd go for me? In this country, football is to track what Goliath was to David. And I don't mean to make any judgments of the worth of the two sports—though I do think track is more challenging and noble—but I'm just saying that track is this kind of underground sport, a kind of cult following thing. I mean, name five famous football stars and then name five famous runners. You can't name that many runners. But here in town, Kevin's more high profile than anyone. He's got the papers covering him, got the TV crews covering him, got national magazines and newspapers talking to him, got recruiters from both coasts calling him—he doesn't take calls from recruiters anymore, did you know that? He has his mother screen them all away! And his whole quiet-guy act pulls everybody in, makes everyone's imagination go wild! Well, it's not an act, I guess. But because people know so little about him, they just imagine what they like and suddenly he's everyone's favorite hero. And what Kevin has going for him is that he's out there every day, running in the city. People see him. He has certain routes that he repeats and people know these routes and know when he'll run by. I talked to these two girls from Zame Smith who made a game to see which one could guess his running route most in a two week period. So each day after school they'd each drive out to a place they thought he'd go that day and if he ran by, they snapped a Polaroid. I don't know which girl won, but the point is, Kevin has become a moving landmark of sorts. In your article, if you publish where Kevin lives and where he does all his morning runs way out in the country, I know there'd be some people showing up there. I run with him sometimes in town, you know, and when we run down, say, Blissmam Road, all four lanes of traffic are slowing down as they pass and half the people lean out their windows and scream 'Go Ke-*vin*'—men and women, I say. And Kevin pretends he hears none of it. I said to Kevin once, 'You're a local mascot, you know,' and he denied it with no expression on his face."

A poll of Sundry Seeley students recently showed that 100% knew who Kevin Schuler was and recognized him when they saw him; 73% of Zame Smith students answered the same—amazing, considering that Kevin never sets foot in Zame Smith. Last month, in the wake of the announcements that the automobile plants in North Bend City would close on November fifteenth, the *Bend City Gazette* conducted a poll in which they jokingly asked a hundred Bend City residents if the city mascot, Lenny Lug Nut (the cheerful steel lug nut, remnant of the city's 1977 campaign to attract the automobile factories to the county, who waves from atop Bend City's scenic River Cliff), should be abandoned in favor of "that ubiquitous, mysterious, undefeated, non-manufactured Go-Boy, Kevin Schuler, who has proven to be more reliable and awe-inspiring and well engineered than any automobile ever manufactured by the two bumbling corporations that graced us with their low-paying jobs for fifteen years." Eighty-two percent of adults presented with this farcical question said yes, Bend City's mascot should be Kevin Schuler.

All hail Kevin.

On the morning of Saturday's cross-country championships, Kevin's mother gave him a letter jacket onto which she had sewn all his patches and medals from his running victories. Though his high school career is not half completed yet, the front of the jacket is already literally coated with medals—gold, gold, gold—the medals overlapping like the scales of a reptile's skin. I asked Kevin why he agreed to wear the jacket—a strange move for this most modest star. "It means a great deal to my mother," he said.

Why do you run? I asked Kevin. Why do you run so fast? Kevin avoided such questions for weeks. Finally, late in the evening after his state cross-country victory, I put the question to him again and he did not dodge it. He said, "If I didn't have to run, I wouldn't."

Kevin has held six state eighth-grade 1A 800-meter records (made while competing for Carton), four state high school 4A 800-meter records, one state high school 4A 1600-meter record, and two state 4A cross-country records. His racing times place him high in national ranks. Last spring, Kevin was rated the fourth fastest high school 800-meter runner in the country.

The three faster runners were all seniors. This season, Kevin is ranked the second fastest high school cross-country runner in the nation—at the front of the season he was ranked first. Despite his prowess, Kevin routinely turns down opportunities to compete in regional and national competitions. "I've defined my territory as Missouri," he says, "and I have to succeed here by my own standards before I'm interested in competing elsewhere."

Immediately following his victory at the state championship Saturday, Kevin left the crowds, sat on the grass beneath a young, leafless maple, and removed the dingy pair of spikes he has raced in since eighth grade. He strapped an ice pack onto his right knee and admitted to me—as a score of reporters descended on him—that for most of the race his feet didn't even feel as if they were touching the ground.

Kevin Schuler is kin to air.

On Thursday morning, Mother dropped me before the doors of Sundry Seeley and Jol intercepted me as I entered the building. He gripped my arm and pulled me across the street.

"What's this?" I asked him.

"You'll see."

We wound through the narrow hallways of Zame Smith, made our way into the administrative annex, where Andanda waited outside Porphorhessohln's office.

"What's this?" I asked her.

"It's the least Jol and I can do," she said.

In thirty seconds we three were seated before Porphorhessohln who nodded appreciatively at all of us. "My gems," he said. "My pillars of the school. To what do I owe the pleasure of a group visit?"

"We want Kevin to be granted his wish of being admitted to Zame Smith," Andanda said.

Porphorhessohln's eyebrows jumped and then dropped.

"Kevin, we've discussed this already," he said.

"He's smarter than most of my classmates," Andanda said.

"He's smarter than all of my classmates," Jol said.

"It's worth this much to you?" Porphorhessohln asked me. "Worth enough to bring in your friends and risk punishment? Some might see this as a very stupid move."

"We don't want anything to turn unfriendly," Andanda said. "But you know who we are and the influence we have upon certain portions of the school."

"I don't want anything to turn unfriendly," Porphorhessohln said.

"It doesn't have to," Jol said.

"It won't," the superintendent said. He laughed, stood up, walked around to the side of his desk with his hands in his pockets. "But it's worth a great deal to you, Kevin, to get into Zame Smith?"

"It is," I said.

"You know it's ranked the best school in the state," Andanda told Porphorhessohln. "You know how much people pay to come here from out of district. How many Zame Smith students from St. Louis and Kansas City live in supervised boarding houses across the street, making Zame Smith into their own boarding school?"

"I'm just amazed by the risk Kevin took to bring you two into this," Porphorhessohln said.

"The school's a magnet," Andanda said.

"Yes, yes," Porphorhessohln said. He stared at me but his eyes became unfocused for many seconds. Finally he said, "When do you want to start?"

"Winter semester," I said.

"We'll have a counselor assess you, see what level you can enter at." I nodded.

"But if your running performances suffer, we'll have to reconsider. . . ."

"They won't suffer," I said, "they'll keep increasing."

"Indeed," Porphorhessohln said. He gazed out the window now, out toward the line of oaks that bordered the campus. "What's better than an outstanding athlete?" he said. "An outstanding scholar-athlete."

In the halls of Zame Smith, I thanked Jol and Andanda. They dismissed me.

"We saw we could do it, Kevin, so we were obliged," Jol said.

"Why don't you come over to Zame Smith with me?" I asked.

"I'm no scholar," Jol said.

"You'd do fine here," Andanda said.

"I'm a welder," Jol said.

Jol left Andanda and me. She told me then that the *Bend City Gazette* wanted to run the article she'd written about me. She asked my permission. I congratulated her and said it was fine by me. Andanda knelt and pulled books from her locker. I leaned against the closed lockers. Henny came by. We looked at each other. Then she looked at Andanda's back and passed us. I had not received a letter from her this week.

After the final school bell rang, Gregory was waiting for me outside my geography classroom.

"Gregory," I said. I patted his shoulder.

"Kevin," he said, "we like each other. But I am angry to have to read in the newspaper that you have injuries. You have runner's knee?"

"You knew that. You saw me ice it."

"That's true. But shinsplints, tendonitis?"

"They don't slow me down."

"They will. I'm furiously upset."

"You're not talking like you're upset," I said. "You're talking like you're discussing a dead aunt."

"That is because I am furiously sad. More sad than upset. I'm sad at you."

"These injuries are tiny. There was no reason to worry you."

"I'm not upset just at you, I'm upset at Brake and E. What are they doing with you each week? Aren't they checking for injuries?"

"No."

"I'm taking you up there today."

"Today's the day I usually go. Brake will be outside waiting for me."

Gregory took me outside and we stepped up to Brake's Cadillac.

"Good afternoon, coach," Brake said.

"I am taking Kevin to Hibernia now," Gregory said. "You can follow us."

"Sure, Greg. That's not part of the agreement, but—"

"The agreement is dog feces. You're ignoring Kevin's needs. Do you know he is complaining of shinsplints?"

Brake looked at me, looked down at my shins as if he could diagnose the injury on sight.

I rode with Brake; Gregory drove behind us. At Dr. E's laboratory, Gregory stood by while they checked for pronation, located my shinsplints, diagnosed my runner's knee, made sure my Achilles tendonitis was gone. Gregory blamed Brake for buying me shoes that didn't match my needs. He accused E of being oblivious. He called Brake a charlatan.

"I should never have agreed to let a doctor who doesn't run treat Kevin," Gregory said. No one said anything to him. He picked up my training flats, the shoes Brake had bought me, and threw them down onto the tiled floor. "You people are bad, bad people!"

"Perhaps you wish to forfeit your part of our arrangement," Brake said.

That said, Gregory shut up. He stepped back and watched Brake test my Achilles tendon flexibility. Soon Gregory left without saying another word.

As Brake drove me home in the darkness he let me use his cell phone to call Mother and report that I was an hour late.

"You can call your girlfriend too," he said after I hung up.

"I don't have a girlfriend."

"I see you with that curly-haired girl. That tall girl."

"She's the reporter who wrote that article about me. She's not my girlfriend."

"Well," Brake said defensively, "I've seen you two walking at cross-country races with your arms linked."

"She's a friend," I said.

"What about that little girl. She was on the track team. Blond hair. Always sitting with you. I see her at the meets with you."

"Just a friend."

"You don't have a girlfriend?"

"No."

"You could, you know."

I said nothing.

Brake said, "Have you ever had a girlfriend?"

"Yes," I said.

"But you broke up?"

I considered this. "No," I said.

Next week, immediately after lunch, Porphorhessohln summoned me to his office. There, he and Gregory sat in armchairs by the window. They both said they were glad to hear that Brake and E had deemed my injuries minor—problems that would heal during the off-season and not recur if they were carefully monitored.

"But in the future," Porphorhessohln said, "we hope you let us know of such problems. We can help you early on."

Porphorhessohln offered me coffee.

"Not for an athlete, you know," I said. "Chemicals."

"We also wanted to inform you," Porphorhessohln said, "that we have spoken at length about your prospects and both agree, off the record, that the state university would be a splendid place for you to compete. Especially considering what you said in that article—that you wanted to compete only in Missouri. Though of course you'd sometimes be competing out of state. But *for* Missouri."

"We think it would be a good program for you," Gregory said. He spoke without meeting my eyes.

"Both track and cross-country," Porphorhessohln added.

I nodded.

"And academically, too," Porphorhessohln said. "And we're sure the university can offer you substantial financial incentives to attend. Right, Gregory?"

Gregory ran his fingers around the rim of his coffee cup.

"Incentives, I am sure," he said. "Track and cross-country."

"We're just thinking of what's good for you, Kevin," Porphorhessohln said. "Informal advice. Banter. Taking care of our own. Looking over you. Just wanting you to be happy. What's more, I understand that Gregory here has a good chance at an assistant coach position up at the university just about the time you'd be entering college."

"That's great, Gregory," I said.

"I would like to coach there," he said. "That would be lovely."

"Though we'll hate to see him leave Bend City," Porphorhessohln said.

Lo and behold, in early December, as I ran upon a treadmill in E's laboratory, Christmas carols playing from a stereo, an extremely tall and tan man came into the room and pointed at me and walked toward me. Bob Popincock rose quickly from his seat and stood motionless.

"Kevin Schuler," the man said, extending his hand toward mine. "It's a honor to meet you. I'm Jetty Rowen, track and cross-country coach here at the university."

"I know who you are. I'm pleased to meet you."

We shook hands. I was still running.

"Bob, stop this dang thing," Rowen said, and Bob scrambled toward us and stopped my treadmill.

"Whatchya testing today?" Rowen asked.

I explained. "I'm running at a perceived effort of fifty percent while I keep bread toasting in these three toasters. This toaster is for the white bread only. This one for wheat. And this one alternates between the two. I am restricted to using my left hand. Bob is recording how efficiently I accomplish the task of keeping toast going in all three toasters at the same time. I am also judged on the degree of toast-edness—you know, no burnt toast. All this is happening while Christ-

mas music plays to see what effect the carols have upon my performance. See, last month, we ran the same test with no music."

"Then I seem to have simply barged in here and disrupted the
experiment," Rowen said. "Blammo. You'll have to shoot me now."

"No, no, Dr. Rowen," E said as he emerged from his inner office,
"there's no problem with the interruption."

Rowen nodded. "Kevin," he said, "you're aware of your running
prowess and the press is aware of it and I'm aware of it, so I won't dish
up what must seem to you to be dull flattery—though believe me I
could—and instead I'll simply tell you that we're honored that you're
taking part in Dr. E's experiments and I hope perhaps you are giving
thought to the possibility that you might run for us in a couple of
years."

"Sure I have."

"Have Brake shuttle you over to the field house sometime and I'll
show you around. It's the off season right now, of course, but we'll be
up and training for the indoor track season after Christmas, and
there'll be a lot of excitement then."

"I hear you're considering hiring on Gregory Altrabashar."

"Yes we are. He's doing a fine job down in Bend City we see."

"He is a wise coach."

"He was one of our best distance runners ever. His times in the
5000 and 10000 are still school records, even after ten years."

"I didn't know that."

"He was a lucky recruit, a walk-on, really. We'd never really
worked very hard for any international recruits, so it was a nice surprise
when he appeared. His coaching wisdom comes from first-hand experience, I'll tell you that. He's become quite a marathoner, too. He did
well last summer at a couple of regional events. What was that race, E?
The Corn Classic or something like that? Some half-marathon he won
up north. Iowa."

"I didn't hear," E said.

"Anyway, I hope you come by sometime, meet the assistant
coaches, meet the runners—they're excited about the possibility of you

coming here. And come see our facilities. We've just moved into the new field house, you know. Very nice."

"I'll try to come by."

"And let me know if there's anything I can do for you," Rowen said.

"Can you get some specific tests run on me?"

Rowen glanced at E. "What do you want?" Rowen said.

I gave the list: determine my VO_2max, measure the ratio of slow twitch to fast twitch muscles in my major leg muscle groups, measure my aerodynamic drag and the alterable variables that affect it, measure my biomechanical efficiency, especially in my stride, to locate lost energy, and measure my body fat.

Rowen tapped E's shoulder. "Do it," he said.

Dr. E's jaw hung loose and his eyes skipped rapidly between Rowen and myself. Then he closed his mouth and nodded.

T w o   n i g h t s   a f t e r   C h r i s t m a s , Fitz Sickle died of a heart attack. Annabelle Wicke—a close friend and neighbor of the Sickles— told Mother that after the ambulance had made the half hour trip out from Bend City, it wandered up and down the Sickle's gravel road ten minutes before it found their driveway. There were no street numbers out on the gravel roads of our county, and the Sickle's mailbox, though it had once been painted with "F. Sickle," had not weathered well through the years and now appeared to bear the faint name "F ick." When Mother told this story she spoke with conspiratorial urgency. I recalled the unstable pitch of Mr. Sickle's voice when he had cornered me in the hardware store and begged me to come to the Sickle farm and work for them.

I didn't tell Mother that I had heard that ambulance at two in the morning. I had heard it whining up and down Vance Road—a mile to our south as the crow flies. In my 2 A.M. state of mind, I had briefly believed that the ambulance was coming for me, that I was dead and would be taken away. This delusion had given me momentary satisfaction, as if the world had suddenly been put right.

Mr. Sickle's funeral occurred during the first serious snow of the year. While Mother and Father attended the service, I ran. I ran out into the snow, which fell in clots, fell as slowly as ashes. Tufts of snow capped fenceposts and sat atop the heads of cows. Two days later we received another four inches of snow. And on New Year's Day eight inches fell. The next morning, I entered Zame Smith Woolstonecrapt for the first time as a student.

Mother bought light-reflecting decals to paste our name and address on our mailbox.

Porphorhessohln lurked about the halls of Zame Smith that first week of school, chirping greetings to students and staff like an eager bellhop. He had begun to wear pastel shirts with white ties beneath his blue blazers. Gone were his brown suits. He wore glossy, zippered half-boots.

"He doesn't usually prowl like this," Andanda assured me. "He likes to think his mere presence in the administrative wing exerts a certain aura to keep us duly inspired toward overachievement."

Porphorhessohln introduced me to a pale, beanpole boy one morning.

"Kevin Schuler, this is Young Stan. Young, this is Kevin Schuler."

The boy shook my hand tightly. His black hair was mussed, English schoolboy-style.

"I'm honored to meet you, Kevin," Young said. "You were one of the reasons I decided to transfer to Zame Smith."

"Young here is a runner, Kevin. He's a freshman, but his 3200 and 1600 times are very promising—probably the top eighth-grade distance runner in the state last year. He also posted some sub-two-minute 800s."

"Well, I'm glad you're on our team," I told him. "I heard of some of your races. Weren't you with Kirkwood West?"

"That's right."

"But," Porphorhessohln said, "our academic reputation and the rising strength of our running programs drew him here." Porphorhessohln knocked Young between the shoulder blades.

The next day, Porphorhessohln introduced me to a sprinter named Onslow Byrumbie, another outstanding athlete who had also transferred from a distant school. Later in the afternoon I met new-student Lisandra Litaska—IQ 134; 200-meter dash 25.10.

The snow continued. I welcomed the snow. The blanket. One after-noon, a wind-blown snow coated all the west-facing windows of school. Winds haunted the February nights, so that snowdrifts formed and reformed regularly, giving one, each morning, the impression that in the night the snow had undulated like a great sea, only to freeze at dawn. I ran in the afternoons through the white world, protected by wind pants and a ski mask. By late February, as we drove down our county blacktop, the snow stood higher than the car on either side of the road. Dad called from Tampa and complained of the humidity. Mother spent evenings dusting her silk plants or applying iron-on dec-orations to sweatshirts. She stood beside me on the afternoon when the City Council of the City of Bend City presented me with a key to the city upon naming me the town's new "Symbol of Pride."

As part of the ceremony, I was driven by limousine onto the Jack Schnae Floebuss Memorial Bridge where, as the wind rocked me, I dumped a pail full of nuts and bolts over the railing. This winter, though, for the first time in sixty years, the Missouri River had frozen over, so the three hundred nuts and bolts I launched simply bounced and skidded across the white ice—to remain there until thaw.

To conclude the "Symbol of Pride" induction ceremony, a motor-cade accompanied me as I ran a mile across the bridge, up Banner Street, past the courthouse, and then up to the top of River Cliff (three city bulldozers had cleared the hilltop of snow), where for the ninth time that day I shook hands with Mayor Gina Bing. Crowds lined the streets—seven thousand people had been laid off in the autumn, and today the automobile unions urged their members to come see me run. *Come Watch Kevin Go* read their newspaper advertisement.

Andanda covered the day's events for the school newspaper and asked me during the post-induction press conference what I would do with the key to the city. I held up the key. It was a wooden key as long as my forearm. It was painted gold and had a velvet ribbon tied to it.

"First I'll get it duplicated in case I lose it," I said.

The reporters laughed.

"Then I'll sew it right here," I said, and held the key against my letter jacket. The flashbulbs popped.

"Has the weather this winter impeded your training?" a reporter asked later. "We don't see you running in town."

"I run at home this winter," I said.

"Are you pleased by the series of outstanding runners who have transferred to BCHS, citing you as one of the major factors in their motivation?"

"I think the academic reputation of Zame Smith Woolstonecrapt deserves primary credit for such transfers."

The week after I became the city's Symbol of Pride, displacing the joyful Lenny Lug Nut, Andanda asked me before school what my motivation had been for accepting the city's offer. Likewise, Henny slipped a note into my locker—the first communication we'd had in weeks—asking the same question. I told them both that my motivation was a mixture of civic duty and desire for greater public recognition.

Henny wrote one sentence back: *Who are you?*

The city's mascot seal no longer bore the happy lug nut and his slogan, FASTENING ONTO A STRONG TOMORROW. Now the seal depicted an anonymous runner silhouetted against an outline of the city's courthouse. It bore the words BEND CITY: UNBREAKABLE STRIDE!

Through the days and nights of that deep, white winter, I could not draw my thoughts away from the rivers and streams, could not withdraw my imagination from the black waters running beneath the heavy ice. At night, I envisioned the continual movement of the waters and lost sleep. When March came the weather warmed; the ice cracked; the rivers revealed themselves; and the tightness in my chest dissolved. I felt the forces within myself rising again to where the world could view them.

It was time to run hard again. It was time to race. The excitement made my fingers quiver.

Track season had arrived.

This is my season, I told myself. *This is my season.*

seventeen

But my feet fell heavily. My feet were stones. My bones ached dully, as if the winter's ice remained within them. I became overly aware of that flashing moment, mid-stride, when neither of my feet were touching the ground, when I was indeed detached from earth, airborne. I became aware of this moment because it now seemed so brief, so ill-fated and cruel. It was the moment before impact, the moment before I fell. It was false flight. It was folly—to defy gravity, defy the inevitable.

As I sat by myself at track meets, I chewed on my hangnails. The muscles around my eyes spasmed, ached. And for the first time ever I fell prey regularly to the awful curse known as runner's trots.

After a race on a cold night, Gregory came at me with a large towel to drape about my shoulders. I met his kind eyes and decided to tell him of the iron weight of my legs, the jackhammer force of my footfalls, the flesh-gnawing worm in my gut, the slivers of steel that impaled my eyes. I would tell him all this. I would tell him that my speed was caused by fear. The fear had caught my body.

He pulled the towel around me and said the thing he always said after I won a race, "You did this for you? Did you win this for you, Kevin?"

That was the thing: I was still winning each race. I set a state 1600-meter record at our first outdoor meet of the year. I anchored the new 3200-meter relay team of Bobolink Crustacean, Young Stan, and Ezekiel Bly—a team which won no race by less than fifteen seconds in March and by mid-April had closed in on one of the oldest records in the state. I appeared lighter than ever on the track. Andanda, in a small newspaper piece about the team's victory at the pivotal early-season Grace Invitational, wrote this: "If Kevin's increased speed training, transfer to Zame Smith, and civic mascot duties have impacted his racing in any way, they have sharpened it, taught him to focus more precisely, made him an even smoother runner than before. His legs turn over like a sprinter's; he no longer cocks his chin slightly to the left as he races; he glides like a puck on ice. As I heard one PAC 10 college scout say last week while Kevin accelerated down the final meters of the 800: 'I would marry that stride.' "

So instead of telling Gregory about my pains or even implying their existence, I pointed to my race time on the digital scoreboard and said, "Evidence of well-being."

How could I complain when my races continued to improve?

In the winter I had run in snowstorms and on afternoons when the temperature never topped five degrees. In the spring I ran through storms, through hail, through ninety-degree days. I won races, broke records, let myself go further into a territory that promised more speed, and yet I had not remembered anything new about my old life, my Carton teammates, since running the cross-country championship in November. Nothing new came through the curtain; yet the curtain rustled and waved from the commotion behind it. My eye-aches increased. I had abdominal pains at night. I slept less. I blamed myself for my inability to recall all my past. And sometime that spring, I began blaming myself for blaming myself.

*　*　*

Bend City hosted a small invitational in late April—a new meet that had been Porphorhessohln's idea. Porphorhessohln scheduled the meet to start immediately after school so that the students could simply walk to the stadium and begin cheering. His ploy worked and the stadium filled to capacity. Jol won the 100-meter dash. The crowd rippled with energy. The mayor watched from beneath the coaches' awning. Henny was there, watching with Tinka from the grass across the field from the grandstand. Henny had not joined the track team this year.

I waited near the starting line of the 800-meter run. It was a sixteen man box-alley start. The crowd stood. Bend City students started the cry of "Go boy! Go boy! Go boy!" Then the students began a synchronized cheer: The girls screamed "Go!" and then the boys yelled "Boy!" As we stepped up to the starting line, a new chant came from the crowd: "Record! Record! Record! Record!"

The race started. The silence clasped me. I set a pace to let the other runners stay with me. I passed Henny and Tinka on the back stretch and they neither waved nor cheered. Tinka positively frowned at me. As I finished the first lap Jol flapped his arms from the grandstand, yelling toward me. Andanda waved her cigarette at me from the infield as I passed.

Two runners were on my shoulder. I held back. I concentrated to pull my stride in, to slow down. I wanted to see how far I could rein myself in. My pursuers were working hard. I gritted my teeth. I breathed through my nose. *Slow down, you bastard,* I told myself. Finally, here was a Lower Bend runner passing me. His gait was labored, choppy—his form was eroding quickly. But he managed to run even with me, then pull inches ahead. I had to hold back my energies, keep myself slow. It was like holding my breath: I couldn't block the speed for too long. My neck burned, my forehead burned. I became aware of an ache in the region of my kidneys.

The Lower Bend Runner inched ahead. His head wagged. Sweat flung from his earlobe. We entered the final curve. I wanted to scream at him to take the damn race. But he couldn't hold the curve. He would fade soon. In his wobbling stride he shouldered me, then faltered, then stepped onto my foot. I threw out my arms to keep balanced, but he veered into me and we leaned forward, unbalanced. I hated him now. He was a loser; he had lost control, shown poor form, poor control, poor stamina. I watched my feet as we broke stride to keep from falling. Then I calculated, aimed, and spiked his ankle. He began to fall and I slowed myself, watched him tumble into my path. The next moment, I jumped coolly over him. There I hung, midair. The runner lay below me like a strange landscape. Again I calculated, aimed, brought my foot down onto his hand. I wanted that. Then I opened my stride. I could not hold back. My heart vaulted. My legs released themselves. I sprang off the curve. The straightaway opened up gorgeously before me, like the returning sailor's first view of his homeland. Speed entered me, fear held me, crowded my consciousness and pushed me into another territory, a lost memory:

When it was time for science class at eleven, Miss Palmer, our fourth-grade teacher, stood smiling before the class with her hands clasped beside her neck. She stood silent for what I counted to be twelve seconds, then said, "Shall we retrieve our egg vessels?"

We nodded, eager but polite.

Miss Palmer stood absolutely still. "Your mission," she said, "was most challenging: to build a container to carry an egg through a thirty-foot drop in such a way as to protect the egg from damage."

We nodded.

"Most challenging," Miss Palmer repeated.

And on her signal—a nod—we scrambled to the back of the room, to the coat rack. We each had brought a container we had made at home, maybe a box filled with Styrofoam peanuts or a coffee can choked with shredded newspaper.

We returned to our seats with our containers, sat obediently silent as Miss Palmer handed an egg to each of us. I cradled my egg in both my palms, then held it softly against my cheek. The egg was cool and had moisture on it.

"Where's your box?" Pim Blotto, a town boy, asked Ellie Butter-bit. Pim poked a cracker box into Ellie's face. In the box were cotton balls.

"I don't have a box," Ellie said.

"No box!" Pim said. "You people are dirt poor."

"Dirt rich," Ellie countered.

Pim cackled.

We filed outside, crossed the courtyard where dandelions shone like coins, passed the bus garage where Tyler Arkass waved with greasy hands. He yelled, "I'll take mine sunny side up!" We passed farther on, walking beneath the wide spring sky, and mounted the bleachers beside the track. Miss Palmer unlocked the door to the old scoring booth—our high school no longer had a football team because our school was shrinking—and climbed the ladder onto the roof. She had changed from heels into sneakers. Gina Daley was designated to hand the containers up to Miss Palmer. There was a great rustle among us as we arranged our eggs inside the containers and bragged about the efficacy of our contraptions.

"I could jump on it," said Bobby Sickle of his double shoe box egg shuttle. "I could kick it . . . and roll it behind my bike, I could . . . I could . . . let the bus bump over it. . . ." Everyone had similar notions.

Georgia Teeter slid close to me.

"You can help me," she said.

The containers began flying. Trolley Catchell and Tom Poolcall opened them as soon as they rolled to a stop on the slope behind the bleachers. Some of us complained that Miss Palmer was actually throwing the containers *up* instead of simply letting them drop.

Two containers failed. Three. Four. One succeeded (Heather Garnet's box with trailing balloons). Six more failed. Another succeeded (mine—an egg within a foam football within popcorn within a box). Two failed. Only a few remained. Ellie Butterbit, who sat away from us, asked if she might go to the restroom. Miss Palmer assented with a glittering eye.

The final boxes fell. Eggs broke.

"There's none left," I told Greg French.

He didn't acknowledge me—he was sullen because his toilet-paper-tube egg shuttle had failed spectacularly.

Miss Palmer, though, heard me. From the scoring booth roof she said, "I think there may be one more." She pointed toward the school.

There came Ellie Butterbit, hauling a large wooden box. She labored.

"That's too big!" Pim screamed. "That's too big!"

"Lend her help," Miss Palmer said, and Bobby Sickle and Jason Blick rushed out to Ellie. Immediately I wished I had gone.

They hauled the white box up the bleachers and into the scoring booth. Then Jason and Bobby came out of the booth and Ellie closed the door. Miss Palmer had come down from the roof into the scoring booth, but we could not see what Ellie and the teacher were doing. Presently, the door opened and Ellie came out. Then Miss Palmer appeared again on the scoring booth roof, holding, beneath her arm, a white-flecked hen. To the bird, Miss Palmer said "Hello, hello, hello."

Our teacher walked timidly to the booth's edge. Her tongue stuck out of her lips. The hen's head bobbed.

"That's junk," someone said.

I looked down onto the broad apron of unmown grass behind the bleachers. Beyond, on the tarred roof of the school, pools of water reflected the sapphire sky. Far away and below, third graders were beating erasers against the brick school. Hills stitched off toward the horizon, a road silver among them. I shuddered. I looked at Ellie. Her brow had dropped. She appeared agitated in her silence. And suddenly I knew what she feared: She wondered what she had forced the hen into. Hens don't fly. They flutter; they scatter leaves, hop fences, little more. Ellie now feared she had done a cruel thing, a torturous thing—captured a hen, taken her from home in a dark box, and now would be responsible for her death. I wanted to help Ellie. We needed to stop Miss Palmer. I saw Ellie raise her hand, open her mouth. But teacher threw the hen . . .

Indeed, Miss Palmer *had* thrown the hen *up*, and at the top of her rising arc the bird hung perilously fat, orange feet clasping the air. The sun illumined the saffron hues of her neck feathers; she extended her wings to a surprising length; and she fell. She flapped like a wind-up toy, furiously, but almost noiselessly, amid a halo of her own down, and descended slowly, spiraling to earth, where she tumbled forward onto her gizzard upon landing, then walked to a spill of popcorn and ate. To me, though, it appeared not that she had fallen, but that the earth had risen to hold her. Perhaps my classmates had experienced the same vision—we were silent.

Then we cheered.

The aluminum bleachers hummed beneath the jumping, and the few cynics and unbelievers were cured when, gathered on the grass of the slope among popcorn and strung egg yolks, Ellie held the gentle hen honey-belly-up on her lap and everyone had a chance to feel the fully formed egg in her tummy. Heather Garnet asked the bird's name.

"Bawk," Ellie said—and I understood her to mean bawk as in *bawk, bawk, bawk*, that universal chicken sound.

"You named your bird after the music guy?" Heather said. She slid close to Ellie.

I looked at Ellie for a moment and we both understood, I think, the beauty of the misunderstanding.

"She's a beautiful clucker," Ellie said softly, "like a singer."

"Ellie," Miss Palmer said, "how fine."

"She hasn't clucked," Pim said.

"She's just shy," Miss Palmer replied.

Aided by eighteen pairs of hands, Ellie brought Bach into the school and set up a wire cage for her in the back of the classroom. When Miss Palmer needed the class to be quiet at any time during the afternoon she mentioned that Bach couldn't lay her egg amid a cacophonous din. She wrote "Johann Sebastian Bach" on the board and had Mr. Tanner, the music teacher, play a Bach song off a record—this saved the class from fifteen minutes of math. Because the sharpener was beside Bach's cage, a good deal of pencil sharpening went on that day.

I watched Ellie. At the end of the day, as we lined up at the door waiting for the bell, I grew eager for the bus ride home. For Ellie and I shared a bus, and I resolved to tell her, on the bus, how much I admired her solution to the egg shuttle game. But Ellie did not ride the bus that day, of course, because her father came in his pickup to carry Bach and Bach's cages home. As I watched from the bus window, Mr. Butterbit placed the caged hen in the bed of the truck and then got into the cab with Ellie. Ellie smiled and laughed and talked to her father, who laughed as he drove away from the school.

In the morning, I maneuvered my way to stand in line behind Ellie at the water fountain and I tapped her on the shoulder and said, "I liked Bach." And further: "It was good."

Ellie said, "Thank you."

Past the finish line, I doubled over. I sat on the track. I had not released all my energy and now the residue made my stomach cramp. Nausea swelled within me. I shivered.

Gregory and the track officials gathered around me. "Your shoe's untied," Gregory said as he pulled it off and began cleaning the spike wound atop the bridge of my foot. The officials told me they were waiting for word from the other runner—who was being treated by paramedics at the moment. But when they finally did speak to me, they said, "Can you verify that he pushed you maliciously?" I looked up toward the faces. My foot was in Gregory's hand.

An official: "The foul play was clear—he pushed you, spiked you, knocked you off balance. . . ."

"I landed on his hand," I said.

Official: "He knocked you off balance. He fell into your path."

"I smashed him."

Official: "What we need you to verify is that he made the first contact. Then we can start the procedures to reprimand him."

I laughed briefly—even as rubbing alcohol stung my spike wounds, even as bile rose in my throat. I shook my head.

"He didn't come after me on purpose," I said. "He tripped on my shoelace," I lied. "It was untied and he snagged it and that rocked his balance and that's why he hit me and then everything he did after that was just an attempt to keep from crashing."

Gregory and two officials verified that my shoelace had indeed been untied when I crossed the finish line, and the Lower Bend runner was cleared of any suspicion of wrongdoing.

Twenty minutes later, as I sat again alone on my blanket, Henny approached me.

"Are you okay?" she asked. She approached no closer than ten feet. Tinka hovered behind her. The sun threw their shadows all the way to the fence.

"I'm fine," I said.

"I just wanted to make sure," she said.

"Thanks."

"I'm not done being upset with you," she said.

I didn't respond.

She said, "I think you spiked that guy on purpose."

I shrugged, said, "I think you're disappointed in yourself for still having a crush on me."

Tinka yanked Henny behind her. Tinka sneered at me. Her blond hair swung across her breasts.

"Shut up," Tinka said. "Shut up, asshole."

Tinka dragged Henny away.

"Why do you sit with your back to the track all the time now?" Henny yelled in retreat.

"Ignore him," said Tinka.

"What's wrong, Kevin?" Henny asked.

They left. Jol came.

"I was working against the grain in that race," I told him.

"I saw."

"I hate what I did."

"You were provoked, man."

I shook my head.

"Look at this," I said, and showed him a rash that covered my back.

"Weird," Jol said. Then, "Recruiters asking me questions about you."

At the opposite end of the track, the starter's pistol cracked. Cracked again. False start. I could also hear the buzz of the stadium lights far above us.

I said, "Tell them I'm in love with a flying hen."

eighteen

On May first, after I had won the 1600 in Bend City's big dual meet with Lower Bend, half the stadium lights went dark and Porphorhessohln met me on the track.

"Congratulations, Kevin," the stadium announcer said. "And happy birthday!"

"Happy birthday," echoed back from the hill across the street.

"Sweet sixteen!" the announcer said.

The crowd cheered. Porphorhessohln shook my hand. Gregory lurked behind him. Brake appeared, shook my hand. He pointed to Dr. E and Bob Popincock waving in the grandstand.

"Hello Bend City!" a female voice said over the PA. "This is Mayor Gina Bing, here tonight in the scoring booth to help celebrate an important birthday for our important city Symbol of Pride, the Go-Boy, Kevin Schuler! Happy sixteen, Kevin! Can we give him a cheer?"

A cheer.

"Did you see that race he just ran?" Gina Bing asked the crowd. "He's simply unstoppable! Unfettered!"

A cheer.

"He's got unbreakable stride! Just like Bend City!"

I looked to Gregory in the dim light. Gregory appeared sad. His beard drooped.

Gina Bing: "And now some of Kevin's friends and family have a sweet sixteen gift to present him with. If the crowd will accompany me in singing 'Happy Birthday,' we'll bring his present around the track."

Thus commenced the song. And on the far side of the track appeared a small car with its parking lights on, driving slowly around the circuit. It was a red roadster. A convertible two-seater, Japanese. It was the same car Brake had tried to give me six months ago. It coasted onto the straight stretch before the grandstand. In the car sat Mother and Father—Father driving. Mother held a round cake balanced on one hand. The cake had candles and the candle flames blinked in the breeze and some of them blew out. The car rolled down the straight-away toward me. Mother hailed me. The birthday song ended. The car stopped. "And it's not a car made by either of the second-rate companies that have abandoned their commitment to our community!" the mayor announced. Cheers, cheers, cheers—like waves rolling onto shore. The parents came to me, hugged me, clapped. Everyone clapped. Father handed me the keys. I took them, made myself grin. Hugged the parents. Waved to the crowd. Sat in the car. Waved to the crowd. Let the photographers shoot me. Saw the radio announcer in the scoring booth laughing and talking quickly, watching me. Saw the mayor clapping near the radio announcer. Saw Andanda standing trackside with her arms crossed, smirking. Saw the line of city council members clapping in the infield. There, too, was the Bend City principal and two vice-principals. And now a pack of cheerleaders surrounded the car, posing in victory attitudes. I saw Brake standing near. I saluted him.

I got out of the car, pushed politely through the cheerleaders, stumbled into a television cameraman. I handed the keys back to Dad—after all, I didn't have a license—and let him drive it away to the parking lot.

"We're all proud of you, Kevin," the mayor announced. "Unbreakable stride!"

As I shook Brake's hand for a final time that night I whispered to him: "Fuck you too."

Gregory waited outside my last class of the day—American Politics— and hugged me as I walked through the classroom door.

"I have acquired it!" he said.

"Acquired what?"

He held up a manila envelope. "The report from the university. Dr. E's report on you!"

We went to Gregory's office—a windowless, cinder-block closet inside one of Sundry Seeley's locker rooms—and spread the pages of the report on his bare desk. He had already gone through the report and highlighted particular data. Now he pointed to each highlighted finding.

"Slow twitch muscles, fifty-two percent—this is very perfect for a mid- or long-distance runner. Very prime!" His smile broke through his beard.

"Vertical stride motion—unmeasurably small. Good . . .

"Pronation—none. Yes . . .

"Foot: a bit slightly hypermobile. Easy to control with proper shoes. We knew that.

"Resting heart rate, thirty-eight beats per minute. Extreme fitness. Genetics! Nearing world-class!

"Maximum heart rate, one seventy-seven. Very good! Very good! You have lowered it with training!

"Heart volume, eleven hundred millimeters—remarkable! High! High!

"VO_2 max, eighty-one point one. This is amazing. This is genetic luck!"

"Quite remarkable," I said.

"See, there's a reason you run so fast, Kevin. There's a reason! The reason is that you're built to run this fast! The fastness is inside you! It's stamped on you. What we should do now is release this report, along with a summary of your career, to the top college programs in the nation."

I reminded Gregory that the university owned the report and barred unauthorized distribution of the findings.

Gregory nodded, then shook his head. "Right. Yes. I knew that. I mean I should have recalled that. I mean, I am thinking ahead of myself."

After a long pause, he said solemnly to me, "The state university has a fine running program, and I think it would be a most excellent choice for your college career."

"So I've been told."

"They are a very . . . good program. You should attend there."

"Do you have any idea," I asked, "why the dates here on pages five and nine and nineteen do not match the more recent dates elsewhere?"

Gregory flipped through the pages.

"No," he said. "Clerical error. Those dates should match the others."

"That's right. A clerical error of a sort. And do you know why Dr. E finally released these statistics to us?"

"No."

"Because after Brake gave me the car on my birthday, I told him I'd return the gift publicly if he didn't send us this report. It wouldn't look right for a university to be handing out new cars to young high school athletes, would it? Even if it was technically the medical department of the university giving me 'research recompense,' and not the sports department."

"Right."

"I'm saying they've had this data sitting around for months, that's all. They weren't going to release it. They've had it from the very start, way before I asked Rowen for it."

Gregory ran his fingers across a page of the report. "I think," he said, "the contract might allow them to keep their findings private."

"That's true," I said. I wasn't sure why Gregory was repeating the obvious. "But why did they go to the trouble of trying to doctor the dates of the study?"

"They are great researchers up there at the university. They are great coaches. It is a good school for a runner."

I nodded.

I came in from a weekend run. . . .

Here was Father, can of strawberry soda in hand, resting in a lawn chair behind our house, looking out over Jim Toto's pastures, out toward the fat herd of shorthorns. Father's green cap sat crooked atop his head. His nose whistled like a piccolo. A sweat bee danced in the air near the soda can. And Father's face appeared to me like a proud, firm hill that had rather recently turned to mud and begun to slump away.

"Jim has built a good herd after all," I said from behind Dad.

He looked up over his shoulder, smiled.

"What?" he said.

I repeated the comment.

"Yes, he has," Father said. "That he has."

He sipped the soda. A black ant walked on the toe of Father's boot.

I crouched beside Father, squatted on my hams.

"You must like running," Dad said.

"Sure," I said.

"I mean, being out in the air all the time, underneath the sky," he said.

"A bird shat on me once."

"What?"

"A bird shat on me once."

Dad laughed, said "Fertilizer from heaven." He drank again.

"Me," he said, "I'm trapped in a machine all day."

A few lean yearling heifers had wandered near the fence and chomped on the grass. I could hear the grass being ripped up by their teeth.

"I sleep in a machine," Dad said. "I have a ringing in my ears that is always there. I have a ringing in my ears from driving a truck in Vietnam and from driving a truck all over this country. There's no way to lose the ringing. Sometimes when I'm at home for a quiet week like this and maybe I catch a flathead or two in Keen Creek, and maybe I sleep until eight o'clock, and maybe we three play cards up to midnight, and maybe I go and watch my spectacular son win some races—well, I get in the cab of the truck after a nice week like that, a quiet week, and then I'm on the road, and my engine's roaring for nine hours, and then it rumbles all night even as I sleep in the bunk."

He drank the strawberry soda.

"What was I talking about?" he asked me.

"Ringing in your ears."

He nodded.

"Machines," I said.

He nodded, said, "And your mother has a line of machines for me to fix each time I come home. The toaster is blowing fuses. The rooftop antenna has been knocked off signal. The electric pencil sharpener is spitting pencil shavings. Just spitting them all over. I love your mother. Her watch needs a new battery. The car's burning oil. The sump pump rattles. I love your mother."

"A lot of work," I said.

"What?"

"Lot of work for you."

"I like to fix things."

"Do you wish you weren't driving anymore?"

"My ears ring," he said. Then, "Well . . ."

He looked at his soda can.

"That's good strawberry soda," he said. "That's good soda."

I won my races at district. I won my races at the state meet. Three races. I set two state records before the huge crowd. I threatened to break the four-minute mark in the 1600, which meant I was close to breaking four minutes in the mile—a barrier not crossed by an American high school runner since the sixties.

The four-minute mile.

"If you want to beat four minutes next year," Gregory told me, "you can."

"With your help," I said.

My speed came ever easier to me in those last weeks of the track season. It seemed to have no limit, as if I were running constantly down a hill and could open my stride as much as I wanted—simply let gravity push me down, speed me on. In other words, I felt like I wasn't straining to run faster, but straining to hold back—because I knew if I ran too fast down a hill, I could lose control. And, more importantly, every hill has a bottom, and I didn't particularly want to rush to the bottom of my hill. I was headed there, I could see, but I could slow the process. I could. Perhaps I could even stop my descent, I told myself. Perhaps I could even turn around, climb the hill.

Imagine that. Ascension.

nineteen

Summer arrived as a needed gift, supplied me with solitude, with time, and with that salve that hardened runners gleefully call LSD—long slow distance. I ran once a day, early, before the heat of the day, before most of the state had even awoken. Eight miles, or ten, or twelve. Cupped in silence I ran comfortably, away from the trappings of competition, away from fear. This warm off-season was my balm.

I had taken, for the summer, a fifteen-hour-a-week job as a shelver at the largest discount store in Bend City. On Tuesdays and Fridays, after my early morning run I showered and Mother drove me into town. I worked my shift and Mother picked me up at four thirty. "How'd the shelving go?" she'd ask when I got in the car. My stock answer was "Beautifully." Mother laughed at this as if it were witty.

Sure people recognized me, hooted "Go-Boy, Go!" at me as I stacked boxes of panty liners or pushed a cart of motor oil across the store. But most of my workday I spent in the stockroom or low traffic aisles.

It was in just such a secluded aisle—gardening wares—that I found myself face to face, one noontime, with a charming girl who smiled pixie-like toward me and who, I finally realized, was Henny with a new short haircut—a bob.

"I heard you worked here, you puke," she said.

"I do."

"I hate this store," she said, "but they're the only place within walking distance of my house now that carries garden goods."

"I hate this store, too," I whispered. "That's why I work here."

She arched her eyebrows. "Observing the enemy from the inside?"

"This scourge of Mom and Pop stores," I said, "destroyer of downtown business districts. Unabashed cornerstone of suburban sprawl, of profit-over-people, of anti-unionism, of the rankest form of petty materialism, of low-quality merchandise, of crap and ugliness. Crap and ugliness."

"Oh you make it hard to hate you," Henny said.

"I try."

"You do not, you prick. You try with every ounce of your non-running energy to make yourself bitter, cynical, cocky, and unreachable. Untouchable. Impenetrable."

She pushed my chest. She pushed again.

"Don't touch the goods," I said.

"Damn your goods."

"I like your haircut," I said.

She walked away.

Three days later, I began receiving letters from Henny again. She wrote: "I had tied myself into a knot simply because I didn't know how to tie a bow—and so I relent and repent and drop these grudges against ghosts and facades. *Facades*, Kevin. I will not be envious of Andanda Dane."

In early July, I was working on a display near the front of the store in the high-traffic impulse-buy alley that ran parallel to the line of registers. I had arranged the final bottles of sunscreen with meticulous care when a man ran past my display. He ran very fast, I noted, with a smoothness that betrayed a gifted runner. He held a small box in one hand. He dashed through the entry doors, brushing past a clot of senior citizens with such speed that the octogenarians spun ninety degrees

on the heels of their loafers. Now two plainclothes loss-prevention officers ran past me in pursuit of the thief.

"Stop the shoplifter!" Curtis, the fleshy loss-prevention manager,
yelled. "Check this brash incursion!"

In trying to exit via the entrance—as the thief had—Curtis was
intercepted by an automatic sliding glass door that knocked him backwards onto his bottom like a toddler learning to walk. His younger,
wiry companion, Nat, made it through the doors and streaked across
the parking lot.

The race was on.

I joined.

I exited, sighted the thief far across the black parking lot. The air
stunk of sulfur. Heat waves rose off the asphalt and made the thief
shimmer and appear as if he were teleporting himself into another
dimension. A pickup truck made an abrupt stop, nearly striking Nat
twenty paces in front of me. Nat stopped, flustered. I passed Nat. I
came into the nether regions of the broad parking lot, where drainage
grills were the only landmarks and a lone shopping cart rolled through
the afternoon heat. An empty plastic bag ballooned and hovered.

I ran alongside a minivan. A mother drove the van and observed
me coolly through her sunglasses. In the rear seat of the van, one child
beat another child with a loaf of sliced white bread. The van stopped at
the end of the parking lot to turn onto the busy, five-lane Blissman
Road. I did not stop. I ran onto the boulevard, just as the thief had,
making one dash into the middle lane—the turn lane—and then signaled my intended left turn until the traffic in the remaining two lanes
cleared and I completed my crossing.

The thief ran before me along the shoulder of the road, running
toward the oncoming traffic. Cars brushed past by my right shoulder.

Now I set a stride. Now I opened my speed, and closed on the
thief. I still wore my blue apron from the store and it flapped between
my knees. The thief vaulted over the hood of a hatchback that was trying to turn onto Blissman Road. The thief's loose blond hair coursed
behind him.

The humidity of the day lapped my neck and bare arms like a bath.

We passed an auto parts store, a discount shoe store, a plaza that included a pet store, a music store, a submarine sandwich shop, a futon store. There were no trees on the boulevard. No sidewalk. It was a country of cars, power lines, and signs. We passed Slaney Drug, Furniture Factory Showroom, Dana-Dana Pizza, Stix Drive-In Burgers and Shakes, Showstopper Video Rental, Replay Used Sporting Equipment, Bertram Begman Collection Agency, Kwik Loan Money Shop, Fidelity Northpoint Insurance, Rodman's Motorcycle Zoo, and the crafts store called Kuntry Kullectables.

"Stop now," I said as I came within earshot of the runner. He looked back at me, and I had never seen a stranger face—bland and cheese-pale and sad and puckered.

I tackled him, pushed him into the ditch. Perhaps we had run three-quarters of a mile. He toppled like a sack of potatoes. I found myself sitting upon his back—he was facedown. He didn't resist. I looked up the road. Nat was a fair distance away, limping. I looked back down at the thief. He had sweated through the back of his T-shirt. He had no strength left. He twisted his face around and peered at me.

"I know you, you," he said.

"A fan of mine?" I asked.

"I got so tired of losing to you that spring I quit track for good," the thief said. He wore an earring.

"What spring?"

"When we were eighth graders. I'm Jamie Torffelson."

"Jamie Torffelson?"

"You know me, man. I cheated and still couldn't beat you. You and your janitor coach."

"Jamie Torffelson," I said. I moved off of him now. "You were in that race."

"Which one?"

"Where do you live?" I asked.

"In town here."

"You transferred? To Lower Bend?"

"I'm not in school," he told me.

"I don't run anymore," I said. "I hate fucking running."

"Me too," he said.

His contraband lay scattered in the grass—a portable CD player, a baby's bottle, and a container of sunscreen. Then I realized I must have brought the sunscreen with me and dropped it when I tackled him.

I knelt and Jamie rolled onto his side, as if we were chatting at the beach. The passing cars threw a fitful breeze onto us. Jamie had a scar above his eyebrow.

"Do you need these?" I asked, pointing to the stolen goods.

"Look, man, I—"

"If you need these to fulfill your life, then take them."

He stared at me.

"Take them quick, before the loss-prevention guy gets here."

He picked up the bottle and CD player.

"Now knock me over," I ordered.

He hesitated.

"Do it!"

He pushed me down and hovered above me. A cardboard cup lay near my ear.

"Now tell me who spiked who in that race at Bryceville," I ordered.

"What?"

"Did the Carton kid spike you, or did you spike him?"

"It was an accident. Neither one of us meant to do it, I think."

"That can't be right," I said.

"I think it is."

"Hit me and get out of here," I told him.

"But you can turn me in. You know who I am."

"You only have a few seconds to pull this off."

Jamie struck the soil near to my shoulder three times. I cringed, curled up into a ball. As he stood I saw his fist was bleeding. He dashed off behind a blue-shingled seafood restaurant. I rose to my knees. Glass glittered in the dry grass where I had lain.

"Jeez," Nat said when he reached me. "What did he do?"

"Nothing," I said.

Nat wheezed, twisted a knob on his two-way radio, barked a report to the store. He coughed.

"You got the CD player back," he said.

Indeed, it lay near me.

"I didn't do anything. He left it."

"And a bottle of sunscreen. So the poor guy made off with nada," the officer said. "That was all he had, right?"

"Yeah," I lied.

"You gave him some exercise at least," Nat said. He shook an asthma inhaler, sucked on it, held his breath in a manner similar to a pot-smoker, then said, "He'll have some sore muscles at least. Maybe he'll finally stop coming into our store. You know who he was?"

"No."

"Want a job in loss prevention?"

"Not at all."

"It's more money."

I declined again.

Several newspapers found the incident humorous, even though Jamie had escaped:

SHOPLIFTER HAS BAD FORTUNE TO BE CHASED BY SCHULER
BEND CITY THIEF PURSUED BY STATE RECORD RUNNER
SHOPLIFTER LOSES ILL-FATED FOOTRACE

In late July, a series of rainy days ushered in cool weather, early autumn weather. I took advantage of the coolness by running home from work one afternoon. I changed into my running gear, Mother picked up my work clothes, and I started the run. Heavy traffic rolled along Blissman Avenue—minivans, jacked-up pickups, multitudinous American-made sedans. The low clouds slung drizzle as I turned onto the access road that paralleled the four-lane federal highway. I hoped the rain would continue. Cars turned their headlights on and the wet asphalt gleamed like icing on a cake. I came to the highway's last exit in Bend City. On the east side of the exit was the mall, a plaza, several fast food restaurants, and two corporate buildings. On the west side of the exit was forest. I continued running west on the access road, ran through the forest, past the country club, past the mattress factory outlet, the concrete company, the salvage yard, the trailer parks, the Little League park, the sawmill, the limestone quarry. Dust rose like smoke from the quarry. Nearby, bulldozers pushed down trees, clearing a plot for a new church. After three miles I came to the next exit, where I ran south on the overpass. Now I was on a county road. I wound into the hills. I crossed Keen Creek—far downstream from the point it passed our house. I went on into the country. Houses became more scarce. A row of high capacity power lines—borne aloft by wide-shouldered metal towers—ran across the hills, cutting a swath as wide as a football field through the woods. The slow rain continued. Because the store I worked at sat on the western edge of the city, in the most recently developed section of the county, the run from work to home was only sixteen miles—a long run, but one that didn't drain me if I kept a slow pace. I was home in a little over two hours.

A week later Missouri still lay under the weather pattern that depressed our temperatures and threatened showers every day. So I ran home again.

There, on that last stretch of the access road before I turned onto the county blacktop, I saw another runner approaching from the opposite direction, up on the highway. He was a slender runner, dark haired, with a shuffling but obviously efficient stride. He wore red shorts and no shirt.

He was Gregory Altrabashar.

We made no gestures toward each other, but he took the exit onto the access road, and I slowed my pace to meet him near the intersection.

I was running that way, south, I told him—running home.

Could he accompany me for a while? he asked.

We headed down the county blacktop. The road dropped beneath us. Pickups passed. Round hay bales bobbed in the fields.

I shrugged off the silence that smothered my runs and talked to Gregory.

I told him the rumors about him. Pakistan. Turkey. Three wives. Nine daughters. Soon-to-expire passport, work visa. Political refugee.

Gregory didn't laugh. He still wore his beard and I could not discern his facial expressions through the thicket of hair.

"It is not so mysterious as all that hoopla," he said.

We ran a half mile in silence. A bit of sun gleamed through the feathered clouds. Then the clouds drifted, closed the gap. Gregory said, "I grew up in India. I attended good schools, run by the British. I had a shiny school record, so I applied to study university in the States. I didn't want to be stuck always in my home country. I had no family. But I had dreams. One university gave me a rather okay amount of money. That school was the state university."

"So here you came," I said.

"So here I came. Then I studied. I ran track and cross-country for the university—not sports we Indians have much success at, but I did fine. I married another student whose parents had immigrated from India. So I then became an American citizen. I entered the master's degree program in sports education. I worked. I coached some. I ran. Here I am."

We crossed Keen Creek. The water ran brown. A tree lay in the channel. I explained to Gregory that this creek ran very near my house.

I said, "Rivers don't like me."

"I am thirty-three," Gregory said.

"You should bring your wife around sometime so we can meet her," I said.

"We are not married now."

"I'm sorry," I said.

"No, not at all."

Several seconds of quiet.

"If a wife leaves a husband," Gregory said, "everyone assumes it is because he is doing something crappy. And if a husband leaves a wife, everyone assumes it is because he *is* crappy."

I said nothing to this. A delivery truck passed us, honked.

"What shakes you, Kevin?" Gregory asked.

"What do you say?"

"What do you brood on?"

"That's a funny question," I said.

Gregory looked at me. "It is no funny question."

I looked at my feet.

"What shakes me is doubt," Gregory said. "And loneliness. Maybe nothing shakes you, Mr. Kevin."

We passed a trailer home. A child's bicycle with no front wheel lay in the yard. A brown dog barked at us, pulling on his chain. The chain was tied to an old truck tire and the dog pulled the huge tire several inches while we passed.

"I have come too far," Gregory said. "I am too far from home. I should be turning back now."

I assured him it was only about five more miles to my house, that we could run there and I would drive him back into town.

He declined, said good-bye, and turned around.

twenty

Porphorhessohln's secretary called me in late August and asked if I could meet with the superintendent the next day. Mother dropped me at the school on the morning of the meeting and I wandered through the vacant halls of Zame Smith toward the administrative offices. The floors of the school all shone brightly—the wood, the tile. The gray lockers gleamed. The warm halls smelled of new paint. Bolly Shinbone, a janitor, strutted. He saw me and starting singing: "I love that clean schoolhouse. The late summer schoolhouse. That dustless and uncluttered time. . . ."

"Hi, Bolly."

"Welcome back, Kevin."

"Good song."

In his air-conditioned office, Porphorhessohln introduced me to two business-suited adults—one Jimmy Bledsloe and one Freeda Van-derhoffenblau.

"We represent the State High School Athletic Association," Jimmy Bledsloe told me. He was a bald man with drooping eyelids. He and Freeda Vanderhoffenblau sat on the leather couch. I sat in a captain's chair. "I am a member of the Association's Board of Control. I represent the South Central District. Mrs. Vanderhoffenblau here is an executive officer. Are you familiar with our organization's role in state athletic events?"

"Yes."

Porphorhessohln, who stood near the windows, asked me if I had any idea why the Athletic Association might be scrutinizing me.

"No."

"Let me put it this way," Porphorhessohln continued. "Do you recall cheating or misleading any Athletic Association officials at track or cross-country meets?"

"There was an incident," I said, "during my eighth-grade year."

"We don't police junior high athletics," Freeda Vanderhoffenblau said.

"They've uncovered a string of serious infractions on your part, Kevin," Porphorhessohln said, "and I find it hard to watch you sitting there all cool and detached like you're ignorant of your own crimes. Or as if you don't even care. They've gathered a lot of evidence. Do you hear? Undeniable evidence. So now would be the time for any person who wishes to retain one scrap of integrity to admit his wrongdoing."

I went rigid in my chair.

"God damn it, Schuler," Porphorhessohln said, "you've pulled some dumb-ass stunts, and you and your team are going to pay for it! Not by my hand, but by the Athletic Association's."

"I do not know of any rules I have broken."

"Don't make me wish I'd never taken you into this school!"

"I apologize for my ignorance."

"Just tell him," Porphorhessohln said.

Freeda Vanderhoffenblau read from a sheet of paper:

"After due, peer-reviewed process, the State High School Athletic Association of Missouri finds Kevin Kendrick Schuler of Bend City High School at fault for violating SHSAAM track and cross-country regulations by wrongfully and willfully misinforming SHSAAM Field Officials, Meet Directors, Meet Officials, and Referees."

She stopped reading and looked up at me. Porphorhessohln and Jimmy Bledsloe watched me, too.

"I don't know what that means," I said.

"You lied to officials," Porphorhessohln said. He had removed his jacket. Sweat ringed his underarms despite the sixty-five-degree air conditioning.

"I lied?"

Jimmy Bledsloe nodded. "After many races—no less than seven but possibly as many as thirteen—when you were approached by an official who had reason to suspect that foul play had been directed toward you during the competition, you denied all such suspicions, even to the point of fabricating alternate explanations for your opponents' cheating."

"I'm being penalized for my refusal to blame those who aggressed against me?"

"Obstruction of justice, really," Jimmy Bledsloe said.

Freeda Vanderhoffenblau said, "We were alerted to the possibility that you were misinforming officials and were able to confirm, via observers and even the actual runners who had attempted to hinder you in the first place, that indeed you had willfully concealed their actions. The fact that your misinformation of officials can be traced through your entire high school running career is clear evidence that these weren't isolated misjudgments on your part."

I nodded.

"Do you admit to this?" Porphorhessohln said.

"Yes."

"If you admit your guilt you automatically waive your right to an appeal," Jimmy Bledsloe said.

"I admit I committed the acts you have described."

Jimmy Bledsloe hunched his shoulders. "The Board of Control of the Association voted unanimously for the maximum possible punishment in this case, because of the repetitive nature of the infractions. Therefore you are hereby banned from competing in any SHSAAM sponsored sports between September first of this year and September first of next year. In other words, the next season you may compete will be a year from now—your entire junior season is blocked."

"I have one question."

"Yes?" Jimmy Bledsloe said.

"What happened to the runners who during the course of your investigation admitted to or were otherwise proven to have tried to interfere with my running?"

"Many of them have graduated," Mr. Bledsloe said.

"And the others?"

"Well, there aren't many others."

Freeda Vanderhoffenblau said, "The others were granted immunity from prosecution by agreeing to testify against you."

"I see."

Jimmy Bledsloe passed a dark look toward Freeda Vanderhoffenblau.

"Whizbang," Porphorhessohln said, looking out the window.

I signed an admittance of guilt, an acceptance of the terms of the punishment, and an agreement that promised unreversible expulsion from all Athletic Association events if I repeated my particular crime in the future.

When Jimmy Bledsloe and Freeda Vanderhoffenblau had left, I remained sitting beside Porphorhessohln's desk—where I had signed the papers—and the superintendent leaned against the windows. He opened one window, put his hands out onto the sunlit brick ledge for several seconds, then brought his hands in and shut the window.

"This thing is pretty unconvincing," he said without looking at me. "But if you hadn't been so open in admitting your guilt, we could have leveraged for a shorter suspension. Or no suspension."

I said nothing.

Porphorhessohln turned toward me.

"I hate competing anyway."

Porphorhessohln snorted. "You do not and you know it. You wish you hated competition. You wish."

I smiled.

"Don't get smart," the superintendent said.

"There's no way to dodge this thing," I said. "Jimmy Bledsloe is the father of a runner who hated me, you know. One of the runners who interfered with me at the state meet last year. One of the runners who I'm sure helped 'inform' the Athletic Association about me. Of course it's a sham."

"Well, then we can appeal with that—tell the Association that Jimmy Bledsloe is not impartial."

"The only way to make any appeal to the Association is via your district representative. And that would be Jimmy Bledsloe."

"So he's the father of a Lower Bend kid?"

"Father of a graduate. Rye Bledsloe. Very good runner. He would have won the state 1600 and 800 last year but for me."

"So Jimmy Bledsloe's probably after this school as much as he's after you."

"I don't know," I said. "I suppose."

"But we can't get into a PR war with this," he said, looking out the window again. "Not right now." He walked to his door, peeked out into the secretary pool, shut the door, then came toward me. He raised his voice: "Why did you go and do such stupid things, lying to officials? You screwed our running programs, your career, your potential college career. How old are you?" he asked. "How old are you? You're sixteen. Sixteen years old. You think you know everything? You think you know anything?"

"I don't have to explain myself."

"The hell you don't! There's people depending on you! You're not a boy living in a bubble! There's people out here who depend on you. You're walking around with a fucking seventh-grade attitude, and now it's finally gone and knocked the house down. You *do* have to explain. You have to explain to me. You have to explain to your teammates. You have to explain to Gregory. You have to explain to Brake and Dr. E and Coach Rowen. You have to explain to your parents. You have to explain to those little pup kids who buzz their hair to look like you and hang over the railings of the bleachers trying to get your autograph. You have to explain to Gina Bing and the city council and the whole entire city who looks up to you as a symbol of something just a bit purer than the filth we see around us most of the time. That's who you have to explain to."

"You know Coach Rowen? I didn't know that. How do you know him?"

"What? You're the one on the spot here."

"You're trying to put me on the spot. I won't go for it."

"I don't see where you have a choice about it! *Your* actions and decisions have put you where you are! You did this to yourself! You can shrug off your mistakes. You can cower or waver and act like a boy, or you can stand up and answer, admit your responsibilities!"

"Why didn't you let Gregory come to this meeting?"

"Oh, there's a lovely reason I didn't invite Mr. Coach Gregory von Hindu-land to this morning's little legal session. The reason is that I fired him at approximately four o'clock yesterday afternoon, after I learned the details of the case against you."

"You can't just fire him. He's an excellent coach."

"Oh, I *can* just fire him. His contract was up for renewal—such convenient timing. And besides, he freely admitted that he knew you were covering up your opponents' cheating, but he did nothing about it. Very bad coaching. Very bad example. And you must admit he's not the most dynamic leader, nor the most domineering presence. I understand he's had a rough time in the past two years, but he has to learn to separate his personal life from his job. He can't mope and ignore his team all the time."

"He took a relatively unremarkable team to two state track championships."

"He got lucky with a sudden turnout of good runners."

"His gentle encouragement and wise advice improved my race times."

"That, Kevin, is a lie. We both know it. I respect you for standing up for your friend, but there's nothing to gain by it. If you think Gregory was a good coach, then you'll be surprised what a truly distinguished coach can do."

"You're going to get a new coach?" I asked.

"A very experienced coach. A coach with an impeccable record."

"I will not run for Bend City High School under a new coach."

"What?" he whispered.

"Unless Gregory is my coach, I will not enroll at Bend City High School this semester. Or any other semester."

Porphorhessohln put his palms on his desktop, hovered, leaned toward me so I could feel the air leaving his mouth as he spoke. "You, young Mr. Schuler, don't have the courage to return to Carton—you can't face it!"

"I will transfer to Lower Bend City High School."

Presently, Umber Porphorhessohln, M.S., M.A., Ed.D., father of four, grandfather of five, proud Oldsmobile driver, decorated Korean War veteran, and former state track champion, took from his desktop a small paperweight of clear Lucite, in which was suspended a yellow scorpion and many wee bubbles, and launched this heavy half-orb, by the power of his own right arm, through a triple-pane window with a view of a line of high and straight oak trees. From my vantage point, I saw the paperweight arc like an artillery shell toward the lawn, where it skidded to a stop, reflecting the sun.

I said, "Yow."

Porphorhessohln paced the room, clapping his hands together in front of his breastbone. Eventually, he pressed the button of his intercom.

"Ms. Hoyle," he said.

After a pause, she answered. "Yes, Dr. Porphorhessohln?"

"Ms. Hoyle, peel your ear off my God damn door for half a minute and get Gregory Altrabashar on the phone. And send for a custodian."

I wiped my palms on my jeans, and retrieved, minutes later, Mr. Porphorhessohln's ejected paperweight from the well-groomed lawn below the school. In the car, when Mother asked me how I'd come to possess the paperweight I said, "It's a gift from Mr. Porphorhessohln."

"What a nice man," she said.

"And a good role model," I replied.

part three

twenty-one

Following my suspension from running, I breathed with vigor. September, I walked barefoot around our yard, read Chekhov beneath the maples during these waning days of summer. Yellow ladybugs walked in circles on my knuckles.

I waded in Keen Creek. My toes burrowed into the sand of the sun-warmed shallows. Fat, tar-hued tadpoles, even this late in the season, knocked their brows against the arches of my feet, which shone like pale sticks of butter beneath the clear water. With no cross-country practices to monopolize my afternoons, I began to feel giddy. Into our mailbox came the JC Penney Christmas catalog— that glossy, fun tome of wishes—and I leafed through it repeatedly, circling in red ink the items I desired, no matter how fanciful or impractical or costly they were.

Look here, I told myself, you're free. And if you desire a gumball machine–piggy bank, do not fetter this craving.

I wrote Henny a nine-page letter—the longest yet—in which I described my overwhelming desire to disassemble my perky red convertible and then further sever the component parts into many tiny pieces which I would slowly distribute throughout mid-Missouri. I'd bury a brake lightbulb behind Sundry Seeley, drop a scrap of the seat leather into the Missouri River, sprinkle bits of windshield glass along a gravel road, fashion a new flag for our battered mailbox from the cherry red body of the car. And so on.

"You're discharging negative energy in a creative manner," Henny wrote back. "You're sounding very healthy and sane and young for once. God damn that damn cross-country and track, if indeed that's what had bound your channels."

I gave Henny a portrait I had made of her by gluing tiny alphabet macaroni onto a large sheet of sturdy black posterboard (a medium I had not employed since the age of eight). Above her three-quarters profile I glued these words:

—HENRIETTA INANNA BULFINCH—
SOUL-PURE
SALVE OF CYNICS
QUEEN OF BEAUTY
TUNE-WRIGHT
SAINT

She blushed when I gave the thing to her at school. I blushed in sympathy. Later she wrote me: "But I must point out, Mr. Perfection (Mr. Great Athlete, Mr. IQ 130, Mr. Adonis), that some of us are not so accomplished in all fields of achievement as you are. That is, we'll let you keep running fast (if you wish) and let you retain your good looks and intellect, but perhaps we won't stand for it if you choose to flaunt your obvious artistic talent, too. Maybe we're not interested to know that you are also a genius with blank-verse poetry or musical composition or magical tricks or the baking of diverse pastries."

In October, as winds combed the leaves from the sky, I dreamed a little dream of Carton. Of my classmates from those years. We all stood assembled in a vast stone courtyard with nothing to occupy us. We could see the walls surrounding us, but above us was only darkness, as if perhaps there was no roof on the place. Cold air poured from above. I could see all my classmates, every detail, it seemed—unlaced basketball shoes, mousse-abused bangs, bony thirteen-year-old wrists. My classmates and I looked at each other. We didn't speak. I ventured a smile. I wanted to say something like, "Hey, I know you all now. I remember you all," but the silence of the group made me wonder at the appropriateness of any such announcement. Jason Blick sat down. I could hear Trolley Catchell's nasal breathing. Heather Garnet crossed her arms on her chest. "You've got us all now," Bobby Sickle said to me. Then Tom Poolcall touched Pim Blotto's shoulder and the two of them walked away from the group toward one of the walls, which suddenly seemed to be much farther away than previously. Tom and Pim headed toward this wall, disappeared in the gloom. Very soon, then, we heard a door closing, and Ellie Butterbit, who stood comfortably close, said to me, "Here we go." Then everyone in the group took one step toward me.

I tried to wake up. My heart felt flooded, felt jammed. Everything was dark now and I couldn't wake up. Someone was sitting on my legs. I tried to kick. Someone pushed my torso. My head bounced against the floor. My classmates were going to take me apart. They had a case against me. In the darkness, I threw out my arms, swung at adversaries I couldn't see. My knuckles beat against shinbones. Still my legs were held down.

"Kevin! Kevin!" they screamed. Light flashed. I closed my eyes. I yelped.

"Kevin! Stop it!"

This was Mother.

She stood before me, above me, in her long nightgown and robe. The overhead light shone down on me. I lay on the floor, in the corner of my room. My sheets were twisted around my knees. The wall beside me was cracked—the drywall had been hit hard by something.

"Where are we going?" I said.

"You were belting out!" Mother said in an accusatory tone.

"Yelling?"

"That's right!"

"Bad. Dream," I said.

"You broke the drywall!"

I was sweating.

"I didn't know where we were going," I said.

"Are you okay?"

"I'm fine here. Just staying here."

"Well," Mother said, "I should think so."

I sat up reading, then, from three-thirty until five, when I fell into a shallow sleep with my head resting on my desk. I woke at five-forty and began the day.

I still ran each morning. My legs, my head, they thanked me for running. During the second week of October, Gregory asked me to come to a cross-country meet. "The team will rally around your presence. And I wonder if you could offer me your opinion on the team's performances. It seems to me they are having problems gauging pace. They have disparate strategies. They need a leader." I agreed to attend and stood with Gregory beside the starting line on a wet Saturday morning at a meet near Hibernia. The varsity boys' teams lined up across the hill. There, seventy boys breathed into the cold air and their exhalations hung suspended and visible as they stood motionless between the starter's announcement of "On your marks!" and the gun. As the runners accelerated, the starter sprinted behind them, watching for tussles and thrown elbows.

"Okay," Gregory said, "you see how Bobolink charges out perfectly, and the other boys try to follow his example. Come on." He began jogging toward the one-mile marker, where we would check the splits and observe the runners on the course's longest hill.

"Kevin! Let's go!" he called after me.

I started to follow him, but fell.

"Kevin!"

Gregory stopped, looking back at me. I took to my feet again but just as quickly toppled onto the grass. My knees had no power.

"What is with that?" Gregory yelped.

"Go on," I said, "go on."

Reluctantly, Gregory jogged away, crossed a gulch flanked by cedars, disappeared.

Across the way, striding down a treeless ridge, the runners coursed like an avalanche. The mist that shrouded the view seemed to darken as I watched, and I could not discern the individual identity of any of the distant runners. But I could hear the muffled thumpings of their spike-clad feet meeting the soft earth.

After the runners disappeared into the oak woods, I regained my feet and walked slowly toward the parking lot. Near the lot the many cross-country teams had erected their large team tents—square tents with one open side—and as I passed near the Bend City tent a gaggle of small girls from the junior varsity team, none of whom I really knew, called to me and beckoned me into their dim cavern. I turned and went to them and as I neared they curled their lips and let their eyes leak honey. Some of them reclined on the thick tufts of grass, posed in different stretching postures, and some of them stood as I came inside the tent. Thus, when my knees gave out for the third time that morning, I tumbled forward into a thicket of thin girls who caught me softly and surely and lowered me smoothly to the ground.

"We had heard that this suspension thing was just a sham," one sly-toned sophomore named Rhea said as she held my head on her thigh. "Just a coverup for your irreversible illiotibial band friction syndrome, which had failed to respond even to hydrocortisone injections and excision of the tendon that rides over the femoral epicondyle."

"You Zame Smith girls are dreamy," I said. "But your theory is incorrect."

When Gregory found me in the tent after the varsity boys' race was completed, he crouched next to me.

"What is wrong with Kevin?" he asked.

The junior varsity girls had left when they saw Gregory approaching, so we had the tent to ourselves.

"I don't know," I said. I wagged my head, shrugged comically. Gregory wasn't moved.

"I do hope you have not begun to forgo breakfast," Gregory said.

"What it is," I admitted, "is that I wanted to be in the race."

Gregory nodded.

"I would have won," I said.

"I know."

"I need to race. I'm all stoppered up. I'm backwards."

"You need to race."

"I'm full of fuel and there's no way to burn it. It sours my dreams at night."

"We have to find a way to burn that motherfucking fuel," Gregory said.

"You can help me."

"I will, Kevin."

"Thank you."

"Yes."

"You know, I've never heard you cuss before," I told Gregory.

"Well," he said, "dang."

twenty-two

Here they had finally come to me, all assembled. But they wouldn't leave.

Again, again, again this dream:

My Carton classmates and I, standing surrounded by stone walls. No visible ceiling above us. Pim Blotto and Tom Poolcall leave. "It's all you guys!" I tell my classmates, thinking they are waiting for affirmation from me. But they care not. "I'm trying to put you all together," I say. "I'm close." Someone snickers. "You're stuck," Trolley Catchell says, "so we're stuck." I have no response for Trolley. Georgia Teeter buttons her shirt's top button. Heather Garnet scratches her arm. "Here we go," Ellie Butterbit says. "Here we go what?" I ask. "Flood," Bobby Sickle says. "A big flood is coming." "Then we have to get to higher ground," I tell them, and soon I am leading us all up narrow stairways in a stone tower. There are occasional narrow windows in the tower but they look out only on darkness. Heather Garnet holds a handkerchief over her mouth. The tower is frankly medieval, but very clean. We reach a staircase so narrow that we can only pass up it single file. Bobby Sickle pours a canteen of water onto his shirt and then holds the shirt over his mouth. Ellie Butterbit has put safety goggles on. She hands me several folded maps. I have trouble holding the maps as I lead my classmates on, farther up. I feel confident—the tower is so tall we will be impervious to any flood. The shell of the tower is stone, but the innards are all wood—thick beams and wide plank floors. Some of the rooms hold heavy wooden tables. "Come on, Kevin!" some disgruntled classmate yells from below. What is the problem? I am the problem. We should be climbing faster. And I must admit that I don't know exactly how high the tower is—which seems like a serious oversight on my part. Ellie comes close to me at some point, is climbing the stairs directly behind me, and I slow and put my hand on her shoulder and lean on her. "What do you think's best?" I ask. Or: "Let me know if you have any ideas." She answers nothing. She has replaced her safety goggles with what appears to be a fireman's oxygen mask—this covers her entire face and even if she were to answer me I deduce that I couldn't understand what she might be saying. Everyone's coughing. This seems silly at first. We hear a tumbling noise and I wonder who's fallen down the stairs. The lighting is so dim here, I can't see more than ten feet in any direction. I pause at the top of one flight of stairs and let some of my classmates pass me, hoping I can find out who fell and see if they need help or moral support. Gina Daley passes me and she is crying. Her eyes are frightfully red, and she's holding her hand over her mouth and nose. I hurry back up to the head of the procession. "Why are you slowing us down like this?" Trolley Catchell says to me as I pass him on the steps. He yells after me: "Is this what you think of us?" "Trolley," I say, "come on. You've never been mean to me. Come on. We're fine." Trolley has passed out of sight. Later, once I am leading the group again, I try to climb faster. The windows of the tower are now showing signs of light—a pale yellow light which makes me glad to think that dawn is coming and soon I will be able to see what is outside. That will answer questions. If I can place this tower in a landscape, then I'll be on my way to handling some of the larger questions surrounding this situation. I think, as we continue, that the light outside is growing brighter, and I can see clouds floating near in the dawn. These narrow windows, though, only allow me to peer outside with one eye at a time. But the fact that I see clouds floating below us bodes well for our chances of outpacing the flood. Jason Blick pulls the sleeve of my shirt violently. "What do you think you're really accomplishing?" he asks in a bitter voice. "We could have walked right out down at the bottom!" "I dropped the maps," I say. Now we enter a low-ceilinged room that has no apparent exit. That is, the stairs have ended. We are at the top of the tower. There is nothing in the room, only the wood floor and one window on each of the four walls. The ceiling is wooden too and there I can see a trapdoor and if we could somehow reach the trapdoor I figure we could get onto the roof of the tower and therefore be quite impervious to any flood and have a fine view of the world. "Hoist me onto your shoulders," I tell Greg French, but he doesn't budge. He has balled his T-shirt in front of his face and breathes through it. Gina Daley wears a swimming mask and snorkel—and I note her practical gear choice, even if it betrays her paranoia and perhaps even her distrust of my ability to lead everyone clear of the rising waters. "We'll get up on the roof," I say. "If someone can boost me I can reach the door and then we'll pull one another up. Up onto the roof. The sun will rise soon and then think of how the sun will shine across all the floodwaters and we can enjoy jam on bread with the peculiar kind of blackberry brandy we have brought along. Or we can have melba toast." No one cheers or smiles at my suggestions. In fact, I notice that everyone seems to be quite gloomy. "Now," I say, "there's no problem." "What do you mean?" Jason Blick asks. "We're very safe," I say, "and now we'll have a long time to rest and just hang out." Gina says, "We're in a tower with walls made of stone and interior made of wood, and you think this is a safe place to escape the fire?" "What do you mean, fire?" I ask. I do, though, smell smoke. "The cathedral's on fire," Greg French says, "and we go up the old cathedral tower, you lead us right up the tower." "What do you mean fire?" I ask. "You said flood," I say. "We were having a flood," I protest. And I do feel heat now, remarkable heat, surrounding us, holding us, rippling the air. And outside the windows, I see that the clouds are not clouds but great plumes of smoke and the sunrise is not sunrise but the light of the fire in the cathedral below us. "Maybe it's a flood *and* a fire," Greg says. Both Gina and Ellie shake their heads at me, disappointed. "How high are we?" I ask. "Three and a half miles," Ellie says. I am surprised I can understand her through her fireman's oxygen mask. I face her squarely. "And this is a fire?" I ask. "And not a flood?" She nods. "Well, we're all here," I say. "We can still figure out something." "We're not all here," Greg French says. "Bobby Sickle passed out in the smoke and we left him." Indeed, Bobby Sickle is not among us. "Where's Bobby Sickle?" I ask. "Trolley Catchell couldn't keep up with us," says Gina. "He rolled down a flight of stairs into a room that was already on fire and we didn't see him again." Trolley Catchell is not here. "Where is Trolley Catchell?" I ask. No one is answering me. "We had to climb this tower very fast to outpace the fire," Gina says. Then she says, "Hoover Garfield got left behind. He passed out in the smoke. He didn't have any water to wet his hand-kerchief so he could breathe through it." "Where is Hoover?" I ask. "I mean it," I say. "Where is he?" "We went very fast," Greg says. "Heather Garnet has asthma and the smoke got her," Greg says. But I feel certain that I have recently seen Heather in this very room just as we were discussing how the flood is really a fire. I look around now, determined to find her. But I do not find her. "Where is Heather Gar-net?" I ask. There are only three people in front of me. "Where's Heather?" I ask. Only Greg French, Gina Daley, and Ellie Butterbit stand before me. I see that my hands are black as if marred by soot. "Is all this true?" I ask, but no one seems to hear me. I take Ellie by the shoulders. Her mask has gone cloudy and wavy from the heat, so I can barely see through it, but I do see through it, and I see that Ellie's eyes are rolling up into her skull. I shake her shoulders. Her eyes stop rolling and she sees me. "Is all of this true?" I ask her. "Yes," she says. "Boost me up to the trapdoor!" I say. "We can get up onto the roof. Maybe someone will see us! A helicopter! Maybe there's a bridge off the tower!" No one moves to boost me. I jump toward the trapdoor. I hit it with the palm of my hand and the trapdoor jumps open a few inches and then falls shut as I drop back to the floor. The floor, actu-ally, is leaking smoke through the cracks between planks. "We'll get up on the roof," I say. "You can't do anything," Ellie says loudly. I look at her. She has removed her oxygen mask. "Stop trying to do stuff," she says. "It won't work." Her eyes wobble back into her skull for a moment. "We could have walked out of the cathedral on the ground floor," she says. "Get this back on!" I say, and try to strap the huge mask onto her face. The straps are apparently fastened around a person's head by tying them like shoelaces. "Get it back on!" I yell. Ellie is lying on the floor. Her face appears smaller than before, younger. The rubber parts of the mask have gone soft in the heat. They seem to be melting. I try to hold the mask against her face, but it slides off again and again.

Quite suddenly, though, I am not in the tower. I am in another tower. I am on top of another tower. I can tell that indeed it is morning because the air is cool and the sun in fact is rising somewhere behind me. I am on top of another tower, by myself, and I am looking back toward the tower my classmates are in. Through the billows of smoke, I can see the tower burning, the flames sprouting from the stone windows of the tower, climbing higher until flames come from the windows of the top floor of the tower, and then flames break through the ceiling of the tower so that the thing looks like a huge stone candle. From my vantage point—on this tower which is not burning, which has a trapdoor that leads down into the tower, which has a sturdy ladder leading down through the trapdoor into the tower—from this vantage point, I cannot see the ground, I am so high.

twenty-three

In October, the clocks retreated, relinquished an hour, the sun began setting before six, the first snow of the year dusted Burt Kahl's soybeans, and Mother knocked on my door one Sunday evening as I held my cold hands beneath my armpits and studied at my desk.

"I read here," Mother said, shaking the newspaper, "that you won a race yesterday. The paper says it's very impressive. That's very impressive, Kevin, to run in a race and beat people like Gregory and this fellow Deek Hazystrump who won this race for the past seven years. But what is '5k'?"

"Five kilometers."

"Oh. Is it a European kind of race?"

"It's just a road race, three-point-one miles, the same distance as cross-country."

"And I thought you went to the library yesterday."

"That's just where I had you drop me off and pick me up."

"Did it feel good to race again?'

I shook my head.

"What is this?" she asked. She poked at a pile of letters on my desk. She picked one up. "Henny Bulfinch?"

I shrugged. "Girl at school."

"Isn't she that little girl you talk to at the races sometimes?"

"Yep."

"You haven't even opened these."

"Uh," I said.

"Don't be rude. She must be nice. Look at all these. I think there's perfume on some of these. Or it's just the nice scent of a nice girl's stationery."

"Put those back."

In fact, I did open the most recent of Henny's letters very late that night. I read the first words my eyes fell on—"You've swung away so suddenly. You look sickly."—and put the letter back in the envelope.

When I gave up on sleep for the night, I wandered out to the kitchen table, at about 4 A.M. On the table lay the article about the 5k race. Mother had cut it from the paper. The headline, which I had not seen before, read, BEND CITIANS SAVOR SCHULER'S VICTORY—FIRST APPEARANCE SINCE MAY. I read on:

> Earl Spooner, a fifty-one-year-old ex-manager with the automakers north of the river, is no picture of athletic fitness, and admits to being no particular fan of running events. But when Spooner heard on last night's ten o'clock news that Bend City 5k River Classic organizers had discovered suspended high school running superstar and Bend City Civic Symbol Kevin Schuler on their registration list, he awoke before six this morning and drove downtown to secure a seat for himself and his wife near the race's finish line. He was joined by an estimated crowd of twelve thousand— creating traffic problems and shattering all attendance records for this race that is well known among runners, but ignored by most Bend Citians. "The state athletic association," Spooner says, "knocked this boy out on a whim—this boy who did no wrong. And people like me relate to that. But what does he do when he's banned from school races? He comes out here and, in front of his home crowd, he tears the asphalt off this race."

> Mayor Gina Bing, in awarding Schuler the River
> Classic trophy, lauded him as an inspiration to Bend
> City. She addressed the crowds: "We don't have to
> enjoy hard times, but, like Kevin, we should adapt
> and seek creative solutions in order—

I put the paper down. I turned the story over and began brewing coffee. When Mother finally appeared after five-thirty, as I was about to suit up for my morning run, she blinked at me and smiled and poked my ribs.

"Who would have thought I'd build a boy that goes to bed after me and gets up before me! Who woulda thunk it?"

My arm twitched and coffee splashed from my cup onto my toes.

It so happened, later that morning, that I arrived at school forty minutes early—to use Zame Smith's library—and walked from where Mother dropped me between the two schools to the unlocked, early-hours rear entrance of Zame Smith. As I opened the door, I saw Dr. Brake entering the back door to the administrative wing of the school, not twenty meters away from me. He did not see me. I jogged across the frosted lawn and followed Brake. He was no fast walker. His girth gave his gait a lurching quality. I slunk behind him in the dim, vacant hallways. He entered the secretary pool outside of the administrative offices. The lights were low and the only secretary I could see was at the far end of the room. Brake walked immediately through Superintendent Porphorhessohln's open door, and I heard the two men exchange low-toned greetings. Porphorhessohln's office lights were bright, and I felt secure in the darkness of the secretary pool. I moved forward over the scarlet carpet to a point where I could see Brake reclining on Porphorhessohln's couch while Porphorhessohln, in somewhat atypical fashion, lounged casually opposite the doctor in a captain's chair. I could not discern the words of their conversation, but Porphorhessohln's face carried a light, almost gleeful expression, and when Brake handed him a check, this expression did not alter.

I, though, retreated.

* * *

Of course I did sleep. No matter how I fortified myself with caffeine and dread, I did eventually, most nights, sleep about four hours. I never slept under the covers. I would lie on my back, eyes open or closed, the lights of my room all burning, and my body would twitch every few minutes. If I did fall asleep, I would wake when a car passed our house, or even if an airplane passed close enough. I would wake if Mother flushed the toilet. I would wake if the wind kicked up suddenly. Once, as I slept, the telephone rang, and I vaulted from bed to crouch beside the dresser. Sometimes Jim Toto's cattle would bellow through the night, constantly pulling me from sleep. And when the coyotes raised their yaps and howls across the snowy fields, my sleep was usually ruined for the sum of the night.

But these noises that woke me sometimes were my salvation: They would pull me from the dream of the burning tower, which came a few times each week, and which I could not pull myself from. The dream replayed itself with remarkable clarity. It did not change. I began each dream with the same ignorance as before: thinking I was saving my classmates from a flood only to later find I had led them to their doom in the burning tower. And at the end of each dream I was instantaneously transported to a safe tower with a view of the fire.

Mid-December, I succumbed to the flu for the first time since junior high. That sickness stayed with me through to Christmas—which we celebrated on the twenty-eighth when Father arrived home—when I dragged myself to the couch of the living room and lay mired in such weakness that I could not even unwrap my own presents but had to ask Mother to do so. In my fevered and balloon-headed state the lights on our aluminum Christmas tree burned playfully onto my retinas and entertained me more than the gifts that piled before me. The gifts were more numerous than ever before. For me: a yellow beanbag, an expensive digital watch that monitored air temperature and altitude, a gumball machine–piggy bank, a 4.5-inch-diameter-mirror reflecting telescope, a small pinball machine, and a complete 228-piece tool set in its own rolling storage cabinet.

"Is that a garbage can?" I asked when presented with the tool set.

My gifts to my parents were both contained in envelopes. Mother opened hers first. She pulled a sheet of paper from the envelope. Her hair appeared buoyant to me.

"Your gift," she read, "will be delivered this afternoon."

"That sounds right," I said.

"Ee!" she said. "Sounds glamorous."

"I don't remember what it is," I admitted.

"Sick Kevin doesn't need to worry."

"I wonder what it is. What is that?" I asked, pointing toward my gumball machine–piggy bank.

Father had quickly adapted to my illness by talking much more slowly than normal. "That there," he said, kneeling before me on the carpet and holding the gumball machine up to my eyes, "is your little piggy bank that you put your loose change into, right here, and then, out of here, this little slot, comes a gumball."

"Oh."

"You circled it so much in the Christmas catalog, we couldn't disappoint you," Mother said.

"Did I circle it in red or black?"

"Red circles with black stars."

I considered this.

"Then I must have really wanted it. And now I have it. I will finally be popular at school."

"You circled all this stuff so we wouldn't miss it."

"My gift," Dad said as he opened his envelope, "says, 'Your gift will be delivered this afternoon.' "

"Uh oh," I said, "I got you both the same thing."

"Isn't it afternoon already?" Father said.

"I think that for your gift," I said, "we might need a fence around the yard. I'm not sure. I can't remember."

"We'll see when it gets here."

"How do the gumballs get into the gumball reservoir?" I asked, holding the piggy bank on my stomach.

"Well, we put them in there," Mother said.

"Where do they come from, though?"

"You can buy them most anywhere."

"Oh. So you use the piggy bank to save your change to buy the gumballs so you can fill the gumball reservoir so you will be enticed to save your money by being rewarded with a gumball so that you can save enough money to go and buy more gumballs."

Later in the afternoon, a delivery truck arrived and one very small man in pastel-blue coveralls deposited, onto our kitchen table, an eight-setting collection of dinner china of a design Mother had salivated over for decades—Primrose Day—including cups and saucers, serving platters, serving bowls, a gravy boat, punch bowl, and candleholders.

"Oh, Kevin. This is too much. This is so fine. Primrose Day! You knew all along how much I wanted this set. Goodness gracious! Look at the punch bowl. Isn't that a charming pattern, Dad?"

"That's a charming platter," Father admitted.

"I said *pattern*, dear, not platter. Finally we have china to match Grandma Skuttle's silverware. Kevin, you didn't have to go and spend this kind of money."

"But it's okay," I said. "I have the money." I felt dizzy standing there on the kitchen linoleum.

"But you give us so much already. You helped us insulate the crawl space and fix the Buick's transmission. We don't deserve all of this . . ." She held her hand against her mouth then and cried. "And we were only able to buy you such nice gifts this year because you've been giving us so much money . . ."

"Emmy, now," Dad said, pulling her to him. "Now, now. We have a generous son."

"Oh . . ." she said. "You're right, and we'll be able to buy that new table soon and then we can seat eight people in here, finally."

"I think a table might be my gift to Father. I'm not sure."

When Dad's gift arrived, it proved to be an overstuffed, button tufted, wall hugging, reclining easy chair, which the delivery men brought through the front door by turning it sideways, as if it were as light as a toy, and plopped it down next to the couch where I lay in a semi-delusional state after expending so much energy to watch the arrival of Mother's china.

"Look at that," I said, eyeing the chair.

"Thanks a bundle, son," Dad said, and he dropped into the chair and pulled the lever. A footrest rose silently from the lower regions of the chair and the chair itself reclined to a comfortable angle and then further to a dangerously horizontal angle.

"Now wait," Dad said, and he rose from the still-reclining chair and with the help of the delivery men lifted me and my cocoon of blankets onto the chair.

"Oh lord," I said, from the ridiculously comfortable chair. "I picked a good present for Father."

"Maybe I can buy another one and bolt it into the cabin of my truck," Dad joked.

The delivery men assured him that just such a scheme had been successfully employed many times.

After the men left, Father began collecting wrapping paper from the floor. Mother busied herself with dinner. Soon, Dad went outside to shovel the drive and I felt sleep pulling me. I was pumped full of antihistamines and had eaten only chicken broth, Jell-O, and bananas in the past three days. I saw that the Christmas tree lights were blinking—something I didn't think they had been doing before. "What's going on over there?" I asked the tree, but no one answered. The cloudy afternoon waned into an early dusk. Passing cars and trucks slid quietly past our house on the snow-packed road, and I fell asleep. I became ridiculously hot in my blankets. I dreamed the little dream. Finally, I struggled, pulled myself awake. My head and neck were in pain. The walls and ceilings were not in their correct position. I cried out something. Mother and Father were both soon at my side. "I heard that thump all the way outside," Father said.

"What happened?" I asked. The walls were realigning themselves and the Christmas lights suddenly reappeared.

"The chair fell over backwards," Mother said. "You must have been jerking in your sleep."

"I'm okay now?" I asked.

"See, we've set you back upright," Father said.

Inside my blanket cocoon, I had sweated through my T-shirt and pajama pants. I saw my new yellow beanbag on the floor beside the chair.

"What's that?" I asked.

That winter, my hitherto perfect attendance record at BCHS was broken. December's flu became January's bronchitis. Then the flu returned. I suffered colds. My legs cramped at night, headaches wrapped themselves around my eyes. Dr. E and Dr. Brake paid for all the medical expenses that Father's insurance wouldn't cover. Father's insurance had changed recently and forced us to leave Dr. Spittle, that reluctant Carton doctor, that wannabe agrarian, and take a new physician. This new doctor, Dr. Rowle ("Row-lee") Pennysquat, was a fine example of the corpulent, chain-smoking medical practitioners not uncommon in mid-Missouri, most of whom held backwater D.O. degrees. Pennysquat treated me much like a sick cow. That is, he betrayed no feelings for me and did not make eye contact with me and did not talk to me but only to my mother, as if I were an animal and she my owner.

"Is he experiencing chills?" he asked Mother as I sat slumping on the examining table and Mother sat in the chair beside the door.

"Are you experiencing chills?" she asked me.

"No," I said.

"No," Mother told Pennysquat, "he isn't experiencing chills."

"Has the Tylenol brought his fever down?" he asked Mother.

"Did that Tylenol work for the fever, Kevvy?" she asked me.

"It did," I answered.

"It worked," she told Pennysquat.

And so on.

Once, though, when Pennysquat had absconded to Las Vegas for the first week of March, a young M.D. from his group saw me, Dr. Katherine Awn, asked my mother to wait in the reception area, made me get down from the examination table and sit in a chair, knee-to-knee with her, assured me I did not have strep throat but simply a cold, and asked me to rest as much as possible and sleep like a cat.

"You mean sleep curled up?"

"I mean two words: a lot."

I don't know how she sensed my uneasiness with the idea of sleeping a lot, but she stopped writing on her clipboard and laid her hand on my shoulder and said, "If you are having difficulty sleeping, tell me and we will fix the problem."

I assured her I was fine.

She had earned a throne in my thoughts with her earnest manner and simple proclamation: "We will fix the problem." Also, I was impressed that she knew "a lot" was two words.

twenty-four

Frankly, spring surprised me when it arrived. Spring seemed a very unlikely thing to occur. But it did. Daffodils trumpeted. Rain tortured the remaining snowbanks. And after my sickly winter, I began running again. I found myself not much out of shape at all. In fact, I seemed to carry a new reserve of energy and steadiness, as if sickness had hardened me.

"I hate all of this driving, you know," I told Mother as we drove home from school one Friday afternoon. "I think it's sick."

We were driving west, toward the sun, and we had come to the stretch of road that paralleled the under-construction, twelve-mile, four-lane extension of the federal highway that passed within a couple miles of our house. The limestone hills had been blasted away, the topsoil had been scraped off, wasted. Bulldozers pushed trees into tangled piles.

"I hate cars and trucks and highways and bridges," I said.

"Well," Mother said after a moment. "Fret, fret, fret," she said, and nothing more. But I had tripped some wire in her, for Monday morning when I emerged from my room at the normal hour for my ride to school, she was still sitting in her dressing gown with her coffee.

"From now on," she reported, "you are your own chauffeur."

Though I explained how ridiculous and wasteful it was for us to drive to town separately, she would not agree to take me and so I began to drive my own little convertible each day, the car which still had less than a hundred miles on the odometer.

At the state university, after a session in which Dr. E drew blood from the artery in my wrist to study my blood gases and then had Bob Popincock count all the hair follicles on my chin (one of E's pet interests was the relationship between hair growth and athletic efficiency), Coach Rowen showed up at E's laboratory and asked if today would be a good day to visit with him. Rowen took me in his German coupe across campus—where Frisbees hovered nearly motionless above a grassy quad—to the new indoor sports complex. Here he introduced me to the assistant coaches and to several track team members. "I don't know how I feel about talking to a guy who posted faster 800 times during his freshman year of high school than I ever have," Tommy Toomnis, team captain, joked. The weight rooms, the locker rooms, the meeting rooms, the offices, the sponsor-supplied gear, the indoor track, the hot tub—it was all brand new and brightly lit and smelled of Ben-Gay and vinyl.

Rowen and I sat in Danish designed chairs in his office and reclined and nodded.

"Any questions?" Rowen asked.

"Why aren't there any windows in the building?"

"Good question." He yelled toward the open door of his office: "Patty?"

"Ahoy," his top assistant coach answered from down the hall.

"Kevin wants to know why there are no windows in the building. Find out."

"Aye aye."

"You're aware of our scholarship programs, Kevin. It's all there in black and white for you to see. We will supply you with the highest tier of funding should you choose to attend here. There will be nothing shadowy about the process. Your grades will get you into the school, even get you into the honors program if you wish, and I will award you the highest tier of scholarship support available. It's not many undergraduates that can make a profit from attending college."

"I never thought of college as a business venture."

"Kevin, we know every running program in the country wants you. You can pick and choose between the best in the country—Arkansas, Stanford. We're not the strongest running program. We're not the strongest academic school. We're good, though. And we're Missouri. You would be close to home—but not too close. You would probably be running with some of the same boys you're running with now at Zame Smith. And when you go out and run races, you'll be winning for your home state—that'll feel good."

I nodded.

"You should also know that I have spoken to Dr. E and we have only recently discovered we can guarantee that if you attend this school, you can continue with Dr. E's research, if you wish. The funds you gain from the research would be yours in addition to the scholarship funds. If you attend any other school, Dr. E cannot continue to offer you compensation for his studies. Because of intercollegiate athletic codes. Everything clear?"

"Translucent."

Patty knocked on the door frame. "Coach?"

"What's the million-dollar answer?" Rowen asked.

"There are no windows in the building because of construction costs and energy efficiency and the architect's desire for unbroken planes of sheet metal which communicate an aura of speed and modernity."

"Ah," said Rowen. "So there you have it."

Late in the spring I received an evening call from Tyler Arkass.

"The thing is," he told me, "the school board's having me dismantle the memorial. People won't leave it alone. Kids spray painted it.

And the shoes got stolen twice. Once the sheriff found them in a pig lot. We had to clean them up. Other time they were thrown through a window at school."

I agreed to meet Tyler in front of the school Saturday morning—I ran in through the white sunrise. But when I arrived, Tyler sat on the half-dismantled brick column with his hat in his hands. He shook his head.

"Someone got to them last night," he told me. "I know word leaked out that we were taking them down today, and someone got to them."

I told him it was no big deal. I had the real shoes, after all.

As I turned to leave, Tyler stood up and I saw then that the brick pillar of the memorial was not solid brick but hollow in the middle.

I ran through town, past the churches and houses and the old downtown, where the long abandoned railroad depot was now a machine shop. As I ran on the sidewalk parallel to the railroad bed, a pickup passed by me and ran through a long puddle that lay by the sidewalk for fifty feet or more. The water from the puddle splashed onto me. Many seconds later, the pickup passed again at a greater speed—it must have circled the small block—and splashed me again. I did not look into the pickup's cab.

I drove to Bend City myself one evening after supper. There in Zame Smith's theater, the school's award-winning orchestra performed selections from Holst's *The Planets,* and then the whole of a Mozart symphony. I sat in the back row of the auditorium. A slight breeze blew off the stage and bore the scent of old velvet. The Holst struck me as crass and unformed, but from the first lilting strains of the Mozart, the music saturated my mind, slowed my breathing, soaked my limbs with warmth, and eventually gave me a sensation of being weightless. I listened to most of the concert with my eyes shut—for that way I lent my full attention to the music—but could not resist occasionally watching the first chair clarinetist, who exuded grace.

This musician was Henny.

And when, in the *lento* movement, Henny's clarinet suddenly ascended like a butterfly through the swaying grasses of the strings, I had to, for a moment, grip the wooden armrests of my seat very tightly.

I stayed until the applause began, then quickly exited the auditorium before the crowd and crossed the lobby, but found myself feeling compelled to say something to Henny, or make some gesture of appreciation, some sign of affinity. I stopped in the lobby and thought. After several moments, the crowd filled the lobby and milled about me. I remained standing still, locked into a wordless debate between the parts of me that sought to flee and the parts that did not. This was a trying debate, and before I had decided on anything, Henny herself came into the room and made her way toward me.

"Kevin? What are you doing here?" she said.

"Oh," I found myself saying, "the orchestra came highly recommended by various people in the know, including Andanda." This was true, though it was not the reason I had attended the performance, and the statement itself sounded artificial, especially in light of the fact that Andanda had not attended the concert.

"What's wrong?" she asked. "You're shaking."

I made a noise through my nose, a combination of a sigh and a laugh.

"I'm a little tired."

"Congratulations on making first-tier honors," she said. "You make people like me look dumb."

I pointed to her. "Congratulations on your . . . music playing. Very much."

The crowd had grown and now congealed around us and pushed us closer together.

"Thank you," Henny said.

"I mean it," I told her.

I looped my thumbs beneath my belt and then unlooped them and then touched the back of my head and then crossed my arms and uncrossed them.

"I order you to write me a letter," Henny said.

I laughed.

"I mean it. If you get to see me perform, and if you enjoyed it, then you owe me. We won't let you keep drifting off like some iceberg, trying to melt."

"Okay," I said.

"You're trying to melt, damn it."

I rolled my eyes.

"You have to write me," she said, fervently. "Also you have to tell me what you want for your birthday."

"I don't need anything. Really. I'm tired of gifts. I don't need these things."

"Okay."

"My parents give me silly gifts and I stack them in my closet."

"I wouldn't want to take up your closet space."

"It's not a big closet."

"I wouldn't suppose so," Henny said.

"I don't want anything at all," I said.

"Then don't worry about it. You won't get anything."

She leaned toward me and touched my arm and said quietly, "Do let me know, though, if you someday acquire a larger closet or, ridiculous as it may sound, find yourself actually needing something—God forbid—or *someone* or even some silly immaterial thing, some emotional gift."

Her tone disarmed me and I doubt she heard my soft, "Will do," as she shouldered away through the crowd.

twenty-five

I did not write Henny.

Nor did I receive any gift or card or letter from Henny on my birthday, which was celebrated, at Mayor Bing's invitation, in the company of the city council at the new seafood restaurant by the mall. It was the kind of seafood restaurant with plastic shingles and neon-light lobsters pointing their pincers toward the entrance. In other words, the majority of the menu selections were deep-fat fried.

The next thing that happened was summer. I worked again at the discount store on Blissman Road. Mother still would not drive me any-where, so I had to drive myself to my job three days a week and there-fore I could not run home. Fewer people recognized me this summer, perhaps because my face had not been in the papers much during my running suspension and also my hair had grown somewhat shaggy.

"Time to crop that top," my manager, Aleen Eanly, suggested in late June. I let Mother trim my hair. Even after that, though, Aleen watched me closely. She complained that I was not as fast in finishing my tasks as I had been last year.

"I 'spose you got notions that if people love you so much, you don't have to work as hard. Big sports hero," Aleen said.

At first I let her allegation go unanswered, but finally I explained to her that often my hands and forearms were somewhat numb and not as nimble as last summer. I also pointed out that I was still her fastest worker.

She looked at me blankly. Her jowls hung. "Ain't no carpal tunnel from shelving," she said. "So forget it."

I ran in the mornings, began speed training sessions in anticipation of the cross-country season. The summer loped along, the heat rose, the humidity pulled on us in such a way as to make time slow. Though I was against the idea, I bought my parents a window-unit air conditioner, which they ran through the nights of that summer. I kept my bedroom door closed, though, and sweated through the nights. Often that summer I found myself drawn toward Burt Kahl's ponds—which had become eutrophied and therefore supported no fish but, in the absence of bass, became home to thousands and thousands of frogs. Few rains came, the ponds shrank, and on the muddy shores the frogs crawled in ever greater numbers. Perhaps there would be fifteen tiny frogs in one square foot of mud, perhaps twenty-five. Most of the frogs were the size of my thumbnail, though there were larger leopard frogs and bullfrogs the size of rats. Though I never set out to visit the ponds with any overt designs, I found myself, nearly every day, hunting the frogs with my walking stick. It was not an easy sport—the creatures were skittish as I stood over them, and often could avoid my strikes—but nonetheless I killed many frogs every day, smashing them into the mud with my stick. These tiny frogs died unspectacularly. Afterwards, in the evenings, I grew frustrated at my senseless, childish acts. Why slaughter frogs? Was I that immature? Then in July I recalled another time I had enacted the same frequent ritual: the summer immediately following my last semester at Carton, the summer after the accident. That summer I had run many miles, compiled many lists, reconstructed my classmates' names, and killed frogs. When I remembered this, I burned my walking stick and did not visit the ponds again.

*   *   *

In August, Mother offered to drive me into town. She still visited Bend City nearly every day, busied herself with comparison shopping. She had not offered to drive me anywhere in months, and I accepted the offer and spent the day at the city library. Mother picked me up at six o'clock. The streets wept tar in the heat.

"I've just got to drop something off," she said as she turned off the expressway. We passed the mall, the west side hospital, turned onto the commercial-zoned access road that ran parallel to the north side of the highway, then turned onto the road that ran parallel to the access road and allowed entrance, on its north side, to several planned neighborhoods. We turned off and dipped into the valley of houses known as Edgeknoll. The winding concrete streets were all named after tribes of midwestern Indians. It was a neighborhood I knew from my running. Now, in the summer evening, water arced lazily from the lawn sprinklers. Waxed European sedans sat idle in the driveways. A lawn service crew lifted their mowers onto a flatbed truck.

Soon, Mother stopped the car before Andanda's house. I said nothing.

"Now," she said, "This is the right address. I'm supposed to deliver this here for my club." She handed me a slim package, wrapped in plaid gift paper. "Take it up," Mother told me, "ring the bell. They'll know what it is." She gave me a small paper bag, too, stuffed with something. "And this might be needed."

Warily, I climbed out of the car. Surely Mother didn't know whose house this was—though I recognized the ridiculousness of the idea that Mother and the Danes might share a club. As I followed the front walk to the wide wooden door, the Buick sputtered behind me. I rang the bell. I heard footsteps approach. The door opened and a woman taller than Andanda, but with the same beautiful angular face and curly hair, opened the door.

"Ah!" she said. "You're Kevin. I recognize you from the papers. I'm Jessica Dane. You could have just gone around back if you wanted, but then I wouldn't have had the chance to finally meet you."

She shook my hand.

"I brought this," I said.

"Thank you. She'll appreciate it. William!"

Mr. Dane came into the foyer, dressed still in his suit, and greeted me.

"We read much about you," he said, "but Andanda's opinions of you are even higher than the press's—if such a thing is possible."

Mrs. and Mr. Dane laughed.

"She's a good friend," I said. I considered the wrapped gift in my hand. I held the present out, but neither Dane made any motion to take it.

"Pass through, pass through," Mr. Dane said, waving me into the house. "They're entrenched on the patio."

"My mother . . ." I said, glancing toward the street, but the Buick was gone.

"Pass through, pass through," Mr. Dane repeated, guiding me away from the door as he closed it. "Lady Dane and myself have celebrations of our own to haunt this evening and need to prepare ourselves."

He led me to the basement stairs and watched me descend. "Revel well!" he shouted as I turned on the landing and left his sight.

The low-ceilinged basement was dimly lit by fixtures over the pool table and the light from the patio doors. Those doors were open, their curtains swelling in the breeze, and I could hear music and laughter coming from outside. I passed through the doors, onto the flagstones, and there found assembled Andanda, her friends, Jol, some people I recognized as Andanda's fellow journalists from the school paper, and a few unknown faces. Most of the party sat on canvas lounge chairs, drinks in hand, but a few people were in the pool.

"Hicks alive," Andanda said, holding her cigarette beside her ear, "it's Kevin Schuler."

A few people clapped.

"So your mother persuaded you into coming?" Jol said. He was wearing bathing trunks and a tank top. All of the party wore bathing garb. Andanda wore a black bikini top and wrap skirt.

"Mother can be convincing," I said. Everyone laughed, and I

laughed. One lilting giggle among the crowd caught my attention. I looked to the pool and now recognized one of the wet-haired swimmers as Henny. She smiled up at me.

I sat by Andanda. "This is for you," I said.

The present, it turned out, contained a beautiful and not inexpensive gold-nibbed fountain pen. Somehow, somewhere, my mother had bought something rather tasteful. And not only tasteful but appropriate; for this party was not Andanda's birthday party, nor simply a party for the sake of a party, but a celebration of the recent election, during the summer strategy meeting of the school newspaper staff, of Andanda as editor in chief of *The River Messenger*. In pure Andandan style, she had arranged her own party, decided I needed to attend, and then called me to invite me; but finding me not at home informed my mother of the plan. Mother, ever happy to oblige the girl who she still regularly referred to as "that gorgeous newspaper girl," saw that the best way—indeed, the only way—to get me to the party was through deception. I did not tell Andanda that my attendance at her party was not of my own volition or that the present had not been chosen or purchased by me.

Knowing the poolside nature of the party, Mother had sent with me, in the paper sack, a new pair of swimming trunks, and so as the sunlight dropped into the hedge I did swim and participate in water games—against Jol's beautiful flips and gainers from the diving board, I played the ham, executing technically perfect belly flops and aerial screw-ups—and, much later in the evening, riding a sangria-induced slope of merriment descending toward serenity, I declined for the moment to follow the party's retreat into the basement for boisterous card games—spoons—and remained resting in the pool instead, where the semi-weightlessness of my submerged limbs gave me pleasure by easing my fatigue and the sense of heaviness and general physical dysphoria that had hounded me through the past months, and even now hounded me in recent days as I neared peak condition again for the autumn racing season—neared, in fact, what appeared to be the greatest fitness and capacity for speed of my running career.

The pool's pump hummed across the yard. Someone shuffled cards in the basement. I leaned against the poolside, extended my arms along the lip of the deck, felt the warmth of the underwater light against my lower back. The chlorine-scented air soothed my lungs.

I, in fact, fell into a doze—a light slumber where I was not haunted or hunted but buoyant, loosed from gravity, from history, from my body.

I woke when something caressed my chest. Little waves in the previously still pool were lapping at my chest. Across the pool, Andanda had entered the water—she had created the waves. She swam breaststroke to reach me, and moved her body close against me. She leaned her head against my upper arm and looked at me. In my sleepy and relaxed state, I had no averse reaction to her sudden intimacy.

"The light is warm," I said.

She placed her palm below my collarbone.

"What do you do out there all the time?" she asked. "Why don't you tell it to someone?"

"Tell it?"

"You don't have to say it. You could write it down. Henny tells me you used to write letters."

"There's nothing to tell."

"Pretend you're not yourself. You're just a narrator."

I breathed through my nose for several seconds. A single-engine airplane hummed far above. "Well," I said, "this summer. July. I walk a lot. I went out through a neighbor's pasture, up to an old stand of oaks." I was speaking very slowly. "These oaks are quiet trees. Maybe some of them are older than the government of this state. Through this grove I went, then down against the creekbottom. And there's the old railroad bed. Railroad's long gone, and the line is choked full of cedars now. But along one stretch I found a stand of blackberries a quarter mile long. And the berries were at peak. They were black and heavy. And no one had picked them. No one. If I stood still I could sometimes hear a berry fall to the ground. The brambles were bent over with the weight of the berries, and they were just dropping to the ground, and no person knew it."

I stopped talking, but Andanda didn't say anything. Inside the basement, someone hooted and the party suddenly laughed.

"Is that good?" I asked. "Is that what you want?"

"That's good," Andanda said. I felt her breath on my cheek. "If that's what you want to say, then it's what I want to hear."

I nodded.

"I mean, it's perfect," she said.

"I just have one question," I said.

"Hm."

"Now that you're editor, are you going to send out brash young reporters to harass me at my house?"

She laughed softly.

"I mean, will you tell them to manipulate my mother and blackmail me by getting Porphorhessohln on your side and other such tactics?"

Rather than laugh, or answer, or dunk me beneath the water, Andanda kissed me with expert gentleness. The tastes of alcohol and tobacco smoke matched my mood. For several minutes we kissed gently, until Andanda rolled her eyes toward the house. We dried off and entered the basement. To my surprise, no one in the party commented on our absence or reappearance and we were both dealt into the next round of spades. It was not until half an hour later that I noticed Henny was ignoring me.

Still deeper in the evening, the late hour warped the atmosphere. The lighting seemed suddenly bright in the basement, and everyone's face radiated an exaggerated portion of our common energies. At what I recognized as the crux of the evening, at a point when a few among us had abandoned themselves fully to the alcohol but most of us had regained sobriety, I realized Henny was not in the room, nor Jol, and when the two appeared, some twenty minutes later, from outside, I recognized clearly that Henny had been crying. I at first attributed her unstable mood to the alcohol, only to remember that neither Jol nor Henny had imbibed.

The party broke all at once. A cuckoo clock upstairs signaled 3 A.M.; all conversation ebbed; someone picked up a bottle cap from the table, then carefully placed it back exactly where it had lain.

Circumstances then set me in the backseat of Andanda's car, next to Henny. Jol rode in front with Andanda. As we moved through the sleeping city, we all pretended to be extremely fatigued. For some reason, the traffic lights around town still remained on their daytime cycles—at this late hour they should have all been switched to blinking red or yellow—so we often found ourselves stopped at intersections by red lights when there was not another car in sight. To my surprise, Andanda obeyed all these lights. When one red light switched to green, I said, "Tally ho!" Henny giggled at me. She threw her cardigan at me and I smelled it. She laughed more. The cardigan smelled of ginger.

We let Jol off. We let Henny off. Then Andanda and I drove into the country. We opened the windows of the car.

When we finally turned into my driveway, Andanda yelped.

"What is that?" she asked.

My father's semi occupied the driveway. He must have arrived home within the past few hours. I told Andanda it was my father's truck.

Andanda turned off the engine of the car.

She said, "Kevin, Kevin, Kevin."

"Me, me, me," I said.

She was wearing only her bikini top and wrap skirt, as only Andanda would have the gall to do, as only the humid August night would allow.

"I could show you inside the truck, if that's what you want," I said.

She faced me squarely.

"I'm not going to force you into anything, Kevin."

"I," I said.

"I wonder if you'll ever do anything for yourself, though," she told me.

She gave me a peck on the cheek. I got out of the car, closed the door. I leaned down to look into the car.

"I'll see you in three weeks," Andanda said.

"Yep," I said.

She nodded.

"School days . . ." she said.

I said, "These carefree days of youth."

twenty-six

Jol first asked to borrow my car during the opening week of school.

"It's just that coach wants me to see this doctor up in Hibernia once in a while, and he can't always drive me up there," Jol explained in the locker room after school. I was changing into my running clothes.

"Is this doctor by chance affiliated with the university?"

"Nah," Jol said. "I wouldn't ask you, but you know how my dad is about me borrowing the truck."

"It's no problem," I told him. "You know I hate that car and if you have it back by five-thirty, like you say, then that's fine."

"I'll fill it up with gas for you."

"Relax. Don't worry about it."

Jol was back before five-thirty. He threw me the car keys as I stepped from the shower.

"I don't happen to have any pockets on me at the moment," I muttered, then walked to my locker.

Jol didn't laugh. He leaned against the red lockers. I began dressing.

"How'd the doctor thing go?" I finally asked.

"All right. He's just monitoring me, watching out for potential injuries, you know."

"Good deal," I said.

"He's a good doctor," Jol said. "This guy. Dr. Jones."

"That's good."

"Thanks for the car," Jol said.

"If you need it again, it's yours."

"It's a peppy little thing."

"It is peppy," I agreed. "Just like me."

"You're not peppy," Jol said.

"Fuck off. Fucker."

We laughed. I had finished dressing and now put on my letter jacket.

"Did you pull your arm?" Jol asked.

"I don't think so. I just hold it like this sometimes. It goes a little numb sometimes. Nothing big."

"We'll be old before our time . . ." Jol said.

"They run us like greyhounds."

"Like racehorses," Jol echoed.

"Fight the power," I said.

Because I was a senior with a high grade-point average, I spent my days in senior seminars—small classes taught by faculty with advanced degrees. The seminars met on a different schedule than the rest of Zame Smith, including a different lunch period, so I rarely saw the rest of the student body. Henny had also qualified for the seminars, though we didn't share any classes. Andanda had opted out of the seminars to devote much of her day to her editorial duties, but she often managed to corner me in the library before school. She would ask my opinions of different topics in the news.

"I should get credit in the masthead for all this," I told her one morning in mid-September after we'd debated what stance the paper should take on the pending retooling and reopening of both of the automobile plants. "At least you could call me an advisory editor or something. An editorial consultant."

"I don't think so," she said. "But if you ever want to write anything for us, let me know." She slapped her hand onto my notebook. "That's a compliment, Kevin—c-o-m-p-l-i-m-e-n-t."

"Thanks."

"I have more writers than I can use. And most of them ridiculously mediocre. People forget how to write anything even slightly creative. Writing should be organic, not mechanical. I guess I should be in magazines, not newspapers. That reminds me, though: I have this little freshman who's submitted several pieces to me. I haven't taken any of them, but I think she's a great writer. She just doesn't understand form yet. But I'm going to ask her to be a staff writer—which is a big thing for a freshman—and then I can work closely with her to really shape her stories. She'll catch on. I was a staff writer when I was a freshman. Anyway, the whole reason I bring this girl up is because she says she knows you."

"I don't know any freshmen."

"She says she lives out near you. Her name's Tam Butterbit. Says she's known you forever."

"She must have transferred."

"She did."

"Tam Butterbit's just a little girl," I said. "But I guess that's right. She's three years behind me in school. So she's a freshman now."

"She's very cute."

"I know."

"How did you know her? Just a neighbor? Saw her at school?"

I shook my head. Then I nodded. "Right. Small town. People know people. That's all."

Andanda was sitting on the table in front of me. My books and papers stretched neatly across the table.

"That world . . ." I said, "resurfaces . . ."

The morning bell rang.

*　*　*

I watched for Tam, but did not see her—my seminars kept me clois-
tered. September passed away. I won the first two cross-country meets
of the year. Gregory shaved his beard off and his pale cheeks glowed
like pears, lent him an infantile appearance. He took me aside. "You
are holding back again," he said, "and that is not what is good. That is
denying yourself what you do deserve. You know that runner Jim
Ryun?"

"Yeah. Kansan."

"Kansan? Is that some manner of tribe?"

"He's from Kansas."

"Yes. This Jim Ryun, he made world records when he was nineteen. You could be coming onto that territory if you let yourself. The
records should not be feared."

"I'm not scared of records," I said. "Records . . . I mean, they
don't bother me."

"Then stop with your scaring yourself."

Word came that the state's cross-country championships would no
longer be held on the flat Jeffer Lake course but on a new golf course
south of town. The name of the golf course was Maple Nut.

"Maple Nut?" said Bobolink Crustacean. "That's a silly name.
You'd think people could come up with decent names. I mean, what is
a maple nut?"

Bobolink told me this as we ran warm-up laps on the track.
His dreadlocks bounced. He was a very slight runner—possessed
the narrow-hipped, small-chested body type of a world-class
marathoner. His parents were Kenyan expatriates who taught college in St. Louis.

"The silly name is misleading," I said. "I've seen the course and it's
the toughest course in the state. It's all hills, nothing else."

"Just hills," Bobolink repeated softly. "Then we'll train for hills."

"In fact," I said, "we'll do everything in our power to forget that
there is any terrain *but* hills on this earth."

* * *

Yes there are hills. There are peaks and valleys, crags and vales, tors and hollows, hills and dales, mountains and canyons. Gravity holds the world together, brings us back down each time.

When I began to doubt her presence, she appeared beside my car after cross-country practice in late October.

"Hello, Tam. Good to see you."

"Hi, Kevin."

"My sources informed me you had enrolled in our fabulous school."

"My sources told me I could find you here at five-thirty," she said. "And that perhaps you could give me a ride home."

It was an overcast day, and dusk was approaching. My hair was wet from the showers, my feet ached from the run, my medals clinked gently against each other on my jacket.

"Stayed after school, did you?" I asked her.

"Working on the newspaper."

"That's right," I said. "Very impressive. Andanda praises you. Makes me proud to be a country boy."

"Thanks. My father can come pick me up if you're too busy, it's just that—"

"In fact, I am going to meet someone just now . . ."

"That's all right. It's no problem," she said. "I'll call my dad."

I stopped her, though, called her back, told her I could give her a ride and would be happy to do so. I admitted I'd lied about having to go meet someone just now. Though she asked for no explanation and her gentle expression did not alter at all, I offered this single excuse before I unlocked our doors: "My backbone isn't what it used to be."

Tam had grown to resemble her sister, though as we drove out of Bend City I realized that Tam was now older than Ellie had ever been. I asked Tam about her classes, her teachers. She told me she liked everything too much, couldn't decide on a major.

"That's the sign of a healthy person," I said.

I asked her why she'd transferred from Carton.

"Carton's a mess," she said. "I guess it always has been, but my parents lost hope when Mrs. Eisenreich and Ms. Julip quit."

"I didn't know they were gone," I said. "That's bad."

At the first opportunity, I turned off the four-lane highway and took to the county roads. We drove through the hills around the old railroad town of Gagling. Along Lippenswitch Creek the sycamores shone white in the dusk. Finally, we came out onto county road Z, passed my gravel road, continued south, then turned onto Tam's gravel road. Darkness had arrived. We rolled down the long hill and I saw, on the left, floodlights shining toward the road. There were new houses sitting up in the terraced field—three blocky houses.

"I didn't know those were there," I said.

"Hm," Tam said. "Built in the spring."

"That's the Sickle farm, right?"

"Mrs. Sickle sold it. Moved to Illinois where her sister lives. A developer bought it. There will be more houses built up by the road, and one or two in the woods."

"The woods next to your house?"

"Yeah."

"It's just ugliness is what it is," I said.

"I know," she said.

We neared the old Sickle driveway at the top of a hillock. I couldn't see the house sitting back under the elms; there were no lights. At the end of the driveway the mailbox bore this message: F ICK.

Further down that straight road—over another hill—I turned into the Butterbits' short driveway. The centenarian gable-front-and-wing house looked as neat and clean as ever. The Butterbits' small pickup was pulled up alongside the old barn. The eyes of the horses in the pasture reflected my headlights.

Inside the house I could smell the woodwork and oven's pilot light. Shelves of home-canned jars lined the back porch. The short-snouted, long-legged mutt named Pawn leaned against my legs. A box of matches lay on the kitchen floor and a few matchsticks were scattered there. "Pawn's eating matches again," Tam said. In front of the kitchen was the study, where bookcases climbed to the ceiling. There was no television in the house—never had been—and the rooms of the house were each still painted a different pastel color, which, taken together, resembled a melon salad.

I crouched, stroked Pawn's chest. "Where have they been keeping you, Pawn?" I asked. "What have they been doing to you? Here you are—here you are."

"My parents must still be in the barn," Tam said. "A calf was in breech birth when I talked to them after school. That's why they couldn't pick me up. A calf born in October. Kind of embarrassing."

"You're lucky I'm not a snob when it comes to cattle breeding."

Tam invited me to go up to her room and see the water clock she had built—she had designed it from descriptions of medieval models.

"Water clock," I said. The stairs to the second floor of the house, where there were three bedrooms, rose into the darkness. "Drip, drip, drip?"

"Basically," Tam said.

"I would but . . . I have to get home," I said.

"That's fine," Tam said.

"No, that's not the truth," I said. "What I mean is . . . I . . ."

Pawn sniffed my shoes.

"You don't want to go upstairs," Tam said.

"Yeah."

"You're sweating, Kevin."

"I need to get outside."

In the barnyard, Tam went to the chicken coop to close it for the night. I peeked in. The biddies hunched in the nesting boxes, blinking at Tam as she checked their water and shone the flashlight in the corners.

"Pawn, are there any snakes?" she asked.

Pawn sniffed into the coop.

"Pawn whines if there's a snake," she said.

"He knows the score," I said.

Pawn coughed, then left the coop. I stooped through the low door and entered.

"Is there a hen named Bach here?" I asked.

"Bach . . ."

"A very nice hen."

"Wait, I do remember Bach. I was very little. Bach was one of our first hens. Probably half the hens in here are her progeny. Her grand-daughters and great-granddaughters and so on."

I stood surrounded by Bach's legacy.

"Huh," I said.

We stepped out and Tam closed the coop.

"I'm not against you, Kevin," she said. "I have no bitterness."

"You should."

"That's stupid. I thought about you. I was glad when you trans-ferred. We're not members of any of the Carton churches either, you know, and they treated us poorly too, and I know how they turned people against your family. You transferred. So you could breathe. I was only ten, but—"

"I owe you something."

"You do not," she said. "You owe yourself."

I drove back out the gravel road. As I passed the Sickle mailbox, I saw that the letters on this side bore a different message: F ICKLE.

"Then there's no way you can waive her tuition?" I asked Porphorhes-sohln the next morning before school.

"I can't make exceptions for one student," the superintendent answered from behind his desk. His hair, thick as steel wool, stood at a strange angle, uncombed.

"You made an exception for me," I said.

He nodded. "You were exceptional."

"Just how much is the out-of-district tuition for the full year?" I asked.

"Sixty-two hundred."

"Is there a sliding scale?"

"What is this? We're not a charity. We do offer a payment plan."

"I suppose you charge interest."

"Only eight percent."

"What a bargain."

"It is a bargain. What are you doing?"

"I'm writing a check, Umber. And here it is. A year's tuition. Apply it to Tam Butterbit's account."

"What the hell kind of stunt is this?" the superintendent asked.

"It's not the kind of thing I'd expect you to understand."

"What am I supposed to tell her parents?"

"Say that benefactors occasionally pay tuition for exceptional students, not just exceptional athletes."

He glared at me.

He said, "You can throw your money away if you want."

"It intrigues me that the superintendent of the best school in the state considers education a waste of money."

"Is this stuff you've learned from that damn socialism class?"

I left.

twenty-seven

ILL-RECEIVED VICTORY
by Tyson Lorry, Staff Writer

BCHS's Kevin Schuler won the Jim Rod Southwest Invitational cross-country meet Saturday, besting the field of 159 runners by a margin of twenty seconds, spearheading the varsity team's domination of the race (full results, p. 7). His top-place finish, though, was met with boos from the crowd of over a thousand spectators. "We came out to see him set a course record," Tonya Bilirubin said, "not to see him cruise in like he was out for a jog."

Cross-country coach Gregory Altrabashar admitted the crowd's reaction was something Kevin will have to deal with more and more. "They feel insulted if they don't think he's run his heart out," Altrabashar said.

Girl's varsity cross-country team captain, senior Tina Brown, said, "I have no idea what Kevin's motivations are, but I'm sure he doesn't run simply to woo the crowd."

Kevin declined to comment on the race.

"What . . ." I said. We were eating meatloaf and mashed potatoes and peas.

"What?" Mother asked.

"What . . ." I said, dragging furrows into my mashed potatoes with the tines of my fork.

"What's that?" Dad said.

I said, "What."

My parents, between themselves, had drunk an entire pitcher of instant iced tea, which they alleged put them in a summer state of mind, even in autumn.

"What ho?" Mother asked and she and Father laughed and Father's upper denture plate slipped loose and he clapped his mouth shut.

"What what?" Dad said.

A gush of wind blew leaves against the windows.

"What what," he said again, shaking his head, looking at his food.

"What I mean is . . ." I said.

"What?" Mother said.

She and Dad giggled.

Before their giggle was expended, I said, "What I mean is: On the night of the accident, Ellie went up into the bleachers to talk to you. I sent her up to talk to you guys. And she went and she walked all the way up into the bleachers and she opened her arms toward you as she neared and she stayed up there for at least five minutes. I remember this now. And I want you to tell me what she said."

"What did she say?" Mother asked.

"No, see, I'm asking *you*. She went up to talk *to you*. Damn it, it was the last time you ever talked to her."

My parents glanced at each other. After a moment, Mother's head began to shake very slightly.

"Ellie didn't come talk to us that night," she said. "I don't remember her coming to talk to us that night. Dad?"

Dad said, "I don't remember talking to Ellen that night."

"That's wrong," I said.

"Well . . ." Mother said.

I put my napkin on the table, put my palms down on either side of my plate.

"Okay, see," I said calmly, "I'm the one with the fucked-up memory, kids."

"That's right," Dr. Langley Pipperschnell said as he bent over me, peering into my mouth. "The hygienist was correct."

"Io ut ut?" I asked with the doctor's dental mirror jammed into my tongue. He withdrew from my mouth. "Right about what?" I repeated.

"What we have here, Kev, is wear on your molar enamel. On the crowns. The tops of your molars."

"Erosion?" I asked.

"Abrasion, really."

"But that's what teeth are supposed to do. Mastication. You know, chewing food. The teeth abrade against each other."

"I'm talking about abnormal wear. What's happening is that your teeth—which I admit are beautiful and clean—are rubbing against each other. Do you ever notice yourself grinding your jaw while you're asleep?"

"I notice very little when I'm asleep."

"Do you sleep well?"

"No."

"Are you weathering some stressful times?"

"It could be seen that way."

He said, "You should wear a plastic guard." He rummaged through a drawer behind me, then waved a clear retainer-like thing before me. "Fit it between your teeth at bedtime. Then you can grind your teeth all you want." He hummed a bar from a Pink Floyd song, then sang: "Grind on, you crazy diamond."

As usual, Gregory talked alone to me before the race. "On these big downhills, keep your arms down. Don't be letting them come up, or you'll be wasting energy. You've done that in other races. You have to be putting the clutch in and rolling." I nodded, knew his advice was correct, a timely reminder. This Maple Nut Golf Course was all hills, and the people in the know had estimated the winning time would be 16:50—extremely slow because of the terrain.

In our team tent, the boys gathered around me, the girls listened from outside. I told everyone to be quiet. I could hear the powerful Bridgeway South team beating their war drums. Somewhere, a whistle blew.

"We will win," I said. Elvin and some of the girls smiled. "There will be a big pack at the front of this race—no one will be able to break out. I expect Bobolink and Partridge and Young and Englander to have no problems holding onto the pack. Elvin and Tim, try to stay in sight of the pack. If other runners break from the pack, let them. Then at the two-point-one mark we will all open up. The ending is no easy stretch. That uphill slope is misleading. But that's where we'll stamp our win on the day. We've trained for the hills, but most of the other runners will crash in the last mile."

Everyone nodded. Though I was technically cross-country team captain, this was by far the most leadership I had served up all year.

"The only other thing," I said, "is Gregory's advice of not letting your arms come up when you're running downhill. He's correct."

SATURDAY IN THE PARK WITH KEVIN
By Andanda Dane, Editor

In his second and last high school cross-country state championship race, senior Kevin Schuler surprised the crowd of eight thousand and the field of 220 competitors by hiding inside the huge pack of about thirty runners that led the race. Some spectators thought Kevin had withdrawn or fallen. "We saw five of his races this year," retired schoolteacher Pettis Orgrove said, "and when that pack came by I said to my wife, 'We must have missed him. He must have gone by already.' But he hadn't. We were sitting in our lawn chairs at the mile marker and when the pack came around again we didn't see him then either so I said to my wife, 'He had an injury, or fell down.' And she said to the young people next to us, 'Kevin Schuler had an injury. He fell down.' "

But soon after the two-mile mark, a hand rose from the pack, one finger held high. This was Kevin's hand. Immediately, then, Kevin emerged from the pack with Bobolink Crustacean on his shoulder and took the pace up to a level that no one else even tried to follow. Kevin had blood on his right calf. With half a mile to go, Kevin began the long, rising spiral toward the finish line. Crustacean was two hundred meters behind him, and the pack three hundred meters behind. What the crowd saw in Kevin's last half mile seemed to rival the speed of his 800-meter track performances. As in his track events, Kevin in fact accelerated through the last section of the race, striding beautifully, smoothly, crossing the line with the time of 15:37—a full minute faster than the estimated winning time for the inaugural run on Maple Nut Golf Course.

Bobolink Crustacean, struggling visibly, finished second with 16:32, followed by senior Don Englander at 16:52. The race marked the first time in state history that the top three finishers of any state championship cross-country race all ran for the same team.

The remnants of the pack began struggling in after seventeen minutes, including Young Stan in 8th, Partridge Johnny in 9th, Elvin Crowley in 14th, and sophomore Tim Diderot in 23rd.

Bend City High School's winning team score was a state record 23 points, followed by Bridgeway South's impressive 48 points, and Vicksley's 101 points. Lower Bend City High School finished 9th overall, led by Rene Bloomberg's 10th place run.

Kevin Schuler granted an exclusive post-race interview to *The River Messenger*. He admitted to holding himself to a slow pace for the first two miles. "I saw that I could control the pace while keeping our team together. We were in excellent shape to make a late-race surge, so that's what we did. The Bridgeway South runners could have broken the pack and forced us into a risky over-paced duel; but they were scared to pass me and so the pack remained a bit slow and we were in the perfect position for the final surge."

Asked if he regretted forfeiting his own shot at an even faster time, Kevin shrugged. "Does that matter?"

When this reporter suggested that the one-finger victory sign at the two mile mark was an uncharacteristically immodest gesture, Kevin, shocked, said, "Oh, geez, no. It wasn't a we're-number-one sign, it was just a signal that meant there was exactly one mile left. It was a signal we'd agreed on before the race, given at the two-point-one mile mark, the point where we'd planned our break."

Kevin confirmed the report that he has recently agreed to compete in cross-country and track for the state university after graduating from BCHS. By NCAA rules, verbal agreements are non-binding; the official signing will occur in the spring. Kevin's flankman Bobolink Crustacean has also voiced a commitment with the state university, as has Young Stan, girls' cross-country team captain Tina Brown, sprinter Onslow Byrumbie, and long jumper/200-meter topman Pettis Demeister, among others.

Henny had not been at any of my cross-country races this autumn. Her birthday was the week after the state cross-country meet, and I mailed her a tiny birthday card I had made myself which said "Welcome to your majority. Happy 18." I also sent her a square of paper marked with a magic-marker-drawn "1"—the slip that had been handed to me on winning the state cross-country meet. Inside the birthday card I wrote, "I take these first place finish cards and turn them sideways and thus they are transformed into a symbol of stability and grace and continuity: the horizon."

The next week, I received in the mail a manila envelope with no return address inside of which was the "1" card and a handful of alphabet pasta.

I forbade my parents from buying me useless Christmas presents. I made certain to circle nothing in catalogs.

Mother sewed the autumn crop of medals onto my letter jacket. "There's no room," she lamented. "You've excelled past the capacity of this jacket. What should we do?"

"Maybe there is a letter coat—a long coat that comes down to your shins and so gives you more surface area on which to apply petty tokens."

"Maybe . . ." Mother said. "Or I could start sewing the medals onto the sleeves."

"That would work."

"But the patches and letters. Some of those just won't fit."

"And a bloody shame, too," I said.

And so by Christmas I wore a letter jacket with medals hanging from my shoulders and biceps.

Now, with the leaves off the trees, the nights below freezing, and no snow on the ground, I could hear, as I sat through the nights, the whine of traffic on the new highway two miles to our north. The noise sounded to me to be a kind of wailing, a mourning song with no meaning.

"We will put it together," I wrote repeatedly.

"It is our job alone."

"It is one story."

"Here we go."

Above my doorway, I had taken the "1" cards from all my cross-country races, turned them sideways, and taped them in an attempt to form a single line. The result, instead, resembled Morse code or a string of subtraction signs:

— · ‒— —— ··— ——— ·· —— —

twenty-eight

What had been forecast as a late-evening two-inch snow arrived early—just before school let out—and blew across Bend City with a silent fury that seemed to suggest it resented having been underestimated. I was five miles from school, running by myself, before I realized the snow wasn't going to stop. Then the hollow peals of thunder began. Thundersnow. It was a heavy, wet snow, and I plodded through it as best I could, making it back to the locker room forty minutes later than I'd planned.

Apparently, basketball practice had been canceled, for the gymnasium and locker room were empty. As Elvin Crowley dashed into the locker room, his footfalls echoed from the cinder-block walls. He shook his hands above his head. "God, man," he said. "We gotta get out, man. We're not gonna make it home, man. Forget it, man. Forget it all! And a Friday night, too! Jeez, man. Shoot! Man!"

He seemed to be airing his own anxieties more than actually speaking to me. He had trouble stuffing his towel into his backpack. He punched the towel frantically. "Don't! Have! Time!" he yelled. "Must abandon!" He left his towel on the cement floor and then dashed out. Again I sat alone in the locker room. Pools of snowmelt moved slowly from my shoes toward the drain beneath the bench. I judged I had time for a dip in the hot tub, and so used the key Gregory had given me to go through his office to the hot tub room.

Twenty minutes later, as I emerged tenderized from the hot waters, the lights went off in the locker room. I groped my way to the door, wrapped only in my towel, then peeked into the gymnasium. There were no lights there, either. I flipped the locker room light switch and nothing happened.

Therefore, I dressed in the dark, packed my duffel in the dark, and walked through the gymnasium, which was lit faintly by a row of windows high above. There were no lights anywhere in the school. The lights in the parking lot were out also, and from that vantage point, through the blowing snow, I saw that there were no lights at all in any direction, and that my car was buried beneath at least eight inches of snow and resembled a beetle or giant confectionery.

The January sun was gone. The snow itself seemed to be the only light source. So I walked back to the school building, was somewhat surprised that the doors were still unlocked, and called home from the pay phone in the lobby. No answer. Mother was probably en route.

I had no shovel in my car, no emergency cold-weather kit. No food. I had only my letter jacket as a coat, only running shoes for my feet.

I called Andanda. Her answering machine picked up. I considered calling her parents' line, but realized her house was a good four miles away, anyway.

Jol's house was nearby, but out of the question.

I looked up Henny's number.

"Henny, this is Kevin."

"Kevin?" There was a bit of silence.

"I'm stuck at the school."

I walked through the dark neighborhoods, where no cars roamed, and arrived at Henny's house half an hour after leaving school. The door opened and Henny, looking Nordic in her Fair Isle sweater, yanked me by my arm into the yellow, kerosene-lamplight of the house's front room. Her parents closed in on me.

"You look colder in person than you do in the papers," Henny's father, Byron, joked.

Hot cider was put into my hands. My letter jacket, medals jingling, was hung by the door.

"And how is metal as an insulator?" Henny's mother, Jane, asked.

"Metal, bad," I said. Jane and Byron laughed.

Jane demanded that I take off my wet shoes and put them by the wood stove.

At the round, lopsided dining table we ate a rich mushroom soup, made by Henny, and a fresh loaf of bread, made by Byron—the gas stove worked, of course.

"I read that you'll attend State U. in the fall," Byron said.

"That's right."

"You can get a fine education there, if you want to."

"I hope to get into the honors program."

"It's a good program. You'll get in if you're half as smart as Henny tells us. You'll get in. I taught in the honors program from the time it started until, oh, eight years ago. I taught there for fifteen years."

"What did you teach?"

"Here he goes . . ." Henny said.

"English. Then I taught here at Midstate for a while—which was a relief to me because I could walk to work instead of driving the fume-shitter. And now I'm fifty-nine and have the best job of my entire life. Best job of my entire life."

"What's that?"

"I'm a janitor over at Highpark Elementary. I tell you: For twenty-nine years I was in academia and each year there were fewer and fewer professors and students who cared about beauty and creative thinking, and more and more packaged political dogma and witty scorn for artists. And so *Huckleberry Finn* is no longer taught at the state university of Missouri. Mark Twain, no longer taught in his home state!"

"We hear this often," Henny said.

"What? You won't let me speak my mind? Tell this good boy what kind of ignorance he's up against?"

"We agree with you, Byron, you know that," Jane said.

"And so *Huckleberry Finn* is no longer taught in the state university of Mark Twain's home state!"

I nodded.

"Here's what I say, if it's worth anything to you, if you don't think I'm completely out to lunch: The best jobs are the simplest jobs."

"Yeah," I said.

"And the best meals are the simplest meals," he said, waving his hand over the table. "The best times are the simplest times—no electricity, no phone ringing, no television. The best works of art are based on the simplest ideas. The best questions are the simplest. The best *lives* are the simplest. That's what I say. I'm just an old farm boy but that's what I say. If it's worth anything. If it's worth anything."

"It is," I said.

After dinner, I tried to call home, only to find the phone now dead.

"Suddenly we find ourselves inhabiting the nineteenth century," Jane said.

"We must not forfeit the opportunity to frolic in the new snow," Byron declared.

"We should walk down to check on Mrs. Bittering while we're at it, get her wood stove going," Jane added.

"Will we be a foursome?" Byron asked Henny and me.

"I've already run ten miles in this snow," I said.

"We'll clean up," Henny said.

"Good enough," Byron said.

After her parents had left, Henny built up the fire in the wood stove while I soaked the dinner's dishes. Then we brought most of the candles and lanterns into the kitchen. I washed the dishes while Henny dried. My hands were swollen and numb from being outside without gloves, so I had to work slowly, cleaning each glass and plate with deliberate strokes of the washcloth. Henny and I didn't speak. The wind whistled at the house's corner. The cat stared contentedly toward us from a shelf. When the dishes were done, we unloaded the refrigerator's contents into the glassed-in back porch, where the thermometer read thirty-five degrees.

Henny showed me her small corner room. I looked through her books, commenting on some of them. The one candle provided little light.

"How's Andanda?" she asked, finally.

"She's fine. You see her as much as I do."

"I do?"

"Yeah . . ." I said, somewhat puzzled. "I think you two are applying to some of the same colleges."

"How's Jol?"

"I don't really know. I almost never see him. Colleges are flying him all over the country, trying to recruit him. He borrowed my car five times last semester to go see some doctor. When I see him, he's kind of glum."

"You don't seem so glum as you used to be."

"I don't?"

"You're kind of chipper."

"Imagine that," I said.

"Your shirt's buttoned lopsided."

I looked down. Indeed, I had not matched the buttons to the appropriate holes. I nearly mentioned that I had dressed in the dark locker room, but I did not. I was reclining on my side, propped on my elbow, on Henny's bed, and I tried to undo the top button of my shirt but my hands were nearly useless.

"Here," Henny said. She was sitting on the wood floor by the bed and now she moved close and knelt and removed my hands from my shirt and unbuttoned each of my buttons from the top down. When she reached the bottom of the shirt, there was still one button tucked below my beltline, and she paused very briefly and her cool fingertips rested on my T-shirt very near my belly button and then she tugged my shirt, untucking it, and undid the last button. She then returned to the top and refastened the buttons correctly.

Byron and Jane returned, snow encrusted.

"We rolled down St. James Street," Jane reported.

Henny and I had made hot cocoa for them and they took it somewhat reluctantly, informing us that Mrs. Bittering had made them drink nearly half a bottle of brandy.

We played Chinese checkers by candlelight, and later I reached my mother on the phone. "Henny Bulfinch?" she asked. "Is she that cute little girl?"

"That's her."

"You're staying put," Mother said.

When it came time for bed, the Bulfinches set me up on the couch.

I mentioned I'd rather sleep on the floor.

Jane said, "Then let us get you a comforter or something to lie on."

"Actually, I like it hard," I said. "For my back. This will be perfect."

Jane and Byron disappeared into their bedroom. I blew out the last candle and lay quietly on the floor. Henny's door was open—to let the stove's heat in—and she still had some candles burning. They burned for another two hours. I heard no sound from her room. No pages turning. No bedsprings flexing. Finally, her room went dark.

I lay motionless on my back. I heard no traffic in the city. The snow was still falling, brushing against the windowpanes. The cat approached me after a space of time. She sniffed the length of my body and then settled between my shins.

As usual, I did not sleep. The house creaked. The fire in the stove popped.

After a long time, the lights of the house suddenly came on, the refrigerator began humming, and classical music blared in the kitchen. In the sudden light I saw Henny, wearing pajamas, sitting in her doorway. Her eyes were shut, her head bent forward, but a few moments after the lights came on she woke, saw me, jumped into her room, and closed the door.

I stood up, turned off the lights and radio in the kitchen, came back into the front room and turned off the light there. I sat by the window as the streetlights went from dim to bright and I saw that the snow had stopped. I cleared my throat. The cat, in response, began purring and climbed into my lap. I sat there for many minutes, then checked my watch—2:49—and got back into bed.

twenty-nine

In February, three weeks before track practice officially began, Gregory and Porphorhessohln sat calmly, each wearing a mild smile, when I entered the superintendent's office.

"Kevin, my boy," Porphorhessohln greeted me. "Sorry to drag you away from the library. I know you love to barricade yourself in there every morning. But Gregory and myself have some important news for you. Please sit here."

"Thank you," I said, sliding onto the leather couch.

"You have a big season in front of you, don't you, Kevin?" Porphorhessohln asked.

"You could say it that way," I answered.

"You're ranked top in the nation in the 800, second in the nation in the 1600."

"That's a misranking," I said. "I should be ranked first."

Porphorhessohln laughed.

"I'm sure you'll soon claim your rightful ranking," Porphorhessohln said. "And you've got a strong team to back you up. Bobolink will rake in the silver medals. The rest of the distance runners are superb. The sprinters, led by Jol, of course, are stronger than ever, too. And for the first time, our field athletes are top notch. A very complex team, a team fueled by your example of perfection."

I nodded. "This sounds like the kind of propaganda you pump into someone right before you fire him."

Porphorhessohln guffawed. Gregory bit the end of his mustache.

"In fact," Porphorhessohln said, "it's not you we're taking off the circuit, it's Gregory."

Gregory nodded.

"You're trying to fire him again?"

Gregory spoke up. "This is voluntary, Kevin. I cannot coach this most complex team. I have so little understanding of sprinters. I have not enough experience with field events. I was botching these things in the past."

"But you're an excellent distance coach. Why can't he just stay on as the distance coach?"

Porphorhessohln said, "Gregory has led this team to the best of his abilities. But this year, because of the age of our team, is a crucial year. Under the appropriate leadership we could dominate not only the state track arena, but take top ranking in the nation."

"He is positive," Gregory said. "There are coaches who can do more than I can. There is no reason to gamble by taking a chance on me. I'm not being fired, really. I am keeping my full salary, because my superintendent is generous. But now there will be four new coaches— a head coach, an assistant coach, a sprinting coach, and a field coach. The head coach will lead the distance runners. He is a more experienced and accomplished coach than myself by a very giant margin."

"This is silly," I said.

"Listen, Kevin. You have to agree with us," Gregory said. "This is me talking to you. This is Gregory. If the team sees you accept the new coaches, then they will accept the new coaches. As team captain, you are being responsible for the team's attitude."

"I haven't been named track captain."

"Now you have," Porphorhessohln said.

"Oh."

"This is all for your best," the superintendent said, "and for the team's best."

"I see."

Porphorhessohln continued. "The new head coach is named Artlink Boonslick."

"Isn't he an assistant coach up at the university?"

"Correct. But he's agreed to spend this semester with us. Next year, though, he'll be back with the university, so you'll be working together for some time to come."

"Artlink is a masterful coach," Gregory said. "He coached me when I was in college. He knows how to support the runner. He knows how to guide athletes with extraordinary talent. He will not bungle."

"Bungle?" I said.

"You need to stay with us on this issue," Gregory said.

"If you will it, Gregory."

"I do, Kevin. I do will it."

"Then I'm with you."

"Very good," Porphorhessohln said. "This is the making of a dynasty. The cross-country team took state, the football team took state. Now track will wind it up, take the nation."

"Only a fool would misunderstand the situation," I said.

"We can count on you," Porphorhessohln said.

"I will come through," I said. "Now if you'll excuse me, I do need to get back to the library before class starts."

As I rose, the lamplight shone upon the sweat of Gregory's brow.

"My Kevin," he said timidly, smiling weakly. "Glorious, wise Kevin."

"I cannot comment on it," I told Andanda several days later.

"Come on," she said. "We'll quote you anonymously. We'll paraphrase you."

"The nature of the coaching changes will make itself apparent to all in time."

"Give me a scoop," she said.

"I have a feeling you will be content with the events that will unfold this spring. You will have enough scoops to make a banana split."

"Jackass," she said. "Funny guy. I've got a job here. You're not telling me what is rightfully mine."

I sighed. "Just be patient."

"All right. All right. I'll back off. I'll leave the fragile little superstar alone."

"I will come forward on my own terms."

"I gotta go outside and smoke before the bell rings. Come with?"

"No," I said. "Thanks. Cough cough."

"Is your shoulder okay? Why are you hunching it like that?"

"My back," I said. "It's hurt for a while."

"A while?"

"A few months. Or more. Or something."

"Well shouldn't you get someone to look at it before the season starts?"

The next day was Valentine's Day, and I received from Andanda two dozen roses and one red condom. I received a dozen roses from a girl named Evaline who was in one of my classes. I received another dozen roses from the high jumper Sasha Liddy. Four other girls and two anonymous admirers sent flowers that day, which also happened to be the last day Gregory would occupy his office. I took the flowers that had been sent to me, used Gregory's key to get into his office before he cleaned it out after school, spread the flowers upon his desk, and left a small card on which I had written "Thank you for being honest."

I sat on the examination table. Dr. Katherine Awn entered the room and shook my hand.

"Tell me about your back pain," she said, so I explained how long I had had it, how sometimes it was just an ache and sometimes stiffness and sometimes a tightness in the muscles. Sometimes it seemed connected to a numbness in my shoulder and arm. Sometimes there was a tingling, sometimes a throbbing. Sometimes a tiny, persistent itch in my wrist.

"You are a student?"

"Yes."

"Where?"

"Zame Smith."

"Ah," she said. "A smart student. What year are you?"

"Senior."

"Ouch," she said.

"You know it."

"Do you participate in any sports or other strenuous activities?"

"I run track and cross-country."

"I ran cross-country in high school back in Nebraska," she said. "I was no good. Are you good?"

"I do all right."

"You're very modest. I know who you are. Tell you what. Let's take a walk down the hallway. Bring your jacket," she said, pointing her pen toward my letter jacket, which lay beside me.

We walked down the hallway toward the waiting room. She was much shorter than me and I could see the neat part in her dark hair as I walked behind her.

We stopped by the scale.

"Hand me the jacket," she said, "and get on the scale."

I did so. The number was the same as it had been ten minutes ago when the nurse had weighed me.

"Now put on the jacket," she said.

I wrestled with the jacket. The medals knocked against one another.

"Very nice," the doctor said, observing my new weight. "Now, come back to my office."

Once there, we sat opposite each other in soft chairs. A ficus tree thrived in one corner. On the wall I saw a picture of Dr. Awn standing in the middle of a stream holding a trout out of the water. For the first time in my life I suddenly had the idea to check a woman's hand for a wedding ring. There were no rings.

"Kevin, I read the papers. I can guess what is weighing on you. You're a senior facing the end of one phase of your life. You're captain of one of the most touted track teams in the country. You're expected to set numerous records this season, perhaps even national records. You're enrolled in a very rigorous high school. What are your career plans?"

"I don't really know."

"Another source of stress. And do you have a girlfriend?"

"There are things . . ."

"Another source of stress. And there are probably more."

I nodded.

"To top it all off, your letter jacket weighs fourteen pounds. How often do you wear your letter jacket?"

"All the time. It's my winter coat, and my spring coat, and fall. My mother is very proud of it so I wear it for her."

"What you need to do is this: first, stop wearing the letter jacket, or take off all the medals; second, seek some means of balancing out the stressful parts of your life, some counterweight. Perhaps your running is a stress reliever?"

"It used to be. Kind of."

"You must find a balance. Perhaps this means releasing tension somehow. Perhaps it means something else. Perhaps you carry too much emotional weight. Or maybe you're carrying your emotional weight in an inefficient or unhealthy manner. If you want me to refer you to a psychiatrist or therapist, I will."

"But my back's okay?"

"Most likely. If after two weeks of not wearing your letter jacket your back still hurts, let me know and we will fix it."

"Yes," I said. "Thank you very much."

"Okay?"

"Yes," I said. My hands were trembling.

"Okay."

Dr. Awn stood up. No sooner did I stand too than a rush of heat and weakness saturated all my muscles and I tottered and my vision darkened and I slumped forward against the small doctor. She caught and supported me. My nose was against her collar and I smelled her. I thought, momentarily, that perhaps I could tell her some things.

"I am from Carton," I muttered.

But I quickly regained my strength and composure and vehemently assured her that I felt a tad weak only from a small lack of sleep and the fact that I had eaten only an apple for lunch. I maintained that I had simply blacked out briefly as I stood up from the chair. She eyed me not with suspicion, but with concern. I put my arms into my letter jacket.

"Hold it," she said. "No jacket."

I laughed and took the jacket off. "Ya ya," I said. I smiled foolishly and even shuffled my feet comically in a jester-like jig because I was uncomfortable beneath Dr. Awn's steady gaze of concern, which carried behind it, it seemed, all the weight of the wide green world, the firm earth beneath our feet, the stability of her own native Nebraska where even the rivers cannot carve deep channels into the land, and against which I could muster no shield, on such short notice, but pure buffoonery.

The first night of March, I sat home by myself. Father was on the road and Mother was still in town. Since she no longer shuttled me to and from school, her daily shopping excursions had slowly extended later into the day, so that she rarely arrived home by five. This night, the rain blew against the house. It was a cold rain, and the back door jolted restlessly in its frame. I bent over the table, soup on my right, magazine on my left, tall, green glass of water standing between the two.

The storm grew stronger. The door began to make even more of a racket than before, shaking quite rhythmically. No sooner had the back door quieted, than the front door began to rattle.

It was only when I heard a bizarre clicking against the kitchen window that I looked up and saw a wan hand on the glass, like the pale flipside of a starfish, and beyond the hand, a face.

Gregory.

I let him in at the back door.

"I tapped on all these doors," he said.

"I thought it was the wind."

"I was out running and the rain came up and I kept running, even through the dark. It was very much dark. And I was nearing and nearing your home."

I brought him a towel to dry off with, but he simply held the towel on his lap as he sat at the kitchen table. He dripped. His tan wrists rested on the white towel like recently unearthed potatoes.

"I came out here because I have lied to you, Kevin. I lied to you about the new coaching."

"I know."

"Yes, I thought maybe you did."

"I knew you were lying because you were talking too calmly. You were echoing Porphorhessohln too closely."

"I did. I did do that! I was shutting myself off."

"I knew you were lying, but I didn't know what exactly you were lying about."

"And that is why," he said, "this storm has brought me here: so I will tell you. Kevin, there is badness about."

Over the next ten minutes, as Gregory spoke, his face grew progressively redder. I listened without interrupting. By the time he had finished, the rain had stopped. I offered him soup then.

"What kind of soup is here?" he asked.

"Mulligatawny," I said.

"Oh my. Oh. Very comforting. Very. And I thought I smelled curry, but I was thinking it was just my memories becoming confused and taunting me."

"I made it myself."

I warmed him a bowl of the soup.

"Now," he said. "What will you do? Now you know the badness."

"I will keep running."

"Yes," he said. "That is right. Do not let these things impede you."

"I will attend the university."

He looked up in surprise, opened his mouth to speak, but lowered his head back toward his soup without saying a word.

"How they treated you was not right," I said.

"But I am guilty, too."

"In a small way. But you came forward, and that is more important. That matters. You were just a pawn like myself. You deserve better than they promised you. You deserve more than a coaching assistantship at the university."

"They will not hire me now because I have revealed their tricks."

"You could get another coaching job. A better coaching job. Just look at your record at Bend City. An excellent record. You coached me. I can serve as a reference for you. Any high school and a lot of colleges would surely take you on."

Gregory said, "But that is not what I want."

"What do you want?"

"To go home."

I nodded.

"To India," he said. "And I will be sad to leave you. But I will stay through this season. I will see you finish your high school career. I will watch you break more records. But you have to do it in a certain way, Kevin. You can listen to me now because I am not concealing anything anymore. I am not coaching in fear anymore. You have to run in a manner that you have not done before. This season, you must to run *for yourself.* Do not run for your team. Do not run for your fans. Forget any obligation to your past or present or even your future. You deserve to take credit for your accomplishments and to be prideful with yourself. You must do this for yourself. You are old enough now to face this directly. Run for yourself: then you will break barriers. Real barriers." He tapped his spoon on the rim of his bowl. "Then you will break the four-minute mile."

"That's it," I said.

Two days later, I called Andanda.

"Here's your first scoop," I said. "Get pen and paper—you can quote anything I say. I'm breaking this story with you."

I told her this: On March twenty-sixth at Bend City's first home track meet of the year, I would, in front of the home crowd, be the first high school runner since 1967 to run a sub-four-minute mile.

"Why now?" Andanda asked me. "What is the motivation for this run?"

"I want you to print this," I said. "I am dedicating this race to Gregory Altrabashar, my deposed coach, who knows more about motivating a runner than all four of the new coaches combined."

"What do you mean, 'deposed'?"

"I can't comment on that."

"And just what do you think your odds are of actually breaking four minutes? I mean, this isn't an easy task. How many American high schoolers have done it?"

"Three."

"Off the record, then: What are your odds?"

"On the record," I answered, "barring illness, accident, foul play, or act of God, I will break four minutes. I guarantee the outcome. I will break four minutes by a solid margin. I will do it for Gregory."

"What's your fastest mile time to date?"

"I've never run a mile in competition. In Missouri we do the 1600-meter run. A mile is 1609.344 meters. Porphorhessohln will have to get permission from the state track association to set up the mile at our meet."

"Kevin, what does this mean? Why are you doing this? Talk to me."

"About what?"

"About what?" she echoed. "Maybe it's time you tell me."

"This isn't about me," I said.

thirty

The stocky, balky Artlink Boonslick took exception to my plan. I cornered him in his office, stood so close to him that he wheeled his chair away from me until it was wedged into the cinder-block corner. His heavy neck shuddered as I told him my plan.

"You're setting yourself up for disappointment," he countered.

"Thank you for believing in me. The fact of the matter is that I don't believe in you either."

Artlink was one of the surprisingly common track coaches who had never run competitively.

"What's your plan?" he said softly.

"Negative splits. That's how most records are broken. I treat each of the four laps as a separate race, as if I'm simply running four quarter-mile races in succession. On the first quarter mile I aim for 1:00, say; 59 for the second, 58 on the third, and 57 on the fourth. What is that? 3:54? That's faster than is realistic. I think I'll aim for 3:58."

"What is the record?" Coach asked.

"3:55.3. Jim Ryun, 1965."

"And second?"

"3:59.4. Tim Danielson, 1966. Then Marty Liquori with 3:59.8 in 1967."

"Your goal is unrealistic."

"Shut up," I said. "What I need are pacesetters—to draft off of. Quick, tell me how much of a runner's energy is used in overcoming air resistance."

"Uh . . ."

"Between two and eight percent. Therefore drafting can save me between one and four seconds per lap."

"We can only enter three runners in any one race. Your pacers will poop out."

"I'll start off behind one pacer who will essentially run the first two laps in a steady 800 time—exactly two minutes. Bobolink can do that easily. Then he'd be burnt out after the second lap and I'd need someone else."

"No one else could keep up that kind of pace after two laps."

"What we do is have someone run a lag-lap. That is, our third runner starts the race real slow, running the first lap in exactly two minutes, letting the entire field lap him. Then, just as he's finishing his slow first lap, Bobolink and I are coming in after our second lap, so Bobolink passes me off to this third runner and then he takes off at full steam, having conserved his energy on the lag-lap."

"That's crazy."

"But not illegal. The third lap will be crucial. That's when I will have to push beyond my ordinary pace. The thing is, no one on our team can be counted on to run a 1:58 800 after the lag lap. So, instead of risking a burnout, the third man runs a solid 400 for me—a 59, say—then peels off and I run the last lap on my own. I can do that. I can pull myself the last 400 meters. *409.344 meters.* It's the foundation laps one through three that would be hard to do alone."

"Maybe we should enlist a 400 runner."

"We have a lot of people that could run a 59."

"Who do you want?" Artlink asked.

*   *   *

"I'll do it," Jol agreed.

"You'll be my slingshot man," I said. "You shoot me into the fourth lap."

"You don't even need me. You could break four minutes on your own."

"I want you there. I can go faster with you."

"I'll do it," he repeated.

We were in the cavernous Sundry Seeley shop building. Jol was disassembling a car chassis and it lay before us in pieces. We were squatting side by side. Air compressors hummed behind us.

"We never really came together," Jol said after a while.

"Who?"

"I mean me and you and Henny and Andanda. I thought we would come together like a group, you know. Like we'd hang out each weekend and stuff."

"Things don't come together on their own," I said.

"That's true," Jol replied. "It's easy to take things apart." He waved toward the pieces of the automobile in front of us.

"I have to skedaddle," I said after another pause.

"Yeah."

"How's the college decision going?" I asked him. "You know, the sooner you decide, the sooner they'll leave you alone."

"I got Notre Dame on me," Jol said. "They made a good offer. I haven't told anyone but you and coach."

"That's amazing, Jol. They're like the best in the country."

"They are the best in the country," he said, expressionless.

"That's wild, man. Do you feel good about it?"

He shrugged. "I should feel great, right? It's like it's supposed to be some kind of dream or something, right? I should feel great."

"You should feel how you feel, Jol."

"It just doesn't mean anything to me."

"Football is something you do," I said. "Football is not who you are."

"Real deep."

"Maybe I'm just talking out my ass," I said.

Jol looked up at me. He put his gloves on, picked up his welding mask.

"We'll break that four-minute mile for you," he said.

"For Gregory," I said.

"That's good," Jol said, standing. "Deflection."

As yet, Porphorhessohln had no reason to suspect Gregory had squealed to me, so Gregory was still allowed access to the track. He wandered over to where I stretched by myself on the lawn. Behind him, the bleachers had filled to capacity, even though Porphorhessohln had raised the gate price to six dollars for the meet. Though the competition started at four-thirty, the mile was scheduled at five-thirty so people would be off work to see it.

"All this yawning, Kevin. What is this yawning?"

I admitted to him that I slept very little of late.

"Nervousness?" Gregory asked.

"Dreams," I said.

At five-twenty the sun dropped from the clouds and lit the track and bleachers vividly. Cars passing on the street beyond the track honked. Spectators stood outside the chain-link fence. Jol and Bobolink and I waited calmly in the infield. We wouldn't know what starting lanes we would occupy until the last moment.

"You, sir, owe me," Bobolink said. "I'm going to burn myself out on those early laps and forfeit my race for you."

"You can stay in the race," I said. "This field is not formidable. Lower Bend, Jocoro West, Kickingpoo, and Licking—they don't have any runners who will come in below 4:12."

"I've never run the mile before," Jol joked. "Give me some advice."

"I haven't run one either," I reminded him.

There were sixteen runners in the race, a box-alley start. I drew lane two, Jol lane three, and Bobolink lane eight—meaning he would have to sprint hard to come inside with the lead before the first turn.

He tied back his dreadlocks as we took our lanes. Jol fidgeted with his shirt, tucking it tighter into his shorts.

When the gun fired, I felt no relief, no elation, no comfort in the silence. I felt gravity, pulling me downhill.

Bobolink floated before me. My limbs felt cool.

The sun shone off the lens of a television camera.

I had shaved my head for this race. I had shaved the hair off my arms and legs. I wore new spikes, lightweight and laceless. In lieu of the usual tank top and floppy shorts, I wore a sprinter's one-piece speed suit. I wore no socks, no watch.

After half a lap we passed one of our team's student managers standing in the infield. He flashed hands signs at us to let us know we were dead on the target pace.

I breathed through my nose.

I smelled lawns.

At the quarter-mile mark, Artlink Boonslick gave us a hand sign. We were one second ahead of pace.

"Stay on," I said loudly to Bobolink. I wanted to keep that one second lead from lap one. When I said, "Stay on," I heard myself. I had never spoken during a race before, never spoken during the silence of my running. My own voice, I now discovered, was exempt from the silence.

"Hey," I said softly.

I heard myself.

"Putting it together," I said.

My pace felt slow.

I looked into the bleachers as we passed. Mouths were open.

On the curve, we passed the high jump pit. Members of a visiting track team lay on the high jump cushion like lounging seals. Their heads rose to watch me.

On the back stretch again, our signaler told us we were still up one second.

"Stay on," I said.

Far above the field, a small airplane dangled.

We came into the turn. On the other side of the turn, I could see Jol jogging along. We were coming up behind him.

Somewhere in the stands, popcorn flew.

In the infield, the shot put arced.

We neared Jol on the straight stretch. He sped up, watching us over his shoulder. We came within ten feet of him. Eight feet.

Bobolink peeled off to the right. Jol and I came together.

I looked into the infield. The only face I recognized was Artlink Boonslick's. He signaled that we were on pace. Bobolink and I had lost our extra second.

I looked into the grandstand. I found no familiar faces.

Without socks, my feet were sweating and slipping in my shoes.

Jol pulled me along. His short legs worked furiously. He set the pace well. On the back stretch, the student manager signaled that we were still on target.

Then, though, Jol's speed slackened almost imperceptibly. I stayed on him, hoping he would correct himself.

He did not correct himself.

On the curve I made an assessment of myself.

The assessment was promising.

As we neared the end of the curve, about the 1100 mark, I said clearly, "Peel off," and Jol immediately obeyed, veering into the second lane, leaving me an open track. Jol had dropped the pace and so I jettisoned him early.

I passed Jol.

I passed Artlink Boonslick. He signaled I was on pace. I saw the lap bell being rattled in the air.

On the last lap, then, running by myself, pushing through the air, I did not resist the pull toward greater speed. I let myself fall into the speed, the smoothness.

The lap passed quickly.

The back-stretch timer signaled me: over pace. This was easy.

The air around me seemed to become colder.

The air around me seemed to have weight, texture, grain, color.

Gray-green.

As the speed coursed through me, there came a point where fear took over. I had descended that far. And fear made speed.

My shoulders burned. My crown burned. Only the final strech lay before me. Only this last distance. I could see the finish line of the 1600. And beyond it, freshly painted onto the track, was the finish line for the mile, and the finish tape stretched tautly.

The final stretch passed without incident until I reached the finish line for the 1600. I still had nine meters to go, and I expected a fight. I expected a struggle from my body. Or at least a question from my body. What's this? I was ready for any sensation. I was ready for heightened senses. I was ready for the feeling that I was running through a dark and narrow tunnel. I was ready for a blurring of the world, or a veil of red pulled across my vision, or a smell of carrion, or even a thunderclap penetrating my silence. I was ready for a sensation of drowning, or falling, or both.

But none of this happened.

I anticipated strangeness of some sort, and that's what I got, but it was a strange bit of strangeness, one I didn't see coming: The brief time it took me to pass from the 1600 line to the mile line did not exist for me. One moment, I saw myself cross over the 1600 line, and the next sensation I had was the pressure of the finish line tape across my chest. That time between the lines had not been.

But I crossed the finish line, and that's what mattered.

3:57.18.

In my periphery, flashbulbs ignited en masse.

The silence collapsed—the noise of the crowd jostled me. I braced myself for an implosion or a crack in my consciousness, a jumbling of my perceptions. These did not occur. I awaited the arrival of a memory from my past or a sudden retrieval of narrative coherency. These did not arrive. My fingernails, sweat-slick, felt as smooth as the interior of an eggshell. I stroked my fingernails with my thumbs, waited for a sense of buoyancy to enter me. This did not arrive.

People were coming toward me, running at me. People were jumping into the air and hanging there for what seemed to be long intervals. Hats came off midair.

I looked over my shoulder to see Bobolink finishing in second place. Quickly, though, my view of the wider world was occluded by people surrounding me, touching me, speaking. Here was Porphorhessohln, shouting in my ear. There was Andanda smiling coyly. Two timers held my arms. One official read from a script explaining the verification process that would make my record official. Bobolink tackled me from behind, rode my back momentarily. Gregory's hair moved through the crowd, but his face was hidden. Somewhere, the chant "Ke-*vin*, Ke-*vin*, Ke-*vin*," rose. Microphones held by disembodied arms were thrust toward me, questions were shouted. Through the crowd came two city policemen, guiding my mother toward me.

"Where's Jol?" I asked Bobolink.

He shrugged.

Calm returned slowly.

Eventually, I agreed to make a statement for the press. I would answer no questions. I would speak on the stipulation that the reporters and camera crews had to stay in the infield while I stood on the other side track—about thirty feet away.

Thus arranged, I told them only this: "I ran this race for my former coach, Gregory Altrabashar."

The questions descended like sleet. The reporters pushed against each other, leaning over the track.

"Why has Mr. Altrabashar been fired?"

"Do you plan to attempt to break Jim Ryun's record?"

"Who conceived the lag-lap pacesetting plan?"

"Why have you shaved your head?"

"Have you scheduled your signing date with the university yet?"

"How does it feel to have broken the four-minute barrier?"

"Are the reports that your training schedule has lessened true?"

"Why did you jettison your second pacesetter?"

"Do you have designs on the 800-meter national record?"

"What was your motivation in this race?"

"Why have you gotten rid of your trademark spikes?"

After observing this wall of inquisition for many seconds, I turned away. This barrier was not porous. I could not penetrate it. But I turned back toward it. I held up a hand. The reporters went silent.

I said, "I'll add this: I am disappointed in myself."

thirty-one

This was still late March. Freezing rain fell at noon. The sidewalks shone. Then the ice melted. When school let out, Zame Smith students exited the school with unusual sluggishness. We had been beaten down by winter.

"It's not a problem," I told Jol.

We stood in the locker room after track practice. He had asked to borrow my car the next day.

"The thing is," he said, "I won't be back until late. The only time Dr. Johann can see me is at eight o'clock."

"This is that same doctor, right?"

"Yeah. It's my knee, you know."

"Take the car. If it were up to me, you could have the car. My mother's visiting her sister in Kansas all weekend, but Andanda can drive me home tomorrow night and then pick me up Monday morning for school. You just bring the car back to your house and I'll pick it up Monday after school."

"You sure?"

I put my hand on his shoulder. His flesh felt like clay.

"I don't need the car this weekend. This is the least I can do for you. You helped me set my mile record."

"I hit a wall. I broke pace. I botched."

"You did fine. I came in over target."

"I botched. I haven't run well in a long time. I don't want to run well, I guess."

"I got energy from you in that race. I was proud to be paced by you." Jol shook his head.

"I'll tell you something," I said. "My car, it's not mine at all. Dr. Brake bought it for me. The university bought it. I didn't want it. I didn't ask for it."

Jol looked puzzled. "Is there something going on? Is the university doing something? I don't understand things these days."

I nodded. "If that car disappeared, I would be a happy man. I hate that car. So you can see I certainly don't mind if my friend borrows it."

"They can't give you a car."

"It's all under the guise of the research. Listen, Brake owns it, technically. In my mind that car is just an intrusion into my life, my balance."

"Balance," Jol said.

"Or my lack thereof."

Jol nodded. He threw his socks onto the floor. "I registered with selective service after Christmas," he said. "This winter I watched the news every night and hoped the draft would get activated so I would be sent to war so maybe I could find some new way of being me."

"There's nothing wrong with that fantasy," I said. "Maybe there's a way to achieve the same goal without participating in organized murder."

Jol didn't appear to hear me.

"I have to register soon," I said. "My father got drafted for Vietnam."

"If I stay here," Jol said, "I become a welder like my father. If I go to college I have to play football, which I don't want to do. I was wishing for war. That's what I was doing, Kevin."

We both zipped our duffel bags. I put on my letter jacket, which now bore no medals. Jol stared at the concrete floor.

"That's just like them," he said, "to give you a car. As if a car means anything. You should give the car back to them."

"I did once. It didn't achieve anything."

"You should fill the car with cow shit and send it back to them."

"Maybe . . ." I said. "Maybe we're letting them use us."

"I guess we are."

"We get something out of it, too," I said. "I mean, we do."

"I don't," Jol said. "Not anymore I don't. That commitment you saw me sign with Notre Dame: It's a curse on me. I would break it if I could. I don't care about it. But suddenly my father is on my side. He made the decision for me. And now he's my friend for the first time in years. His son is suddenly a Notre Dame football player, and so he's become my pal. He wears the Notre Dame hat, Notre Dame sweatshirt, Notre Dame necklace. There's a good chance he'll become Catholic."

"Conversion by football," I said.

"I'm sorry, man," Jol said. "I'm real sorry."

"About what?"

He didn't answer immediately. His eyes slid away. "About botching your pace. You know."

Friday, I gave my keys to Jol after practice. Andanda picked me up. She refused to take me straight home.

"We have reservations at Ticci's," she told me. "Because you need some kind of celebration of your record, and I knew you wouldn't do it yourself."

"I don't need any celebration," I said. "It's kind of you—"

"You'll shut up and like it, damn it. I'm sick and tired of your modesty. There's something very pompous and egotistical about modesty."

Ticci's was the only place in town that offered valet parking. The restaurant occupied a huge Italian Renaissance house on River Street. The rosebushes were wrapped in burlap. As we walked onto the triple-arched entry porch Andanda took my arm, leaned into me. She wore a black velvet dress and I felt doltish in my jeans and sneakers. The doorman sneered at me.

We sat by the windows looking out over the river. Ice flowed on the river. The sun had just set. Glasses clinked at the bar. Andanda helped me order.

"I'll tell you what's pissing me off," she said. The house lights dimmed.

"What?"

"You," she said. "God willing, I'm fleeing the state in five months for some far-flung college, and you're staying here. First of all, that's a waste of your intelligence. I've seen enough people go to the state university, even into the honors program, to know that most of them stagnate there. The university just doesn't deserve you. That pisses me off. Your grades and scores could get you admitted anywhere. And your running could get you scholarships up the wazoo. But you're going to waste away here. I don't have any problems with Missouri. Well, I do, but I think it's only logical to get educated out of state and then decide whether you want to return. You limit yourself too much if you don't. You've never even been outside the state. What bothers me more, though, is that I know I won't hear from you next year. You won't write or call. You won't try to visit me. And on holidays and over the summer I'll have to hunt you down myself, and then I'll be lucky if you'll agree to come see me. That's the way it will be, you bastard."

"I am a bastard," I said.

"I've considered having your baby just to insure that you'll keep in contact with me. How's that?"

"Good luck with that."

"Bastard. I like you a lot," she said. "I like you very much, Kevin Schuler. Someday, some girl is going to get you to open up and I'm so fucking jealous of that girl right now that I've lost my appetite."

"I'm flattered to be an appetite suppressant."

"You should be."

"I am."

"Good. I don't know what to do with you. You're pissing me off so much. I've tried to be as much of a friend as you'll let anyone be. I've tried to let you have your space. I've tried to get naked with you, tried to get you drunk. I've tried to blackmail you and ply you with gifts and flattery. I've tried to find out about your past. Nothing works. It's like trying to a woo a swamp. I'll tell you, though. I'll tell you who I wonder about. I wonder about Ellie Butterbit."

"And who, pray, is she?" I asked.

"Very nice. But I have spoken at length with my protégé, Tam Butterbit, and found out a good deal more about you than I've let on. I don't mean to breach any subjects that cause you undue discomfort—God forbid—but I'm too curious now and too short on time to play footsie instead of coming out in the open with things. I wonder about Ellie Butterbit."

I answered simply, "So do I."

"Tell me about her," Andanda said point-blank.

"No. I don't think . . ."

"Tell me about her," she repeated.

I forced a laugh. I moved my napkin from the right side of my place setting to the left side. Andanda was staring at me. I looked at my fingers. Then I looked out the window. I rubbed my eyebrow. I rubbed my shoulder. I sat up straight. I took my elbows off the table. Then I slumped again.

"What was her smile like?" Andanda asked in her journalist voice.

I lifted my hands, held them palm-up above the table as if to show I held nothing—no information to give her.

"Tell me," Andanda said. "Tell me that much."

"I don't remember enough."

"That's a cop-out."

"It's not my fault. I mean, it's not. I don't remember enough."

"It's impossible to tell when you're lying, Kevin."

I shrugged.

"Maybe you didn't care about her," Andanda said.

All the breath went out of me. My limbs felt waxen. A thin fuse had been lit in some cavity of my chest. For several seconds the fuse burned and I sweated and then the fuse reached its end.

"Fuck you," I whispered.

Andanda blinked at me. She didn't say anything. Her brow softened. Our entrees arrived. They steamed our faces. Far below us, along the river, a train clattered and wailed. Andanda did not speak or eat.

"I hate being young," she finally said. "I hate having no experiences."

I nodded. "There's only one way for us to go, though," I said. "We get older. We get experience. It's too easy."

"I'm not hungry," she said, sliding her plate of marinara aside. She pushed her hair back from her face, held it there momentarily. "I'm a cynical girl," she said. "And I'm pushy and cocky. I know who I am and I don't pretend to be modest. My parents are rich. I am spoiled. I'm already overeducated. But I want to let you know that I'm not lying to you, Kevin. I never have. My concern for you is sincere. My adoration . . . and . . . that's what I want to say."

She picked up her fork.

After the meal, after torte and espresso and chalky mints, we stood together outside, waiting for the car, and the breeze blew Andanda's hair against my neck. When the car came, Andanda pushed me toward the driver's door, and so I drove us out of Bend City. We drove with the stereo off—a rarity for Andanda—and didn't speak. Her car drove smoothly but tightly, a better engineered sports car than mine, European engineering compared to my Japanese efficiency. As we came down the long stretch of blacktop before crossing Keen Creek, I put in the clutch and turned off the headlights for several seconds and we glided along, hearing the wind and the wheels. Our eyes adjusted quickly to the light of the nearly full moon, which illuminated the broad floodplain pastures as if they were one smooth, clean lake, atop which many black cows happened to be floating.

At home, the driveway was empty, the house unlit.

"Do you want me to invite you in?" I asked.

In the dim cabin of the car, Andanda said quietly, "Of course I do. But more than that, I want you to do what you want to do."

I thought for a moment. "I don't want to invite you in," I said. I heard no sound from Andanda. "I want to invite you out."

I climbed from the car and went around to open Andanda's door. I took her hand as she stood. She wobbled on her heels.

"Actually, you'll have to come in for a bit," I said.

Inside, Andanda changed from her dress and hose and heels into a pair of my jeans, one of my old flannel shirts, some of my clean socks, and a pair of Mother's weekend shoes. She changed in my room while I waited in the kitchen. Wearing these clothes, Andanda's face retained its city-girl sheen.

Back outside, we walked across Jim Toto's high pasture, along the creek bluff, and stopped at the place called Cissy Point. The moon lit the view. From here, I told Andanda, we could see two counties—Graham County and River County. I used to think you could see three counties, I told her, but for a few years now I only counted two. Andanda didn't say much. She leaned on me. I saw that she was smiling a very small smile. A very simple, un-Andanda smile. But I smelled the mousse in her bangs, and that, as much as anything, clenched the evening.

I held her hand as we walked back to the house. She remained quiet. She changed back into her dress. I set her in her car, shut the door, and kneeled by the open window.

"Do you want to do something tomorrow night?" Andanda said.

I shook my head. "I don't want to hurt you."

"Hurt me? A cliché from Kevin Schuler? If you hurt me, that would be a change. At least you'd be doing something for once. At least I would have something to hold against you."

"You have plenty to hold against me. One thing you can hold against me is that I resist giving you anything that you can hold against me, knowing full well that that infuriates you."

Andanda looked at her lap.

"What you can hold against me is that I'm too stupid and too blind and too self-involved to go for a girl as magnificent as you."

"I'm entering a bad territory," she said. "I'm entering the territory where the object of my affection, having refused me, becomes my consoler."

"Would it help if you knew there was another girl?"

She looked up at me. "I wouldn't believe it."

"It's plain but true."

"Who?"

"Henrietta."

"Henny? I didn't know that. I would never have guessed that. But she's crazy about you."

"Used to be."

"Oh, Kevin, she still is. I'm sure she is."

"Those aren't the signs she sends me."

Andanda smiled. "Is this the point where I'm supposed to start helping you get together with Henny in an ill-fated attempt to please you at any cost?"

"I can't made that decision for you."

Andanda shook her head. "Henny is great," she said.

For a long time we didn't speak.

"I gave up smoking," she finally said.

"I can tell. That makes me happy."

"That's why I did it," she answered.

"You did it for yourself," I said.

After she left, I went inside. She had folded my clothes and put them on my bed. The clothes held many of her scents: perfume, hairspray, soap, makeup, deodorant, baby powder, but no smells of flesh or sweat, no human smells.

The phone rang after 2 A.M. I was reading at my desk. The phone rang twice. Then three and four times. I went down the hallway and into the kitchen. The phone kept ringing. I turned on the overhead light, looked at the phone hanging on the wall. It rang again. It would not stop ringing.

At ten rings, I answered. "Andanda?" I said.

"Uh, it's . . ." the caller mumbled. "Is this the Schuler home?"

"This is Kevin Schuler."

The line popped with static. "This is Dr. Brake."

"Hello," I said. "This is later than you usually call."

The line remained silent for the moment.

"I'm sorry to call you very late at night."

"I'm up," I said.

"This is Kevin Schuler?" Brake asked.

"Yes."

"I got a weird phone call. I'm not sure what's going on. I thought it was a prank at first. I thought you might not be at home."

"What do you mean?"

"Do you know where your car is?" he asked.

"It should be in Bend City by now."

"It's not with you?"

"I lent it to a friend."

"I thought you were dead."

"What are you talking about?"

"I got a call, Kevin."

"What call?"

"The highway patrol called me just now."

"Highway patrol?"

"There has been an accident. That's the way to phrase it, right?"

"An accident at this time of night?" I asked. I realized my question was ridiculous.

"Someone was driving your car, Kevin, and they crashed it. The highway patrol called me because the car is registered to me. The driver didn't have identification."

"Wait a second," I said.

"No," Brake said. "You wait a second. You mean you know who was driving the car? You loaned your car?"

"Yes," I said. "I lent my car to Jol Brule."

"What do you mean?"

I repeated myself, "I lent my car to Jol Brule."

"The officers talked to me. There was no identification on the driver. I thought the driver was you. There was no identification and they said it was a young male and they asked if I might know who it was and I said of course I knew who it was, it was Kevin Schuler."

"No identification . . ." I said.

"I'm confused," Brake said. "I don't know what's going on."

"You are not confused," I said. "Just calm down. Tell me where the accident happened."

"On highway 64 between Hibernia and Bend City."

"Tell me when the accident occurred."

"They called me just now. They've barely been on the scene twenty minutes or so."

"Was there a passenger?"

"No. They didn't say there was a passenger. Just a young male driver. They asked me if I knew who he was. I said yes, that's Kevin Schuler's car. I mean, it's my car, but it's driven by Kevin Schuler. They asked me if I was sure and I said sure I'm sure. They told me they would call your house and see if your parents could verify that you were out driving somewhere and then could come and make a positive identification of you. But I called you as soon as they got off the phone with me. So they're trying to call your house right now to get your parents to identify you but you're there and you're saying that you're not with the car and that Jol Brule is. Who is Jol Brule?"

"He's in my class. He's in Sundry Seeley. He's the football star."

"That's right," Brake said. "I know him. Sure I do. Notre Dame. He's black, though. They didn't tell me the driver was black. Then I would have known it wasn't Kevin Schuler. It's not Kevin Schuler, you know. And Kevin Schuler's not black."

"Tell me what happened to Jol. Where is he now?"

"I've been trying to tell you that. Haven't I been trying to tell you that? Who is this?"

"I'm Kevin."

"That's right. I'm calling your house. I thought you were in the car and—"

"How is Jol?" I asked.

"Jol is not alive. Or . . . is that the way to say it? The driver did not survive. I've been telling you that for a long time now. The driver was pronounced dead on the scene. You're confusing me. What time is it? I think I've got everything straight. The highway patrol is trying to call you and you have to tell them the same thing that you told me or they'll ask your parents to come and make a positive identification."

"I will tell them the same thing. My parents aren't here, anyway. So they couldn't identify me if it were me that needed identification."

"You're saying you don't need to be identified?"

"Correct," I said. "You're getting straightened out now."

"And you can help them locate this Jol Brule's family? I don't know who he is. I don't know who his family is. I've seen him play football. I didn't know he was driving the car. How was I supposed to know? Maybe there's some lawsuit that will come from this. Somehow, I let a stranger drive dangerously in my car. I mean your car. Maybe I can be sued. If they had said the driver is black, I could have said well, then I don't think it's Kevin Schuler. But they didn't say that. They just said young man."

"I know who his family is. I'll tell them. And there's no lawsuit. Jol took the car because I said he could."

"That sounds okay," Brake said. "That's how it happened, I guess. I didn't know what was happening. Now the highway patrol will be calling you as soon as we hang up."

Moments after our call ended, the phone rang.

"Officer?" I answered.

At 2:32 I called Andanda, told her.

"You have to get up there," I said, "see the accident."

"I'll come pick you up."

"No—they're going to move the car soon. You have to leave now. I'm counting on you to witness it for me. And the whole school, too. You'll have to tell it in the paper, you know. You can't rely on the accident report; they're up there still confused whether it's me or Jol in the car. I talked to them on the phone. I don't trust them to record the details. You have to see this thing. You have to get the details."

"I can be up there in about fifteen minutes. Then I'm coming to your house."

"No, follow it through. Write the story fresh. Talk to the officers. Whatever."

"I'm coming to your house right after I see the thing, damn it!"

She did show up at my house as the sun first rose. We sat at the kitchen table, drinking coffee. Andanda wore plain jeans and a drab polo shirt. Her hair was tied back in a ponytail. We spoke of the chill of the morning. We spoke of the clear sky. Andanda said she had seen a dozen turkeys in the creekbottom. At first, she admitted, she thought the turkeys were peacocks. She's not a country girl, didn't have any context in which to place the unidentified birds except a zoo. When we came to a lull in the conversation, I held my hands over my hot coffee.

Andanda stood.

"Let's go up," she said.

It took forty minutes to drive there. Highway 64 between Bend City and Hibernia is a four-lane, interstate-style road cutting through the karst hills north of the Missouri River. The accident scene was on the southbound lanes—he was heading home. I wouldn't have seen it if Andanda hadn't known where to stop. There were faintly discernible tire tracks leading off the right side of the road and down a grassy embankment. At the bottom of the embankment were woods. A few saplings had been bent and snapped. One large maple bore a fresh gouge at knee height, a wheel rut at its base. Several yards into the woods was a marshy area—pools of water shone back there.

We stood beside the trees with our arms crossed in the cold.

"A pickup behind him said he just veered off the road very smoothly," Andanda said.

"He must have fallen asleep," I said.

"Do you know why he would have been coming back so late?"

"He told me his doctor's appointment was at eight, I think. So that's no reason he would have been late."

"The thing I have to tell you, Kevin, is not pleasant."

"I know he was thrown from the car."

"Right. But . . ."

"What?" I asked.

"He wasn't wearing his seat belt."

"They didn't tell me that."

"Do you think that's odd?"

"I think he always wore his seat belt. Not like I drove with him a lot. But I remember he wore the seat belt on the track team bus. Hardly anyone wore their belts there."

"The other thing . . ."

"What?"

"Jol bought two rolls of duct tape very late at night before leaving Hibernia. The receipt was in the car. He wrapped both rolls of tape around the steering wheel and steering wheel column in such a way as to block the deployment of the air bag."

"Oh," I said. I became conscious of cold water seeping into my shoes.

"Is this it?" someone yelled from above.

Andanda and I looked up to see a man coming down the embankment.

"Is this the accident?" he asked, nearing.

"What accident?" Andanda said.

"It's on the radio. It said that Kevin Schuler crashed his car here last night." The man's blond hair was wet and he wore an orange hunting vest over his blazer.

"I didn't really follow that Kevin Schuler too much," the man said after giving Andanda and myself ample opportunity to speak. "But I think it's a shame anyway. I know he was a bang-up athlete. I think it's a shame and I was driving down to Bend City for work and I thought I'd stop off and look."

"I'm Kevin Schuler," I said.

"You are?" the man asked, leaning back. I guessed he was an appliance salesman. He was not old, but not young, and his forehead was narrow. "Well, you're not dead," he said.

"I am not," I said.

"Then you walked away? You're lucky."

"I wasn't in the car," I said. "A boy named Jol Brule was in the car. He died. He was a friend of mine. I do not appreciate you gawking at the spectacle of his misfortune."

The man blinked at me, then at Andanda, as if waiting for an interpretation of a foreign language.

"Get out of here," I said.

The man backed up the embankment.

As we drove into Bend City, Andanda talked. "If one radio station got your name mixed up in it, you can bet there'll be others." I shrugged. It was, after all, the second time my death had been broadcast on the public airways of our nation, and in the long run such reports had little impact.

"I've spoken with the *Gazette*," Andanda continued, "and they're going to report it simply as an accident, leave out the details. I'll do the same, and I'm pretty sure the rest of the media will, too. The *Gazette* reporter and I were the only reporters who were at the scene before the car was removed, so we're the only ones with first-hand knowledge."

"Is that the right thing, to report it like that?" I asked.

"It's the safe choice."

"But it's not the truth. I don't know if that's the right thing."

"Well, I don't either, but that's the way we're reporting it."

"Can we tell anyone? Will anyone else know?"

"His family will know. The coroner and officers know. The insurance inspector knows. The accident report will be confidential because he's a minor."

"Can we tell Henny?"

"Yes."

"Will Porphorhessohln and Notre Dame know?"

"No. Not unless Jol's family tells them."

"I guess I wish they would," I said.

"Do you remember the name of the doctor he was visiting?" she asked. "Maybe I can find out more about his visit to Hibernia."

"Dr. Johann," I said. "No, wait. I think he told me it was a Dr. Jones once, but later he said it was Dr. Johann."

"Sports medicine?"

"Either that or bone and joint."

"Something was wrong," Andanda said. "What was wrong? Why would Jol . . ."

We were driving through Bend City now and I noticed Andanda was crying. The early Saturday traffic was light. Andanda pulled into the parking lot of a diner, wiped her eyes. Her cellular phone rang. She waited a moment, breathed deeply, answered.

"Hello? . . . Yes . . . Yes . . . No, listen, it was Jol . . . I know . . . It was Jol . . . I know . . . He's with me . . . Do you want to talk to him?"

Andanda gave the phone to me. It was Henny. She had heard the conflicting reports on the radio, thought that both Jol and I had been in the car. "I'm still here," was all I could tell her. "It's me."

thirty-two

Jol's father arranged a private funeral—no visitations.
When we tried to track down the burial plot, we discovered there was
none; Jol had been cremated. At school, an optional memorial assembly was held. Porphorhessohln spoke, Jol's football coach spoke—both
spewing rather glorified rhetoric about the tragedy of losing such an
outstanding young man. I stood near the door of the gymnasium. Porphorhessohln had tried to get me to speak at the assembly, but I
declined because the only thing I wanted to say was that Jol hadn't
died in an accident, but he had made the decision to leave his life, he
had made the step to leave Porphorhessohln and football and Notre
Dame and his father. At the assembly, Henny saw me and came and
stood with me. I shook my head as some of Jol's classmates spoke
about how great an athlete he was. "This is what Jol wouldn't want to
hear," I told Henny. She nodded.

Mid-week, Andanda stopped me in the hall after the final bell. "I
have information," she said.

She led me to her office—a small room in Zame Smith off the
main newspaper room. She closed the door and we sat in the old
wooden chairs.

"There is no Dr. Johann in mid-Missouri," she said. "There are four Dr. Joneses—two pediatricians, a gynecologist, and an ear-nose-throat man. None of these doctors has any records on Jol.

"What I found, though, was that Jol had been visiting a hospital each time he borrowed your car, including the night of the accident. He was visiting a patient. The patient he was visiting is named Lucinda Brule. She is being treated at Jerico Valley Mental Health Hospital. She has been in residential treatment for three years but has recently taken a very bad turn. She is Jol's sister."

"A—" I said. This vowel was I all could manage.

"Jol visited her. He borrowed your car a few times because his father had stopped visiting Lucinda and wouldn't let Jol take his truck. For several years, Lucinda had been under custody of Mr. Brule's ex-wife, Jol's mother, and lived in St. Louis. There was no contact between the two sides of the family until Jol's mother died about two years ago and Lucinda, who was already in an institution, transferred to Jerico Valley. That's when Jol starting visiting her. But soon Mr. Brule forbade Jol to visit her, and Jol had to find ways to get up there on his own. She is very sick. She is schizophrenic and heavily medicated. She's two years older than Jol."

Andanda stopped talking, but I sat there for at least a minute before I spoke.

"He . . ." I said. "Jol never mentioned a sister to me."

"He didn't tell anyone."

"He never even talked about his mother, though I assumed there had been a divorce. But a sister . . . That . . . Jol kept that inside himself. And it didn't work. It didn't."

Andanda nodded.

"How did you find all this out?" I asked. "Aren't these hospitals very private?"

"I asked Jol's father."

"He told you? He didn't chase you off?"

"He was the only primary source there was. I had to ask. I expected to be turned away, but he was very humble. He remembered having seen me with Jol. And I had written nice things about Jol. Mr. Brule wanted me to print the whole story of Jol's sister in the paper with Jol's obituary, along with lengthy accounts of Jol's football success, of course."

"But the story doesn't exactly flatter Mr. Brule."

"He knows that, but was more concerned for his son's image. He expressed regret at the way he kept Lucinda and Jol apart, though I don't know if the regret was sincere. His breath smelled of whiskey, though he wasn't visibly drunk. He showed me Jol's written commitment to Notre Dame. He seemed very proud of Jol."

"I suppose he finds it easy to be proud of his dead son. Are you going to print the story of Lucinda?"

"No. And no lengthy glorification of his athletic career, either."

I smiled. "Good."

"In fact, I told the writer assigned to the piece that she could only use the word 'football' once."

"Who's doing the piece?"

"Your own Tam Butterbit."

"Ah," I said. "My own dear Tam. She'll do well."

Brake very quickly delivered a new car to my house, paid for without any insurance settlement from the convertible. He had asked me, this time, what car I wanted.

"I don't really want any car," I said.

"Come on, you need a car. You'll be at college next year. You need a car. We'll get you another convertible."

"I don't want that. I never once took the top down."

"You never took the top down? That's a waste of a convertible."

I told him to buy me a small hatchback of a particular make that was reliable and fuel efficient. When the car arrived, it was the correct model, though Brake had done his best to purchase the most expensive options packages: the bigger engine, the premium sound system, the anti-theft package, aluminum wheels, power windows, et cetera. This time, I held the title and insurance to the car, not Brake.

* * *

Track meets passed. The absence of Jol crippled our sprint events, but we won every meet regardless. I kept the haircut I had adopted for the sub-four mile: a once-a-week eighth-of-an-inch buzz cut. I did the haircut myself at home, and by mid April had stopped shaving my beard and instead cut it at the same length as my hair each week. Thus I innovated what one sports magazine dubbed "the Schuler sub-four, low-drag, low-maintenance head."

I took Porphorhessohln's scorpion paperweight out of my desk drawer and spent many nights looking at it.

Andanda was accepted to her first-choice college: a very prestigious school in the San Francisco Bay area. Henny got her first choice, too: a top-ranked liberal arts school in central Massachusetts.

I walked her home from school one day.

"And how far is that from Boston?" I asked.

"About an hour and a half."

"In the Berkshires?"

"Not quite that far."

"You've heard that I've scheduled my official signing date with the university."

"Yeah."

"I want you to attend."

"If that's what you want," Henny said.

"It's what I want."

Three nights later, Henny and Andanda and I met after dark in the middle of the unlit football field, encircled by the track, and buried, beneath the turf, a pocket-sized portrait of Jol on which we had each written a message. Henny and Andanda sniffled and I looked around the field, wishing we had chosen a place that suggested liberation. But what place? Had Jol had such a place? Certainly not the playing field, not the track. Not the welding pits. Not his father's house.

We had stood there no more than a minute when an ominous hissing rose all about us and we suddenly found ourselves under the gun of the field's automatic watering system.

thirty-three

The signing day itself was a sparkling day, a warm day, a day when traffic moved sluggishly through town, as if the spring wind had distracted everybody. And, yes, as Porphorhessohln shuttled me downtown after school, my heart did quiver with a certain kind of glee, my pupils dilated, and my toes wriggled ceaselessly in my shoes. I sat in the front seat of Porphorhessohln's sedan, and at a stop light he looked at my squirming feet.

"Why are you wearing your running shoes?" he asked. Indeed, they did not particularly match my khaki shorts and shirt and tie.

"Oh," I said, "I wouldn't feel right signing a running commitment without them. They're the tool of my trade. And I thought some of the reporters might ask me to demonstrate my skills . . ."

Porphorhessohln giggled.

There, in the grand rotunda of City Hall, solid Corinthian columns and Nikon-toting journalists and obese television cameramen surrounded the oak-veneered podium, behind which stood a state flag and national flag and many potted palms and before which sat ranks of chairs. Mayor Bing greeted me with an enthusiasm that drew attention to itself. Coach Rowen and Dr. E and Brake were in attendance, as well as Bob Popincock, Andanda, Henny, Gregory, Mother, Tyler

Arkass, Principal Brill, Dr. Awn, Artlink Boonslick, Tam Butterbit, Mr. and Mrs. Butterbit, Mr. Brule, Deek Hazystrump, Todd Halverstadt, Billy Sommers, Jim Toto, Carl Otto, Young Stan, Bobolink Crustacean, Onslow Byrumbie, Lisandra Litaska, Bolly Shinbone, Mark Marchinson, Tinka Restitution, Tim Diderot, Don Englander, many other acquaintances, and a sizable assortment of strangers, most of whom, it seemed to me, were quite overdressed and therefore perhaps were city administrators that Gina Bing had ordered to attend the event, which had not been widely publicized for fear of attracting a crowd too sizable for the building.

As Porphorhessohln delivered a short speech, his peculiar, jumpy, public-speaking voice echoed from the star-bedecked dome above us like the barks of a distressed hound. ". . . . And we can look back *fondly* on Kevin's meager, meek, *freshman* self, who entered Sundry Seeley *like a mouse*, and gradually *made himself into a lion*, academically and, *most* impressively, on the track. . . ."

I had trouble following the metaphors. At different points, Porphorhessohln compared me to his buddy who died at Inchon, to a racing horse, to a bull, to a lion, to a mouse, to a thunderstorm, to a computer ("a very deceptive computer, that appears to be doing nothing, but is, in fact, thinking all the time"), to a brain surgeon, to a hornet, and to a pinecone.

"Watching Kevin leave my halls will not be painless. Neither will it be joyless, for he is a compliment to our school and an asset to the world."

Then Porphorhessohln introduced his "dear friend" and "enviable inheritor of the phenomenal Kevin Schuler," Coach Jetty Rowen. Rowen took the podium. He was so tall he leaned down toward the microphone, getting too close to it and therefore shocking the audience with the sudden, god-like volume of his voice.

"Thank you, Umber," he said. He paused, surveyed the audience for many moments with a glare that seemed to suggest they were guilty of some moral shortcoming. Then his eyebrows rose. "For many years, many years, the University of Arkansas has dominated collegiate track and field and cross-country in the Midwest. Now, though, with the miraculous transformation of a home-grown Missouri country boy into the top mid-distance high school runner in twenty years, and this runner's common-sense, admirable decision to attend the venerable flagship public university of his own state, Missouri has, as of this moment, effectively tapped Arkansas on the shoulder and said, somewhat wryly, 'Peel off.' "

The crowd laughed appreciatively at the phrase made famous in newspaper, magazine, and television reports of my sub-four mile.

"Kevin's remarkable athleticism, impenetrable discipline, subtle leadership, and national prominence will solidify the core of the strongest Missouri running team ever, and generate the clout and reputation to continue to recruit the best athletes from both in and out of the state, drawing strongly on Umber's own well-developed running programs.

"Please help me welcome to our university, Mr. Kevin Kendrick Schuler."

I walked through the applause, shook Rowen's dry hand. Nodded to Porphorhessohln, nodded to Gregory in the audience, who nodded weakly back, smiled to Mother, who grinned deliriously, pointed to Andanda, who winked at me, waved toward the cameras, which flashed in joy, and then made a small movement that I had promised I would do for Henny, as a kind of secret sign of friendship: I tugged my earlobe.

I pulled the microphone toward me.

"Thank you," I said. "Thank you, Coach Rowen. Thank you, Dr. Porphorhessohln.

"As anyone who knows me can testify, I am not a gregarious person. And as many of the reporters present know, I avoid media attention. An event such as this is not a place where I feel at ease. So I will say what I have to say quickly: In the autumn of this year, I will attend our state university."

Here, cheering and applause interrupted me. I nodded at the crowd. Their outburst subsided and in that sudden silence I could hear traffic passing on the street outside. A door closed rather loudly somewhere. A phone rang. I could smell the store-scent of my newly purchased tie.

"And now," I continued, "what I have to communicate is rather complicated and lengthy, so please excuse me as I read from my notes." I arranged my paper before me on the podium. I noticed, then, that Porphorhessohln had left a note card there and I saw a few underlined words, such as "very deceptive computer," and "the remarkable, exponential potential of a pinecone."

"I will," I said, "matriculate to the university's honor program in the autumn. I will accept one of the university's in-state honor scholarships. I will accept the additional High Flight Scholarship from the state government." I paused, inhaled. "But I will not be accepting any of the athletic scholarships that have been offered to me by the university. I will not accept these monies because come autumn, I will not join the university's cross-country team and, springtime, I will not join the track team."

The audience gasped collectively, quite melodramatically. Someone dropped loose change onto the marble floor.

"I must thank Superintendent Porphorhessohln for teaching me to tell the truth, even when the truth will harm wrongdoers. This was the lesson I learned from my junior year suspension. Now I must apply what I learned.

"Certain suspicions I have carried for the past few years were verified in detail recently. There has been an unpublicized agreement between Bend City High School and the university. This agreement is neither legal nor ethical."

The crowd remained funereally quiet.

"Since the summer after my freshman year, the university has funded research of my athletic abilities through the sports medicine laboratories of Dr. Lucian E. These studies, to date, have supplied me with twenty-seven thousand dollars and two automobiles. These funds were given to me under the guise of research, though the vast majority of the research was meaningless. Furthermore, this year, Coach Rowen notified me that if I attended the university, this research could continue and the money would keep coming. If I attended another university, the research could not continue. Thus, the research money amounted to a bribe. Under the research contract, I was forbidden to publicize the research. Therefore, I have hereby broken the contract.

"The man who arranged the false research scheme is Dr. Allyn Brake, an independent sports doctor who has seasonal contracts with the university. He accepted a twenty percent fee for laundering the research money, keeping the payments and one of the cars under his name. He later funneled university money directly to Superintendent Porphorhessohln to help Bend City High School recruit some of the best runners in the state, such as Young Stan, Lisandra Litaska, and Onslow Byrumbie. These funds were used to pay the runners' out-of-district tuition and provide a stipend. The recruited runners were ignorant that these monies were illegally acquired, but thought simply that they had earned athletic scholarships at Bend City High School. In exchange for the university's money, Porphorhessohln made every effort to encourage these outstanding athletes to attend the university. Some of these runners, as you know, have already signed with the university.

"Furthermore, Superintendent Porphorhessohln personally arranged to have Bend City select me as their Symbol of Pride, and then threatened to transfer me back to Sundry Seeley when I voiced my aversion to such a plan.

"My coach, Gregory Altrabashar, was promised a coaching job with the university upon my graduation if he helped convince me to matriculate there. He, though, has stepped away from the lying and told me the truth of the matter. For his reluctance to coerce me into attending the university, he was suspended from coaching at Bend City this year—replaced by Artlink Boonslick, as you know, a university-paid coach who was 'loaned' to Bend City High School for the season. Now for coming forth, Gregory will be fired.

"I cannot, in good conscience, participate in an athletic program that has no commitment to honesty and decency. I will complete my season with Bend City as a courtesy to my teammates, but it will be the last time I run competitively.

"I feel compelled to say now, before everyone, that running has answered no questions for me. It has failed.

"Thank you for listening."

Cameramen stirred. Porphorhessohln and Rowen sat motionless, watching me serenely. The crowd did not rise. But Gregory stood, came into the aisle between the ranks of chairs. He held a paper bag. He took three steps toward the podium, then stopped, addressing me from a distance as if he were addressing a king.

"But you can answer your own questions," he said. The crowd quieted. "You have yourself! You are not trapped! You are not trapped unless you let yourself be trapped!"

He then reached inside the paper bag and withdrew the pair of bronze spikes that had sat atop the track team memorial. He held them toward me, above his head. He closed his eyes as he spoke:

"Take what is yours."

I descended from the podium, approached Gregory. He placed the heavy bronze shoes into my hands and before I could say a word to him or touch him or meet his eyes he left, entered the crowd, which was standing now. The reporters began shouting questions.

Never has anything felt so heavy to me as those shoes—those brown shoes with the spikes filed off, those spikeless spikes.

Cameras flashed. I shouldered through the reporters. I walked through the tall front doors of City Hall, out into the spring air. I descended the stairs and began to run.

Five minutes later I stood on the Jack Schnae Floebuss Bridge, high above the chocolate waters of the wide Missouri River—that child of the plains and the Rocky Mountains.

I let drop the bronze shoes.

I did not watch them fall.

thirty-four

Porphorhessohln, for the first time since I had met him,
seemed relaxed. He leaned back in his chair behind his desk, exhaled
slowly, smiled a molasses-slow smile. His usual bottle of antacid tablets
was nowhere in sight. His yellow tie was loosened, his eyes were not
bloodshot, and even his white hair, which usually stood firmly at attention, had reclined.

"This is quite a situation, isn't it?" he asked. "Quite a situation."

"You don't seem worried," I replied.

"No. I'm not worried. I'm just not. They can probe and poke and
trace cashed checks and somehow it feels to me not like an investigation, but some kind of routine medical procedure, like a dental cleaning. Something relatively harmless."

"I'm not sure if that means you recognize your wrongdoings or
not."

"The thing is, Kevin, I'm retiring this summer. I've not
announced it yet, but the school board knows. My pension is locked
in. They might condemn me, might cripple this team I have assembled, but I will be unscathed. They might even destroy the two-school
system I've pioneered. How would that make you feel? To be party to
the homogenization of the most prestigious high school in the state?"

"This kind of lovely selfishness must make it easy for you to sleep at night."

"Look," he said, "I can't bump you off the track team. That would simply make me look guilty, and it would ruin our state championship. We can't win without you. No way. And I can't even find it in myself to condemn you for coming forward with the information you have. But I can admit now that I dislike you a great deal. I never have liked you. You don't work for anything. You don't seem to care for anything. You walk around all the time with the same blank expression on your face. You win races, set records, and then walk around looking like you have a bad headache. It's no wonder you've never had a girlfriend."

"Maybe I do have a bad headache all the time."

"You just don't impress me."

"That makes me think that perhaps I am on the right track," I said. "For if I act with decency, surely I will not impress indecent people." These would be the last words I would ever address to Umber Porphorhessohln.

"I don't care to have this conversation anymore," he said.

I removed from my pocket his scorpion paperweight, returned it to his desk, and left his office.

E called me at home.

"I'm sorry to say," he told me, "that the university's new budget has tightened up things around here, and my department head has terminated my research of you."

"You don't say."

"It's true," E said. "There's just no money for you."

"And what a shame," I said. "Just when you were closing in on some real answers."

"Well, yeah. Well, there's just no money."

"I understand. I really, really do. Really, really, really."

* * *

Mayor Bing called me at home.

"A city has changing needs, changing aspirations," she explained. "Right now, with the automobile manufacturers moving back in and the new industries coming, we've entered a new phase here in Bend City."

"That you have."

"Construction starts are up. Property values are up. Population growth is up. Retail sales are up."

"The beautiful signs of a booming economy."

"Yes, and most places in the United States aren't nearly so lucky right now. We're very fortunate."

"I'm happy for you."

"But what I'm getting around to, Kevin, is that our identity has changed. The city council and I have discussed the matter at length and we cannot find an appropriate reason to keep you on as our Symbol of Pride."

"I'm sorry to hear that."

"I know you are. And you know it breaks our hearts to have to let you go. You've been an inspirational symbol for our city for the past few years, and you've helped us maintain our vision. We're very sad to see you go."

"Of course."

"It's not easy for us to do this. But seeing as you will be leaving town in the fall for the university, we couldn't have kept you on for much longer anyway."

"May I ask what the new Symbol of Pride is?"

"Right. We're busy now with the formalities, but I'm certain that within the month we'll name the new Route 180 extension on the edge of town as our Symbol of Pride."

"Ah," I said. "A highway. What a gorgeous Symbol of Pride. It will be very beautiful. How lucky you are. A glorious, gorgeous symbol. A magnificent symbol. How very appropriate and beautiful and inspiring."

"Yes, it is. It is, isn't it?"

"Oh, lord," I said, "it is."

* * *

I was drawn, the weekend before the state track meet, across the pastures toward Cissy Point, from where I could see Keen Creek winding far below me, black water sliding beneath the waxy leaves of sycamores. Beyond the creek, the recently sprouted cornfields lay green and clean. Further still, the hills shouldered the horizon. Cows were specks. Stands of hickory marched upslope. Crows rose and fell, climbed and landed, cawed.

I did not notice Henny arrive. When I saw her standing several paces away, looking out at the same view as me, she appeared to have been there for some time. Her arms were crossed over her chest. Her gray cardigan looked hand-knit. Her bangs rolled to and fro over her temples in the wind.

She nodded at me, smiled a greeting.

"How'd you get here?" I asked, shocked by her sudden appearance. Against the backdrop of sky and pastures, she glowed.

"It's your birthday, you puke," she said. "May first. May Day."

I had no words.

"Don't worry," she said, "I didn't buy you any crappy presents. I decided to visit you instead."

"You've never been out to my house. I should have invited you a long time ago."

"Actually, I've been here. I admit. I admit I've driven past a few times. Twice at night. Twice in the daytime. There. How's that?"

I motioned for her to sit by me. She did.

"You'll have to excuse me," I said after several moments. "I've been rather out of sorts for four years."

Henny giggled. "You're being melodramatic."

"The before and the after. . . . The before and the after are not reconciled. I cannot put the two things together. I don't have coherency. The things before do not work with the things after. Some things have even changed outright. Like my body. Like my sleep. Or like this place, Cissy Point."

Henny and I observed the view together.

"That's Keen Creek?" she asked.

"Very good. An old road used to come up the bluff here. Way long ago. And you can look across there and see Graham County, and those hills that way are River County. So you can see two counties at once. Someone told me once that you could see three counties from here. But for a long time now I only count two. I come here a lot. Each time I only count two. A whole county disappeared. How's that? That's the kind of thing that's happened to me."

We sat in silence for at least a minute.

"Well . . ." Henny said. "You're mistaken. There are three counties. I mean, this is the first time I've been here, but if I know my local geography, there are three."

I looked at her. She had freckles on her ears.

She pointed southwest, said, "Graham County."

She pointed northwest, said, "River County."

Then she turned her finger toward the soil between us. "Croop County," she said. "Three."

"God damn," I said.

I had forgotten to count my own land, where my own feet rested. The land where I slept and ate, ran and read. For four years I had made this mistake.

"Thank you," I told Henny.

That evening, I formulated my plan for the state track meet. It was a plan that would lift me up, lend me a buoyancy I had lost: I would set an 800 national high school record in the last race of my life. I had no doubt I could do it. I would do it for Ellie, for Jol, for Gregory. Then things would come around. I would break this barrier, then things would come together. My speed, perfected, would deliver me.

thirty-five

But as I warmed up on the Midstate State College track beneath the golden sun, on this the second day of the state meet, having won yesterday the 3200-meter relay and the qualifying heat of the 800, and having won an hour ago the mile run (newly revived for the state meet) with a time of 4:00.00—which gave me the singular distinction of being the only high schooler to ever run *the* four-minute mile—I saw, upon the track, a strange stain. The stain was a pale ruby wash—hard to discern on the track's red rubber surface—and seemed to describe the shape of some unknown continent, and when I saw the stain I stopped jogging and crouched there and traced the stain with my fingertips. I recognized the stain, but could not remember where it had come from.

Andanda, seeing me crouch on the track, hurried over from the infield press tent and squatted beside me.

"What is this?" I asked, tapping the stain.

"You don't remember?"

"No I don't remember or I wouldn't be asking," I said. "I don't remember."

"They are your stains."

"What do you mean my stains? I own them?"

"You made them."

"Made them?"

"When you collapsed after your freshman-year state 800. You had been badly spiked. I was covering the meet that year and saw it. You were spiked, fell, then got up and won the race anyway. But then you ran right through the finish line and didn't stop for about thirty meters and then fell down here and sat here while they patched you up. You bled and made these stains."

"They've been here for a long time, then."

"Three years."

"But I haven't noticed them before."

"Well . . ."

"I didn't notice them then, I didn't notice them the next year, I didn't notice them junior year when I was on the field as a student coach. And I didn't notice them yesterday. And I didn't notice them today until just now. I must have run past them or walked by fifty times and I didn't notice them. They were mine, and I didn't notice them and I didn't know they were here."

"So what? They're very faint."

"It just doesn't bode well," I said.

"You're having an anomalous reaction. You're jittery for your last race."

"I still don't recognize older parts of myself."

"You're under a lot of stress."

"I am not. I am under no stress. I'm running in a world without friction. It's like running downhill—gravity is on my side. So don't say stupid things about me being under stress to perform well."

"I didn't say you were under stress to perform well, I just said you were under stress."

She took my hand then, as we crouched on the track, and made like she was going to kiss the back of it. But as she drew my hand toward her she turned it over, and kissed my palm instead.

*   *   *

I was limber, loose, ready. I was so loose I had no sensation in my muscles—in their numbness, they could withstand the acid build-up necessary for me to set a national record. I sat by myself, as usual. I pulled my blanket over my head, created a little tent for myself, blocked the sun, tied on my spikes—my old spikes. My fingertips tingled. This year, Midstate State had brought in many sets of portable bleachers so there was seating for over a thousand extra people. The old grandstand sat to the east of the track as usual, and portable bleachers lined the southern and western lawns. Only here, on the northern side of the track, was the lawn open.

Periodically, the day smelled like diesel fuel. Flat-bottomed cumulus clouds scuttered past.

I did not look into the crowds, and I began to feel more and more exposed and isolated. I didn't like sitting on the wide, bare lawn all of a sudden. I was conscious of being watched by who knows how many people, even though I wasn't running at the moment. I tried to distract myself. I counted the huge light poles that ringed the field. Fourteen. But even they seemed to be watching me at the moment, their floodlights angled toward me.

I rose and walked away from my camp. I walked behind the portable bleachers, along the tall chain-link fence that encircled the track complex. The grass back there was that wonderful thick green grass that only May produces, and the sounds of the track meet were distant. I could look up at the aluminum bleachers from beneath them, behind them. I could see all the legs and feet of hundreds of people. I could see their sweatpants, jeans, calves, ankle socks, bare feet, sandals, loafers. I could see their Achilles tendons. I could see their running shoes and their spikes. It was a landscape of feet. It was a display case for feet.

I continued walking the perimeter to where, in a break between the bleachers, a score or so of cars had pulled off the street and parked with their noses to the fence. These were the cheapest seats in the place—the free seats—but the view wasn't great.

I think Gregory and I saw each other at the same moment. He was looking like a beachgoer, sitting in a lawn chair on the roof of his hatchback. He was barefoot and shirtless, and wore small black shorts, a baseball cap, and sunglasses. His hands were folded on his belly and a pair of binoculars rested in his lap. He smiled at me and came down from his car. I smiled too.

"Who is this I'm seeing?" he said. "Is this Kevin Schuler, my friend, my hero?"

We smiled some more, standing there with the fence between us. He crossed his arms and sighed through his nostrils. "Are you feeling very ready?" he asked.

I nodded, then shrugged. "I always feel ready," I answered.

"Of course you do."

"Yep," I said.

"Are you feeling that you are ready for this being your last race?"

"I don't feel that I'm in control."

"Are you in control of your speed?"

"I have never been. It has been in control of me, maybe. Maybe. You know this by now."

Gregory looked around. He looked up at the sky. He took off his sunglasses. "The 800 is your race," he said. "The 1600 has just been like a hobby to you."

I agreed.

"So this final 800 is . . ." He scratched his neck. "So how would it feel not to win a race?"

"I haven't lost a race in four years."

"You can have control."

"If I set the record like I plan, that's control."

"Kind of. But maybe not. Not for you. You just told me you're not in control of your fastness. We've seen this for four years. I've watched this for four years. It's not a most fun thing to watch. Tell me how many records you have broken? And were they making you feel in control?"

"But if I run this race for you, and for Jol. Then that will work. That can do it."

"I don't think so. It sounds too true to be good. I'm thinking it won't achieve what you wish. It won't be a hill of beans. It will be poppycock. Yes? Yes? I want you to make your own decisions. I'm just talking here. I'm just coaching. I'm thinking of how you can be your best self. Today. I don't even know if I'm right. How can I know?"

"I'm listening to you."

"What's your plan, Kevin?"

"Speed," I said.

"The same as always," he said.

"Yes."

"Do you even need another victory? Another record? Is this something you are wanting to have?"

He knew me well. "I don't want to answer that," I admitted.

"That's right," Gregory said. "But I don't want to say too much. I don't want to make decisions that are not mine to be making. I don't want to be implanting ideas that aren't truly and surely yours to begin with. So I'm kind of bound up here. I'm being specifically unspecific."

I shivered. After a while I said, "Porphorhessohln doesn't think the team can win without my 800."

Gregory went to his car and got the meet's program and brought it to me. Like the good coach he was, he had filled the back of the heat sheet entirely with different team-scoring scenarios. He showed me the current situation, already added up and triple-checked: With the 300-meter hurdles, shot put, triple jump, my 800, the 200, and the 3200 yet to be decided, we were behind Lower Bend's team. Then he showed me what was likely to happen in these last events, how we were certain to pull ahead, even without my victory in the 800.

"I don't know," I said.

"I'm thinking that it's not a matter of knowing or not knowing," Gregory told me. "It's a matter of action or inaction."

"I really don't like this fence," I said. "It's really pissing me off." I shook the fence. "Should I feel like I'm in prison? Or should you?"

Then the first call for the 800 came across the field.

"First call," I said, by way of good-bye.

"It's kind of your last call, isn't it, Kevin?"

There is a particular sense of stillness and serenity that one can receive from crossing the infield at a track meet. Perhaps it is like standing within the eye of a hurricane and looking up at the blue sky or stars of heaven, and forgetting the storm. It always takes longer to walk across the infield than you expect, and it is always quieter in the infield than you expect, and the view from midfield is splendid; and you arrive at the other side with a sense of self-possession and a renewed affinity for the possibilities of the world.

So as I walked through the infield toward the starting line, hands on my hips, looking at my toes, my mind emptied itself. I felt, in fact, like someone without an identity, without a past.

The other 800 finalists were gathered already beside the track.

"I just want to say what an honor it is to be included in the final with you," one runner said, shaking my hand.

"Thank you," I said.

Two other runners shook my hand. Then they stood away from me, as if admiring a celebrity, leaving me standing alone.

"This won't do," I told them, and asked them to gather back around me. Bobolink was in this race, too, and he trotted up and we made fists and tapped them together in solidarity—like clinking mugs together in a toast. He was one of those runners who is always in motion before a race—hopping, bouncing, bending, jiggling—and he was a bundle of action next to my stillness.

"Is this really your last race? No college running?" the starter asked me as he loaded his pistol.

"I believe so."

Someone rubbed my shoulders. Someone clapped me on the back. We took to the track. The track was soft. What was I expected to do here? The race was announced over the grandstand's PA. I heard my name in the announcement. I heard children yelling my name, but other than that the crowd was remarkably quiet as we were placed in our lanes. The boy beside me said, "Glorious, glorious . . ."

"Here's the drill, gentlemen . . ." the starter began. "Old hat. We have the three starting phases today, not two. When I say 'marks,' step up to your line. I want to see your toes behind the line, not on it. I'll then wait until there is no motion on the line. At that point, I will say 'set' and raise the pistol. I don't want to see a single hair twitch. Then I fire.

"If any part of your toe or foot crosses over the line between the times I say 'set' and the firing of the pistol, you will be disqualified. If you hear the pistol fire twice or more, there has been a false start. Return to the line. This is a one-fault disqualification situation here, boys, so let's just relax and have a smooth start. You all deserve to run the race. If you see penalty flags on the course, disregard them. But there won't be penalty flags, will there, boys? I don't want to see any contact. We're going to run a clean race here. Wait now."

The signals went up around the field. Timers ready. Clocks ready. Officials ready. Turn one ready. Back stretch ready. Turn two ready. Front stretch ready. Finish line ready. Lap bell ready. The final clearance came from the meet director over the starter's radio: "Fire clear to go. Say back."

"Fire clear to go," the starter said, then clipped the radio onto his belt.

The starter, with his neon-sleeved firing arm, checked the caps in his pistol. He was still standing only ten feet or so in front of us, in the middle of the track. He looked down the line of us, meeting our eyes, and then he said, in a voice that few of us could have heard, "This is your race, boys. Okay? Now let's blow this popsicle joint."

He backed up, down the track, and took his position in the infield.

"Gentlemen, take your marks," he said.

I stepped to the line. *For Jol,* I told myself. *For Gregory,* I told myself. *For Ellie.* My eyes had become momentarily unfocused. I stood tensed, leaning over the starting line, my quadriceps flexed and visible.

I held one hand in midair before me, one hand beside my hip. It's all too easy, I thought. All too effortless and light. Just let myself be taken by gravity.

"Set."

The starter's arm rose. The black pistol was aimed at the sun. The crowd had hushed.

I looked forward now, looked at the track. The color of the track, I reminded myself, is red. The color of my shoes, I told myself, is white. The sky is blue; the grass green; the birds are colored black or blue or brown or red.

The lane lines blurred before me, nearly disappeared for a moment. I blinked.

Is the answer simple?

The pistol discharged.

The pistol fired with excruciating slowness.

"*Crack*," went the pistol.

The runners bolted forward. We moved, coursed. The race began, and I, without effort, commanded the front position before we reached the turn. My silence, I noticed, felt particularly smooth today, almost silky, as if it were an old shirt that had grown softer and softer with wear. The silence was comfortable, safe, familiar, but it still seemed bottomless.

That is to say, I ran fast.

That is to say, I set a record pace. And gliding down the back stretch I had the lovely but not unfamiliar sensation of flight, of mastery over gravity, of control. The crowds in the portable bleachers were on their feet. Gregory, atop his car, tracked me with his binoculars. I came into the curve, my eyes fixed softly on the mid-distance, my feet tracking along the inside of the track perfectly, inches from the infield. There was no one behind me for at least fifteen feet. This was my race, as it always had been, handed to me four years ago. This was my race, and it was lovely.

How smooth was my stride? How lightly did my feet trod? How evenly did I breathe?

How efficiently did my heart beat? How beautifully did my blood flow?

Oh, this is the world. That is the world. This is the world. That is the world.

It isn't a dream at all.

Off the curve I sprang, still full of energy. In fact, I wasn't expending energy, it seemed, but *gathering* it, *collecting* it, *generating* it. The stark geometry of the straight stretch was breathtaking—wide and enticing. Who couldn't love it? Who couldn't love the present moment? Who would dare? Let me run you down. Let me course over you. Let me through, let me past, let me show you.

Because I will show you all. This is my world too, and I deserve it, and I will love it, too, and everything, eventually, will be okay. Let me lose this race. Let me have that much. But also let me win.

I will have both.

Sometimes you lose by winning, and win by losing.

I neared the starting line. It marked the race's halfway point exactly, and would be our finish line, too, of course. I watched an official hold a cow bell above her head and shake it, ring it. I couldn't hear it, but I saw it. One lap to go. As the starting line approached, I shifted myself, slowing slightly, from lane one to lane four, the middle of the track. Then I crossed the line. Then I stopped running.

I heard at that moment a sound I had not heard in one of my own races in four years: the crowd's ecstatic roar. But it was over quickly. The silence returned. I was running again, with all the speed inside me. This was the last lap I would ever run and I was going to do it right.

What I had done was turn around. I was running the wrong way, back the way I had come. I had approached the starting line, moved to the middle of the track, planted both feet on the other side of the line, stopped short, pivoted, and begun running back up the stretch, against the current, so to say, clockwise versus counterclockwise, backward. The other runners blurred past me on the inside lanes. Though my new route was obviously illegal, and I was immediately disqualified, it meant that both I and the other racers still had exactly one lap to complete.

That lap passed easily. It passed lightly. I felt light. I felt an ascension. I sensed the approach of a completeness, a self-recovery. I experienced, above all, the sensation of speed, which is like escaping, for a moment, the grip of mortality. But speed is not sustainable, and it warps your relationship to the world. At these speeds, in fact, your destination is obscured, made irrelevant, and it becomes unclear whether you are running toward something, away from something, both, or neither. The experience of speed, eventually, is not instructive.

On the back stretch, I faced the approaching pack of runners, baring down on me. Bobolink ran out front, and everyone, on his cue, moved to the second lane, so that I passed down lane one unhindered. I know I was smiling when they passed me. I felt their wind. I left them behind. Or we left each other behind.

The last two hundred meters of the race, after I passed the other runners, felt like a long and smooth exhalation. I came around the last bend. I came onto the home stretch. *This is me out here*, I told myself. I came to the finish. And I tricked the electronic eye which monitors the finish line. As I crossed—well before Bobolink and the others—my time was frozen on the infield scoreboard. I also broke the finish tape.

Numbers are beside the point. I did not break the national record. But I won the race with a good time, my personal record, even though I had stopped in the middle. Even though I had turned around. The time was void, yes, but I had done it. It was mine.

I stepped into the infield, ignoring everyone. The roar of the crowd was immense. I untied my spikes, stepped out of them. I removed my socks. I surveyed the field, saw that it was surrounded by crowds except to the north, so I walked up the track, northward. I continued north, left the track. The lawn felt as soft as mud beneath my feet. A wooded hill rose before me. I climbed over the short chain-link fence. I looked back at the crowd now. All heads were turned toward me. My finish time was still frozen on the scoreboards. Everyone in the grandstand, in the infield, in the portable bleachers—all watched me. They were not cheering, though. Good for them. But I still heard a roar.

I listened carefully to the noise, the roar I had mistaken for the crowd. I recognized now that it didn't sound so much like a crowd but like a river flowing, like whitewater, like a waterfall. The sound was not the crowd's. It was my own. The opposite of my silence. It was my fear made audible. How long had it been in the background? Here it was, now, out in the daylight.

I entered the woods and began climbing the hill.

Clouds drifted past like schooners. Now, below me, I saw familiar figures. Four. Five. Six. They stopped at the fence, talked. Only one figure crossed the fence. Henny. She entered the woods. What had the figures been discussing? Why did only one figure come? Why?

Twice in the same month she sought me out. This blessing I could not account for, could not explain.

If there is bad luck, misfortune, curses, then also there is blessing, grace, and good luck.

She found me.

Blessing, blessing.

"What are you doing?" she asked.

"Crying," I said.

"I see that," she said.

I heard her kneel beside me.

Blessing, blessing.

"Why are you crying?" she asked after many seconds.

I looked up.

I said, "Can I tell you?"

In 1997, when I wrote this novel, many people claimed there would never again be an American high-school runner who would break the four-minute mile. I was happy to have Kevin Schuler do it, even if it was fantasy. But in 2001, a remarkable runner from Virginia named Alan Webb, in his senior season of high school, shattered the four-minute barrier not once, but twice. His mile at the Prefontaine Classic was a spectacular performance in all respects, and his finish time of 3:53.43 made him the fastest American high-school miler ever, even surpassing Jim Ryun's historic 1965 run and, I might add, besting the fictional Kevin Schuler by more than three seconds (although I think Kevin could edge him out in the 800).

Rather than alter my novel to reflect Alan Webb's accomplishments, I left it unchanged, and it makes me quite happy to have Kevin's claim on being the first subfour high schooler since the '60s made anachronistic before it even goes to print.

My hat goes off to Alan Webb, who now runs for the University of Michigan.

Like running, writing a novel is a test of endurance and focus, and without the aid of others, my task would have been more difficult. My friend Laura Gates was my first and best reader. David Dunton, my agent, deserves a medal for his determination. And Carin Siegfried, my editor, helped bring out the best in the book.

In addition, I am indebted to James Michener and the Copernicus Society of America for their support.